W9-BEJ-666

Chelan

By Thomas Lion

LEOBRAND BOOKS
MILILANI, HAWAII

Pages from Paradise

LEOBRAND BOOKS

All rights reserved

Copyrighted © 1996 by Thomas Lion

Published by Leobrand Books

All rights reserved. No part of this book may be reproduced or transmitted in any form or by any means, electronic or mechanical, including photocopying, recording, or by an information storage and retrieval system, without permission in writing from the Publisher.

This is a work of fiction.
All characters and events portrayed in this book are fictional,
any resemblance to real people or incidents is purely coincidental.

For information address: Leobrand Books.
P.O. Box 893548
Mililani HI 96789

Printing History
First Printing 1997

ISBN: 0-9658515-0-8

Printed in the United States of America
10 9 8 7 6 5 4 3 2 1

TO MY MOTHER, GEORGETTE: ETERNAL OPTIMIST; PROFESSOR OF COMMON SENSE; POSSESSOR OF UNCOMMON STRENGTH, WARM HEART, THAT ELIXIR CALLED HUMOR…AND INFINITE PATIENCE.

ALL MY LOVE…ALWAYS.

Table of Contents

Chapter 1

Big Creek Cove

HE SAT STILL in the black Zodiac, one hundred yards from the dock of the Lake Chelan Yacht Club, watching and waiting as lingering last light faded from the Indian Summer Pacific Northwest sky and was replaced by his favorite color—black. When solar winds died and night calm set in, he zipped up his insulated black wet suit, spat in his snorkel mask, and slipped overboard.

He swam with eyes open, inches below the surface, absorbing darkness from the cold, deep water below—concentrating on the mission ahead. Upon drawing close enough to see the reflections of tiny lanterns which lit the dock, he raised his eyes above the waterline and sized up *their* boat—second from the end of the pier. He latched onto the ladder with one gloved hand, tossed his flippers on her deck, and slipped on board the vacant pleasure craft.

HE LOVED BOATS. He learned to love them growing up in Seattle sailing with his father on Lake Washington. He loved this boat. He had watched it and its owners for weeks now, motoring away from this slip to remote coves for midnight cruises, bridge games, and after dinner drinks. The forty-two foot Eldo was a classic craft out of New Jersey, made by a company that produced PT boats for World War Two. This one was built back in 1947 and no doubt had quite a history behind it. He respected each board on its two-inch double planked mahogany hull. He was aroused by the fine interior cabinetwork, all done in teakwood—probably from Thailand. He was saddened by the fate which had been chosen for the *Connie Joe*, but consoled by his belief in the premise that all is fair in love, war—and well paid work.

A round of laughter rang out across the lake from the Yacht Club's restaurant. The dock creaked beneath boater's feet shuffling toward their 'ship'. Clutching mask and fins, he peered intensely over the stern rail, only to see two lusty lovers stagger aboard the second boat from the beach, a full fourteen berths from him. The foursome he was interested in, were just being served their dinners on the outdoor patio.

He opened deck doors to the twin big block engines below, leaned in probing the rough textured cavity between her hull and fuel tank, and quickly left his calling card. He secured the engine compartment, and went straight for the life preservers. There were eight of them, all the old cloth type. He unzipped his waterproof fanny pack, and carefully uncapped the vial. He dropped the acid expertly on each of the jackets, and while they sizzled right down to the fiberfill, he relieved pressure in the fire extinguisher. One gloved hand slid the *Connie Joe's* CB radio from its mount, the other snipped the red power wire. He pointed his pen tech-light at the wire wonderland beneath her dash to make sure the tiny transmitter was alive and well, then carefully repacked the perforated preservers in their hold. A large beach towel with *Maui* printed on it became a makeshift mop to absorb the telltale water he had left behind. After dusting his trail all the way to the ladder, he tossed *Maui* toward the cabin, and silently slipped back over the side of the *Connie Joe*.

THEY LEFT the club tipsy, as often was the case. A bottle of Dom Perignon, a Woodward Canyon Chardonnay—several hundred bucks worth of gourmet food and drink had insured that. The wives wove arm and arm a good way back of the two men, who were puffing on the biggest and best cigars the club had been able to provide them with. The women decided to use the land facilities before casting off. The two men continued on ahead.

They climbed onboard the *Connie Joe*, completely unaware they'd had an uninvited visitor. They stared into the star-filled sky, and they began to speak.

"Dad, I'm really glad you'll be living up here at the lake from now on."

"Me too. Now you won't have an excuse for not spending more time with your old man, the tree killer," the silver-haired gentleman said with a snicker.

Russell Warwick frowned, and thought about how radically his father's environmental viewpoint had changed over the years. "You have to admit that it's is a little ironic for an ex-Louisiana Pacific man like you, who made his fortune clear-cutting swaths through the old growth forests of the great Northwest, to be retiring here to enjoy them."

"And fighting to preserve them as well, Russell. Speaking of which, that law firm from Vancouver called for the fourth time this month about our land."

A troubled look came over the face of Russell Warwick. The knot in his stomach that dinner had loosened began to draw taut again. "They must not understand the word no. Huh, Dad?" he said, knocking a two-inch ash from his ten-inch stogie.

Kenneth Eugene Warwick nodded. "God only knows what kind of clients they represent. Crap! They probably want to build a damn Disneyland or something."

Russ evaded his father's questioning eyes and fixed his gaze on the distant horizon and soothing snow-capped Stormy Mountain. He couldn't quit thinking about the promise he had made to the corporation when he signed on as their environmental public relations man.

The concerned father's hand came gently to rest on his troubled son's shoulder. "Russ? Promise me something."

"Sure, Dad. What?"

"If anything should happen to me or your mother, don't sell the land—ever! Never let anybody butcher the trees, or disturb the wildlife. Remember, you're the sole heir to our estate."

Russell Warwick broke his eye-lock on serene Stormy Mountain, hoisted one hand to his old man's arm, and attempted to shake the seriousness from his face. "Come on, Dad! You know damn well you're gonna out-live me."

Kenneth Warwick broke into his customary smile. "Not if I keep smoking these cheap cigars, I won't."

The women were approaching now. Russ Warwick wrapped his arm around his father and squeezed. "Dad, you know I feel the same as you about that land and this place. They remind me of my childhood. And now that Angy's pregnant..." He paused. "I want my kids to have these kind of memories, too. Maybe we should consider putting it into one of those land trusts you were describing at dinner."

"Maybe. It's probably not a bad idea, Russell. Let's look into it next week."

The wives took their seats at the teak table inside the cabin.

Russ cast off the lines.

Kenneth Eugene Warwick slipped the keys into the ignitions of the '47 Eldo, and ever-so-slowly switched them to the *on* position. The twin Chevy engines roared to life—as always—and they motored north toward the privacy of Big Creek Cove.

BLACK ZODIAC motored north also, hugging a shadowy shoreline, evading illumination from the first-quarter moon, and remaining within required range of the *Connie Joe*. The predator in black listened intensely to the conversation of his intended prey on a miniature high-tech headset. He kept a steady hand on the silenced Honda outboard engine, and maintained a well-trained fixed gaze through night-vision goggles.

THE *CONNIE JOE* cruised past Kelly's Resort and Cottage Beach, with father and son sharing her wheel on the upper deck beneath emerging, magnificent Aurora Borealis. Behind them, lights from Manson Bay and Wapato Point twinkled, marking the extent of man's encroachment upon the northern shore of this pristine valley.

"Look at them, Russell," the senior Warwick said. "Let's hope men like ourselves can contain it all. You know, there's rumor of this entire valley turning into another Lake Tahoe, or another Maui. Folks are choosing sides. Chelan is changing from an agricultural region with recreational opportunities, to a resort community with agricultural roots. Now's the time to set guidelines for growth—plan carefully and correctly—or ten years from now we'll be sitting in traffic jams trying like hell to make it back to the safety of our homes, *or* stuck in lines at the *latest* Safeway, waiting two hours to get our weekly groceries!"

Below them, the wives conducted an entirely different conversation.

"So, Angela, what are your plans when the baby arrives?"

"Russ insists I quit teaching," she shrugged.

The elder woman sat her crochet work aside, giving full attention to her fidgeting daughter-in-law. "Still getting nauseous in the mornings?"

Angy Warwick nodded to her amiable mother-in-law.

"And the nursery? How's that coming along?"

The *Connie Joe* rounded the bend at Field's Point, turning her nautical eye toward majestic Stormy Mountain. On the poop-deck, conversation continued, with father prying to pinpoint the source of a perceived uneasiness in his generally jovial son.

"What's this *tension* at the office you were hinting of, Mr. Corporate Public Relations Man?"

The knot tightened another notch in the gut of Russell Warwick.

"Things have been hectic at our Seattle Division. I...I've been swamped with paperwork, Dad."

"Nothing my only son can't handle. Right?" he encouraged. To which his only son responded with a nod. "So, how do you see the future with this outfit?"

"The future with the corporation is *big*, and the *future* is..." Russ shook his head, snorting into the cooling night air.

"The future is what, Russell?"

He hesitated, took in a too-long puff on his cigar, and began coughing uncontrollably. "Here, Dad," he uttered between outbursts.

"Here?"

"Yes, here. The future is *Chelan!*"

"You're not making much sense. What exactly do you mean by that?"

Russ tried containing his cough. "I'm beginning to think the corporation's plans are going to bring a lot of changes to the Lake Chelan Valley."

The senior Warwick plucked the cigar from his son's lips, and pitched the slimy thing overboard into the shimmering wake. "Is this what's been troubling you? What kind of *changes* are we talking about, son?"

"Some I like—some I don't."

Kenneth Warwick lowered the engines' roar to a whisper, and guided the coasting craft by moonglow into the mouth of the protective cove. He centered his free hand between his boy's shoulders. "Son, we've both seen what change can do to *special* places. Are the goals of your employers going to endanger the quality of life in this valley? Be straight with me."

Russell Warwick reached for his crystal snifter with a wavering hand. "For Christ's sake! I am their conscience. That's *my* job." He took a sip of Grand Marnier, and shook his weary head. "Change is inevitable, Dad. You're the one who taught me that."

"I'm also *the one* who put you through college hoping you'd get a degree in a field which would give you the power to help make that *change* as painless as possible for the people and the ecosystems effected by it."

Russ Warwick knocked back the rest of his liqueur, then strained to seize a fleeting flicker from the artificial lights of man as they descended into darkness, surreptitiously upstaged by the remarkable radiance of the resplendent Northwestern sky. A falling star skyrocketed across the cobalt horizon, and he made a wish.

"Did you say you plan to get together with your old college roommate tomorrow up at Granite Falls Lodge?"

"Yeah, Dad."

"Going to talk about the environment with Billy Baker? Or about the differences between *office work*, and *field work*?"

The son's frustration exploded. "We're just gonna talk! Is that all right with you?" he said sharply. "I'm sorry, Dad."

"What's eating you, Russ? Everything all right with you and Angy?"

Russ's eyes rested on the bridge of his nose. He nodded.

"Is the thought of becoming a father soon starting to get to you? What is it, son?"

RUSS WARWICK thought about the wish he'd just made. He thought about the promise his father had asked him to make earlier, and he thought about the document he had signed when he agreed to work for the Ming Yaht Corporation. It seemed like a reasonable request at the time. After all, they were working with billions of dollars of international investment capital on projects ranging from high-speed rail systems to classified environmental cleanup experiments. And *he* would be privy to their plans—or as much of them as they would allow him to be privy to. Ming Yaht had a legitimate right to guard against technological leaks to their competitors. Accordingly, all high-level employees had been sworn to secrecy. The air temperature around the lake had cooled considerably, and yet, young Russell Warwick began to sweat.

"Are you happy with your work? Do you miss being out on the battlefront—out in the field, with your old college buddy? Is that it?" Kenneth Warwick did not want to push his son any further. He did not have to.

Russell grimaced, and slammed his glass down hard. "The Environmental Cleanup Division is getting very sloppy, Dad. I have every reason to believe there are environmentally unsafe experiments being conducted, and some questionable decisions being made concerning waste disposal."

"Doesn't your opinion carry some weight when it comes to environmentally sensitive decisions?"

"It's supposed to. But every time I schedule an on-site inspection, I get loaded down with public relations work. Every time I write a report, it gets edited. Cut to the bone! And lately, there's been a strange array of government goons in three-piece suits parading through the building."

"Corporate Headquarters are like that, son. Politics and progress go hand in hand. There's bound to be some high-level traffic at an outfit that size."

"Maybe," Russ muttered. "But it's a damn strange mix. There's been immigration officials from Canada and the United States. There's been a swarm of people from the Bureau of Land Management."

"BLM? Some of the old timber industry's best friends," sneered the father. Ken Warwick's curiosity was getting difficult to contain. "Who else?"

"The governor showed up last week for a four hour, closed-door session with the big-wigs from the Home Office. There were security people stationed everywhere. American, Canadian, and Chinese."

"The head honchos are from Vancouver, aren't they? I thought Ming Yaht was a Canadian Corporation?"

"Evidently, the show is run from Hong Kong, Dad. We may answer to the Vancouver office, but *they* answer to Hong Kong. Last week they told us they're moving a new Security Chief and a Chinese CEO down here to head up operations in Seattle and the Pacific Northwest. They've even demanded that most of us take Chinese language courses, starting next month."

"You're a bright kid. The language should be a breeze. Is that what's making you so damn uneasy?"

He took a deep breath. "No, Dad, there's more..." Russ Warwick thought he saw something, or someone, moving across the dark surface of the water near shore. He strained to focus, but the silhouette forest backdrop made the task an impossible one. Russ was well aware of how sound traveled across such tranquil waters as those of Big Creek Cove's at night. Suddenly, he felt strangely uneasy. "I-I really shouldn't be talking so much about work," he stammered, while scanning the shoreline again. "But it's been on my mind a lot lately. Maybe it's all the wine we drank."

"Maybe. But if you can't talk to your old man, who can you talk to?"

Kenneth Warwick cut the engines on the *Connie Joe,* and dropped anchor about one hundred yards from the mouth of Big Creek. They were close enough to hear waterfalls caressing granite beds, and thirsty coyotes yip-yip-yipping from the ridge above before they descended to drink their fill. They were close enough to hear an owl cry out in flight, and a lonely loon signaling its mate across the bay. They were just close enough to be appreciative peasants in the realm of the protective cove without disturbing its natural order, and far enough out to preserve their view of sacred, Stormy Mountain, and half an October Moon. The Magic of Chelan had a grip on them.

"Son, I've traveled the world. I've bought and sold commodities like gold, silver, platinum, and timber. But I've come to learn that the rarest commodities in life are peace of mind, tranquillity..." He patted his son on the back. "Family and nature, the luxury of taking this pure air we enjoy into our lungs after it sweeps down from these ancient peaks, this pristine water, the rare and healthy fish population it supports—that star-filled sky you keep staring into." Ken Warwick cupped his hand around his ear. "Ah, the sights and *sounds* of nature! Modern man needs—"

"I *need* those things too, Dad. I need 'em bad."

"We all do, son. Some of us just don't realize it yet."

The girls, who had been setting up the teak table in the main cabin below, called up to them. "Are you two ever going to come down from there and take us on in a battle-of-the-sexes bridge game?" challenged Connie Joe Warwick.

"Come on, Russ! You'll have all weekend to talk to your Dad," pleaded Angela Warwick.

Kenneth Warwick pointed to the ladder. "Angy's right, you know. We have *all* weekend, son. Shall we?"

As he descended to the main deck, Russell Warwick gazed up into his father's reassuring face and beyond to the vast array of star clusters exploding in the Northwestern Sky. "Dad," he whispered. "I want to talk some more. You're right, you know."

"About what, Russell?"

Misty eyes transmitted raw emotion spilling forth from a healthy young heart. "Change, for one thing. And about talking to your dad." Russ drew a deep, long breath of fresh night air. When his feet hit the deck, he exhaled it. Dead weight of burden fell from his shoulders. Goose bumps of anxiety set sail across the surface of his skin. "There are definitely some things I need to get off my chest about work, Dad."

Kenneth Warwick smiled down upon his son as he lowered himself onto the first rung of the ladder. When he reached the deck, he gave his boy a one-armed bear hug, and whispered in his ear. "Not in front of the girls, Russ. Let's just relax, and whip their tails in some bridge. Okay?"

"Sure, Dad," he agreed, as a feeling of relief big as the night sky swept over him.

At the table moments later, mother-to-be Angela War-wick rubbed her hand in a circular motion across the front of her protruding maternity smock, and offered up a pregame toast with her glass of Perrier Water. *"To the future!"* First her husband, then her in-laws, echoed her wishes.

Future father, Russell Warwick, looked across the teak table into his bridge partner's—into his father's eyes—and offered another long term, meaningful toast, *"To Chelan!"*

"To Chelan!" they echoed enthusiastically.

HE WATCHED THEM gather at the table and drink their libation. The transmitter had picked up every utterance. He made his decision. The Warwicks were all in the *target zone*. He heard their crystal click for that *final* toast. It was time. He laid down the night-vision goggles, removed his headset, and produced the remote control detonator from the jet black nylon gymbag. He held the device out in front of him, aimed in the direction of the *Connie Joe*...and depressed its one and only button. The explosion was instantaneous.

When the fireball faded he cranked up the zode, twisted it, blew a crater in the surface of the tranquil cove, and motored to the scene, ready to ensure there were no survivors. The saboteur was quite thorough. He scanned the waters. He scanned the skies. Then—satisfied that no one had witnessed the flaming end of the *Connie Joe's* last outing—he revved up the silent Honda again, and motored north to the retreat.

UPON THE SECLUDED deck of the corporate retreat, he popped two locks atop an eel-skin briefcase, and activated his cellular phone and scrambling device. Then, sipping ginseng tea, he scanned the vast celestial stage for the constellations which had intrigued him in the days of his troubled youth.

He placidly punched in the code for the party in Vancouver, British Columbia, and recited the five words they were waiting to hear.

"The leak has been plugged."

Chapter 2

The Lodge at Granite Falls

THOMAS BAKER loved Saturday mornings at the lodge. Each and every Saturday, he awoke hoping to catch sunrise over Cooper Mountain on the far side of the lake. Every Saturday morning he ground beans he had selected from Paradise Grocery the day before for the guests' weekend coffee. By the time steam was rising from that first cup warming him, the sun had likewise risen above the North Shore's Echo Valley, warming Chelan and waking everyone, but tourists and fishermen, to another working day.

Sun shafts swept in through the aquamarine stained glass panel above him, caressing his fingers as he warmed them on his cup. And as always, the siren-like lure of the Lady's magic, the magic of Lake Chelan and the mountains which framed her, drew him to the window—*his* window.

Thomas Baker drank in the priceless beauty of the valley in which he had chosen to live out his dreams—the dreams of owning and operating a unique adventure lodge, and pursuing his passion for the written word. They were big dreams for any man, but especially one who had taken the route he had to arrive at them. He may have traveled most of that lonely road alone, but there were a few good people along the way who understood the true meaning of words like friendship, and love. They were the people who provided him with such staples as encouragement and financial—as well as emotional—aid during his five-year stint behind bars. They were the people like his younger brother, Bill, and his silent partner, Jimmy.

Baker broke one of the three vows he had sworn to during his era of incarceration when he invited Jimmy Collins in on his dream: *Never have a partner!* But the dream was realized years sooner, with all the class he had envisioned, because of the Englishman's backing and business experience. No, he could not have done the physical aspects of the lodge justice without his British friend. Not only did he put up half the building costs, but he decorated it with a fine arrangement of antique English furniture. And true to his word, the limey used his worldly connections to introduce a myriad of international and American clients to the simple treasures of the Lodge at Granite Falls. It was those same contacts which helped a starving artist named Thomas Baker get his first novel published from behind the walls of a United States Penitentiary.

Not just anyone would've taken such a chance, investing their time and money so heavily with an ex-con. But Jimmy Collins wasn't *just anyone*. *He* had been a covert freedom fighter for the gypsies of Hungary, ran one of the finest clubs in London in the late fifties, and given birth to the largest antique shipping company in the United Kingdom, before eventually settling in the north of England, where he also opened an Inn and Club of his own.

Jimmy Collins oozed with class and charm, and yet the silver-fox was no stranger to adversity. Jimmy Collins was also gay. That is why he did not concern himself with any social stigmas which went hand-in-hand with his association with a terrible, convicted marijuana salesman like Thomas Baker. Jimmy was a *hands-off* partner in every sense of the word, and though they spoke often, he could only find time for a few weeks a year at the lodge.

It was a partnership tailor-made for both of them, in which trust was not an issue. They had cleared that hurdle in the years before Baker's arrest—back when Jimmy shipped antiques to Thomas's *Lion's Share* antique store down in Lake Tahoe. And the only time that trust had been broken, was when Tom lied about the source of his own investment capital. That's the way it was *back then*, when some things were better left unsaid. Anyway, everything came out at the trial, just before the feds took it all away. All but the land at Lake Chelan, that is, which had been in his mother's name. And so, unlike his dear mother, his dream of living here had never died.

Thomas Baker pulled away from the window's grip, and cruised to his personal computer. He was energized spiritually from the view and physically from the caffeine buzz! It was time. Time to wrestle some stories out of that mess of notes stashed in the cubby holes of his S-curve roll top desk. It was time to play author. He flicked on the monitor, and pulled up page sixty-nine of the first draft.

Since the marginal success of his last novel, Baker was forever in search of new ideas and storylines for future works. It had taken him all of three years in the valley to get close to an interesting local floatplane pilot by the name of James Shawn Wolf. Wolf was an odd-humored, good-hearted, brawler of a man, not unlike many who had settled these parts; but unlike them, he was an ex-CIA contract fly-boy, and consequently—full of very good story. Via a series of sessions, which began over margaritas at the local Mexican restaurant, the writer began transcribing Wolf's thrilling memories of the covert world and integrating them into an action suspense novel set *(where else?)* in the Pacific Northwest. To date, there seemed to be plenty enough action shaping up, but Baker felt he was lacking the fabric needed for the weave which would transform the loosely knit tales into a publisher-tempting manuscript. It was nearly eight a.m. He pulled a wad of lipstick-and-ink-smeared paper napkin from Signor Frog's Tavern out of one of the cubbyholes, and started typing.

"It was 1969. I got a call from the old crazy Cuban exiles' group. They were still contracting for the Agency out of Opa-Locka, Florida…" Two hours, and six hard-thought pages later, Thomas's writing was interrupted by the telephone. It was his pilot friend.

"We still on for a session today, Wolf?" Baker asked.

"Negatory! Gotta cancel, Baker. I've been assigned a mission."

"You're kidding. What's your mission?"

"Search, find, and hopefully, rescue."

"Who's lost?"

"That hip old couple from Tahoe. Your friends and mine, the Warwicks. Word is their son and his wife were with 'em last night too."

There was a moment of silence. Baker drew a deep breath. "With them where? What's the story?"

"Relax, Writer Man. There's no story, yet. Some drunk claims to have heard an explosion echo across the lake last night. He was probably smoking this year's homegrown crop. But the *Connie Joe* never did return to her Yacht Club slip. Oh well," Wolf sighed. "They're probably camping in some peaceful cove. You know? Sleeping off one of those expensive dinners the old man's so fond of? Anyway, Sheriff Hilo asked me to do a fly-by of the north end of the lake."

"Need an extra pair of eyes?"

"Wolf don't need any more eyes, Baker. Wolf's eyes are still the best in the biz. And I can't wait no twenty-five fuckin' minutes for your turtle-ass to get here."

"You sure? I can leave right now."

"Don't worry, Writer Man. If they're out there, Wolf will find them. Bye."

The call of the Wolf stole the morning's surge of creativity from the writer. Reluctantly, Baker switched gears to his *business mode.* The first item on the agenda was the completion of the 1996 brochure for Granite Falls Lodge—the one that the travel agencies and the printer had been hounding him to wrap up for the past two weeks. He lowered the blinds to half-mast, blocking out the flood of mid-morning sun which had made the monitor difficult to read. Beautiful, silent-explosions of autumn foliage spread out between green conifer seas soon led his eyes to the water's edge, then far beyond to where the billowing, colorful sails of the Saturday regatta were rounding Willow Point.

The Lady had a grip on him again. Just one look made him long to take out his kayak and walk it proudly to her shores, made him lust to glide massagingly over her liquid epidermis. Warm desire melted to cool concern across the great expanse as his thoughts drifted to the disappearance of the Warwicks. *Enough!* He broke away from the lure of the lake, and the suddenly morbid direction of his thoughts. He raided the fridge for a shot of fresh-squeezed O.J., and dug back in at the keys to edit his brochure.

Granite Falls Lodge offers the rare combination of pampered luxury and adventure opportunities for any level of outdoors person. Nestled in pine scented forests on the shore of one of America's last remaining pristine lakes, our Lodge can be your jumping-off point for the outdoors adventure you always dreamed of, but never had! Warm sunny days, clear azure skies, cool blue waters, swimming, boating, wind surfing, owner-accompanied kayak outings, professionally-guided fishing trips for King and Chinook salmon, trout, walleye, and other native fishes on 55 miles of beautiful Lake Chelan and the surrounding waters, are only a part of what awaits you...

IT WAS AROUND NOON when Bill Baker knocked on the door of his brother's room. Bill was employed by the Environmental Protection Agency's Office of Groundwater Management, Region Ten, and lived at the lodge with his wife, Nan, and his son, Nathan. Nathan was the son Thomas Baker never had, and Bill was that special sibling everyone dreams of having. Together, they shared a closeness as magical as the lake itself, and the hope of creating an environmental consulting firm in the coming years. But for now, Bill moonlighted as the resident fishing guide between flights to various Northwest groundwater trouble-sites. Nancy, his native Eskimo wife, helped to run the lodge's organic gardening operation, and shared in the midweek meal preparations as well. Nathan was the resident *kid.*

"Who goes there?" Thomas inquired.

"Your Blood, *Hoss*! You alone? Or did you drag some yeti home from last night's hunt?"

"No yetis, Blood. Come on in," Thomas responded, kicking out his chair, and rubbing his eyes a moment. "What's up?"

"Wish I knew. My friend Russ is in town, remember me telling you?"

Thomas nodded.

"He was supposed to show up here for Saturday lunch. He was *supposed* to be here over an hour ago. That's not like him."

Thomas Baker thought about the call from Wolf. He thought about how much his brother had been looking forward to his college buddy's visit and some like-minded interaction with a specialist in his field.

"Bill, listen. There may not be anything to this, but Wolf called here this morning."

"Yeah? What's that wildman up to?" Bill asked casually while gazing at the computer monitor screen.

"Did Russ go to the Yacht Club last night with his parents?"

"He was supposed to. Why?"

"The sheriff called Wolf this morning. Word is the *Connie Joe* never returned to her slip last night. So he's asked our fly-boy to go over the north end of the lake to see if he can spot her."

Bill looked into his brother's eyes. "Is that *all* he said?"

Tom thought about the report of an explosion. "Yeah, that's all."

"Shit! That's nothing. They probably had mechanical problems. Russ Warwick and his old man have been cruising up and down this lake for almost twenty years. Wolfman will find 'em. Don't you think?"

Tom assumed his position behind the monitor screen. "No doubt, dude," he said.

Bill exhaled a sigh of relief. "So, you working on the book?"

"I was. Now I'm trying to put together our new brochure. Wanna let me bounce some ideas off you?"

"Will they hurt?" Bill laughed, rolling his eyes. "Sure. Do it, bro-therrr!"

The writer read his tenth rewrite of the opening line. He read the parts about the gourmet chef, and the Northwest wine tastings. "Well? What do you think, Blood? Should I mention that the gourmet chef only does his thing on the weekends?"

They stared into each other's faces seriously for one minute, which was about as long as they could stay serious when they were together. Bill began scratching the billy-goat-scraggly beard on his chin. "Naaa! Let them figure that out for themselves after they get a serious case of indigestion from Nan's Native Alaskan midweek menu," the younger Baker replied.

The Baker Brother's broke into their routine.

"Tell them we'll issue snares so they can catch something *woodsy* if the fishing sucks," Bill babbled.

"Right! A true, primitive experience for the newlyweds."

"What about the nature trips, bro?"

"I still like the thought of having you dress up like Big Foot, so we can offer *guaranteed* yeti sighting excursions."

"Righteous, dude!" Bill tapped Tom on the shoulder. "Ahhh, Tom…"

"Yeah, Bill."

"You gonna fool 'em with that line about your fine *owner-prepared* campsite fares during your midweek kayak camping adventures?"

"That's low, man! I guess I did fail to mention they have to pay extra for some of the luxury items when they're at the more primitive sites."

"What luxury items?"

"You know, shit like biodegradable toilet paper, water purification tabs, firewood, and rolling papers."

"Did you mention the new guest chalet we built this spring?"

"Does the Pope shit in the woods? Is the bear catholic?" Thomas switched to his deep and silky radio announcer voice. "This year at the Lodge, we've added yet another of our intimate guest housekeeping units to the grounds. *Yeti Chalet*, located at the edge of our tranquil mountain meadow, is custom designed for those couples who are a little more *vocal* in the sack, and need a little *distance* from the main lodge." Again they laughed; then

Tom read the serious content, describing the organic herb and veggie gardens, spacious dining area, and impeccable grounds. "When the weekend warriors occupy the hiking trails, and the lake takes on heavier boating traffic, *you* can relax in a hammock in the midday sun, listen to hummingbirds buzz about a mountain meadow, and—"

This speech was coming up on a minute of seriousness. Bill Baker had to do it. "I hate to interrupt."

"Then don't."

"But how is our hummingbird stock? Should we order more?"

A belly laugh followed. Thomas continued.

"Or just drink in the million dollar views, and experience the weekend gourmet feasts—featuring a tasting of Northwest wines—without ever leaving the grounds. And when the weekend is over? It's time for you to begin the outdoor adventure you've selected to undertake with one of our *in-house experts,* or numerous local contacts. There's something for everyone at Granite Falls Lodge! You may choose to stay behind and just unwind, or take advantage of the Lady of the Lake ferry boat excursions to the majestic Stehekin Valley, and the awe-inspiring Rainbow Falls."

"Awe inspiring? Sounds like your mind's on the novel."

"Okay, smart ass. How 'bout this? And the *wet* Rainbow Falls, where you will stand in rainbow mist below a 312 foot waterfall, and hear the lecture series offered by rangers from the National Park."

"Cool," Bill said nodding. "But, Tom?"

"Yeah, Bill."

"What about mentioning the Colville Tribe's Mill Bay Casino?"

"What do you suggest I say about it?"

"Oh, something like, 'for the couple that likes great scenery, but is hopelessly addicted to pulling dollar slot handles until dawn, we now have—' "

"Bill, please. I'm trying to sell Mother Nature here! Even though most guests' adventures are prepaid, we still don't want them coming back wearing nothing but a barrel. Get the picture?"

Bill nodded. "Speaking of pictures, gonna use any of the ones I took?"

"Yeah-yeah. The one of the lodge grounds is great. That one of Wolf's plane will work, too. Although, having *him* in it might scare off some potential customers."

"I'll tell him you said that."

"You better not—*younger brother.*"

"Oooo! Threatening–boy. Relax—*older* brother. What about the pictures you took of Nan and me in the hot tub?"

"Yeah. I sent the one of you mooning the camera to the printer already. Want to hear my closing paragraph?"

"More than anything else in the entire world. Go on, lay that famous Baker-poetic-prose-schmooze on me."

Thomas cleared his throat. "Sooner or later, all vacations end up with your return to reality, but—"

"Doo-doo, doo-doo, doo...*The Twilight Zone!* Do not attempt to adjust this brochure. You are about to enter another space and time. You are about to enter—doo-doo-doo-doo...*The Chelan Zone!*"

Thomas Baker shook off his brother's lovable lunacy, and went on. "But you can take the memories of a lifetime back to the hustle and bustle of the city with you, if you choose to indulge yourself in the intimate personal attention afforded you by the owners and staff of beautiful Granite Falls Lodge, where environmentally conscious people gather to enjoy the magic of the Chelan Valley—and each other's company."

Bill Baker applauded. "I especially liked that *intimate personal attention* remark. May I make a suggestion?"

"Coitanly!" Thomas responded in his *Three Stooges* voice.

"How about this? A *special* adventure awaits qualified, single *female guests* who wish to share a really invigorating outdoor experience with the owner and manager, Thomas Baker."

"No, seriously. What do you think?"

"You're the writer in the family. I don't *do* brochures, bro. Only masters thesis and boring Environmental Protection Agency reports. And I don't—"

"I know. I know. You don't do windows!"

Bill Baker cleared the impish grin from his face. "You could have said that our grounds were completely unaffected by the greatly over-publicized forest fire. You could have mentioned the fact that we have four mountain bikes, and a shitload of trails available nearby. You could have brought up the wind surfing gig, especially since you know that towns like Hood River down in Oregon are attracting quite a following with that crowd. I didn't hear a damn thing about the alpine lakes they can fly into with Wolfman for some killer fly-fishing. And you failed to mention the llama packing and horseback outfitters we're in cahoots with. What about hang gliding at Chelan Butte, or our plans to install our own cross-country skiing trails? You could have—"

"All right-already! I could've written a stinkin' book. And I would have wrote part of one, if I hadn't tried to do my job. Look, the idea is to hook 'em and get 'em to call Sun Travel, or us, direct for the real clincher. Speaking of which. All I think I'm lacking on this first draft is a good closing line. Something soft and magical—like the lake herself."

Thomas Baker watched his brother's animated face contort in the reflection on his monitor screen.

"Something magical, you say? By Jove I've got it! Besides the guaranteed Big Foot sightings, you tell 'em about the magic mushrooms that grow wild in cow shit in these parts. Something like: Hunt wild shrooms! Pick Pacific Northwest funky fungi for free from fresh cow crap, and get shit-faced with your fellow guests at no additional cost to you."

"Bill!"

"Tom, baby! It's a winner. Did you catch that alliteration? Funky-fungi-for-free—"

"Heavy alliteration's for poetry, man. Book and brochure publishers hate the stuff. Now get serious. I'm stuck here. I'm thinking something…something with an environmental slant for a kicker."

"All right. This is serious?"

"Yeah, Bill. Straight up serious. I'm getting tired of screwing around with this thing."

"You want serious? I'll give you serious." Bill drew a deep breath, straining to keep a straight face. "You ready? Get them fingers on the keys, bro! You won't wanna forget this line."

Thomas Baker took the bait. "Okay, shoot."

"No Fucking Hunters!"

"Cute, dickhead," Thomas said. "Take off, hoser!"

Bill Baker doubled over laughing as he headed for the door. "I'm going to go type that report on the contamination of Yakima's shallow aquifer due to agricultural pesticides and improper irrigation ditch leeching practices," he announced.

Thomas Baker never ceased to be amazed by the metamorphosis of his fishing buddy brother into a full-fledged environmental specialist, which had occurred during his prison term. "I love it when you talk that technical EPA talk, William B.," he sighed.

Bill's face grew flush from the slick flattery behind his brother's remark. "Yeah, right. Let me know when Russ calls, will ya?"

"Count on it. Hey, you still going to go play pool with the Neonman tonight?"

Bill nodded as he pushed open the door. "Got to, Blood. 'Cause Live, from beautimous Lake Chelan, Washington—*it's Saturday Night!* Want to come down a few brewskies with us? Russ is gonna be there too."

"Yeah, I might just do that. I'd love to get an earful of corporate America's plans for the great Pacific Northwest. And I'm sure that Neon's got the inside scoop on which Halloween parties will be happening around the lake. Do you realize I haven't been to a Halloween party in almost nine years now?"

Bill Baker did indeed. He'd tried three years running to get his brother to go into town on the thirty-first, like in the days of old. He thought about the party Neon was planning at his shop, and reflected upon all the good ones they had attended down in Tahoe—even hosted themselves—before Thomas went away on pot charges, and their parents died. How could he forget that Halloween had always been one of their favorite holidays? He could not. Ever since his older brother had walked him through the neighborhoods of Tahoe City on those cool October nights with the smell of fresh raked leaves burning in the autumn air, it had been as special as Christmas or the Fourth of July to them both. He was intent on talking Thomas into attending Neon's bash, convinced it would be great therapy for them both to cut loose and enjoy the company of the people and the place they had adopted as family.

Bill Baker thought about his old college roommate, Russ Warwick, and how strange it really was for a punctuality nut like him not to have at least called the lodge by now. His sense of humor took its leave at the thought. His stomach got queasy. His face grew pale.

Thomas knew what Bill was thinking about because—as usual—he was thinking the exact same thing. "Guess I'll go play charming host with the Saturday lunch crowd. Care to join me?" the older brother quizzed.

"No, I'll pass. Nan took Nate down to Lakeshore Bumper Boats to terrorize the other kids," Bill said. "Think I'll take advantage of the peace of mind and get my work done. That way, I'll have some free time to go out fly fishing with Russ."

Bill Baker bit a slice of skin from the inside of his lower lip, and looked toward his brother with worried eyes. "Would you—"

As so many times before, one Baker Brother finished the other's sentence for him. "Yeah. I'll call you as soon as I hear from Russ, or Wolf," said Thomas.

"Thanks, Blood," Bill replied.

Chapter 3

Funeral

THE WELL-CHARRED corpses of the Warwick family floated to the surface on Sunday afternoon. They were cremated, as requested, on Thursday. And now, this sunny Saturday morning, a solemn crowd gathered on the lawn of the late Kenneth and Connie Joe Warwick's solar environmental retirement dream house to pay their last respects.

Rows of wooden folding chairs had been arranged in two distinct hemispheres which were divided by a wide patch of grass manicured down to the consistency of the Lake Chelan Country Club's putting greens. A vast array of flowers framed the fellowship like a living, colored matting. A podium and simple quilt-covered table were situated at the edge of the wild-flower and granite embankment, which dropped to a sandy beach. And parallel to them, a line of potted Norfolk Pines spread like an earthy green curtain before an immaculate arena captivated by the various shades of flowing blue folds on the surface of Lake Chelan. Upon the simple quilt sat four urns containing all that remained of the Warwick family.

It was ten minutes in front of eleven. The eulogy was scheduled to begin on the hour. Slowly, everyone found their way to the section of their choice. And there were clearly choices to be made.

Kenneth Warwick had served as an executive of the Louisiana Pacific Timber Corporation for over thirty-five years before going for the voluntary buy out offer, and retiring to Chelan on the 1000 acre parcel he'd had the foresight to acquire. Consequently, many of his former associates in the timber industry—from both management and labor, as well as the local mill operators—were present. Many of these people had not seen or spoken with the senior Warwick for years and yet— because of the effect that men like Ken Warwick had on people, and the memory left by his friendship—they all made the pilgrimage when they heard of his *accident*. This group then, occupied half of this assembly.

The other hemisphere of thought was occupied by a variety of locals, who knew the *other side* of Kenneth Warwick, the side which had developed with the wisdom of his years spent on *both* sides of the Northwest logging issue, and the side which endeared them and their cause to him as much, or more, than any other member of their environmental watchdog group called the Chelan Alliance. The summer of 1994 may have been the one in which K. W. sold off his property in South Lake Tahoe and made the permanent, year-round, move to Chelan, but he'd been summering here now for quite a spell. And as a lake-frontage property owner, he was actively involved in the future planning of the valley.

Several members of the Yacht Club who'd come to know and love the Warwicks were also in attendance. Most of them were still in shock over the realization that such a terrible accident could befall any of them in their sacred golden years of sailing, and many murmured of the rash of mechanical reviews of their crafts which had immediately began—and would undoubtedly resume come spring—due to the Warwick's untimely, and *alleged* fuel tank vapor lock explosion.

The people who had come to know the young environ-mentalist, Russell Warwick, during his years of vacationing here with his father, came to pay their respects as well. That group was headed up by Russ's old college roommate, Bill Baker, his wife Nancy, and son, Nathan. They sat in the back row on the environmental side of the aisle. Thomas Baker, Wolf, Michael Johnson (the local neon artist), and his Asian lady friend, were sandwiched between them and Chelan City Councilman, Timothy Alan Barnes, the spokesman for the Chelan Alliance, former corporate attorney, and Kenneth Warwick's best friend.

The councilman sat quietly, hands on his lap, eyes drifting out across the water, thinking about his old friend and how much he was going to miss him. He reminisced fondly upon the first day he'd invited Kenny Warwick to *his* valley to go salmon fishing. He weighed the words he wished to impart in his defunct friend's honor, but only for an instant. Praise from men like Barnes came easily for wise and courageous men like Kenny Warwick. The soothing hands of the councilman's wife softly returned to his shoulders.

"How long are we going to wait for *those people*, Tim?"

The councilman checked his watch. "Five more minutes, Martha," he promised.

She released a long, deep, sad sigh. Her weary head sought the warmth of her husband's hold. "I'm going to miss Kenny and Connie Joe," she sniffed. "It was a terrible way to pass on."

The councilman nodded, handed her a tissue, and buried his face in the fold of his hands.

Everyone else had expected them to arrive in a long, black limo, but not Wolf. He hadn't figured the high-tech executives would choose to endure the grueling weekend traffic from Seattle through the mountains like some common tourists. As usual, Wolf's instincts were correct.

James Shawn Wolf, ex-Special Forces, ex-Navy Seal, ex-CIA contract fly-boy, and present owner operator of Lone Wolf Air, heard their engines with his one good ear long before anyone else. The sound brought him to his feet. He strained to listen closer. He sniffed the autumn air, donned his Vuarnet sunglasses, and locked his wolf-vision on the center of the lake.

Upon the brightly-lit stage of sun drenched waters, the big white bird conducted its descent dance. She landed about a mile out without so much as a bounce, or even a visible wake. Every eye was upon her as the graceful goose motored proudly toward the gathering. Every eye strained to see the craft *they* were arriving in. Every eye, but those of the Wolf, that is. He had already identified her as a customized McKinnon Goose upon their final approach. And now, as she swam nearer, he could better appreciate the beauty of the beast. He began to drool with guarded envy.

They docked the executive water-limo alongside his beloved 1947 Dehavilland Beaver—effectively dwarfing it. Wolf watched with interest as two Asian pilots secured the sleek V-Hull which had set his Beaver bobbing on its merely aluminum floats. The pilots made him think of Nam. *Fucking slants,* Wolf thought. *They were no match for Lone Wolf's skills.* He scoped out the twin Pratt and Whitney PT-6 Turbo engines, and bobbed his head approvingly while pondering the myth of their renowned durability. The Beaver could carry eight passengers—*if* they were very friendly. The Goose seated twelve—in style. The Beaver was strictly a solo act. The Goose required a copilot when flying commercially. Wolf recalled the day he was invited to fly second chair in singer Jimmy Buffet's Goose during the height of the outlaw era in South Florida. The McKinnon was but a toy to Buffet, and so he flew her primarily for pleasure—*sans* second chair. It was the only way to fly, as far as James Shawn Wolf was concerned.

If the sheer size of the two planes didn't underscore their disparity to every aeronautical laymen present, the insignias on their tails certainly must have. The Beaver's tail sported his infamous company logo: A large wolf head, fangs bared, wearing an *anything-but-mild* snarl, and a Snoopy-type, Red Baron scarf. Below the call letters was painted in bold black print—*Lone Wolf Air.* The Beaver's fuselage bore a small circle housing the Ying and the Yang (the dark and light side of life), representative of Wolf's personality.

The Goose tail displayed a large, bright, yellow moon contained by a thin blue line. It was strangely familiar. Wolf had seen the same emblem in Vancouver's Chinatown on the leather jackets of gang youths, who once informed him it meant *they* owned the night. The Goose's fuselage was inscribed with

Chinese calligraphy and in English: *Ming Yaht*. Wolf was lost in thought about the plane and those contained within it. The arrival of the Goose had taken him back to Nam, and placed him on involuntary alert mode.

"What the hell is that?" asked Michael Johnson.

"That, my dear Neonman, is three quarters of a million dollars worth of customized Grummon Goose, care of McKinnon Industries. *That* is a McKinnon Goose. It's the limousine you've all been expecting to see come tooling down that road."

"Wipe that drool off your muzzle, Wolfy," suggested Thomas Baker.

"Wolf envies no one, and no thing, Writer Man," lied the flyboy as he flipped his friend the bird.

The Po Brothers had never made a joint appearance in Chelan. Po Jing had showed his face for the opening of Ming Yaht's industrial park years earlier, and Po Lin had reputedly toured the countryside through the tinted windows of his bullet proof executive limousine, but the billionaire brothers rarely made joint appearances anywhere.

The locals were surprised when the Pos set foot on the dock. There was nothing traditional about them. They were casually dressed in Western clothes, and looked extremely debonair from a distance. Both hemispheres of environmental thought hummed with a full range of emotional and financial speculation generated by the presence of the pair, who had *double-handedly* helped earn Vancouver, British Columbia, the nickname *Hongcouver* in the past ten years. Practically everyone watched the Pos hover benevolently, in the manner of mandarin patriarchs, making polite conversation with the entourage of local dignitaries who'd come to court them.

But Wolf's attention was captured by the third man to disembark the Goose. He was an American, an American who moved like an Asian! He was every inch of six-foot-three, and the tight cut of his Hugo Boss suit only served to accentuate the well-honed physique lurking beneath its silken lining. He had one of those square-chinned, chiseled-from-granite faces, and wore his jet-black hair slicked back into a small ponytail. He stood alertly, one step behind the Po Brothers, with a faraway look in his mirrored-steel blue eyes. He made every hair on Wolf's hide stand at attention. Wolf had seen men like him before…but they were few and far between.

"Does that dude look like Steven Seagal, the martial arts hero in the movies—or what?" asked Neon.

"He does kinda' look like him," remarked Bill Baker.

"Looks can be deceiving," muttered the suspecting pilot.

To be sure, Wolf's *alert mode* had reached new heights with the emergence of the big man, but the fourth and final passenger to disembark the Goose had an equally powerful effect upon him. *She*, however, stimulated an entirely different part of the animal.

The stunning brunette was helped off the plane by the ponytailed American. She stood around five-foot-eight. Her hair was pinned up. She wore designer glasses. She brushed the wrinkles out of her pinstriped blazer, tipped her hourglass back toward the Goose, and retrieved a tiny, navy-blue briefcase, which matched her pleated skirt to a T. She waited patiently, until her employers and the local politicians concluded their greetings. Then, when the tall dark American had completed his scan of the crowd and waved the Ming Yaht party ahead, she filed in behind, briefcase in hand, showing nothing but class— and a whole lotta' leg to Wolf.

Thomas Baker was entranced by the hot-legged brunette. He and Wolf always noticed such sultry skirts simultaneously, and typically indulged in their individual bachelor responses shortly thereafter, but this skirt sent a serious chill up Thomas Baker's spine. The writer did not have an *alert mode* like Wolf, but something similar was stirring deep within him as well.

Bill Baker caught his brother ogling the secretary. "Nice legs, eh Blood?" he whispered. "She has a brain, too."

Thomas Baker nodded attentively.

Nancy Baker elbowed her husband's rib cage.

The scent of the secretary-in-seamed-stockings wafted its way into a special spot in the writer from Granite Falls psyche, as she strolled to the dignitaries' section. Once, he thought he caught her glancing his way across the sea of chairs.

Bill had met the brunette on several visits to Russ Warwick's Seattle office, and deemed her worthy of his brother's attention. Had she not lived and worked in the Emerald City, he would have hooked them up long ago. He wanted to get her attention, but his wife's eyes were burning a hole in the back of his neck, and his ribs were still smarting. He made a mental note to introduce them after the eulogy.

The Po Brothers and the brunette sat beside the mayor, a former governor, and county planner, Hank Hodge. Everyone else sat as well. Everyone, but the tall, dark, American with the two-inch ponytail, and James Shawn Wolf.

The mystery man positioned himself behind the back row, semi-relaxed in a military *at-ease* stance.

Wolf stood parallel to him, in the left hemisphere, with his hands on the back of Thomas Baker's chair. His hard-on for the ravishing brunette was quickly deflated by the flashbacks this *warrior* was stimulating. And the fact that he preferred to stand in back to observe the others, only further fueled Wolf's speculations about the guy. James Shawn Wolf stared coolly at the mystery man, hoping to generate some response.

The tall one unbuttoned his jacket, turned his head toward Wolf, and nodded slowly. Then, he put on *his* Vuarnet sunglasses and resumed his stance, hands folded before him, observing everything and everyone between him and his employers.

Wolf returned the nod, but he could not restrain the muffled, throaty growl which accompanied it.

A clergyman led the congregation in prayer. The mayor spoke briefly. Bill Baker offered a few emotional words of praise for young Russ Warwick, and Councilman Timothy Alan Barnes delivered a moving eulogy.

The brunette's mascara melted into a cascading navy-blue tear of sorrow, as she thought of the senseless deaths of her former boss, his wife Angy, and their unborn child.

THE PO BROTHERS sat silently—like wax-figures—and studied the ancient Chinese science of *feng shui*. *Feng shui* (literally *wind and water*) ascribes prosperity or woe to the particular *chi*, or cosmic breath, of the space that people occupy, be it a house, office, or—an entire valley.

Vancouver, British Columbia's waterfront real estate had attracted the Pos' billions for several very good reasons. One was the Canadian jewel's resemblance to another city by the bay, San Francisco, and its extraordinary *feng shui*. Eight years earlier, Po Jing had toured the North Shore of False Creek, and envisioned millions of square feet of residential and commercial space on the *then* site of Canada's Expo '86. Like all of the Po Brothers' *visions*, that one had since come to pass. Anxiety about Hong Kong's reversion to the People's Republic of China in 1997, and Vancouver's reassuring stability and evocative resemblance to Hong Kong itself, were also driving factors in the Pos' great exodus to the West. Combine these with Canada's investor-immigrant category (that offered fretful Hong Kong capitalists Canadian citizenship after five years, in exchange for a government approved investment of two-hundred fifty thousand dollars) and the result was a recipe for a major influx of Hong Kong Chinese. But that was before all the Asian resentment set in.

Po Jing saw many similarities between Vancouver and Chelan. Vancouver stood at the confluence of two great bodies of water. "Make Vancouver a good-luck city. But only more of Ming Yaht's buildings will ensure prosperity," Jing told Brother Lin in the back of their limo on that rainy day back in 1986. The Chelan Valley's proximity to the Pacific Rim cities of Seattle and *Hongcouver*, (as the Pos now favored calling it) along with the majestic lake's mountainous meeting with the mighty Columbia and scenic Stehekin rivers, had initiated another vision four years hence in the mind of Po Jing.

THE COUNCILMAN'S oration was winding to a close, and the Pos sensed the speaker's eye contact lingering longer in their direction than any other.

"There are those among us who wish to see the Chelan Valley *liberated* from bothersome environmental regulations, and those who wish to preserve them at *any* cost for the future unborn children of the Evergreen State. Ken Warwick entertained a peculiar Northwesterner suspicion that unbridled prosperity might be a curse for a region which offers so many riches that money just can't buy. Kenneth Warwick was not a man who lacked in wisdom or foresight. After spending much of his adult life on the other side of the chainsaw, he acquired enough wisdom to know that the logging of irreplaceable old growth forests had to end...*somewhere.* So he had the foresight to retire on this land where we are all gathered today.

Ken Warwick was a good father, and a devoted husband. He was a generous man. In 1993, it was his emotional and financial backing which helped the Chelan Alliance defeat the BLM's plan to clear-cut trees in the Chelan Basin Watershed within view of these pristine waters." Barnes gestured to charred treetops on a distant ridge. "Ken also fought beside us to contain that great fire," he said.

"Kenneth Eugene Warwick loved this place as much as he loved his family, and life itself. He loved Chelan for the same reasons most of us do. I guess that's why he requested his ashes be spread out over the lake." His lips quivered. The councilman paused for a moment of silence to regain his composure.

The Chinese custom was to worship the ashen remains of their ancestors for eternity, thus the Po Brothers grimaced painfully at the mere thought of the councilman's announcement.

"Such a deplorable and barbarous act, Brother Lin," Po Jing commented, through clenched teeth in whisper-speak Cantonese.

Po Lin nodded in reverent agreement.

"I am certain that I speak for all of us when I say that we, and this valley, will miss Kenneth Eugene Warwick immensely," concluded the councilman. Barnes glared at the Chinese brothers, then wrapped his weathered knuckles on the podium, and walked away.

The crowd dispersed, and the Pos' ponytailed bodyguard rejoined them in the front of the assembly, along with county planner Hodge.

Bill Baker, determined to introduce his brother to the brunette, led a small delegation to the water's edge, with a curious Wolf nipping at his heels.

The secretary had hoped to see Bill Baker's friendly face when she asked the Pos to allow her to attend the service for their fallen employee, but now she glanced around nervously before acknowledging him. "Bill! Bill Baker! How nice to see you," she shouted. She studied the similarities in the two brother's features, and became entranced by Thomas's warm green eyes and silvery blond hair.

"It's a shame about Russ and Angela," Bill said solemnly.

The brunette nodded. "This corporation will miss him. Russ stood for something. He had a great sense of humor, and he will be hard to replace. He thought highly of you, Bill. Care to introduce me to your friends?"

"Sure! Why not? You've met my wife, Nancy, and my son, Nathan."

Wolf's *alert mode* shifted to *horny mode*. He tugged on Bill's belt loop, and twice cleared his throat.

"Friends, Marla Decker. Marla Decker? Friends. There! That was easy enough," Bill announced.

Wolf's shoed paw came down hard on Bill's Nike sneaker.

"And this hairy gentleman is James Wolf, owner of the local airline. We just call him Wolf. I won't waste your time explaining, but if you ever date him, you'll know why."

Marla Decker offered her hand and a vibrant smile, but her attention drifted past the pilot to the writer from Granite Falls.

Wolf growled lightly and feigned fanging the flesh of her palm, but already he perceived vibes between her and Baker. His attention slowly shifted back toward the Pos and their man, who seemed to be showing some degree of interest in their secretary's conversation.

"This is Michael Johnson and his friend, Miss Ho Pai," Bill added.

They exchanged handshakes, and Marla decided to practice her Cantonese on Pai with a simple greeting. The secretary knew she had screwed up the intonation as soon as the words left her lips. "I'm sorry, Pai," she excused herself, blushing with embarrassment. "I'm just learning."

"You speak Cantonese very well, Marla," the perceptive Asian said politely. "But I am from Beijing." The woman's mind wandered back to the countless hours *she* had endured learning the English language.

Their introduction session was interrupted by another outburst of Chinese, as the Pos singled her out to speak, having overheard their conversation.

"'Ho Pai? What a beautiful name your parents have graced you with," offered Po Lin.

"And quite fitting, I might add," chimed in Po Jing.

Pai assumed an instinctually respectful pose to the elder Pos.

The ponytailed American had made note of the young Ming Yaht employee's file before taking this assignment. He knew everything about her, and yet he asked in perfect Beijing dialect about her work in the valley.

The surprised Pai identified herself as a lab technician at the corporation's Chelan Biotech Research Lab, which invited Po Lin to inquire further.

"And how do you find your work in this field?" Po Lin led off. And for several minutes the billionaire brothers spoke in rapid, singsong native tongue with the captivating expatriate, as if no one else existed.

Soon enough, Wolf's curiosity got the best of him, and he attempted to enter the conversation—in Chinese—by inquiring about the McKinnon Goose that the brothers had arrived aboard. Po Lin glowered intensely at his bodyguard, who immediately intervened on his employers' behalf. Then, the Asian brothers carried on with their own kind.

The ponytailed American locked hands with Wolf for what seemed like an eternity, as both men stared silently into each other's French-made shades.

"Mr. Wolf? Nice to meet you. My name is Nicholas Gordon."

Knowing the guy had been tuned into their conversation for certain now, Wolf's *alert mode* kicked in again. "My pleasure, Mr. Gordon. And what, might I ask, is your position in the corporation?"

Nick Gordon did not hesitate to answer. "I've been assigned to the position of Security Chief for Ming Yaht's Wash-ington State interests."

Wolf tightened his grip on the big guy's hand. "I suppose we'll be seeing a lot of you then?"

Nicholas Gordon out-squeezed Wolf—as if to prove a point—before pulling his hand away. "I'm kind of a loner actually, but I'll be popping in and out of the valley quite frequently." The Pos made a gesture to him, and the Security Chief took his leave, issuing a closing order to the secretary. "Five minutes, Miss Decker. Then join us on the dock for the flight back to Seattle."

"Yes, Mr. Gordon," she replied.

Bill Baker broke the ensuing silence, hoping to restart the germination process he had perceived between the brunette and his brother. "Marla? This is my brother, Thomas. I told you about him already."

Thomas Baker gave his brother a glancing visual blow which screamed out, *"I'll talk to you later!"* before placing a gentleman's kiss upon the lady's hand.

"Mr. Baker, it's a pleasure to meet you," Marla remarked.

"Pleasure's all mine," Thomas replied truthfully.

"I've read all your articles in the Seattle P.I. on kayaking...*and* your first novel, too," she shocked him by saying.

"You have?"

She nodded. "I also attended your first reading session at Elliot Bay Books."

"You did?" Thomas answered, with a twinkle in his eyes.

"Sure did. But it was late. I was in a crowd. You'd been sitting there all day signing those paperbacks. You looked tired."

He felt awkward. "I must have been very tired not to have noticed you," he crooned, as a broad, inviting smile filled his face.

The Seattle secretary blushed. "Hasn't Bill told you any of this? I asked him to introduce me to you a long time ago."

Again Tom scrutinized his brother's impish grin.

"Anyway, I'm very glad to meet you. Sorry it couldn't have been under better circumstances," she lamented.

A pleasant, primitive aroma filled the writer's senses, inviting him to investigate this female before him further. "So, I take it you're an outdoors person then?"

She, too, was invited by a primitive wind. "Yes, very much so, but my job keeps me tied down. I live out most of my adventure vacations these days staring out the twenty-first floor windows of Ming Yaht's Seattle headquarters at the Olympic Mountains, or the Cascade Range. I enjoyed your feature story in the Sunday Travel section this spring about Granite Falls Lodge. The concept of combining nature adventures with pampered personal attention is a great one. It's a sure-fire winner in an era when more and more people like myself are coming to know the value of such experiences and wanting…and *needing* such things in their hectic, corporate lives."

The writer perceived her words were sincere. He drank of her beauty in the noonday sun. He shook his head in disbelief. "And you say you've read *my* novel? Well? What did you think?"

"I enjoyed it. Immensely," she said pursing her lips. "Actually, I'm sort of a novice writer myself. Poetry mainly."

The chemistry was brewing now, and Thomas Baker was facing his ultimate temptation—an outdoors-minded beauty with a genuine interest in the written word! The writer grew weak in the knees.

The secretary checked her watch, then the dock, where her employers were engaged in a lively discussion with the county planner. "Next time you're in Seattle, perhaps you would do me the honor of checking out my work," she said, in a totally unprofessional fashion.

When she glanced back nervously over her shoulder, Wolf planted an elbow in the writer's ribs, and whispered: "At least she didn't say *etchings!*" And when she directed her heavenly hazel eyes back to Baker, Wolf pleaded: "But Marla...I am the main character in his next novel!" Then the pilot threw in a pair of puppy-dog eyes for added effect.

Michael Johnson—the Neonman—had been watching the county planner do everything but shine the Po Brothers' Bally loafers on the dock. "Do you see the way that Hodge is sucking up to your bosses, Pai?" Neon remarked with an ill expression.

"Sucking up?" the Asian beauty echoed with a puzzled look.

Neon quickly explained the slang term, then added, "Shit! You'd think they were some kind of royalty or something."

Miss Pai furrowed her finely plucked brow. "Michael! They are very wealthy and respected businessmen. Do not forget that their investment decisions could have major impact on the lives of the people of this valley."

James Shawn Wolf watched the dock as well, lamenting the loss of hearing in his one bad ear more than ever. He vehemently resented the Pos' presence, and to a lesser degree, felt unwarranted malice toward Neon's Asian companion. The first time he had visited Chelan there was only a small Chinese restaurant, and *Hop Sing's Laundromat.* Peaceful, apple-picking wetbacks were the only foreigners back then. As Wolf's trained eyes zeroed in on the dock, he theorized about how many would follow the *Pied-Piper-Pos* to the promised land in the coming years—especially after the reality of Communist Chinese rule settled into the Hong Kong business community. Wolf was not a man without a conscience though, and deep within him it uttered these words: *"I am not a racist!"* To which the animal responded: "But I am *very* aware. And *that* makes me *very wary."*

Meanwhile, on the dock, the county planner's simple-mindedness continued to irritate the Po Brothers.

"Why this thrust into Chelan, Mr. Po? I mean, why here? Why now?" blubbered Hank Hodge.

"Nineteen-ninety-seven," Po Lin replied as he watched Councilman Barnes entertaining an audience, out of the corner of his sloping eye.

"The world is getting smaller, Mr. Hodge. Did you actually expect such a precious valley as this one to remain cute and quiet little Chelan forever?" added Po Jing.

Po Lin turned his cold, dark eyes upon the planner. "I am deeply disturbed by what I have seen this day, Mr. Hodge," he pronounced.

The face of the planner grew deadly pale. "How's that, Mr. Po?"

"It appears you have failed to inform us of the full extent of opposition to development in the valley." The Great Po's eyes shifted back toward the city councilman. "This *Councilman* Barnes. Is he going to become a stumbling block which will impede our timetable?"

Hank Hodge swallowed hard. "N-n-no s-sir, M-Mr. P-Po. I can handle him. He j-just represents a small r-radical element in America that wants to over-regulate to the point where these regulations themselves become overbearing and unaffordable." The planner wiped sweat from his brow with a silk handkerchief. "Men like Barnes employ scare tactics based on unstudied and undocumented scenarios which foretell of an environmental holocaust, simply so that they will have a cause to fight for. Trust me. What the people of Washington State and Chelan want and need, are jobs and a secure future!" He cleared his throat. "Now as you know, the governor is behind us on this thing one hundred percent."

Po Lin bowed before starting for the water-limo. "Good day, Mr. Hodge. Our Mr. Gordon here will keep me informed of your efficiency level."

The planner had been itching to be dismissed, and disappeared in a heartbeat from the dock.

Nicholas Gordon watched the walrus-faced fool waddle out of sight. "He's a weak link, Lin. Why in the hell do you tolerate his insolence?"

"Because he is a necessary fool for us, Nicholas. And you, of course, do understand why. " The pilots were waiting at the open door of the Goose, and there the Great Po paused to impart his words of wisdom with a glowing smile. "Black cat, white cat—it is a *good cat* if it catches mice."

Marla Decker bit her lip, and scuffed her navy-blue flats on the gray granite pebbles beneath her. She was about to remove a card with her home number scribbled on it from her purse, when Nick Gordon called her the first time. She gazed into the eyes of the writer from Granite Falls. "Listen, about Russ…"

Po Lin snapped his fingers.

Marla dropped her business card back inside her purse, and sighed.

Nick responded. *"Miss Decker!* Time to leave."

The secretary looked longingly into Thomas's eyes. "Nice meeting you, Mr. Baker," she said, as she strolled off toward the seaplane with her card, and a piece of the writer's heart, still in her possession.

As Nicholas Gordon helped the last Po into the belly of the Goose, the elder Lin took note of the entourage of locals gathering the Warwick's remains for what would be their final flight on Lone Wolf Air Service. The secretary was getting perilously close, so Lin lowered his voice to a conspiratorial whisper. "This Barnes…*watch him!*" he hissed. "Watch all of them—very closely. We must not fail in this endeavor, Nicholas. Is this understood?"

Nick Gordon removed his glasses. "Yes, Mr. Po, I understand perfectly," the human hawk replied.

AS WOLF taxied for take-off moments later, he watched the Goose tail and its yellow moon insignia rising in the Western sky…and his ensuing involuntary growl soon drowned out the rattle of the 1947 DeHavilland Beaver's radial engine.

Chapter 4

Party

ON HALLOWEEN NIGHT, 1995, Chelan's city streets were alive with the sound of music and gaiety. Masqueraders meandered door to door on wooden Wild West walkways. A cool breeze born of glacial mountains blew boldly down Woodin Avenue. A warm tequila wind wafted from the open door of Signor Frog's saloon.

The Eskimo, Dorothy, surveyed the scene, and saw a small village called Bethel, Alaska. Her husband, the scarecrow, and his brother, the lion, saw Tahoe City, California, in the days of their youth. Bethel, Tahoe City—they had all grown up in paradise, and been trying to get back ever since. Back to a place where community was not an abstract concept, but a way of life. Back to a place like Chelan.

The threesome paused at the curb to study their attire and second-guess themselves, all somehow affected by the change of seasons and its magnification of the passage of time. They gazed across the street to Lone Wolf Airways and Michael Johnson's *Forever Neon* studio and shop, which was their destination. An eerie incandescent flicker shone from the display window of the lowly lit gallery. In the apartment window above, a neon witch on a brown glass tube-broom traversed the night sky, taking the threesome's curious eyes out over the lake behind it, and the mountains beyond.

Nancy Baker thought about the passing of her father the summer gone by. He was the last family she could claim, and now he was no more. And Bethel, Alaska was just another word on a map to her.

Thomas Baker thought about how long it had been since he'd felt close enough to a group of people to party with them. For the lion's share of his prison experience he became alienated by the infinite inconsiderateness displayed by men to their fellow men. When his mother died of cancer, he had to attend her funeral in leg irons and chains with a U.S. Marshal escort. It was his worse nightmare come to pass—and an experience he feared would leave him irreparably bitter. Again and again he dreamed of isolating himself from the thoughtlessness of his own species when he was free, but in spite of the only lesson that the U.S. *justice* system had to teach to non-violent men convicted of crimes of conscience, his natural tendencies prevailed. For that thought he exhaled a visible thanks to the heavens above.

Bill Baker thought of the last flight of the Warwicks. Again the ashes of his friend Russ fluttered to the blue grave below the open cargo door of Wolf's Beaver, and again Bill lamented the loss.

Slowly the Oz trio turned to one another. A spontaneous group hug ensued.

A piercing wolf whistle broke the spell. *"Hey Baker! Save some hugs for us!"* shouted the good witch/bad witch Deli Twins from the second floor pub of Campbell House Restaurant. The Chevy Suburban with *The Lodge at Granite Falls* on the door had given them away.

Thomas Baker spotted the luscious twins immediately, and waved a lion's paw.

"Where's Wolfy?" lovely Lyla shouted above the roar of the pub's rowdy crowd.

Thomas pointed across the street to Neon's place.

"Wanna party with us after you get bored with all the couples in there?" said Lynn luringly.

The lion nodded, waved his furry tail, and led the skipping trio across Woodin Avenue, roaring, *"Let's Party!"*

Three beers and a deafening group wolf howl awaited them at the door. Neon had gone all out. The sound system cranked out *Crocodile Rock*, while his glass color chart ran top to bottom to the beat. Neon wore a Frankenstein costume. He had his tube-bender's blow hose, and a long thin balloon wrapped around his neck. Wolf was in an outrageous werewolf outfit—same as every year. Miss Ho Pai's face was covered in white base with a painted-on, unblinking smile. She wore a traditional Chinese silk robe. Everyone was in costume.

"Well? What do you think?" asked Neon.

"You know all these people?" Bill asked the host.

"Naaa! The whole town is partying, dude. I know most of them, but I haven't been lifting masks to see who's who."

The Oz trio from Granite Falls studied Pai. Because she had arrived to the Warwick's funeral late with Neon, they had really never gotten a chance to speak to her.

"Isn't it about time you broke down and formally introduced us to your lovely lady friend, Michael?" asked Nancy Baker.

Miss Ho Pai had been curious about Nancy's ancestry from the first day she saw her browsing at Riverwalk Books. She bowed silently, and allowed Neon to do his host thing.

The gray-green make-up and shoe-black hair covered the healthy Swedish features of the Neonman all too well. "This is Ho Pai. Just call her Pai," he said. "She is a biotechnician at Ming Yaht's Chelan Environmental Research Lab."

Bill Baker's eyes lit up with curiosity. "Just what are they working on out there, Pai? I hear it's some pretty advanced stuff."

Pai's painted face wrinkled. "I'm sorry, Mr. Baker. I would be very happy to discuss my work with you, but it is not permitted."

Her answer reminded the scarecrow, Bill, of a similar one for a similar question put to one Russ Warwick by telephone the week before his death.

Upon hearing her response, Wolf cast a suspect glare toward the Asian, then resumed an entertaining yarn for a flock of females.

Local fishing guide, Rick Graybill, and his wife, called out to Bill and Nancy from behind their salmon masks, and the Bakers excused themselves to join them.

Thomas Baker scanned the gallery as he drank his long neck Ranier beer. There were a dozen podiums displaying intriguing glass works. Swaying neon palm trees bedecked one wall, a huge gold Chinese dragon another. A bold black and white ying-yang circle hung above the steel door leading to the back half—the work area—of the building.

Neon caught the lion looking. "That one's for Wolf's place," he explained.

Baker rubbed his fuzzy lion chin. "You are prolific, Johnson," he said.

"Yeah, Tom. Thanks," Frankenstein answered humbly.

"No, man. I mean it. People are saying good things about your work. You're really getting a name for yourself in the Pacific Northwest." He paused to admire another piece of art. "I can't help but notice the Asian flavor you've added since my last visit."

"That's some of Pai's influence on me I guess," the Neon monster yawned. "She's helped me design several radical custom works for Chinese clients in the last couple of months." Mike Johnson appreciated the ego buffing Baker was giving him in front of Pai, but he didn't need it. He *knew* he was good, and he never blew his own horn, too. That's why older guys like Wolf and Baker thought highly of him. That, and the fact that he was mature beyond his twenty-six years—and not some junior know-it-all. Neon saw curiosity on Baker's face. "In case you're wondering, Pai was attracted to the art, and the light, and the science of neon," Frankenstein proclaimed, wrapping his arm around his date and squeezing her gently. "Pai, Gooood!" he growled.

Beneath her painted face, the lady scientist was blushing red.

"I'm doing a little bartering with her," Neon said. "I'm teaching her the well guarded secrets of the trade."

"I'm envious Mikey," the lion admitted. "You've never shown *me* or Bill your work room. What exactly are you... *bartering* for?"

"I am going to teach Michael Tai Chi, in exchange for his knowledge of the neon art," the Asian explained.

"Pai?"

"Yes, Mr. Baker?" she answered respectfully.

"Please. Any friend of Neon's is a friend of mine," the lion blurted, extended his paw. "Call me Thomas."

A warm feeling of acceptance swept over her.

"If you're ever of a mind to take on another student, let Mikey know. I have always wanted to learn Tai chi," Thomas said innocently.

Nancy Baker called the host's date to join her foursome, and Pai looked to Neon for direction.

"Go on! Meet some more locals, Pai. That's why we have these little get togethers," Neon suggested. He placed a kiss on her painted cheek, and let loose a ghoulish laugh. "I'm going to drag Mr. Baker's body to my laboratory, and show him the equipment—so he stops whining!"

Behind the closed steel door, Baker waited in total blackness for too long a time, while the host dragged his elevator shoes in character around his workshop. Then came silence, followed by the twisting of a rusty valve, and the hiss of propane gas escaping from captivity. Baker's pulse quickened. He scanned the darkness with eyes open wide. "Hey, Neon!" he called out nervously. He saw nothing. Heard nothing...but silence.

POOF! Match met gas, and the cannon burner cast a blue flame gleam upon the host's features. "Just call me Frank," Neon laughed. The silhouette shuffled to the next metal stand, lit the ribbon burner, then explained how both devices were employed to bend glass at varying angles.

Baker could see an array of tables, gas canisters, glass racks, and gauges, by the illumination of the twin burners. He watched the shadow of the artist do the monster mash to the rear of the shop. He listened while the silhouette explained non-asbestos pattern liners, and compared European glass to American, along the way.

"Back here, Baker!" Neon barked beneath a ceiling adorned with twinkling copper coils and dangling alligator clips. "You're an author, right? Always wanting to learn about new shit, right? I'm going to show you something that'll make your hair stand on end. Who knows, maybe you'll want a neon-bender for a character in your next novel."

"Never know," said a wary lion, as he carefully approached his host's position.

"In which case you'll need to know all about the most technical and dangerous piece of equipment in the shop—*this!*" Frankenstein slammed the metal arm of the main breaker box like a one-armed bandit long overdue to hit three bells. A red light flashed on the back wall, and a loud, low, mean mechanical growling started up at Neon's feet. The flick of a second switch brought forth a cluck-cluck-clucking sound from a belt and pulley, and a six-inch erection of glass began to glow ghostly white—then just as quickly dimmed. And to this abracadabra duet of sound and light, the Neonman did a macabre metaphysto waltz.

The hair on Baker's limbs stood up and boogied to the beat. Fine fuzzies on the back of his neck rose to the occasion. Even the woolly mane on his lion costume danced rhythmically in the supercharged atmosphere! In deja vu, he reflected upon his hikes in the Sierra Nevada's beneath the great expanse of power lines occupying the firebreaks. *"What the hell is that?"* he whispered.

"That, Writer Man, is a bombarder and its playmate, the vacuum pump. And this, is where I nuke the glass and bring my little creations to life. Behold the power of Neonman!" he shouted, his voice echoing off the far wall.

Baker was amazed by the way Mikey's persona had been altered upon entering the workshop. He began exploring the bombarder area. "No wonder you're dressed like that. This place looks a lot like Frankenstein's castle," Baker snickered, as he reached for the control device on the end of the table.

Neon lunged for the lion's arm, knocking his beer to the floor in the process. *"Don't touch that!"* he screamed. "Unless you wanna look like a dead Buckwheat—or that jive boxing promoter, Don King." Michael Johnson shut down all the gadgets, and quickly regretted his rare nonchalance. "Sorry about your beer, Baker, but this is serious shit here. I try not to forget that," he stated, as they made their way to the door in silence. "Show's over. Let's get back to the party, and get you a fresh Rainier," the host suggested.

Baker changed the topic to romance. "Pai's different from any woman I've seen you with. Are you getting serious with her?"

"Would it bother anyone if I was?" Neon snapped.

The lion looked the monster in the eye. "Sure as hell wouldn't *bother* me. Why would you ask a stupid question like that?"

"I don't know. There's definitely something about her. This may sound strange to you, but have you ever been attracted to a woman by her scent, and her vibes? I...ah, shit! I must sound like I'm losing it. Good thing I'm not into commitments—just like you and Wolf. Huh? She's a *nice* girl. Know what I mean, Tom?"

The lion thought about the Seattle secretary from the funeral for a moment. "Yeah, I hear ya. But be careful, Mikey. Nice girls can be dangerous," he declared.

They re-entered the party, and ran smack dab into Wolf and the good witch/bad witch Deli Twins. Lynn wore white lace hose, and waved a glitter-filled wand with a white star on the tip. Fast Lyla brandished a cat-o-nine-tails, and fanned the air with her overheated leather skirt. They were about to down another chug of Cuervo Gold Tequila with The Wolfman.

"Happy Halloooo—weeeeen, Writer Man!" howled Wolf. "Did you hear the sad news?" He did not wait for Baker's reply. "Our famous, flirtatious Deli Twins here, are transferring from the community college down to UCLA, come January."

"Nice party, Neon!" the twins screeched in stereophonic valley-speak.

"Thanks goils. This true about your leaving?" Neon inquired.

"Hell, yes!" shouted Lyla.

"Like, really! You're joking, right?" echoed Lynn.

"No, I'm not," Neon replied. "Why in the world would you want to leave Chelan? You both are a year away from a degree in Business Management. You have your dad's deli being handed to you on a silver platter, and business is starting to take off. You have some damn good people who love you here. Do you know how many people never have that? Christ sake! You two are a frickin' institution. With all the new offices going in for the industrial park, and the expansion at Field's Point—not to mention those studs on the construction crews—you'd have to be crazy to bug out now. The place is going to be a gold mine, and—"

"The place is deadsville, Tube Bender!" Lyla snapped, in concert with a flick of her leather whip. "We've done our term here."

"Yeah! We're sick of Apple Blossom Pageants, and Apple Blossom Parades," her tipsy twin concurred, while waving her glitter-filled wand.

Lyla's whip cracked again. "We've had it up to our bodacious butts with slimy Salmon Derbies, and funky Fourth of July fireworks! We—"

"Ladies! La—dies! What about this summer's International Hang Gliding Competition? Jet boat races? And those hellacious concerts at the Gorge? Were those hokey and boring, too? This place is just starting to get hip," the lion argued.

"Face it, Baker. Chelan is a long way from being cool. It's like—like, *Andy of Mayberry* around here some days!" Lyla said smacking her ruby red lips, and shaking her frizzy black hair so hard that her pointed hat fell to the floor.

"Hey now. Careful, girls. Andy of Mayberry reruns are making a big comeback in syndication," smirked Neon.

"We're serious!" Lyla protested. "Why do hunks like you three stay around this crummy little place? You all have so much talent."

"Yeah!" echoed Lynn. "You guys could make it *anywhere*. Why are you wasting your time here?"

The Lion removed his mask and shook his merely human mane. Part of him wanted to preach—another part wanted to simply walk away. But a big-enough portion of him was already at attention for the white lace-stockinged Lynn! And so, he bit his tongue, knowing time and tide would have to serve as the young Deli Twins' tutors in the coming months and years.

"I'm not wasting *my* time! You, Baker?" asked Neon.

A subtle smile on the winking Wolf preceded the clearing of his hairy throat. Baker caught his hint, and Thomas, too, knew how foolish it would be to further irritate the objects of their desires.

Neon thought to carry on the conversation, but saw Wolf's *cut* sign, and then thought better. "Think I'll go entertain the troops," he announced gracefully, before shuffling off in character once again.

The Deli Twins suggested heading out to Wapato Point for the party at Katzenjammer's Club, but Wolf whipped out a stash bottle of French Champagne, then asked, "Now wouldn't you rather drink this, and take a moonlight floatplane ride?" To which the witches winked wantonly, then whispered sibling secrets in each other's ears.

The boys beamed lustful looks toward the twins.

"Come on...who's yer buddy?" Wolf growled.

"Who's your pal?" Lion purred.

"You two...*animals* up for a little skinny dipping?" Lyla taunted, knowing full-well they were about to bag their game.

"Ooo, yeah. These outfits are getting really uncomfortable!" Lynn teased, squirming in her skirt.

They wanted to exchange high-five's. They wanted to strut right out of Neon's bash with their foxes in hand and revel in their skills as huntsmen, but the two animals kept their cool, barely exchanging glances.

"Let's step into my *office* ladies, and talk this over," Wolf requested, after laying his claws on bad-witch Lyla and starting for the exit. "You know, that water out there is colder than a witch's tit this time of year..."

"Want some?" Lyla slurred.

Wolf's head bobbed like a dipping duck!

"Then stop whining," the naughty witch said.

Lynn latched onto the lion's tail. "You saying a big, bad wolf like you, and your cuddly writer friend, are afraid of a little *exposure* to the elements?"

"Yeah! Is that what you're saying?" Lyla ribbed, pinching a little wolf hide. "And I don't know how that line *colder than a witch's tit* ever got started, but it's simply not relevant." She peeled back her blouse, blinking extra long extended lashes. "*If*—you catch my drift."

The frothing Wolf certainly did, and consequently, he increased their pace toward the Beaver to a lope.

BILL BAKER and guide Rick Graybill were downing their fourth beer at the bottom of Neon's stairway, where they had been talking about the off year for Lake Chelan's sacred Salmon fishery.

"I've been guiding these waters for over fifteen years now, Bill, and I've never seen it this bad. Fact is, it had been getting better each year," Graybill stated, removing his orange and black Garcia fishing cap to scratch his head. "Maybe you could get someone from the Department of Fisheries to come and check things out."

"Sure, Rick," Bill answered, after a healthy belch. "But it's probably just a cycle." He scratched his chin. "Could be connected to all the fire ash. Naaa! Remind me this spring, and we'll trick one of our government employees into coming out and actually doing their job."

ON THE Neonman's upstairs balcony, the Eskimo Nancy Baker and the Chinese Miss Pai had removed their masks, and begun to share their innermost thoughts.

"And do you miss your China sometimes, like I miss my little village in Alaska?" Nancy asked.

Ho Pai gazed across liquid moon waters to the peak of Stormy Mountain, and saw the mountains of her home province instead. "Yes," she sighed, noticeably chilled by the quickly cooling air. "But I too can never go back to what was."

Nancy Baker shared her coat, a hug, and these words of comfort: "Then we will both make this valley our home."

THE TALL FIGURE in black tux and top hat leaned against the support beam below Neon's balcony and yawned. He was bored by the young Chinese, but intrigued by this *Wolf* and his ways. He laid down his silver tipped cane, and drew the night-vision goggles to the slits in his Phantom of the Opera mask.

He had watched the animals skillfully shed their skins, straddle the plane's pontoons in their birthday suits, and paddle out beyond the view of the party-goers. He had heard champagne corks popping amid aroused laughter as the twins tossed their lingerie piece by piece upon the floatplane's struts. And now, a smiling Nick Gordon concentrated on the trim and supple torsos of the sensuous sisters whose youthful breasts appeared to defy gravity itself.

The foursome disappeared into the Beaver's Nest, and soon the floatplane was rocking and rolling as if it had just encountered an awesome attack of turbulence—without ever having taken flight! A good five minutes passed and then, several long, loud roaring howls, rang out across the bay.

The Chinese and the Eskimo started up again on the decking above, and he listened once again.

Initially, Nicholas Gordon had deep reservations about the overt/covert nature of this assignment, but like the waning Indian Summer, he could already feel them fading away.

Chapter 5

Wolf Session One

"IT WAS LATE afternoon on a clear May day in South Florida, 1969, and now I was a graduate of Emery Riddle School of Flight. I was hung over from a three-day binge. I was dog-tired from tearing through the annual migration of spring break bitches to the beaches..." Wolf sucked the last hit of nicotene from his cigarette, and doused it in backwash and brew at the bottom of a brown glass bottle—right along with the rest. He scratched his fingernails across the gray streak of his beard. "I had just put the phone back on the hook and the son of a bitch started ringing! It was the guys from the Agency I'd gotten tight with in Nam, the ones who worked with our Special Forces Unit. Remember when I told you about their Air America cover and the promises they made to me at that sin bin in Saigon?"

Thomas Baker scraped his knuckles across the stubble on his unshaven chin. "Yeah, I think so. Shit, Wolf. It's been over a month since we've had a serious session. Air America. Wasn't that the CIA's cover company used to create a stable of standby mercenary pilots?"

"Yeah-yeah. Well, I get a call from them...and an offer to do some *outside work.*"

Thomas Baker's finger tips stalled out at the keys of his personal computer. "Explain *outside work* for me again."

Wolf shook his shoulder length mop. "Mercenary. Outside the fuckin' United States. Shit, Baker! We'll never get to the exciting part of this chapter if I have to keep explaining this petty crap to you."

"Lighten up! Go easy, man. Listen, I don't want to insult readers who know this stuff, but I have to walk a fine line and make sure people who haven't a clue get a feel for what's happening. That's why this writing game is such a trip."

"Fuck 'em if they can't figure it out, Baker."

"Come on, Wolfy. I've been waiting for this scene too long. What was the *outside work* they were offering you? Oh, and how old were you then?"

"I was twenty four..." Wolf whispered, looking off toward the window shaking his head in disbelief. "And they were asking me if I'd lost my nerve since I came home from Nam."

"Well? Had you?"

"You're an asshole, Baker!" he snapped back. "Wolf never lost his nerve. I lost confidence in the people up the chain of command. I lost the ability to hear in my left ear, but Wolf *never* lost his nerve. Got it?"

"Got it. Sorry. It's just the writer in me. Say, when are you going to let me know the *real* story on that ear of yours?"

"Patience, Baker. I told you. I lost it in the war."

"You tell everyone that line of shit. I want to know the—"

"*Patience*, Writer Man. You wanna know the entire plot by the middle of the novel? You wanna put the cart ahead of the horse? You aren't one of those closet readers who likes to check out the end of the book before he reads the rest, are you? Tell me it ain't so, Baker."

"It ain't so. What was the mission?"

Wolf settled into the recliner. "They wanted me to fly right seat—that's copilot for your moron readers. They wanted me to fly copilot to their destination, then double as a kicker when we were over the target."

Baker hesitated to ask his question. "Explain 'kicker' for me, please."

"Shit, Baker!" Wolf growled. "A 'kicker' is a guy who shoves, pushes, or kicks out the cargo from the hold when you fly over a drop site."

"Got it. Go on."

"So, I drove from Fort Lauderdale to Opa-Locka..." He paused to clear his throat. "That's an airport north of Miami where the CIA worked out of. We hung out there for six or seven days getting type-rated—that's certified to fly that type of plane," he snarled, half-smirking.

"Very good, Wolfy! I think you're getting the hang of this interview game. Not everyone is an expert on this fly-boy-spy-shit, you know. What kind of people were down there in Opa-Locka? And what else did you do besides learn about the aircraft?"

"People were just coming together...getting the plan ironed out. Every morning we flew the planes. Every afternoon we worked at adapting them for the mission. And every night the crazy Cubans dragged my ass into town to get shit-faced and exchange war stories."

"So, it was the Cubans you were working with?"

"Mostly, but there were some Haitians too."

"What were the Cubans like?"

"Cubans. What do you mean—what were they like? You said you did time with some of them. They were loud as hell. Never could speak in a normal tone of voice, man. Had gravel voices. Sounded like they just smoked twenty packs of generic full-flavor fags. Picture me and those guys loose in the Miami bar scene. They were the same crowd from the Bay of Pigs fiasco. All late sixties rejects. I told you about them before."

"We were drunk in Seattle then, Wolf."

"We should be drunk in Seattle now! Drunk with a couple lanky-legged, long necked cocktail waitresses who like Beaver rides hangin' on our rumps."

"So, what were *these* Cubans like?"

"Crazy, man! Crazy. Could drink my ass under the table every time. And as you know from experience—that's not an easy assignment. As I told you, this was the crew who came here in the sixties convinced they would win the fight to retake Cuba from Castro. But good ol' Uncle Sammy taught them old dogs so many new tricks about flyin', lyin', and covert operations, that by the end of the decade they all said, 'Fuck it, *mang!* Let's make some serious money and take care of our mistresses and our families. Let's make a life right here—in *Miami!*' And any asshole knows they did exactly that. And they used their drug bucks to buy good friends like George Bush's son.   Then, they just brought everyone over from Cuba who they wanted to save, and got them citizenship. Cuban *dinero* carries clout! Which is why south Florida is like fuckin' South America today. Just like L. A. turning into beanerville.   *That's* what's wrong with all this immigration crap, Baker.   America is for Americans," Wolf hissed, drumming his fingers on the writer's desk. "At least I speak-a-da language.   Gringos like you need a goddamn interpreter to vacation in south Florida nowadays."

"And a bodyguard," Baker half laughed. "You really think the U.S. government trained and equipped the early pioneers of the drug trade to finance their covert operations?"

"*Think?* Hell, I know, Baker! From Southeast Asia to Cuba. Hear me now, but believe me later, my literary friend."

"Weren't there *any* Agency boys on that ill-fated crew?"

Wolf considered mentioning his ill-fated introduction to one Arturos Aquindo, but blew it off with a snarl. "Negative, Writer Man. They set this one up like all their hits—made to look civilian-backed through dummy corporations. *All* civilians, in case it was exposed."

"How many planes were involved? And what kind of air craft were they providing you?"

There were only three…" The reminiscing pilot smiled as he rose from the recliner. "Ahhh…but they were beauties, Baker," he sighed. James Shawn Wolf walked to the picture window for this twenty-five-year-old recollection, where Thanksgiving Eve's morning rains were shifting to sleet now—nearly four hours after they'd merged minds in this novel-interview game session. "The Lockheed C-121-A Constellation was President Dwight D. Eisenhower's Air Force One before it was replaced by the newer jets. What a beautiful bird, Baker! One of my all-time favorites. Slick, sleek looking animals they were. Had a range of 7200 miles. Those Connies were classics."

"What adaptations were needed for the mission?"

"Mainly gutting the interiors and installing a roller system on the deck of the fuselage, so we could handle the cargo. We installed a straight shot to the rear cargo hatch, then turned the rollers there, so the kicker could deliver the load over the drop site."

"And what was the cargo on this trip?"

"Each Connie carried ninety fifty-five gallon drums filled with a mixture of gasoline and Ivory Soap. That's a poor man's napalm, Writer man. Make note. Your readers should find that interesting."

"Why Ivory Soap? And what was the ratio used?"

"It could've been any brand. Maybe there was a sale on Ivory," he laughed. "I'm not sure about the mix. Just say twenty to one. No one will ever know the real amount. Hell, I don't."

"I told you, Wolfy…I don't want people reading my work and saying this Baker guy doesn't research his subject material." Writer watched Wolf slip another Marlboro between his lips, and toss the crumpled wrapper in the trash. His lodge was a non-smoking resort. When dining out alone, he always requested the non-smoking section. In his mind Thomas protested, but the protest ended there. For he knew Wolf would be Wolf, and that this story had to be heard to be written. "What about this soap ingredient?"

"The soap made the gasoline stick to whatever it exploded on," the pilot mumbled, mouthing the Marlboro. "Get the picture, Writer Man?" He struck a wooden match theatrically while whirling to face his interviewer with an animated expression shouting: *"Stick and burn! Stick and burn!"*

Baker recoiled at the keys, then cleared his throat. "How 'bout some coffee?" he whispered into his monitor screen.

"Coffee? Screw that idea! How 'bout a couple beers? Beer, Baker, is food for thought. And I am a thinking man today thanks to you. Let's down a couple."

"First describe the mission for me. Then we'll take a break, and finish up with the action scene."

Wolf leaned upon the cedar windowsill. "The mission was to destabilize Papa Doc Duvalier's government down in Haiti. It seems Papa was getting carried away with the repression game and his secret police."

"Wait a minute. Haiti? Even back then? Didn't we install this Papa Doc to begin with?"

"Hell yes, we did! We pumped him up and put his puppet ass upon the stage, but the damn Pinnochio had a mind of his own, like most marionettes do. And here we are in 1995, still messing around with that punk-ass country. We've got good people risking their asses down there right now. For what? Look at Panama *ex post facto*. We got pizza-face Noriega locked up in some posh padded cell so he won't snitch out his American and international banking buddies. And the poor Panamanians got an even dirtier crew in control today—still laundering money, still landing cartel aircraft. The whole world is laughing! And nine out of ten tough-on-crime politicians have fat offshore bank accounts or secret safety deposit boxes stuffed with bloodstained hundred dollar bills. Haiti? Screw Haiti!" the peeved pilot pronounced, pounding the wooden windowsill.

"Shit, Baker! It's only a fuckin' breeding ground for AIDS anyway! I don't know why we don't just—"

"What was the game plan then?" the writer interrupted.

"The plan was to fly straight down to Haiti from Opa-Locka, and take out the airport at Port-au-Prince. Burn its ass up! We had three Connies loaded with 90 drums each. That's 270 all totaled. They told us it would be a milk run. An easy job. No one would expect us. Right? We'd come winging in at dawn and do the dirty deed. The head honcho even gave us a little pep talk. 'The people of Haiti will rise up and join the revolt when you strike this blow for freedom!' Yeah, that's the way it was *supposed* to go down. We come in clean, torch the airport, and then the freedom fighters cut loose on the ground with small arms fire. By day's end they'd have a new puppet in Haiti, and

Wolf would be ten grand richer and drunk on his hairy ass, with some beach bunny sitting on his happy face."

"You say *supposed* to go down. What happened?"

"Oh no, Baker! It's beer break. I wanna keep your ass in suspense, like you do to your readers. Let's go raid the fridge."

"Ten-four. I'll stoke the fireplace. You hit the cooler. And grab me a tonic water while you're in there."

Wolf had no sooner bent beneath the English walnut bar when he was startled by Chef Gary Fisher's emergence from the kitchen. "Ah ha! Caught with your paw in the proverbial cookie jar again, eh, James?" said the lodge's clean and sober chef.

"Shit! Busted by the Alcoholics Anonymous Police," Wolf growled. After grazing his head on the cooler door, he stood rubbing it.

"It's a bit early in the day to be tipping back those bottles...even for you, James."

"Go stuff your turkey, conehead!" Wolf retorted.

Chef Gary removed his ribbed white high-hat, and brushed back his long, moist, straight, black hair with trembling fingers. "I can take a hint," he huffed with an outwardly forced cackle. But inside he was boiling.

"That's nice, Gary," Wolf taunted, after unceremoniously crowning the cook with his paper cone.

Chef Gary's kitchen whites hit the swinging door full stride, and once inside he blurted, " *Macho asshole!*", before burying the big cleaver in the parquet cutting board.

THE BLAZE in the Great Room had once again nearly died, but Thomas Baker was not one to let his fires die so easily. He slid the black screen guard against the vast expanse of stone extending to and beyond the cedar surfaced ceiling. With one gloved hand he opened the damper, and from some faraway surrealistic spot, the specter of *her* memory swept into his breath upon a chilly down draft.

Wolf popped the top of a long neck bottle of the Olympic Peninsula's Kemper Ale, and flicked it into the coals. "Shit,

Baker," he gurgled. "Why in the hell did you hire that chef? Can't even have a beer before dark in peace with him around."

"What's that?" Thomas questioned.

"That fuckin' nag chef of yours you made me fly to Seattle with you yesterday for your holiday wine run. Don't do that again, Baker."

The writer shivered slightly as he plucked the iron poker from its stand. "Don't be so hard on him. He's a good man, and a *great chef*. He just deals with life differently than you or I, that's all."

"No shit," Wolf growled, handing Baker his tonic water. "I'd hate to see him around a pile of cocaine! When a guy talks that much about recovery and abstention, you know damn well that inside he's just dying to indulge. Crap. You never see him without a cup of coffee in that kitchen. And he chain-smokes non-filter Camels like there's no tomorrow."

Baker tapped the poker tip on the oak plank flooring. "At least *he* chain-smokes outside," Thomas muttered. Sometimes his outbursts disturbed him, but overall Baker cherished Wolf's friendship, sharing his glorification of the lonely hero and rugged individualist. Deep down, the writer suspected that Wolf, too, secretly longed to satisfy those innately human yearnings for closeness and connection called 'community'. And so he would continue to promote the evolution of a relationship between pilot and chef—regardless. Besides, one of the writer's weaknesses was gourmet dining. It was a deprivation which he came to mourn as much as sex during his imprisonment. And so, Thomas Baker would have his chef.

Wolf often wondered what had attracted him to Baker, who liked the same sixties music he did, but listened to Tony Bennett, Barbara Streisand, and classical music as well. Baker couldn't even replace the water pump on a simple Chevy engine, when he, Wolf, was a devout machine head. And though he had his strengths, this romantic writer still allowed his prison divorce to haunt him. Pitiful. Wolf suspected the writer relapsing at this very moment. They had talked about her once, when Wolf summarized: "You are *lucky*, Baker. You survived *two* prison bits.

Anyway, marriage is for women. It's an illogical arrangement for men like you and I." And yet, having *said* this, once in a full blue moon, some primitive voice inside Wolf found its existence lonely, and cried out in the middle of the night for a mate. To which, after forty-nine years, there had been no response.

Wolf ventured to the big bay window, which offered a million-dollar view of Lake Chelan. The hard, fast-flowing sleet had developed into the first serious snow of the year—just in time for holiday ski crowds. He thought of when and why he came here, and how he'd turned down an offer to fly tourists on The Big Island to open Lone Wolf Air. As the snow thickened, he envisioned row upon row of tanned Hawaiian honey buns, and this reminded him of his latest business inspiration—a salon of *Wolf* tanning beds staffed by young babe employees at his beckon call. 'Yes, Mr. Wolf...*anything* you say, Mr. Wolf...' He and Neon had discussed the joint venture over margaritas way back in May, before the foolish kid met that chink bitch, Pai. And it hadn't come up again since. His nose twitched at the thought. A muffled growl vibrated in his throat. The snowfall increased further still.

Baker stirred dying embers after filling the hearth with thought and fuel. He wondered why *she* had returned to haunt him after all these years, like some lost soul tormented by the peace and order he'd established in his life again. He poked the hot, dry log, and wondered for the thousandth time: *What if. How is she? What does she look like now?* Looks—that model's face. Body—those amazing breasts. That wonderful smile. Those warm brown eyes. Those humongous hooters! That curvaceous crotch. *Those tits!* His jeans grew tight as he stirred the hot box with delight until the old log exploded in flame sending sparks showering in every direction. Again he wondered how she was, but the smell of burning pant leg broke the spell. *Oh, hell. Who cares?* he thought, as he patted his trousers, slammed the screen guard back in place, and mumbled, *"Out damn spot!"*

"That's what happens when you play with fire," Wolf snickered from behind him.

The Great Room grew uncommonly quiet. Tomorrow, a small group of friends would gather by this fireside to give thanks. By Friday night, the lodge would be booming with a lively holiday ski crowd—courtesy of the present snow squall. But here and now the fire crackled, a clock ticked, and two friends sunk into a black leather sofa to quench their thirsts.

Wolf sipped scanning the chamber's unorthodox array of European and Northwest decor. A hand-hewn canoe hung above the big bay window. Worn old wooden skis, turn of the century snow shoes, a classic bamboo fly rod, mounted trophy fish mouthing ancient tackle, wooden duck decoys, early black and white photos of Portland, Seattle, and Chelan, all tastefully cluttered the cedar walls. There were oak stacking and satin-wood breakfront bookcases filled with volumes of vintage poetry and prose, a Regency rosewood chaise lounge, a window seat and matching tea table, two curved glass display cabinets crammed with vases, ink wells, hat pins, sequined *twenties era* purses and silver thimbles…even an 1800's German carousel lion. Several rainy day game boards stood at the ready. Wolf's eyes returned to the spoon-carved mantle above the soothing flame where a fine French champleve' clock's delicate tinkle tolled the hour. He scrutinized the signed art deco bronze and ivory figures and the old cast iron banks beside the timepiece, then let out a healthy belch, signifying his appreciation.

"You're a goddamn pack rat, Baker," said Wolf.

"So? I've got an entire lodge and several guest chalets to clutter up. What's the problem?" Suddenly Baker remembered doing five years living in a government issue closet without so much as a calendar, and smiled.

"You need a moose head and a couple deer."

Baker shook his head. "Not into dead animals. You know that."

Wolf chose another irritating topic. "Gonna allow snow-mobiling this year?"

"No way! That's not our kind of clientele." They had debated this before. The avid Nordic-skiing Baker Brothers despised the sight, sound, and smell of the trail trashing machines amid the tranquil winter woods.

"What if one of your *clientele* needs to be extracted from the back forty in an emergency? Be practical—like Wolf. Let me leave that extra Skidoo of mine up here so you can get some experience on it."

The writer skillfully changed the subject. "Heard anything on this rumor going around?"

"Which one?" inquired Wolf.

"The one that has everyone but yours truly who is sitting on lake-view property getting offers to sell out from some big Vancouver firm," answered Thomas.

Wolf shook his muzzle. "When you only have one good ear, you don't waste it on the rumor mill, Baker."

"Something's in the wind, Wolf. I think the development battle is going to explode here within the next couple of years. I knew it would, but not so soon." Baker tipped back his tonic water. "I thought the recession would stall out Northwest expansionism, but L. A. has really been taking the express train to hell since the riots. The people with money can't get out quick enough. They're selling out in droves and heading north. Portland is packing them in. Beaverton and Gresham are having growing pains, too. Seattle is jammin'. Several television shows are set right here in the Evergreen State. Suddenly everyone wants to try the Emerald City. And with Boeing landing more foreign aircraft orders every month, real estate prices are soaring in and around Puget Sound. That Los Angeles flight capital is buying up the islands now. Bainbridge and Vashon residents are at war with developers again. Same in the San Juans. Out on the Peninsula, Poulsbo and Sequim are hopping because they lie in that strategic rain shadow of the Olympic Mountains—same reason the Japs snapped up all the land around Port Angeles for some damn mega-resort. And with the almighty dollar doing a nose-dive, foreign investors like the Po Brothers see bargains aplenty in the Pacific Northwest. Yeah, Wolfy…everyone fears the California immigrants, but there's bigger real estate sharks swimming in the local waters. Beware the hungry Asian Tigers, I say. Because I got a really sick feeling we're their next meal," the wordy writer prophesied.

"You gonna give me your old San Francisco/Tahoe-Seattle/Chelan theory again? What makes you think Southern Cal is going down the tubes so quick?" chuckled Wolf.

"I talked to the Greek's son, Georgie, in Long Beach last week. He tells me getting a rental near the water used to be impossible. Now you can get one within a block for $600 a month, with the first month free. And the landlord will help you move."

"You're shittin'?" Wolf gurgled.

Baker shook his head. "Georgie owns a duplex in Long Beach. He says its getting rough. Some lady was murdered on the lot next to his place. He paid $260,000 for it six years ago, was offered 280 grand back in 1992, and laughed in the buyer's face. Now he wants out bad, and the best offer is 190 grand. The place is bleeding him, Wolf. Broken windows, busted-down doors. Vandalism is rampant. He's going to take the loss. Says city rentals are going the way of the dinosaur. Says resort property is the place to invest, but Tahoe is off the wall. He's asked me to scout around Chelan for him.

Immigration, gangs, earthquakes, droughts, fires...the LAPD! Money people have had it with Southern Cal. Trust me. The minute the second O.J. Simpson trial ends, they'll all be looking north. And where they gonna go? We've got all the woods, the water, and the elbow room." Baker turned away from the roaring fire to face Wolf eye-to-eye. "Where will California's deserters go to vacation after they invade the rainy Northwest coast? Back to their beloved Tahoe? No, Wolfy me boy. Eventually, they will all come here to Chelan. Mark my words."

"So? Business will be booming. You should be happy. Right, Baker?"

"Guess again. The big boys will be pushing hard to acquire and subdivide all the view property people have been sitting on for ages. We're talking year-round residents, Wolfy. Why else would these rumors be flying about some super outlet mall in Wenatchee?"

"Screw Wenatchee, Baker! That's thirty miles from Chelan. They have to have electricity and water to develop the big parcels around the lake. And regulations for sewage treatment are getting tighter every day."

"Brother Bill says new technology will allow developers to locate drinking water aquifers trapped inside these granite pockets without the trial, error, and cost of drilling wells. Some kind of new sonar. Think of it, Wolf! If they know which view tracts are sitting on water, they can pick winning investments every time—like having a foolproof system on a roulette table. They can always build filtration plants like the new one at Chelan Ridge. And running electricity into the boonies ain't shit for multimillionaires. There's also the risk of one of these outside consortiums using other local Native American lands to bring Vegas-style gambling to the valley. I'm talking about a complex that would blow the Colville Tribe's neighborly little Mill Bay Casino right off the map."

"You serious, Baker?" Wolf growled, slapping his bottle in his palm and simultaneously envisioning scores of topless showgirls doing the can-can.

"As a heart attack! That's why we've got to hold the Chelan Alliance together," he added, clearing his throat. "Councilman Barnes has asked me to take a more active role in the Alliance come spring."

Wolf pointed his finger at Baker. "You? The enlightened ex-con, and author of the *Three Great Vows*? Maybe I should collaborate with another scribe. Your credibility is eroding fast."

The writer frowned. "How so, oh hairy one?"

Wolf held up his index finger. "First you said *no more partners,* because that's how you went down on conspiracy charges. Taking on the merry ol' Englishman shot that vow in the ass. Then you said *no more marriages or serious commitment.*" Wolf pawed his pal's shoulder. "I saw you give that secretary the ol' stink-eye at the funeral. And now you're letting that kid, Lynn, fall for you.

Trust me. You don't need a woman with that nag-ass AA chef around," he yapped.

"Right," Baker snapped.

"And now you're going to break vow number three by risking your peace of mind, and possibly your freedom to take on the fucking government," Wolf said, with an accusatory stare.

"Wrong, Wolf breath. You act like I'm joining a damn militia! The Alliance will only confront developers, high speed rail proponents, the tree rapists, and—"

Wolf laughed like a hyena. "Who the hell do you think that gang is in cahoots with? Reality-check, Writer Man. Just remember the fear you felt when they handed you your indictment and you read the title page: *The United States of America vs. Thomas Paul Baker.*"

This time, it was Baker who walked to the big bay window muttering. "We live here, Wolf. We're territorial animals—you and I. And this is our turf. We came here for the quality of life. Didn't we?"

"I came here to avoid the lunatics," barked Wolf.

"Whatever. What if the lunatics move in next door? Huh? What then? The day is coming when we'll have to stand up and pay our dues," predicted the author.

"I thought we already did. Listen, you know what I think of the feds, but—"

"But my ass," Baker mumbled, as he placed his hands against the cool glass. "There's some things we just can't walk away from. Or do you suggest we move on down the road to the next valley, the next Chelan? And let this one go to hell?"

Wolf tilted his head like a curious pup. "There aren't any more Chelans, Writer Man."

"Precisely. That's why Barnes asked me to recruit a few more local business owners for the fight."

"Oh no! Not me," Wolf protested, as he flew off the sofa determined to change the subject. "You gonna try to get into that brunette's britches, Baker?"

The writer's concentration was captivated by swirling snow. He did not answer.

"I'm really looking forward to this year's crop of snow bunnies. How 'bout you?" the prowling Wolf asked.

The writer stood silent.

"The problem with women in fancy ski wear is the *grab bag factor*," Wolf snorted, baiting Baker. "Don't you agree?"

"All right. What's the grab bag factor?"

"You never know what you're grabbing under all that baggy wrapping! That's why I, Wolf, wanna open a tanning salon and sponsor a winter tanning contest." By this time, Wolf was whispering in the writer's ear. "I need a *partner*, Baker!"

"Irritating bastard," Thomas hissed, as he started for his office. He had heard this all before.

"Wait. You could be one of the judges! Think of all that tanned boo—"

"Let's get back to the story, Wolf," the writer demanded.

A gray day gloom permeated the lowlit writer's room. Baker pulled the chain on his picturesque reverse-painted-shade lamp, and sat beneath its soothing glow.

The pilot settled back in the recliner with a beer and a sigh. "Where were we, Baker?"

Thomas punched up the info on the computer screen. "The plan was to fly straight down to Haiti from Opa-Locka, and take out the airport at Port-au-Prince. Blah, blah, blah…it was supposed to be a milk run."

"Is that what I sound like? I mean, did I really say blah-blah-blah?"

"How many people were on your plane?" the author prompted.

"We had a three man crew. Me, the pilot, and *Nigger Charlie*."

"Who the hell was that?"

"He was our Haitian kicker," replied Wolf.

"Describe him for me," quizzed Thomas.

The pilot downed his beer and plopped it on the writer's roll top desk. Baker slid a coaster beneath it. Wolf focused on his own reflection in the monitor screen. Baker watched Wolf's expression take on a serious tone, watched Wolf's eyes rise into his forehead…and then he started typing fast as he could.

"Every plane had a Haitian kicker on board, but our guy, *Nigger Charlie,* took the cake. Charlie was a Haitian muscle head. Stood about five-eight—max. Had a round black face like most Haitians. Looked like one of those flying monkeys from the Wizard of Oz. Always hopping around with a Cuban cigar and a bottle of rum in his paws. All Charlie ever talked about was bitches, booze, and that damn voodoo shit. Had arms like Popeye. I mean fuckin' bowling pins! Our pilot was one of the crazy Cubans. All he did was piss and moan about the money the Agency was paying him to fly the mission. He was determined to fly that Connie to Columbia afterward, and fill it with weed. Said it was the only way they could make it worth his while."

"Well? Did they let him do it?" Baker interrupted.

"Hey, Writer Man. Let me finish the story, will ya?" Wolf snorted. "So, everything was ready. Or as ready as could be. Actually, it was really half-assed, man. Like most of this kinda' shit. You think we have this unlimited supply of money and intelligence. Right? Because after all, we are the big, bad ass United States of America! But it was like backyard warfare, Baker. Rusty drums filled with homemade napalm. Three retired pleasure-planes with no defensive weapons or escort fighters. Talk about your skeleton crews! Come to think of it, I believe Nigger Charlie actually may have had human skeletons on board that Connie with him."

"You're kidding. Right? I told you to let me handle spicing-up the story, Wolf. Just give me the real stuff, and I'll bend and shape it into something that will read quick and sell a shitload of copies."

"Dream on, Baker! But just in case you ever do hit the best seller list..." he coughed twice. "Don't forget Wolf. I want my name on the jacket and—"

"You got it. Go on. Did this Haitian kicker actually practice voodoo?" the writer prodded.

"Shit yeah! He always wore this funky necklace with some damn devil-dude medallion hanging off it. And every time we flew practice runs in Opa-Locka, he took chicken feathers with him. When we left for the *real McCoy*, he took a whole dead rooster. That maniac sat atop those drums in the rear of the cargo bay chanting and nipping rum the whole trip down. I couldn't get a wink of shuteye, but then—I never slept on a run, no matter how confident I was in the pilot. I guess it's the adrenaline-high from the anticipation of the shit about to go down. You know? Like moving a load in the weed days must have been for you *middle men.*"

Baker vacated the keys to view swirling snows and recall his pot dealing days. It seemed like a lifetime ago. It *was* a lifetime ago! And like prison—seldom remembered. For him the high Wolf spoke of had been replaced by things like writing, rowing, and this lodge—*his* lodge. To rehash them was as senseless as allowing a failed marriage to ruin one minute of one day in the here and now. "What was your support like?"

Wolf laughed loudly. "Know where the Turks and Caicos Islands are?"

The writer twisted the wiry, rust-red ends of his mustache, then slowly shook his head. "Nope. But I'm sure you're about to tell me."

"Some writer you are! They're right off the Bahamian Coast, and a favorite stopover for smalltime smugglers and big time money launderers," Wolf said, resting his chin in the cradle of clasped hands and donning a docile smile. "Anyway, we timed the thing to arrive at sunrise. It was beautiful, Baker. Those three Connies flying tip-to-tip at dawn, the whole damn island asleep beneath us. Ours passed over the airport first. I left the cockpit, and started pushing the drums on rollers to the back where *Nigger Charlie* was. He was stinkin' drunk. He lit up a mondo-sized Cuban cigar, and started dancing around shouting voodoo shit and freedom crap in that damn patois' French/Haitian/Creole polyglot of his. He tossed in some English for me of course. Shit like, 'We go up in Papa Doc now. Eh, Wolf-boy?' "

"Wolf-boy?" mused the scribe.

"I was young once, Baker," the aging pilot mumbled. James Shawn Wolf focused on a cubbyhole in the writer's roll top desk, and remembered that morning back in 1969. He remembered the black Haitian monkey-man dancing like some crazy surrealistic shadow at the long dark end of the Lockheed C-121-A Constellation's fuselage. He remembered laughing off the chanting, and thinking how easy it was going to be to pick up his paycheck. And he remembered that eerie moment when he thought about the people below who might become innocent victims when the napalm stuck and burned—stuck and burned to their skin!

Old Nigger Charlie threw open the rear cargo doors and started setting charges inside the first set of three drums to be kicked out of the hold. Drenched in pastel hues of Haitian dawn, the monkey-man lit each stick of dynamite by glowing tip of Havana and jammed them in the unscrewed metal spouts. The first three were jettisoned. Young Wolf's heart pumped harder—faster! He put his back into the line-up facing him, feeding the next set, and the next yet, to Nigger Charlie. Within minutes they had dropped a third of the load.

James Shawn Wolf fidgeted remembering the remorse he felt when the first set exploded below them on that tranquil morning over Haiti…then broke into a full-on sweat recalling how those clear blue skies exploded all around them in a thunderous rain of gunfire!

Wolf had been whispering the memory into Baker's ear, having fun with it—just like then. He had been bathing in mellow morning sunlight back in 1969, but now the terror returned to haunt him. "They were shooting the shit outta us!" he shouted. "Bullets zipping through the fuselage! Bullets riddling the wings! Our pilot banked the bitch wildly. We swung around. The crazy Cuban ordered us to dump the load. Charlie chugged his rum and tossed the bottle out the doors. Some drums were hit. There was gasoline and Ivory soap running down the aisles! I fed 'em fast as I could. We were slipping around. I thought we were going up in flames for sure.

Beside us, Carlos' plane caught fire and turned back over the water to ditch. His gravel voice was screaming Cuban cuss words over our radio: 'I told you motherfuckers! Stupid motherfuckin' gringos! *Puta! Merican*—motherrrr-fuckerssss!' **Kaboom!** I saw this billow of black smoke out the starboard portholes. I was scared shitless. I fed the drums faster to *Nigger Charlie*. That dumb shit was slipping all over back there. He couldn't keep the timing of the charges right at that speed. Fucking drums were going off a few feet from the cargo doors. *Boom!* That Connie was rockin' and rollin'. And all I knew was we couldn't land with that napalm at the emergency strip on South Caicos. All I saw was that black-ass monk dancing around soaked in gas and soap...trying to hold his big fat Havana away from the fuckin' fuel. He was chanting and dancing. 'We gonna go to Hades with Papa Doc now! Eh, Wolf Boy? Ha-ha-ha! Ah, *magnifique*'! If the guy hadn't been clear at the other end of the fuselage I would have kicked *him* out the fucking doors!" Wolf slapped the roll top. "Jesus. I swear, Baker, I never saw that much action in Nam."

James Shawn Wolf was dripping sweat when he walked to the window to watch cool winter's snows swirl about the Chelan valley. "Two planes made it to South Caicos that afternoon. Ours had over a hundred bullet holes. We had been sold out by a double agent posing as a freedom fighter. There were no supplies, no medical teams, and no spare parts for the Connies on South Caicos, as promised by the Agency. We were stranded there three weeks. The ten grand I made was big money back in '69, but it was the hardest ten g's I ever earned, Baker," Wolf panted.

Thomas Baker clicked off the PC. Wolf-breath steamed up the window. It was as if the pilot had just relived the mission. Hell, Baker had just relived it with him! It was good stuff. It was going to make damn good story. "Did it ever make the news?" asked the writer.

"There was a paragraph in *Newsweek* about a failed coup attempt. But like most government abortions, it was quickly covered up." Wolf shook his head slowly at the window. "I should've learned my lesson about working with them right then and there. But no, hard-headed Wolf didn't learn." He produced a crumpled pack of cigarettes from his pocket, and looked toward his friend for permission to light up.

The writer tossed a woolly brown poncho to the pilot. "Chill out, big guy. Let's call it quits for today. What do you say? I've got a sudden urge for two shots and a beer."

"You, Baker? Hot damn! It's not even the cocktail hour yet. What will your AA chef have to say about that?"

The writer yanked the brass chain on the lamp, and joined the pilot at the window. He put his arm around his interesting friend. "He won't say shit, Wolf-boy," Baker said, as he led him from the writing room. "Cause by the time you finish helping me bring that rack of firewood in off the front deck?"

"Yeah," Wolf commented cautiously.

"It will officially be Cocktail Hour at Granite Fall's Lodge!"

"Let's go then," Wolf grumbled.

Chapter 6

Forever Neon

IT WAS THE FINAL HOUR of *their* seventh session together, and her seventh attempt to bend the letter *P* before the watchful eyes of her instructor. Small slivers of file-cut glass begged her to scratch her irritated arms and face, but she channeled all energy to the thin tube of glass and the fine flame of the ribbon burner. Her eyes began blinking as frustration and fatigue took their toll.

LEARNING THE ART of neon was not as easy as she had hoped, but then nothing had come easy in her twenty-four years of living. She would endure her own impatience and achieve proficiency in this endeavor—just as she had in biochemistry. Her one and only lover had once told her that art and science were incompatible animals, and her perfectionist ways would always be a roadblock to her mastery of the arts.

Her instructor had been overly complementary of her ability to absorb the technical knowledge of neon. When she carelessly dropped her blow-hose shattering its tiny porcelain mouthpiece, he was too quick to assure her he had done the same thing a hundred times before—before replacing it with another. He was patient to extremes with her. Her instructor was kind, gentle, and she was undeniably attracted to him. Undeniably attracted to a man for the first time since China. He was physically attractive to her—blond hair, blue eyes, fine toned physique. Yes, even-tempered, athletic Michael was a handsome American male, but there was more…there was chemistry between them. She was admittedly strong willed and independent, but a long way from home and family, and very, very lonely. And though she had achieved dreams and freedoms beyond her wildest childhood fantasies, she soon found these hollow without someone to share them with. She needed to get close to someone, and she wanted that someone to be Neon.

SHE WANTED to impress him, and so she strained to complete the *P*, but the glass was too thick—the flame too cool, too thin—too hot! Her hands began to tremble.

He slipped sure and steady hands around her tiny torso—the Neon Knight coming to her rescue *again*—just as he had earlier with the thin glass file, but before he could stabilize her the cylinder shattered.

The student bit her lip. She grated her teeth with clenched fists. For in the ribbon burner's flame, loomed lost memories of a sweltering summer blaze back in Beijing…memories of helping her lover finish the Freedom Statue, and his speech to students fearing government reprisal. *"For too long we have allowed The Party to take heart from the people! Heart can only be given to a cause, or another…"* She remembered how he looked into her youthful soul with soft brown eyes of love. *"…by free will! It cannot be demanded! It must not be extracted! I, Jin Qi, give this heart—"* Pai pictured him pounding his chest, and swallowed the memory hard. *"…to my art and the cause of freedom by choice…as all of us with clear conscience must—regardless of the consequences!"* A vociferous echoing cheer ensued the second Jin finished his moving oration. She begged him not to carry the Lady Liberty into the square with the others. Was it not enough he had created it? He called her a product of the State, told her she too must learn to give her heart freely to the cause if indeed she believed it just, told her the people's need for freedom was greater than the love they shared. And then they spoke no more.

PRESENTLY, tears for that fateful day merged forces with rare tears of frustration. A river of tears fell. The student crashed the remnants of her work upon the table, tossed her safety glasses to the floor, and started for the door.

"Pai, what's wrong?" Neon asked, knowing half the answer. She had pushed too hard, too fast—expected too much of herself too soon. She froze with her back to him. She could not answer. "I told you, every time you bend glass there is a fifty-fifty chance of breakage occurring. You, me, *my* instructor—it can happen to anyone."

"Yes, but it happened to me!" she wailed.

Silence followed her remark.

She wanted him to stop treating her like some porcelain China Doll, preferring he shout how clumsy she really was. She was angry. Yes, angry. But not at him. At herself. She was embarrassed and ashamed for having acted so childish. Worry overcame her, worry she might alienate him and lessen their chances together. Thinking *t'ai chi ch'uan,* she breathed deep and slow, pushing the foul air of Tiananmen Square and the squandered air of frustration from her breasts, before excusing herself to the restroom to regain her composure.

She returned determined to apologize for her behavior, but found the room had been cast into darkness. "Michael? I am sorry. I want badly to learn from you, Michael."

A soft white light arose at the rear of the workshop. "We can learn from each other, Pai. Come here," her instructor coaxed from beside his latest surprise creation—a delicate white crane spreading wings, which was the definition of her Chinese name.

"It is beautiful, Michael!" she squealed with delight. "Can I touch it?"

"*Touch it?* It is yours. A gift from me." She attempted to speak, but he put a finger to her appreciative lips. "One of the first things my instructor taught me about neon, was that when you make something with it, it lasts a very long time," he said softly.

She looked longingly into the misty windows to his soul, and placed her hand in his. "Does it last *forever*, Michael?" she whispered.

He kissed her forehead, and held her in a warm embrace. He told a tale of a very successful, extremely disciplined psychologist, who flipped out at the school of neon he attended. "After three days of attempting the same bend as you, the psychologist tossed his entire project at a tension-relieving bulls eye the instructor designed for just that purpose. 'There! I feel much better now,' the shrink announced to the stunned class. From then on he was cool and collected, Pai. But he maintained a two-foot high stack of failed work for the duration of the class."

"I feel much better now," she chuckled with bright admiring eyes, before asking why a renown psychologist would want to learn of neon.

Mike made reference to her profession. "Why do people do the things they do? To relieve stress, or tension? Because there is too much discipline in their lives? Lives lived on paths chosen for them by people or circumstances—instead of *heart?*"

Neon touched her deeply with his words. It was not the first time, nor would it be the last. The shop had become unbearably hot, and so they made their way to the upstairs apartment.

He watched her out on the balcony from his kitchen, dancing, prancing, whirling, twirling in the swirling snow like an innocent child. She had taken the tie from her ebony mane and set it, too, free in the winter wind! She caught snowflakes on her tongue. By the time he brought the wine, her high cheekbones were cherry red.

They shed their work smocks, and settled into the futon couch. She tucked knees-to-chin facing him, and petted the hummingbirds on her polished silk jacket. They sipped a Chardonnay.

He earlier told her of his upbringing in Michigan and his parents' divorce. He had moved with his father to Seattle, and they had vacationed in Chelan together often. He fell in love with the valley, and resolved to return one day to reside here. And now she wanted to hear how he became *The Neonman*. 'How many years did he ponder this field? How did he know which university to attend? How did he meet his instructor?'

"My parents wanted me to graduate with degrees in Business Management and Accounting. I took those courses to please them, and Commercial Art for me. After two years hard at it straight from high school, I grew very frustrated with my studies. I had serious doubts about the usefulness of a degree, but more important, my heart was not into it. I was cramming for finals my sophomore year. I had talked with my mother on the phone. She had remarried a nursery owner, and moved to Tennessee from our old home in Michigan. I complained to her about school. She suggested I take the summer off and think things over. The next day I was having the same conversation with my father, when this television spot comes on CNN. They showed an old rundown barn and this reporter says, *'You wouldn't believe what's going on inside this old barn behind me in this tiny Podunk town of Chuckey, Tennessee...'"* Neon had to explain *Podunk* to Pai before he continued.

"The CNN camera panned the surrounding countryside. It was beautiful, Pai! Mist hung off the foothills of the Great Smoky Mountains. A small stream meandered beside that old barn, shimmering in the morning sun. They had my attention. I turned up the volume. The announcer talked about the history of neon, explaining how it got its start in the 1920's and peaked in the fifties. With the advent of advance plastics, it faded from popularity in the seventies, but like the old Chinese theory of the *wheel always turning...*" he paused.

She smiled warmly, right on cue.

"It re-emerged in the eighties, and was red hot by the end of the decade. The forecast for neon was glowing and bright for the nineties and beyond. The announcer discussed the financial temptations of the field as well as the type of students the school was attracting from all over the country—doctors, lawyers, teachers, musicians. The camera took my eyes inside that old barn, and revealed a world I had never seen. The lights. The students. The instructor, he was a big guy, always smiling beneath his big, bushy, red hair. Big, yes, but you could see how gentle he was, too, and how *fluid* his motion was when he demonstrated his craft to them."

Neon sipped his wine. "There I was, Pai, sitting in the house of my father. Nineteen years old, never been out on my own, but not the least bit afraid of giving it a try. I had my Marketing book on my knee and my Commercial Art book on the coffee table, and here's this announcer saying anyone with a touch of art and a pinch of salesmanship could go far in the neon trade. It was an omen. A match made in heaven! I had to go. The instructor pointed a tube of colored glass at the sign and said, 'Southeastern Neon graphics: *If you got the dough, we got the glow!*' That was his punch line, Pai," the artist pronounced, pausing to take a breath.

"I clicked off the television, and sat staring into my father's eyes. He knew. I called my mom and told her I was coming to Tennessee to *visit*. Two days later I aced my exams, packed my old Volvo Wagon, and cruised." He smiled as he refilled their glasses. "Pai, you don't know me that well, but I'm the kind of guy who looks toward the future with specific goals in mind, and doesn't like rushing into things. *Good things come to those who wait,* my father always said. That spring was the first and only time I ever rushed into anything simply because it *felt right.* Do you understand?"

She kissed his hand, and nodded. "Did you ever regret giving in to your feelings?" she asked with furrowed brow.

"Never," he replied without hesitation. Their eyes were locked now.

"Fate truly works in strange and wondrous ways, Michael," she uttered softly from wine wet lips. "Is this not easy to believe when a television commercial sets you off upon your life path?"

Neon broke the mood. "Enough about me. I want to know more about you. I am fascinated by you. You're at the top of one of the hottest fields, working under a top-notch Pakistani Biochemist, and all this at the tender age of twenty-four. You're independent. You are *extremely* beautiful."

She blushed.

"You moved all the way from China to a strange place like this, solely to pursue your research? I want to know all about you. What was your life like in China? What made you want to come to the United States?"

Behind her demure smile, she wondered how honest she could be with him. She thought about the real reason she left China. "Michael, do you remember the tragedy in Tiananmen Square?"

He studied her face. "Yes. It was in 1989. Right? Why?"

"June of 1989 to be exact. You are well read. I was there. I was part of it." She looked off toward the window. "It was my first year at the university. I was the daughter of a distinguished mathematics professor. I was dating a boy there. He was one of the leaders of the demonstration."

"What kind of boy was he?"

She sighed, and rested her head on her knees. "He was an artist—like you, Michael. He helped to construct the Lady Liberty Statue the students attempted to raise in the square that night. It was the symbol of freedom, which drove the Party hard liners to use force to crush the movement. That was when the shooting began...then the witch hunts. Michael, I *had* to leave China! There was no choice," she cried. Her tears made damp the blue denim on her knees as she curled into a ball.

Michael wrapped his arms around her silky shoulders to comfort her. "It's all right, Pai. You don't have to tell me—"

"No! I want to...I *need* to tell someone I-I care for. I can *never* go back to *that* China. Your American politicians may forget Tiananmen so they can do business with Bejing, but I can *never* forget! The authorities arrested all the students they suspected of involvement. Many good people died that day," she sobbed. "Many were rounded up and never heard from again."

"And your boyfriend?" Neon inquired tenderly.

More tears cascaded on polished silk shoulders. She slowly shook her head.

"I'm so sorry," he said.

"Don't be. My family feared for my safety. They spent their life savings to secure me passage with the smugglers to San Francisco. My Uncle Lee let me stay with him and finish my education at Berkeley. My studies were the only thing that kept me going. When I graduated at the top of my class, the corporation recruited me to join their team. I was trained in Seattle, and sent here to work with Doctor Habib."

"You left your family in China because you *had* to, then left your uncle to come here?"

"It was a great honor. My mother is very proud." Her face grew stately as she dried her tears.

"And your father?"

She looked away. It was bad enough his only child was a girl, but she was a rebel as well. If he knew of the money she sent home, her father would burn every *yuan* of it.

"But you have no family here. Only your work."

"I have my cat, Ming. And I am falling in love with…with the valley and its people," Pai replied shyly.

"You have me." He nearly choked on the words, they scared him so.

"Do I, Michael?" she whispered, while searching for a sign in his blue eyes. She finished her wine, focused on the swirling snows outside his warm abode, and employed all her *chi* to stuff a painful past back inside the Pandora's Box from which it had escaped.

He took her glass. He touched her knee. "I want you to know—if you ever need me? I will be there for you. I will be your family here in Chelan." She brushed her cheek across his hand, and requested more wine. It was the most she had drank since he'd known her, and he watched with great curiosity from the kitchen when he went to the refrigerator.

She sat her black flats with the little bows on them aside, and stood touching her white-stocking toes. She twisted, turned, and cracked her back so loudly, he could hear it above the Sonny Rollins soft saxophone CD he had selected! She unbuttoned her jeans, sat before the sliding glass door, and effortlessly put her legs over her shoulders. And there with eyes closed, she breathed deep—well aware this demonstration of her limber body had aroused him. "Michael, I want to share something very precious with you," she cooed.

Oh shit! This is it, he thought, nearly dropping the wine. He decided to remain cool, calm, and collected, in case he misread her signals. "Yes Masta' Pai," he mused, when he sat their glasses down. "You have my undivided attention. I am *your* student now. I stand ready to learn what precious secrets you are willing to share with my unworthy self. Just don't expect me to do those stretches!" At long last he perceived the mystery of this sensual, fascinating lady beginning to unravel.

"Michael? What I am about to teach you…"

Teach me? Wait a minute! His curiosity concerning the sexual practices of Asian cultures began to soar.

"Is the exact method I was taught. It is a method perfected over hundreds of years. You must excuse me if this sounds too technical, or is not what you expected to share with me."

The *seducer* in him was seething.

"If my form is too tight, please say," she requested extending her hand.

Neon bit his tongue, thinking: *In America, tight is right!* He helped her to her feet.

"But the way to gain the most from this activity, is to perform the moves correctly," she said. The seriousness of her facial expression confused him. "It is no different than my desire to learn your neon art correctly. As you told me, Michael, you do not know me well." She closed her eyes and rolled her head about her shoulders. "I grew up with perfection all around me. I seek perfection in all things, and at times can be extremely demanding."

His image of her was being shaken. The thought of the innocent child dancing in the snow on his deck earlier in the day disappeared. Suddenly he worried *he* might not perform up to *her* standards!

"Michael?"

"Yes, Pai?"

"It is time. Would it offend you if I removed my jeans?"

"No. Make yourself comfortable," he stammered. "I-I mean—"

"You should remove your trousers as well."

He briefly considered his plain white boxer shorts and three-quarters erection. If only he had known tonight was the night. He'd have worn some fancy *dating* underwear. *Was tonight the night?* Regardless, something about this woman told him it was well worth waiting for her to feel right with him.

She had appreciated his reserve and respect—until now. Now she was sure there was shared emotion between them, and that she must initiate the intimacy—lest it be lost in time. For years she had thought little of men, love, or lust. And when such desires invaded her slumbers by dream, it was always a strong, handsome prince who swept her off her tired feet to take her to his lair! It was not as if *he* was not strong—or handsome.

He felt stupid standing there. For months he had been itching to get next to her. He had an urge to pounce, and drag her to the futon couch, to show her some real Neon *bending angles*, to *bombard* her with passion.

She placed cool hands near his navel. "Do you know what the Chinese phrase is for this area of the body, Michael?"

He shook his head. His erection grew to seven-eighths.

"It is called your Tan Tien," she explained, as she popped the top button on his Docker slacks. "The Chinese believe this area is where all human energy, or *chi* originates from."

Instinctively, he went for the row of brass buttons across the front of her designer jeans. Neither spoke a word as they slipped pants to floor and wiggled free. Each wondered less what the other was thinking, secretly sniffing the sex scent only inches away from their true Tan Tiens. Both longed to lick each inch of flesh they had unfurled.

Neon's tube was unbending at the slit of his shorts.

She stepped back, neatly folded their pants, and assumed some stance which revealed the small black patch beneath the opacity of her panties.

He swallowed hard before choking on the salivary juices he could not yet place where he desired. *Did she desire them there too?* He could not take much more.

"It is time for your *lesson*, Michael. The time for talk has passed. I have been wanting—"

Yes! Yes! I have been wanting you too, he thought.

"I have been wanting to teach you the ancient art of *t'ai chi* for weeks now." She paused to enjoy her play, but when she witnessed his disappointment, it disturbed her. The tent beneath his shorts deflated slightly, and that disturbed her even further. Yet, she continued the mating game, certain now after six years of celibacy—*tonight was indeed the night!*

Neon swallowed harder still, and adjusted his shorts. "I've been anxiously awaiting my first lesson with you, Pai. How about a little introduction before we start?" he said with a sinking heart.

She smiled, convinced the swing of emotion and discipline brought on by delay would only serve to heighten their ensuing pleasure. "Michael, it is told that in China some 700 years ago, a Taoist priest named *Chang San-Feng* journeyed in Hupei Province to Wu-Tang Mountain. Upon the mountain he observed a magpie combating a serpent. As the bird flew down attempting each attack, the snake continuously *avoided* him simply by moving its head side-to-side. The bird, growing tired, flew back to the tree to rest, and consider its next course of action. On the magpie's next attack, he dove upon the serpent and attempted to pummel it with his wings. The snake again neutralized the bird's aggression, this time moving its head and body in quick fluid motions." She demonstrated. "Finally, the bird grew tired and flew away."

How apropos, thought Neon.

"*Chang San-Feng* interpreted this display in his circular *t'ai chi* form." She slowly moved her hands in circular motion, mesmerizing her intended prey. "Michael, to prepare yourself we begin with *Wu chi*, which means, 'that without limit'. This opening posture, as it is called, will help you center your *chi*, or energy, into your *Tan Tien*, or that area just below your navel."

Neon's energy was primarily centered in his lower brain. His focal point was her lacy white panties! He swallowed another sea of saliva, and struggled to listen.

"I want you to stand straight and keep your *spine* erect." She tried to hide her smile as she reached for her wine, but he saw it none the less. The mating game was nearing its climactic conclusion. She drank half a glass, and resumed her spread-eagle stance across from him. "Now Michael, lower your shoulders, empty air from chest, and keep eyes focused on an object of your choice."

Easy enough.

She could feel the heat from his focus. "Let arms hang loose at sides of your body. Bend knees slightly, but do not lock the joints of your knees. The object is to become loose and relaxed."

He half-heartedly attempted the posture, thinking: *Come to papa, Pai!*

"With heels touching, angle toes outward forming a V. Place tongue on roof of mouth, lightly close teeth and lips. Now stand in silence, and allow tension of this day to leave your body." *But do not let the passion go, my Neon lover!* "Try and feel your *chi* sinking into your *Tan Tien*. Use imagination to push all energy down."

Her brown eyes were so close, he could see his awkwardness in them.

"*T'ai chi* is imagination, Michael." She was staring right through him. "Life is imagination," she whispered. "Life begins with imagination, and becomes reality. Reality we choose, and shape, and live for! Imagine the energy running through your body, Michael."

All Neon could imagine was making love to Pai.

"Now we begin posture number one. It is called *Yu Pei Shih*, or preparation. All movement is very circular—very fluid, Michael. Believe the air around you has become thicker, as if a great fog has set in. Think of wading through warm, deep water."

Believe? He *was* in a sensual fog with her, wanting to wade through the warm wetness beneath her lacy panties. She instructed him to shift his weight to his right leg. He shifted his middle leg. She instructed him to lift his left foot and place it apart from his right heel first. He longed to place her in his arms and enter her Tan Tien. He was growing impatient with the lesson, having trouble getting the feeling, any feeling, but the one he was tired of fighting. The one for her.

Pai, too, knew their time had come. She told him his shoulders were too high—too stiff. He moved too quickly with his hands, needed some bend in his body. He needed her assistance and she was ready to give it to him. He needed a physical demonstration of what she desired.

She circled catlike behind him, and pressed his shoulders down into their proper position. She slipped silk arms between his, pulled up his tee shirt, and placed her hands on his chest. She rubbed her lacy bottom against his buttocks, pressed erect protruding nipples through polished silk into his bare back, firmly pushed upon his pecs to rid him of the bad air of indecision—and still he restrained himself! Until she tweaked his nipples, that is.

Michael Johnson whirled into the tight grasp of his *t'ai chi* instructor, and feverishly fingered the buttons between her two hot silk hummingbirds. She did not resist. He cupped her breasts applying a little circular motion of his own...and she did not resist. In her eyes he saw only desire. Her lips were warm and inviting. Fluids flowed freely as she guided his hand beyond lace, where he probed the edges of desire.

Inside, she felt like burning neon!

She bit his lip. He dropped to his knees and gently slid her panties to the floor. En route to her breasts, the artist's tongue detoured at length in the valley of fire, finding sanctuary for saliva he'd been holding at bay.

She came so quickly, quivering...and her nectar intensified his own intoxication. She pulled him to his feet, undressed him, scratched long nails across his tender loin until he twitched and shuddered. And then, she pulled him down...

Neon snatched the futon from its frame, and flung it to the floor.

"But, Pai, what about my lesson?" he teased.

She invited him atop her, took him softly, and rubbed his velvet helmet at the gates of China Town. "I have another posture I need to share with you now," she sighed, easing him inside. Her eyes rolled back. "I want to share my *inner* self with you, Michael. I want...I...I want——"

Neon needed no more instruction from Hao Pai. He moved circularly, fluidly, rhythmically inside her, in a manner that even Old *Chang Seng-Feng* would have approved of. He ran his fingers through her ebony mane, while kissing the appreciative appendages of her breasts. "I have wanted you since the first day I laid eyes on you, my Lady Pai," he moaned.

"And I, you, my love," she whispered softly, with the smile of a contented lover gracing her elegant features.

Chapter 7

The Retreat

IT WAS THANKSGIVING DAY. Nicholas Gordon adjusted the venetian blinds in the master bedroom seeking to see sunrise across icy Lake Chelan. The snow squall had subsided, leaving a foot of fluff at lake-level. Azure skies and sunshine were the order of the day. It promised to be a good one for his work.

Upon the dusted deck, a small squirrel scavenging sunflower seed drove a jay from its feed and chortled pompously. The victory was short lived, for from an overhanging branch, a telltale puff of powder preceded the perfect wide-winged pounce of a great white owl. Snow and squirrel exploded in a squirming-ooze of crimson beneath the attacker's talons!

The large eyes of the bird of prey grew sensitive to the light of day. Dark coniferous forests called, but the creature had seen the human witness his kill. Respectfully, Great White Owl passed Gordon's glare—in that instant blinking twice—before winging to the woods.

Nick had deep, abiding love and respect for wild animals. Love instilled by his mother, respect by his father—early on in the days of his youth. Often then—as now—he preferred *their* company to humans, and sought it frequently in the silence of Washington's woods. The mercenary's mind took flight with the owl.

HE WAS BORN the only child of a Fort Lewis drill instructor with little time for family and his own book of proverbs, among them: *Good soldiers and good marriages are a bad mix* and *The world is tough, so we must be tougher.* Accordingly, Nick grew close to his mother.

It was New Year's Eve, 1959. If Marlena Gordon hadn't found her husband's Studebaker Hawk at the officers' favorite Asian massage parlor—again—she would never have been drunk and doing ninety-five miles per hour in her party dress on the icy I–5 corridor. Part of Nick died that night too.

The repentant parent's New Year's resolution for 1960 was to *make* time for his teenage son, but he never nullified the pain caused by his carousing. Nicholas learned to love boating and the great outdoors, but never grew fond of father. Dad encouraged lad to attend college, set on footing the bill, but the wayward youth enlisted, requesting basic training in faraway Fort Knox, Kentucky. It was the harshest statement he could make to his old man, and they only talked twice in the eight years preceding his father's death.

Army life instilled discipline in young Nick Gordon, and he had eaten, slept, and breathed discipline ever since. He shipped off to Nam with the Fifth Special Forces, destroyed enemy weapons caches, mined harbors, and evacuated Saigon at the finish of the war never fought to be won.

There was nothing to come home for, and Asian massages aplenty in Southeast Asia. Some of his old man's sayings began to make sense. He hooked up with *Spookshop* rogues in Bangkok, eventually being recruited by the Po Brothers triad, which was making megabucks in the China White trade. Nick never touched the junk—only the money—while transporting payments home to Hong Kong coffers from Montreal, Vancouver, San Francisco and L. A. He never failed to collect one dime due his employers, and he never set foot in Washington State again, until this assignment in Chelan.

At the onset of the Eighties, Po Lin transformed his Golden Triangle triad into international mega-corporation, Ming Yaht, and began laundering billions through Hong Kong banking connections. Meanwhile, Nick attempted to exorcise his demons by attending every bloodletting bash the power brokers put on. Afghanistan, Angola, Haiti, Honduras, Nicaragua, El Salvador, South Africa, Sudan…Gordon was there—if only for the blink of an eye—fighting for the highest bidder, with no regard for his victims.

When turf-wars erupted in Hong Kong, Po Lin sent his emissary to retrieve Nicholas Gordon. Arturos found him in Johannesburg buying time for apartheid by keeping various black factions at each other's throats. Ming Yaht made Nick an offer he couldn't refuse. Why not? Po knew his record. He was a man for any task, void of fear or needless emotion, and capable of making decisions in the clutch on his own. He was a man who preferred the shadows, but carried himself well in public. He was an American man born and raised in Washington State, their latest target. He had already earned their trust. Gordon was Ming Yaht's man—*or one of them.*

The reunion was kismet. In those waning days of South Africa's apartheid, Nick saw a direct correlation to a certain middle-aged mercenary. He was tired of traversing the globe, tired of the massacres, tired of collecting his pay from various shady, sticky-fingered operatives. Pos offered stock options and the legitimate position as Ming Yaht's Washington State Security Chief. He was forty-nine now, and a slowdown was inevitable. Years ago he had set the age of fifty as a goal for semi-retirement. Perhaps karma brought him back to Washington State? He felt reborn, respectable—as if the end to a long and mystical journey was somewhere in sight. He almost wished dear old dad had lived to see his evolution…*almost.*

That last week in Hong Kong he'd been disheartened by the sight of all the hawks and large beautiful owls waiting caged in street markets to be bought and eaten by Chinese seeking virility and longevity. The ponytailed American bought four full cages, took them to a remote reservoir, and set them free. Upon returning the next day, Nick was accosted anew by owl and hawk salesmen, who had replenished their supply overnight. On such days he hated Asians and their ways—just as he hated himself some days.

IN THE HERE AND NOW, Nicholas Gordon scanned bloodstained snow for Great White Owl—only to see countless nameless faces staring back at him! He shook this specter by looking to the lake, but there the cool blue waters boiled red around the wreckage of the Warwick's *Connie Joe!* He quickly closed the blinds, and made his way to the kitchen.

Moments later, he stood in the center of Pos' opulent pagoda-style refuge, staring up the spiral staircase to the skylights in the fourth and final floor's upwardly curved teakwood roof. He fed the fancy colored carp called koi, pitching pellets in the pond beyond the outstretched hand of a Buddha fountain figure. Sunlight streamed through thin rice-paper doors on the massive mood room. Behind them, the slender silhouette of a single male canary broke into song. The copper tea-kettle whistled from the kitchen. Nick cinched the sash of his silk robe, donned his cheater specs, and called the interactive digital television system to life… *London FT 100 advancing 22 points in heavy trading. Hong Kong, continuing yesterday's slide, opened on a downward note. Hong Kong gold broke the key $500 resistance level at the opening bell following Tuesday's heated exchange between British Governor Christopher Patten and the Beijing Government over the continuation of democratic rule. The American markets are closed for the holiday…* "Scared chink money is on the run," Gordon remarked aloud, before drinking his ginseng tea.

Cautiously, he peered through the window sheers of Pos' ten bedroom, six bath temple. *No ghosts this time!* The boathouse was still, shrouded in snow, safely housing Black Zodiac and friends. In the oversized garage, Jaguar and Land Rover lay safe from the elements—awaiting the pleasure of his company. Upon the expansive private drive, virgin snow lay unbroken.

As he settled back watching the satellite Ming Yaht's investments had launched beam news of the corporation's increased earnings into this remote retreat, Gordon wondered why they needed more—why the Chinese were born with an insatiable urge to gamble everything—all their lives. Was *he* any better? Why couldn't winners quit while they were ahead? Perhaps their perpetual drive in time became a curse to them all? He pondered Pos' plans to colonize the Chelan Valley, and transfer thousands of faithful shareholders here before the communists took control of their safe haven home in Hong Kong. Was Po Lin losing his touch? Had the wise old man become so accustomed to the ease of their takeover/relocation in Vancouver, that he thought he could effortlessly infuse a white-rural American community with a major Asian population? Why couldn't the Pos just slip away on their own—*sans* entourage—and enjoy their fortunes? Somehow, something deep inside told him this could prove to be a surprisingly difficult assignment in the end.

He drank ginseng tea from a cloisonné cup, and read the Real Estate section of the *Chelan Mirror. Timber and meadows, good chance for water. 500 acres of prime view property. Power available. Close to county-maintained roads. Private! Upper Union Valley area—by owner.* Gordon circled that ad and went on to the next. *Washington Creek area northeast of Chelan, approximately 8 miles. Views, timber, meadows! Great rural living with year-round recreation. 120 acres of good farmland. Private county road—by owner.* There were more of the same "by owner" offerings. He circled four of the larger view-parcels, and read on. Part of his job was to become as knowledgeable as possible about land prices and other on-going development projects, which were sprouting up like weeds around the lake. In a short time he had studied them all with the intensity of a reconnaissance patrol leader—Wapato Point, Fields Point, Peterson's Waterfront, Pinecrest, Cove Estates, Vista View, Morning Sun, Sunny Bank, Chelan Shores, Chelan Ridge...

The Hawk's Meadow project was no kiddy park. Big bucks and brains were behind this one, and it intrigued him. He read their full page ad: *Hawk's meadow at Bear Mountain Ranch ***Overlooking Lake Chelan*** Announcing the first home sites available on the Ranch. We have set aside 600 acres of sunny and spacious meadow land just above our Orchard. There will be 82 home sites. That's right! Just 82 sites on 600 acres. A place for people and wildlife to live together.*

Panoramic Lake Views. 300 days of Sunshine. Horse and bicycle trails connected to 20,000 acres of public land. Minutes to town. Security gate and private roads. **Approved by the Chelan Alliance.** A hawk's silhouette soaring over a serene mountain meadow was their insignia. And in his opinion, they had the right idea.

Nick's last sojourn in Hong Kong only served to underscore his scorn for constrained city living conditions. Why would the Pos or anyone else come to Chelan to build condos? He hated them. *Ant colonies for insecure assholes! He* cringed at the concept of communal living. People escaping the stinking cities' hell only to form another, in a place like *this?* If they have the means they should have the peace of mind as well—like him, here and now, in the corporate retreat.

Lakefront parcels like Pos' and Warwick's were rare—nearly extinct—for now, until zoning laws could be silently, skillfully swayed to open the way to new environmentally sensitive conquests. Till then, they would employ a *shared access* strategy, by creating an enormous community *China Beach* at their Condo City, where wealthy leather-backs seeking skin cancer could be offered the option of owning spacious upcountry 'view ranches' complete with lifetime memberships and boat slips at China Beach. Gordon pictured *sampans* propelled by wrinkly old relatives who caught carp by day and pulled the handles on dollar slots till dawn. Purchasing by Caucasion-owned, Canadian shell corporations, would camouflage Ming Yaht's initial involvement and stem an epidemic of Asian resentment. They certainly possessed the financial firepower. The unknown factor was public resistance to the plan. But the Pos and Arturos assumed that this backlash would come too-little-too-late—long after the actual occupation had begun.

LIKE EVERY DAY, this one began with a strenuous workout for Nicholas Gordon. He slipped on his sweats, and ascended the sterling silver spiral staircase, stopping briefly to view the third floor's gaudy game room. There, once proud predators from hawks to tigers were preserved in action poses in a hellish casino-like tomb with too many ornate chandeliers, rich red draperies, and gold filigree framed mirrors. He tugged down on his neck towel—hard—and ascended to the ambiance of the fourth floor, tramping the treads of his soul upon the silver stairs stridently.

Holding the twin white rhino horn handrails tightly in his grasp, Gordon scanned the glass octagon. Here his ethos was on exhibit. Here he was one with his two worlds. Here six walls of solid glass and four skylights allowed him to commune with nature. Before him lay the lake, beyond it on the far horizon—majestic Fourth of July Mountain. Behind him, giant cedars and ancient Sitka Spruce swayed in silent reverence.

He moved right, approached the weapons wall, and removed a metal shuriken. Pos' promise of ownership in a massive Chelan casino came to mind, and with it came this thought: *If we succeed, I will always be remembered as Pos' Boy—the guy who brought in the Yellow Tide.* He hurled the metallic star forcefully across the matted floor, lodging it in the heart of a life-sized figure! With the flick of a switch, the other solid wall came alive—upon which two full-sized neon men engaged in moving mortal combat. The Warrior-Gordon's blood grew hot. With his breath, he warmed clasped fingertips. His eyes rolled back, completing the trance. Four floors below, the canary's song was the sole sound between Gordon's grunts.

Thirty minutes of stretching (down from forty-five), forty minutes on free-weights and nautilus, and an hour of simulated combat kicks and thrusts with intermittent rounds on heavy bags later, Gordon embarked on his mandatory three-mile morning run. (Which used to be five miles a mere year ago.) "Aging," Nick muttered, panting steam-puffs of breath into the crisp November air. "Ain't it a bummer."

11:20 a.m. He emerged from the sauna to make a final review of his land maps and the blueprint of Ming Yaht's Chelan based biochemical research center, where Po Lin had called for tighter, updated security arrangements. Security was second nature to Nick, offering little or no challenge to a man who thrived on challenges. But zoning laws, environmental regulations, soil composition charts, water tables—lately, *they* intrigued him. He drank his protein drink, gathered his employee files, and set out for the black Land Rover.

A country block from Granite Falls Lodge he saw them—two skilled skinny skiers racing roadside to the sloping entrance. It was his job to observe them, and so he slowed. Cars of friends come for Thanksgiving already cluttered the steep driveway. The Baker Brothers skated uphill side-by-side. They looked so happy! He would hate to have to hurt them, too—should they cross Pos' path.

All his adult life, killing had come easy for him. But these people were *his own kind*. He shook off the thought, and replaced it with: *It's just another job*. But it wasn't. He was no longer the expatriate. He wondered if he should have demanded the Montreal assignment. Seeing the Baker Brothers—their friends gathered for the feast—he wondered: *Had his life come full circle?* A tiny part of him longed for lost youth, family, and friends. *Ha! Friends? Who needed them?* For the first time since he'd met the arrogant Pakistani biochemist workaholic, Ashwan Habib, he halfway hoped the dark doc would show up at the lab later—perhaps with his pretty young Chinese assistant, Miss Pai.

Behind dark shades, beneath the black Seattle Seahawks cap, he watched with a touch of envy, as the younger Baker's Eskimo boy, and the pilot, Wolf, ambushed the approaching brothers with snowballs.

Suddenly, Wolf froze in his tracks behind the lodge's trade-mark totem pole. He sniffed the air while a snarl took the smile from his face. Then, sensing Gordon's presence, he wrapped his mitten paws protectively around young Nathaniel Baker—causing Nicholas to accelerate the black Land Rover on the icy-white South Shore Road, toward the sleepy little city of Chelan.

Chapter 8

Hongcouver

FRIDAY, DECEMBER 30, 1995. Nicholas Gordon was uncharacteristically late. In the Summit, an octagonal shaped structure perched high atop Ming Yaht's Vancouver, British Columbia, headquarters, Po Lin paced impatiently. He clapped his hands, dismissing two teenage Kowloon concubines whose youthful energy he had just absorbed, straightened his tie, and checked his timepiece—fifteen minutes until the corporate meeting commenced.

The vast expanse of windows lured him to their marble sill...and there he stood. Forty-seven floors below, Vancouver's deepwater port bustled with pre-holiday traffic. Po Lin envisioned he and Brother Jing in the carefree days of their youth: Two waifs wading tidal pools, watching colorful sampans, junks, ferries, and other seagoing ships filled with everything from rice and fish to the Golden Triangle's finest opium derivatives, and wishing they were on one of the countless crafts—great or small—headed anywhere, but home to the ghastly ghetto of Kowloon's walled city. He had everything now, but there was a time when he had nothing—*nothing but the hunger inside of him.*

The year was 1950. Hope and fear came courting one sweltering summer night beneath the flickering neon light of the neighborhood pool hall. Leather jackets with bright yellow moons contained by thin blue lines encircled the Brothers Po employing roughshod recruiting tactics—impregnating their young minds with *the way*. Then came the day. They and thirty-four frightened others were round up by their *dai lo* (or big brother) who had sponsored their membership.

There was a large shrine shining down a dark hall. A statue of an ancient Chinese Warlord stood watch over the proceedings. Each inductee was handed scores of burning incense sticks, told to recite thirty-six oaths, and extinguish one incense after each oath. They formed a human circle. The *dai lo* pricked their fingers with a long needle, and mixed the blood in a big brass bowl—from which all were forced to drink. Crude sticks were issued. A large rat was released among them, and struck repeatedly—finally reduced to a flattened, furry fold of blood and guts. Another rodent was released, and the lesson resumed. By beating the rat, triad plebes pledged to seek vengeance against any members who cooperated with police.

From that day on they were triad soldiers—then called *forty niners*. From that day on they spoke to no one outside the group about triad business. *No one!* For if they had, they would have met the fierce Red Pole Fighters dispatched by their *Dragon Head,* and been mauled by these member tigers who roamed the flesh and blood forest—the packed enclave of concrete dwellings. Mauled and left rotting in the dark, dank passageways comprising their shadowy world for all to see. And then? They would have been fed to the fishes, and longed no more to explore distant lands upon the countless crafts—great and small—dotting the harbor of their home.

Their home. A land wrought with history and tragedy from which men like the Pos rose from degradation to unfathomable heights. Their home. Relinquished by China to Great Britain in 1842. The new slumlords looked into the walled city, and deemed it beyond hope, refusing to police or govern its fifty-thousand plus inhabitants. The climate grew ripe for breeding triads. Opium merchants, slave traders, perverse prostitution rings, and gangsters on the lam from Mainland China, all sought refuge there.

From that first summer on, the Po Brothers impressed triad hierarchy with their rare combination of cunning and ruthless determination to succeed in every endeavor entrusted them. Po Lin's business savvy and Po Jing's gift of clairvoyance were quickly recognized, and viewed as valued commodities by their organization's leader, or *Dragon Head.* They shared voluminous victories with their mentor. They also shared a machine gun strafing defending their Dragon Head from an ambush by opposing *Sun Yee On* Triad members. Po Lin did two years in a wheelchair recovering from that act of heroism. Doctors said he'd never walk again. *Sun Yee On's* Red Pole Warriors promised Pos a painful death as payment for their petulance and thus, heeding Lin's pleading, Po Jing took a hiatus from Hong Kong to pursue a belated education in America.

Po Lin labored 717 days to disprove the doctors, then promptly recruited an elite team of mercenaries for a special mission. After emphatically reminding them of their prior promise, his *Sun Yee On* attackers were annihilated by the vengeful Po, to close that particular curve in an infinite circle of killing.

Before the Dragon Head's peaceful passing, his final request was executed in a grandiose bedside ritual, during which Po Lin became Dragon Head. Lin ran the triad with an iron hand, and immediately set about cornering the lucrative heroin market. Their growers soon resided in the hill regions of the Golden Triangle among the slender four-foot stems' voluptuous, vibrant corollas and cores which bulged with the weight of the treasured opium so many were willing to die for. Their fishing trawlers —manned by their triad members—chugged up the coast from Thailand in China White Armadas, off-loading contraband to small triad junks in the South China Sea. Their customs officials turned wealthy, blind eyes, as their packers loaded at Hong Kong's busy international container shipping terminals. Their dockhands delivered the *furniture* in such faraway places as San Francisco's Chinatown. From source to ship—right down to dirty syringes laid to waste in the West's great cities—they paid no middlemen. They regretted no deaths due those endangering the success of their operations. And their men—men like Nicholas Gordon—grabbed the greenbacks of greed and escorted them home to the open arms of their proud new owners.

It was 1980—Year of the Monkey. Competition for U.S. heroin markets had grown fierce, and the Pos' numbered bank accounts had grown fat. Turf wars were once again being waged in the homeland. International banking laws stiffened. World-wide, their colleagues sought to distance themselves from the trade, and weave their organizations into the political tapestries of their native or adopted countries. There was even talk of openly opposing the remaining drug lords in order to appease the people, and prevent entrepreneurial upstarts from challenging their wealth and power. The Pos sought the ultimate goal—to join ranks with all old money throughout the ages, in the safe inner sanctum of the great planetary Parcheesi game board.

Brother Jing likened Hong Kong to a piece of paper in a fire whose edges slowly burn before flames finally rush in to incinerate its center. Jing's visions and Western education, combined with Lin's instincts and longing for longevity, gave birth to Ming Yaht, or *Bright Tomorrow*. Already, they owned scores of shadowy shell corporations, but each of them had tainted histories. Ming Yaht was a clean machine—the vehicle which would transport them proudly into the Twenty-first Century.

Lin, always fond of the term *da gao* (meaning *to do something in a big way)*, gathered the membership at a grand gala to announce his *Era of New Direction*. He set a timetable for their withdrawal from the drug trade, shifted focus to international investments in real estate and technology, and expanded their interests in the surprisingly profitable merchandise counterfeiting racket. He told them Ming Yaht offered the opportunity to jettison a sordid past and sally forth on a different, peaceful, political course, — much like America's early pioneers—into a better and secure future. In the same breath he assured them the British Government's ninety-nine year lease would indeed expire in 1997, placing their fate in the unpredictable hands of the People's Republic of China.

The total ban on drug trafficking took effect in 1987. There was open dissension among the rank and file, but the old guard agreed with the Pos' reading of the *China Card*, and helped keep the *Era of New Direction* on course. The *China Card* had two faces. One offered Ming Yaht a new and equal partnership in capitalism, but *true face* had shown itself to Po Lin in Tiananmen Square, as well as less publicized places. When an old ally, *Rong Yiren*, was appointed chairman of the newly formed China International Trust and given a mandate to seek out foreign investment capital in China, Ming Yaht moved to hedge its bets. Po paid dearly to enhance his *guanxi* (or *special relations*) in the People's Republic—buying into such key areas as shipping, airlines, banking, oil, and the booming private housing market. If China's swinging door could just stay open—the Pos' gamble would pay handsome dividends to Ming Yaht. If not? The lion's share of their assets would be safe from their siren-like kissing cousins in their new North American home.

Meanwhile, several years spent seeking *guanxi* in North America had served Ming Yaht well, paving powerful political inroads to massive immigration and major business agreements, which established stable beachheads in targeted landing zones. Indeed, they were on the verge of owning Vancouver, British Columbia, outright.

The Great Po's foreign policy was unequaled by his rivals, but as George Bush found out in the 1992 U.S. Presidential election, that left the domestic front weak and vulnerable to attack. In *Tsim Sha Tsui*, one of Hong Kong's many neon-lighted commercial centers where the fruits of capitalism were amply displayed in their legitimate enterprise, Po's people faced persecution by re-emerging elements of *Sun Yee On* who were unwittingly basking in the short-term glow of the bloodier-than-ever China White Trade. This *new evil wind,* spawned in the vacuum created by Po's pending exodus, viewed Ming Yaht's *Era of New Direction* as weakness, and was rumored to have forged an alliance with the Red Communist *Regime du Jour* as well. It was one more reason to hasten Ming Yaht's migration to the West.

Po turned away from the window. Again he checked the time—five minutes to go. Where was Gordon? He flipped through the pages of *Newsweek* for the cover story detailing the latest failed wave in an endless tide of illegal aliens fleeing China for the *meiguo,* or *beautiful country.* Misery moaned from their paper features—the hopeless, huddled mass of gray-blanketed bodies in the full-page photo. Po cursed the *snakeheads* (or *human smugglers)* who had brought them so far, knowing they would either die or face deportation. He noted the name of the tramp steamer, which had sunk off the California coast—*The Golden Path*—then crushed the magazine into a crumpled wad and pitched it on the plush carpeted floor. He knew the owner of the Golden Path, and vowed to avenge the death of these innocents upon his return to Hong Kong.

In Hong Kong, old men always spoke of the *meiguo* before passing into pipe dreams. They babbled about modern kitchens, spacious gardens, and healthy baby boys for their grandchildren in America (where their family houses would live on) as they faded from their own harsh reality with visions of grandeur on the *meiguo's* streets of gold dancing in their opiated heads. Theirs was not an impossible dream. Po Lin possessed many material things, but had always yearned for something more: To be a representative of some kind of greatness or spiritual infallibility, to be a modern day Moses—believing it was both his duty and salvation to deliver the extensive extended families of the flock to the *meiguo.* Because of his *Era of New Direction,* the old triad had lost its *guocui,* or *national essence.* And without that precious national essence, which had provided the political balance and continuity with the past, many felt Ming Yaht was reeling directionless into the Twenty-first Century. The Great Po had an answer for these naysayers…

THE INTERCOM interrupted with the long awaited announcement of Gordon's arrival. Po peeled back his shirtsleeve and stared at the Dragon Head tattoo—symbol of his position, power, and responsibility to the triad. (Now the *corporation.)* In the ink upon his forearm he was reminded of his promise to deliver safe passage and citizenship to their people before the summer of 1997—*or die trying!* He cracked his knuckles, slipped on his suit coat, and awaited Gordon's appearance.

Nicholas Gordon laid the thick, accordion file on Po Lin's mahogany partner's desk. "Sorry boss," the messenger explained. "My contact's flight was late getting in to Sea-Tac."

Po gave a slight head nod.

"This is the complete dossier on your Montreal and Toronto rebels. It is extensive. I have prepared a two-page summary," Nick said, handing it to Lin. "Better read this before you call them in."

Po Jing stood beside Gordon now. The clairvoyant had a troubled look on his face. "I'm afraid it's worse than we suspected, Lin," Jing proclaimed.

The Great Po's dark eyes ping-ponged across the pages. He furrowed his brow at first, then struck the desk with closed fist, enraged. *"Liumang!"* he shouted. It was a Chinese term for punk, or hoodlum. *"Liumang! Dangan feng!"* The latter translated to *the wind of wanting to go it alone.* A pleased smile creased Po's face as he placed the pages back inside the file. "This Quebecois separatist movement is a bad influence on our friend, Liu Fuzhi. Pity," Lin declared. "I am afraid this will cost him dearly." Po Lin shook Gordon's hand robustly. "Excellent work, Nicholas. By the way, Arturos sends his regards from Hong Kong."

The old man's strength amazed him. Nick nodded. "How are the negotiations going with the *Sun Yee On?*"

"Very well," the Dragon Head replied. Lin paused to glance at his platinum Rolex wristwatch. "Excuse me, Nicholas, but it is time. Jing, would you please call in the *faithful.*"

Gordon headed for the door, but Po Lin surprised him by requesting his presence. "Stand slightly behind my right shoulder," Lin instructed. "Keep hands at sides. Do not sit or slouch. Be attentive, but do not speak. The hawk should have the opportunity to study its prey. Do you not agree, Mr. Gordon?" he said.

The Canadian executives entered first. Each had an entourage of two. Each bowed respectfully to both Pos. *Liu Fuzhi*, head of Montreal's division, was followed by *Wang Shing* of Toronto. Winnipeg, Regina, and Edmonton's CEOs shuffled in. Seattle, Portland, and San Francisco's soon followed. When all members were present at the massive conference table, two of Pos' security people closed the twin carved teak doors, and Ming Yaht's *corporate meeting* began.

Lin spoke briefly before handing the statistical presentation to Brother Jing. Then, in standard Po style, he sat back in his ornately carved chair and listened to the proceedings, occasionally flashing his alabaster smile, and leading applause. But for the most part he sat silent, stern-faced—eyes fixed on the rebels—with his finely groomed gray mustache unflinching.

The wax figure, Gordon, watched as well.

Overall, the mood was stoic. Few smiled for the first two hours as Jing pressed on, displaying charts and graphs with Ross Perot-like precision. At one point, he showed a short documentary—part of Pos' plan to make Ming Yaht a household name in North America by 2001. He detailed their progress in the international banking arena, noting they were on the threshold of establishing a network which would make BCCI look like an airport currency exchange. Their chains of super outlet malls and resort communities were well on the road to reality, and recent *arrangements* in Mexico had paved the way for manufacturing merchandise there also. American politicians eager for re-election were performing miracles on Ming Yaht's behalf. The passage of NAFTA would nurture the free-flow of goods from Calgary to Mexico City. Waterfront casino gambling on a grand scale was now assured them in *Hongcouver*, and their lobby in APEC (*Asian Pacific Economic Cooperation*), would insure access to booming Pacific Rim markets. In the Twenty-first Century, Ming Yaht would export agricultural products (like Washington State's apples to Mexico and Taiwan) and *borrowed* technology to the world from its new base of operations, and eventually phase out their involvement in counterfeit merchandising as well.

Following Jing's presentation, each division gave a detailed progress report. In Alberta, Saskatchewan, and Manitoba, windswept winter snows had silenced the bulldozers untill spring, but with first weather break would come the crashing of the trees and happy faces of recession-starved workers—hungry for all the overtime that Ming Yaht intended to give them. In return, this contented work force would then spend their hard-earned Canadian dollars in Ming Yaht's super outlet malls—completing the financial cycle. Canadian politicians who had promised Pos' people sanctuary in return for stimulating their sagging economies, were also performing miracles. Consequently, in Canada, from *Hongcouver* in the west, to Winnipeg in the east—at least—they were running way ahead of schedule. Unfortunately, this was not the case in Ontario and Quebec.

The rebels had yawned throughout Jing's presentation, but Po Lin listened patiently to their reports of political difficulties, street wars, and rising Asian resentment, until they became little more than so much background noise. There was much truth in their assessment. *Sun Yee On* triad was rushing to place troops in the eastern provinces—as well as New York—in case their *guanxi* in the homeland dissolved. Their assaults on Ming Yaht were based on a long-standing claim to these disputed regions in North America, where *low-level* killings had increased tenfold. But Po saw the real problem as regional mismanagement and over extension by the corporation. These *paodanbang* (or *running gangs of one)*, and their unbridled urge for *zhuan waikuai* (or *earning outside money)*, were a big part of the problem as well. Their desire for *chaogeng* (or *frying at night)* had gone far beyond what Po deemed *permissible.* Instead of correctly using the authority and opportunities entrusted them to work for the well being of Ming Yaht's minions, they boldly sought benefits for themselves and a handful close to them in every possible way. It wasn't just the money. These unhealthy tendencies and degenerate phenomena had, in Po's mind, severely damaged Ming Yaht's *corporate image.*

Nick's dossier had made it all too clear. Toronto and Montreal had secretly re-entered the heroin trade some time ago. In August, they had smuggled Chinese missiles and Ukrainian uranium to Pakistan, employing not only Pos', but *Sun Yee On's* network as well. Even as they spoke, the corporation's eastern upstarts were arranging mass shipments of migrants, and entering separate negotiations with *Sun Yee On*—should his own fail to satisfy them. Po's black pupils beamed barbarously as he pondered his options.

Nicholas found the well-groomed rebels—with their blue pinstriped suits, maroon power-ties, pencil thin mustaches, and pleasant expressions—a bit of a surprise. Nothing like their mug shots in the classified CIA dossier he had paid fifty G's for that morning! No spiked hair, no French whores, and no diamond earrings. The Sammy Davis Junior jewelry ensemble was noticeably absent also. But there was a distinct cockiness about them. No doubt about it—*these kids had balls.* Nick admired Po's discipline, knowing what he knew. Lin hadn't even demanded they remove their rose-colored glasses when they reported. And Po had this thing about looking into your eyes...

Wang Shing finished speaking, and sunk back in his plush purple armchair. Liu Fuzhi whispered something in his ear. Shing smirked. The Great Po rose, and the strange psychodrama continued.

He was, as usual, immaculate—thinning hair neatly combed, silk tie perfectly knotted, and a healthy Hong Kong tan to boot. He placed open palms on the conference table. The five-carat ruby glistened from his grand, gold Dragon Head ring. He spoke softly, his strong smooth speech oozing sympathy and compassion for the eastern provinces' plight. Then, calculatingly, he played his card.

"Our ancestors taught us that each time one door closes, another opens. Worldwide, the doors to immigration are closing quickly. The United States will soon eliminate the clause allowing asylum for Chinese escaping Beijing's strict family planning policies. The Canadians are considering striking their *investor-immigrant category* which allowed each of you to purchase *your* citizenship here."

A Cantonese whisper of nervous energy rose from the rank and file.

Po skillfully measured their response. "No great cause for alarm!" He cleared his throat. "I am proud to announce, that thanks to the costly presidential election which the new year brings, we have successfully negotiated to purchase the lion's share of *secret* quotas, which sources say have been set in stone by the American and Canadian governments." The representatives rolled their chairs in his direction, packing in tightly—all eyes on Po—just the way he liked it. "This *acquisition* will enable *us* to *guarantee* settlement and citizenship for fifty thousand of our countrymen in the United States." His timing was impeccable. These were the figures they had all been waiting for. "And an additional seventy-five thousand here in Canada. Mexico, of course, remains wide open," he added nonchalantly, between sips of Perrier Water.

The room exploded with laughter and cheers. One by one they stood, until a rousing round of applause resounded off the reflective Belgium glass and New Zealand carpet of Ming Yaht's mighty Summit.

Montreal and Toronto were slow to stand, reluctant to applaud. Liu Fuzhi prodded Wang Shing to speak. "Chairman Po…" With an auctioneer's nod, Toronto was given the floor. "Speaking for Montreal and Toronto—"

Po raised his ring hand. "Please remove your glasses before addressing this assembly again," he commanded. "And let Montreal speak for itself." *Liumang!*

Nick rolled his neck and shook his shoulders. *Finally,* he thought. *Some action.*

Shing nodded. He handed his rose shades to an aide. Signs of sweat formed on his forehead. "Toronto wishes to express its *disappointment* with your announcement," the rebel began. Behind his tinted lens, Montreal's Liu Fuzhi smiled smugly beside Shing. "Each month, snakeheads carry human cargo to our eastern shores. Each day they are recruited into the swelling army of our enemy to confront our *forty-niners* in the streets. We have the resources to bring many more. Frankly, we need additional man-power to hold the line, Chairman Po," Shing declared.

Very tactfully, Liumang Number One, thought Lin. "I now believe present negotiations will solve these problems of which you speak," the Dragon Head responded. "Regardless, only those we have negotiated for will be assured long-term security. The rest would face the fate of stray yellow dogs—serving as slave labor, living in squalor, enduring false hope and humiliation—before facing deportation. This *corporation* will not be a party to such misery!" he shouted, banging his fist on the table. Po took a deep breath, and softened his tone. "Our goal is prosperity for all, but like too many bicyclists on a narrow path— not everyone can ride abreast of one another."

Wang Shing stood speechless. It had not been his idea to voice such futile dissension in Po's presence. He bowed deeply—eyes on shoes for several seconds—in an obvious act of acquiescence.

Liu Fuzhi boldly proceeded to sidestep protocol. "Chairman Po! Is it not enough to deprive us of the opportunities offered by yet another record crop of raw opium in the far-eastern poppy fields? Have you also taken it upon yourself to make this a *charitable organization* as well?"

A mass-murmur rose from the membership.

Shing said something to Fuzhi, hoping to head off any offending remarks.

The Great Po clapped his hands. "Please, let your comrade continue, Wang Shing," said Po Lin, with a sweeping gesture of his ring hand.

Liu Fuzhi straightened his tie and brushed the breast of his suit coat. He cleared his throat twice.

Po took yet another sip of water. "Please remove your glasses before speaking, Liu Fuzhi of Montreal," he requested. *Alias Liumang Number Two.*

Liu let out a nervous laugh. "But...they are *prescription*, Chairman Po," the rebel smirked.

"Remove them. Or shall I have Mr. Gordon, here, remove them for you?" Po said with smiling eyes.

Gordon's glare made Liu Fuzhi fidget. Reluctantly, the rebel slipped his rose shades into his vest pocket.

"Now you see the world as it *really* is. Speak freely, Liu Fuzhi," Po prodded, with perfect composure.

"Chairman Po. Have the years blinded you to the opportunities and obligations of our time? There is an entire generation craving to come to the *meiguo,* and many *snakeheads* willing to bring them. The fare has risen to fifty thousand U.S. dollars per person, and I have personal assurances for landing one hundred thousand on the shores of the Saint Lawrence alone!" He paused panning the faces of the faithful. "We are talking about conceding **billions!**"

Po was quick to respond. "Gentlemen, our comrade from Quebec seeks to debate policy with me on two fronts. My rebuttal will be brief. In 1980, we decided that *drugs* could no longer be looked upon merely as commodities, such as sugar or rice, to be bought and sold *sans* regard for consequence. Since 1987, we have acted in concert to distance this corporation from its past...to enter a *new era,* without the telltale baggage of the besieged drug trade. I thank you all for your steadfastness in the face of great temptation." Lin looked toward Toronto's Wang Shing. "Let me assure each of you gathered here today—this was no mistake on our part. We now stand in the company of many of our oldest, most trusted, most powerful and influential colleagues, in fields from banking to *governing,* who also chose this *abstinence* for their trek into the Twenty-first Century." He scanned each and everyone of their animated faces slowly. "Gentlemen, we are too damn close. We have come too far." His glowering glare came squarely to rest on the man from Montreal. "There will be no lifting of the ban which applies to *any member* of this organization!" He was tempted, but decided not to mention missiles or weapons-grade uranium—wary of tipping his hand—feeling those betrayals would also be charged to their accounts, and settled accordingly.

Nicholas Gordon cracked his knuckles. A great uneasiness came over the Summit.

"As for your concern about lost revenues..." Po was smiling now. "Ming Yaht will *always* make money. Rest assured. It was never said that these 125,000 would be brought to North

America free of charge. They will pay a fair price—with interest —for a complete service. And they will become the backbone of this movement! Satisfied, staunch supporters—each and everyone of them. *Happy customers always pay their bills.* The profits you imagine we are missing, Liu Fuzhi, would never materialize." Lin Po gestured to Brother Jing. "Upon termination of this debate, Secretary Po will brief you on the mathematics of this five-year immigrant payment plan. I trust you will find them to your liking."

"And if we do not?" Liu Fuzhi fired back across the great conference table.

"I have explained my reasoning. You do not have to agree —just obey," Po commanded.

Wang Shing could not silence his associate.

"Chairman Po! Surely you must concede that these *unfortunates* have a better chance for happiness on this continent than in such dark mazes as those you yourself escaped from."

"I...concede...*nothing!*" Po said seething.

The verbal sparring grew vicious.

"Yours is a moral crusade so estranged from reality—" Liu lashed out, pulling his arm away from Wang Shing. "Have you so easily forgotten your past, Great Po?"

An eerie silence encompassed the Summit.

Gordon watched hawk-like as Po's face grew red with anger. The old man had played Liu Fuzhi like a fiddle, coolly cajoling the kid into flaunting his insolence before the flock. But now, those dark eyes sizzled with sinister intent! A blink, and a nod, told Nick to stand ready.

"I...forget...*nothing!*" Po pronounced, removing his suit coat. *Especially your traitorous acts, Liumang Number Two!* He peeled back his shirtsleeve, popping its carved ivory cufflink in the process. He held his flexed forearm before them with clenched fist. Blood boiled in streams of blue beneath the Dragon Head tattoo! Dark eyes narrowed. Nostrils flared. "It is you, Liu Fuzhi, who has forgotten that you are but a tiny cell in the vast body of this corporation—a corporation which I alone control. A corporation which demands unconditional loyalty from its members! A corporation sworn to crush all opposition to its goals, within…or outside its membership. Do you forget that this organization has made you? Your father, Zhugiang Fuzhi, contributed his wealth and wisdom to this organization for the benefit of all as I do now in the golden years of *this lifetime.* I accepted his bequeathal of his shares to you, his Number One Son…but I can not accept your committing *lese majeste.*"

Young Fuzhi was furious. "Great Po! One half of you lives in the past. The other in a future designed for you and your old guard. Not everyone is ready for the rocking chair. Not everyone is willing to sell Washington State Green Dragon apples to Taiwan, and California rice to Tokyo. This is not Hong Kong. I am not some snotty nosed *liumang* who longs to jump at your every word! I—"

Shing, sensing rising tension and senseless risk to their covert smuggling operations, sought to council Liu on the virtues of acquiescence.

Po Lin longed to pull the trigger on the automatic weapon in his top desk drawer. In the old days, he would have taken the *liumangs* out then and there! And in the old tradition, he'd have sent the bill for the bullets to their next of kin. But these were changing times. Their bad news would be delivered by an intermediary and be shared by their friends at New Years. *Yes!* Delivered on the wings of the hawk—*sans* addresser. Po put on a fatherly face. "Please, do not force me to remind you of the penalty for questioning the decisions of the corporation." He softened his words to a whisper. "Abide by my wishes, Liu Fuzhi of Montreal."

Montreal's man freed a freshly bitten tongue. "Questioning my loyalty…" he fixed his gaze on Gordon, "is like allowing this *gwai lo* to stand beside you at our sacred meeting—totally unnecessary."

Nick, having just been called a white nigger, ground his gold crowns loudly as he stood unflinching. Inside, he longed to respond with fists of fury. Outside, discipline, as always, ruled supreme.

Po, perceiving all, turned and nodded to Nicholas. This motion did not elude the membership. "Mr. Gordon has proven his *loyalty* to this corporation—and myself—a thousand times! We have an equitable arrangement, he and I. I do not question his loyalty. And he, in turn, does not question my decisions...as *you* seem set upon doing." Again he whispered, "Abide by my wishes, Liu Fuzhi of Montreal and Wang Shing of Toronto."

This time, both *Liumangs* bowed.

"Excellent! And now, if you all will be seated...Secretary Po will conclude this meeting with a detailed briefing of our immigration plan." As Gordon helped him slip on his suit coat, Po Lin concluded. "Oh yes...you may put your glasses on now, if you so desire."

IT WAS LATE in the day. One storm had seemingly passed, and others loomed large on the horizon of the New Year. In the communications center of Ming Yaht's Harbor House Building, the Po Brothers bowed before their *Sun Yee On* counterparts via the security of their wide wrap-around interactive-telecommunications screen, signifying the completion of six months of negotiations. Po Lin had surprised them with his request for an emergency conference meeting. He *shocked* them with his offer—an offer too favorable to refuse! Commencing March 1, 1996, Ming Yaht would initiate simultaneous withdrawals from all its Hong Kong and eastern Canadian interests, which *Sun Yee On* would *purchase* for fair market value. Ming Yaht's complete exodus from Toronto and Montreal would be finalized by the summer of 1997. Hong Kong would follow in the fall. Financial papers were signed by an array of accountants and faxed forth immediately.

Arturos Aquindo, the Pos hired CIA liaison who had arranged for Gordon to acquire the damning dossier, played the perfect straight-man, protesting Po's *rash decisions* live from Hong Kong beside *Sun Yee On*'s Dragon Head. The entire transaction was on tape. The Pos rose from their bow, and the screen went blank.

The holiday spirit possessed the Pos. There was no turning back now. January 1, 1996, would usher in an era of peace between two ancient enemies—worldwide. They locked in a lengthy embrace. Lin, the military historian, had little love for the Japanese people, but he'd always admired their *Pearl Harbor Gambit.* Ming Yaht was about to receive a whole lot of something—for nothing! And about to give generously in return.

UPON PO'S INVITATION, Nick had spent the last two hours absorbing the *chi* from two of Lin's finest female attendants. Now he soaked in the sauna, pleased with the plan. A treacherous *Siberian Express* storm bearing down from Alaska had grounded all flights until the following morning—all but one. The dossier had divulged that Ming Yaht's rebels were attending a gala New Year's affair high atop Montreal's First China Bank building—*a known Sun Yee On holding.* Po Lin wished their celebration to be a memorable one.

Nick had hoped to discuss his progress in Chelan with Lin —along with a rumored bid by a British corporation for the former Warwick Estate. But Chelan was the last thing on the Dragon Head's mind. What had already been a very long day was about to grow longer for Nicholas Gordon.

THEY STOOD in the glassed-in central atrium, staring at the street and watching snow accumulate on the marble manes of Ming Yaht's lions—foreigners in their magnificent isolation, waiting on the limousine.

"If you succeed, the shares will be transferred to your Channel Islands portfolio on Monday," Po assured him, as the gray stretch slid to a stop curbside, with chrome colored exhaust curling skyward.

"If…?" Nick snorted.

Po Lin smiled, shook Nick's hand, and gazed into his soul. "Your contact will be waiting at Dorval. My name is your key to the city." Po patted him on the back. "Go now! You know what to do."

He did indeed. Gordon's heart pumped harder. This is what Colonel Bolen trained all his men to do—kill the enemy. Kill *slants,* the real threat—as opposed to passive pleasure boaters and pregnant *Caucasian* women. He released the grip, grabbed his satchel, tugged his silk scarf, and donned his shades. The automatic doors opened. The back seat of the limo beckoned. Po Lin's Lear Jet was waiting. *One more mission!* Nick swallowed hard, and never looked back. The gray stretch—and Gordon—disappeared upon a white wind, headed for the private aircraft wing of Vancouver's International Airport.

SATURDAY, DECEMBER 31, Ming Yaht's Hongcouver Harbor building: The corporate headquarters' Summit restaurant smelled of sandalwood incense, hazelnut-patchouli oil, and *steamy sex.* Ornately phallic-carved candles burned beside two Tibetan musicians. The glass elevator glistened in the background. Soft pastel neon backlighting painted polished-chrome steel columns. Kumquat trees were neatly arranged in artful clusters around a sunken dinner setting for nine—Pos, Gordon, and six Hunan sisters selected to attend them in the waning moments of 1995.

Tantra—which began with bathing and massage, conversation and dance—had twice passed through shared digestion of the nutrient feast, and now re-entered the stage of surrendering skin to skillful caress. The six sisters shed silk robes—again—and found their way to the floor.

The musicians played soft and slow—guiding the rhythm of giver and receiver's sustained strokes of intimate pleasure. Sitar strings sang slow long notes—hard then soft—sending shivers down spines in the nine. In low light, bodies began glowing from internal illumination, as they entwined into a human sphere of flesh, stitching themselves tighter than the spun gold threads of the Persian carpet beneath their searing skin. Blood ran through their veins like mountain rivers in spring. Breath pulsated like percussion cymbals...*tap-tap-tapping* to the soft and hard, slow extended strumming of the sitar. Hearts *pound-pound-pounded* like tightly stretched drums beat by healthy young warriors with boundless energy telling stories from sacred books inscribed upon their inner skins. *Faster—harder!* Ears heard music that had yet to be recorded. Eyes saw…

Suddenly a servant wearing a crimson jacket with high-mandarin collar appeared. He held a silver tray with the Pos' high-tech picture phone upon it. *The long-awaited call had come through.*

The music softened. And from a frozen push-up stance, Gordon cast a concerned gaze beyond Po's backside, to the tele-picture screen where three-quarters of a haggard, sixty-something-looking Asian materialized. He wore so many layers of sweaters and long underwear beneath his tunic, that his body had lost all human form, yet the old man uttered his brief greeting in Cantonese with the most cultured of accents. That's when Nick recognized the face beneath the fake facial hair. The caller was Montreal's largest tong's leader—the contact who had arranged access to the First China Bank Building. Nick held his breath…*come on, baby!*

Beyond the greeting, the video-caller *said* nothing—as planned. He rose up, and pulled something from his pocket. There were other callers in cubes in the background. It was one of those new twenty-four hour public picture-phone places. The old man yanked the string on a party-popper, shooting colored streamers toward the screen, then bowed.

Po Lin clenched his fists below the videophone's view. "Yes…it is a *very* Happy New Year," he said, with a cryptic smile upon his face. As the servant took the silver tray away, a surge of strength swept into his being. Great Po grabbed the hair of the youngest Hunan sister, and pulled her close.

And the sitar strummed on, soft and hard, long and slow…in the lowly lit *Land of Po.*

Chapter 9

Lodge Luau

OUTSIDE, the Siberian Express steamed over Stormy Mountain, slamming the Chelan Valley. Inside, Granite Falls Lodge's Great Room's fire roared—its radiant gleam fusing with refracted light from six wall-hung hurricane lamps—illuminating faces in the gregarious gathering until they glowed like jolly jack-o-lanterns.

Standing in the steamy kitchen—hands in pockets, face pressed against the portholed-door, contemplating the tempo of his orchestration—meticulous host, Thomas Baker, monitored their motions. He watched them finish their cocktails, watched them mingle about in baggy floral shirts provided by Baker and Baker, watched them snatch sashimi appetizers and pick at poi as they fondled fresh plumeria leis resting on their necks like holiday wreaths. He listened to the mellow microcosm speak in early-evening, civilized accents—English, German, Chinese, *Chelanian*—about such sober subjects as world politics, peace, and the condition of local ski slopes. He listened to his lovely pianist play.

He felt pleasure, pure and simple. Their contentment pleased him. It gave back another piece of something once so treasured, something prison and its accompanying desertion had deprived him of like acute amnesia—purpose, place—just as he dreamt it would all those sleepless nights *back then in purgatory.*

Year by year, the missing parts were returning, bringing him closer to wholeness. Halloween at Neon's place had inspired this Hawaiian Luau New Year's offering. And now…

They were becoming restless, stirring colored swizzle sticks in empty cocktail glasses. He chewed cheek-skin, and twisted wiry mustache hairs, wondering when to do his good-host karaoke thing.

Deli Twin Lyla tapped his shoulder, shouting, "Do we have to wear these grass skirts, Baker?"

"Yeah, Baker!" said Twin Lynn, squirming. "This thing's making me itch! This is really gonna cost you!"

"And where's *our* champagne?" Lyla asked.

"You *promised!*" Lynn projected through pursed, pouty lips.

"Ladies! La-dies," Thomas said, loading their trays with chilled bottles of Ste. Michelle champagne. "And as for your itches…maybe you'll get lucky later." He flashed an impish grin.

"Maybe," Lyla shrugged.

"Maybe," Lynn smirked. "Maybe *you'll* get lucky," she laughed.

"Maybe," Baker said, gesturing to the open door. "Now, fly! Fly, my pretties!"

The twins adjusted their skirts, straightened the floral knots beneath their flesh knockers, and sashayed past, swishing grass and balancing heavy trays of glass. "You're a trip, Baker!" they remarked, feigning disgust, but feeding on his endless energy. They loved the man—*one, more than she could bring herself to say.* He was honest and healthy, intelligent and respectful—a *Writer Man* whose humor was renowned, whose Leo heart was warm and inviting. But his was a heart haunted by lost love, and his bachelor vow was well known to all the local ladies. Most mistook him for just another player in the dating field, but those who came close enough to the man—to the lion inside—knew better.

Baker flagged Wolf, Neon, and Bill from the floor, and with colorful plastic cups the foursome crept backstairs to the balcony. Champagne corks vaulted skyward. The pianist took her cue from above and cut the keys. The chef slipped the old cassette into the system. The voice of Hawaiian crooner, Don Ho, filled the chamber: *Tiny bubbles...in the wine...make me happy ...make me feel fine!* The gang of four sang, fanning air with magic wands. Soap bubbles filled the red-cedar sky, bursting upon the scene below and prompting guests to raise their glasses high in cheer. *Tiny bubbles...make-a-me glad all o-verrr! With a feelin' that I'm gonna love ya 'til the end of time.*

"Everybody!" shouted Thomas.

"Sing along with Tom Ho," babbled Bill.

And they did: *"Tiny bubbles in 'da wine—make me 'appy, make me feel fine. Make-a-me glad all o—verrr. With a feelin' that I'm gonna—love ya till the end of time!* All right!" Bill Baker yelled, slapping his brother on the back.

A quadraphonic howl caromed off the cathedral ceiling, and spread like boysenberry jam across the floor. Thomas Baker poured bubbly for the boys. They flicked fingers on filled flutes, and rubbed crystal rims to a resonant crescendo. The host raised his hands. "Salutations!" he shouted. "Ready for the Last Supper of 1995?" They were. "Our chef, Gary Fisher—the marvelous master of Northwest cuisine—has prepared a feast fit for the kings and queens that you are." He directed their attention to the white baby grand, where the girls awaited. "Let's give a rousing round of applause for the lovely Miss Sherry Blair, our pianist, and the fabulous Deli Twins, Lyla and Lynn!"

The applause was loud. The twins swished their skirts. Sherry curtsied in her floral formal.

"Sherry is a classical music student at the University of Washington, but she can also do the boogie-woogie on them keys, as she'll show you after joining us for dinner. The twins are former Co-Chelan Apple-Blossom Queens." He paused, allowing their faces to turn a deeper shade of red; then pointed to the big bay window where wind-driven sheets of snow whipped swaying strings of small white Christmas lights. "Outside, the storm is frightful, but here our fire is delightful," Thomas crooned. His guests were captivated by the storm. Baker's face grew serious briefly. "I just want to assure all of you this." He made like an Allstate Insurance Agent with his hands. "You're in good hands here at the lodge." The impish smile returned to his face. "We are well-stocked with food and grog. And our multitalented chef has offered to taxi you locals home tonight after you've had your fill of merriment. Fear not, my fellow Chelanians! Chef Fish does not drink. So relax. Cut loose. Enjoy yourselves."

Fish fed the Windham Hill Sampler CD to the stereo monster, and rich woodwind music filled the room. Wolf and Neon returned downstairs to their respective seats, and the Baker Brothers stayed behind, staring at the faces below and the walls beyond to another place and time...

They saw Neon and Pai holding hands—looking like smitten teens gazing into each other's newly bared souls. They saw the silver-haired Englishman, Collins, conversing fireside with glass in hand, head bobbing like actress Katharine Hepburn—meaning he was happy. They watched Wolf make sexual gestures to the German girl behind him, whose macho-mate had meandered to the Mens Room to make way for the repast. They saw the happy family days of New Years Past—*the Tahoe of their youth.* Eyes misted. Minds remembered darker days endured by reaching out with *written words,* never losing touch in the tunnel of darkness, *the abyss,* always looking forward toward the light, forward to these days of here and now, sharing dreams *together.* Intuitively, they turned face to face. Feelings flowed forth.

"Look at them. They're having a ball," Bill said.

"Yeah, they are. Aren't they?" Thomas stammered. "It's nice. Huh?" Both choking on their words, the siblings simply clicked glasses and nodded.

"You know, Tom, I...I used to wonder."

"Wonder what?" Thomas sat his glass upon the cedar rail, sighed, and studied his brother's crooked smile.

"If the prison thing would take the *kid* out of you." Bill Baker couldn't hold back the tear.

Thomas tossed his arms around him, and whispered in his ear, "I *wondered* too." The brothers embraced. Thomas slapped Bill's back, and collected their glasses. "Come on, Blood. We've got some *special* dinners to serve."

"Always the good host," Bill said, as they walked arm in arm to the stairs.

Below, the Englishman Collins, having witnessed the upstaged balcony brothers' act, was overwhelmed with emotion. He fought futile feelings for his trusted friend and partner, turned to the fire to dry his tears, and raised his glass in silent salutation.

The brothers served the main table last. Thomas pecked each lady's cheek—Pai, Nancy, Sherry, the twins. He shook Neon's hand, and Jimmy's friend, Paul's, too. He embraced Collins warmly, drawing muted whispers, then placed a wet one on Wolf's forehead. His fly-boy buddy bit his arm! The hungry diners laughed hysterically. Facing kissing lips, young Nathaniel Baker scrambled beneath the table avoiding his Uncle Tom's craziness. The crowd loved it. Thomas toasted the main table.

"Without these people, there would be no method to my madness," proclaimed the host.

Everyone clicked glass. Everyone applauded. Wolf howled, then growled, when he bit into the rubber dinner Thomas had served him.

"Lovely!" said Paul in thick British brogue.

"Well done!" added Jimmy, head bobbing briskly.

By 11:45 p.m., Baker had sung Tony Bennett's version of *Oh, the Good Life* with Sherry, and the wine had come full circle back to bubbly. The meal had long since settled, the alcohol had been absorbed, and the volume of their voices was raised in anticipation of the midnight hour.

Councilman Barnes broke away from wife, Martha's, grasp to address them. He tapped his glass with a spoon. "Most of you know I was a lawyer by trade," Barnes began.

Playful booing for the profession was initiated by Wolf. Baker concurred, but restrained in respect of the councilman.

"And most of you also know I've been the president of the Chelan Alliance for the past three years," Barnes added.

Baker led the applause. Only the large German and his submissive miss sat silent, as they had for most the evening, finding no humor in their American hosts' childish games. For one week now, they had laughed little, drank often, and been noticeably discourteous to guests and staff alike.

Barnes babbled on with slightly slurred speech. "In a world increasingly run by faceless billion dollar corporations with little or no regard for the consequences of their conquests, we all learned something special together this past year. We learned that a small group of under-financed, concerned citizens, can still stand up and make a difference. We learned that even when we turned our pockets inside-out and found only lint, we could still reach into our hearts—and our *guts*—and say no. Hell no! The buck stops here. Right here in the Chelan Valley!" He was shouting.

They applauded.

Barnes went on. "Japanese PAC money nearly bought Forestry Service approval to rape and plunder old growth forests surrounding *our lake,* so they could ship the timber to foreign mills. But *we* stopped them. We stopped them at the chain saws. We stopped them in the courts." He softened his voice. "This issue has caused a lot of bad feelings in this neck of the woods, but the *sane side* is winning out. I know jobs are important. I know the developers *think* they're right. But I also know we must oppose them. For one day, when they take their grandchildren by their tiny, trusting hands, and walk them through these ancient forests; then, my friends...even *they* will applaud the sacrifices that groups like ours will have made."

They grew quiet. The crackling fire and soothing musical selection serenaded them.

But he wasn't done yet. "Together we successfully defended this valley against a great forest fire. Now, even bigger battles loom dangerously on the horizon. The latest Clinton/Gore Great Northwest Compromise may have slowed the main assault against irreplaceable old growth forests, but by closing one door, they have opened another door that cannot be easily monitored, one which enforces fewer restraints on the use of *private lands.*"

Wife, Martha, cleared her throat, mouthing: *It's New Year's,* to her hyper hubby.

But he wasn't done yet. "Consequently, large tracts of timberland are being bought for record prices throughout the Northwest, as wholesale lumber costs skyrocket. These *acquisitions* lay beneath winter snows on ecological death row, awaiting the song of the executioner's chain saw come spring."

Martha cleared her throat again, and whispered in his ear, *"Give the trees a break, honey. Save that youthful energy for the bedroom tonight!"*

Barnes' face grew flush. He sipped warm chardonnay. But he wasn't done yet. *Almost though!* He let loose a nervous laugh. "It has come to my attention that the midnight hour is nigh." He cleared his throat. "My wish for the new year is to see us all assume larger roles in the battle to preserve this pristine valley, which is home not only to many of you gathered here tonight, but countless *other* forms of *wildlife* as well."

There was laughter.

"I'd like to see our host commit his writing skills to the fray, to offset those well-paid lobbyists in Seattle and Olympia." He gave Baker the eye. "I know *real-life* can be boring, and Thomas prefers *fiction*, but—"

Martha yanked his belt loop—hard.

"I yield the floor," he declared. *Finally!* Barnes was finished.

When Wolf popped up like a hairy piece of toast, Baker pointed to the mantle clock, and motioned him to sit saying, "Thank you, Mr. Wolf. And now—"

"Geeze, Baker. I thought we were friends," the pilot protested.

"Thank you, Mr. Wolf. Thanks too, to Councilman Barnes for his passionate speech," Baker said, sipping a Northwest cabernet sauvignon from Paul Thomas winery. "Commitment is a word which time has taught me to use sparingly..." He paused at length to consider his words.

"I'll say," said Nancy, before leaning towards Pai's ear and whispering, "Speaking of commitments. Is there anything you two want to announce?"

The confused Chinese looked curiously back. "Excuse me?" Pai quizzed.

Excessive wine consumption had released caged feminine Eskimo curiosity she'd held at bay for over three hours. Again Nancy whispered, "Is it getting serious? I don't mean to pry, but Neon is our friend, and so are you now. How are...*things?*"

Pai looked her in the eye. "We are both very happy. Why do you ask?"

The twins were handing out party favors. Bill scrunched a speckled tiara on his wife's head, and blew a curly party favor until it tickled her nose.

Nancy spilled fresh champagne while leaning into Pai again. "Has he proposed?" she slurred.

When Bill Baker overheard his wife's interrogation, he rattled a noisemaker an inch from her ear.

Nan scowled at him, turned to Pai batting her eyebrows, and flashing her friendly woman-to-woman smile. "Well...?"

Pai smiled back. "Never know what New Year will bring," she blurted in broken English.

Thomas Baker resumed his speech. "But there comes a time when commitment is necessary." He chugged his amber colored libation. While swallowing loudly, Deli Twin Lynn looked longingly into his eyes. "That's why I'm committing myself to the preservation of the valley. Because many people with big money will come here soon...from Southern Cal and God knows where. And with them will come development. So, it's up to us to keep Chelan's expansion sane and ecologically sound. Shall we?"

Bill Baker jumped up, glass held high. "Let's do it, bro-therrr!" he declared.

The brothers clicked glasses.

Thomas sighed. "Life's not about blowin' hot air out your mouth. It's about *being there* when someone, or some *thing* you care about really needs you." His voice tapered off. "Believe me, I know." And now, I give you the last speaker of 1995. Ladies and gentlemen, and Wolf, I give you the man whose antiques surround us. I give you my friend and partner in Granite Falls Lodge, Mr. Jimmy Collins."

Scores of spoons were tapped on glasses. Jimmy did toe-tip-ups and bobbed his head like a dipping duck. He checked the mantle clock—*five minutes 'til the magic hour.* "Lovely. Well done! It's a bloody wonderful little party, isn't it mates?" he sighed. "I'm so glad to be here with you lads and lasses. The quaintness and night life of Europe are all well and good, but I must say, there is nothing quite like your American Northwest."

The New Year's Eve celebrants' spoons concurred.

Collins continued. "This week, Thomas walked me 'round the old Warwick estate..." The mere mention of the name brought reverent silence to the room. "...where we shared the most heavenly sights and sounds God graced his creation with—at least by this weary Englishman's account. I saw foraging deer a few meters off the path. Small birds landed at my feet. And the lake view was breathtaking."

Upon hearing this, the large German guest grumbled to his *fraulein.* "Whiny Englishman! Sounds like a woman. Deer and birds are for the hunter's crossbow," he bellowed.

Jimmy looked to his partner, Baker. Thomas nodded. It was time. Time for the big surprise.

"Trees have given much to me in the last quarter century," Collins announced. "Furniture has made me a wealthy lad. And now I want to give back. Thomas found out that the Warwick estate, without heirs, had reverted to the state for sealed public bids. I have entered a generous offer, my intention—my *wish*—being to retire here in the coming year on the future *Warwick Memorial Nature Preserve!* That is...if you'll have a gypsy English-man such as myself in your midst."

His announcement drew a standing ovation.

The New Year's revelers shouted "5-4-3-2..."

The champleve clock struck twelve! Streamers flew, and kisses blew around the room. They howled. They danced—whirling—while snows, swirling, piled high outside the door.

THEIR ENERGY lit a fire under the frauline's skirt. She asked him to dance. Her macho-mate declined, reminding her that New Years had long since passed in Berlin, reminding her of his plan to rise early and challenge the storm outside, reminding her of the adult toys they'd packed inside their matching Lufthansa luggage—toys for the storm now brewing beneath their matching leather lingerie! When Thomas joined Sherry and Jimmy at the piano for a boisterous rendition of *Auld Lang Syne*, the Germans slipped away into the wintry night, melting knee-high snow with body heat all the way to the privacy of Yeti Chalet.

AT 1:15 A.M. the sober chef drove home a cozy cargo of lush locals. 1:40, Wolf disappears with a demanding Deli Twin for the duration. 1:55, a poorly-muted howl escapes from the lodge's Sugar Pine Suite. One by one they faded, until only three remained.

From her fetal repose upon the fireside sofa, tender twin, Lynn, feigned sleep, stared up to the ceiling, and listened to the partners talk of old times and travels. She thought of how little of the world *she* had seen, thought about the family deli, and those crazy clients, about her and Lyla's momentous move to the UCLA campus.

Outside, the storm raged on, rattling windows and dispatching chilling down drafts to the chimney. Thomas felt them too.

Through half-closed eyes she watched him come to cover her with his prized Pendleton blanket; then felt his caring kiss upon her flush cheek. She softly purred and slightly shuddered, warmed by her writer—again.

He had to be tired, too, she thought. And yet, the host of her finest evening had energy enough for his British friend. His friend, one of many distinguished guests she'd seen hold him in high-regards. His friend, a silver-haired gay fox, treating him like a son, or more, and welcome here because of open-minded Thomas Baker. No senseless gay-bashing in Chelan. And *she knew* her writer's sexual preference. The thought of it made her squirm sensuously beneath his blanket!

She watched them sit before the bay passing vintage port, talking in soft, friendly tones, on and on into the night. She wanted to wait up for him—her writer-lover with the closed heart. She wanted to remember him—no matter what the future held. *But more than anything, she wanted him to ask her to stay in the valley!* She wished their timing would not have been so wrong. She faintly heard four bells tolling, dreamt she saw her lover strolling, dimming scented kerosene lamps, carrying her off to his bed, offering his touch—his *feel.*

And then? She slept *for real.*

Chapter 10

Rescue

ON NEW YEAR'S DAY, gray dawn's blanket receded, revealing a sleeping Chelan Valley wrapped in four feet of snow-white linen. Frozen phone lines lay like fancy black tinsel entwined around protruding, traumatized treetops. A county road crew's dozer snored like some gigantic ogre in the distance. Snow still fell. Chef Fish snuffed the non-filter cigarette, downed his fifth cup of coffee, and cruised back to the kitchen to cook up a storm of his own.

Around nine, winds died. Sunshine flooded Yeti Chalet. Heinrich and Gretta Claus set aside toys and slipped into fine Nordic winterwear. They waxed skinny skis, filled goatskin flasks, and stuffed Gortex fanny-packs with fine German cheese. They stretched their muscles, and chided the childish Americans' New Year's Eve charades. They scoffed at the puny snowfall piled upon their door. Submissive Ms. suggested securing a trail map. Macho-mate reminded her of their bloodline, insisted the weak Americans would have hangovers from overindulgence in inferior wine, and reminded her of their vast experience in the far-superior Alps. They shut down the kerosene heater and headed into the blinding snowshine to master Mother Nature.

INTERMISSION LASTED an hour. Initial resurgence turned day to night, ripping power lines in one roof-rattling gust!

Baker had been tenderly watching his Deli Twin, Lynn, sleeping in his bed, mindful not to wake her, reminiscing distant New Year's mornings when he was young and newly wed. But now he knocked upon the door of Sugar Pine Suite. A bottle fell to the floor. Growling followed. Baker cracked the door to Wolf's den, and explained the situation. The snarling pilot gnawed upon a drool-stained pillow. Lyla lunged for a bedside aspirin bottle.

Soon after their awakening, a cheerful caffeine-charged crew carried armloads of firewood, ruining Christmas pajamas with wet, jagged rounds. Baker, Baker, and Wolf snow-shoed back to the emergency generator shed, and saw no sign of the Germans' awakening through a driving snow. By eleven, guests found their host's *good-hands promise* fulfilled in forms like roaring fire, running water, and electricity. A tiny high-tech satellite dish beamed digital airwaves to a big screen TV. Snacks were served. Stomachs appeased, worries abated, they drifted back to naps or books, anticipating a two o'clock Rose Bowl kickoff, a Washington Huskies football victory, and a Duck Zanzibar dinner.

THEY WERE three miles away, trudging through thick, sticking, snow, over logging roads—rejoicing in their grand German conditioning and gear—when the next white wave rolled in, causing tree tops to tremble and beseeching the ancients to bow before their master, as a roaring snow-tsunami bore down, making breaking trail become a punishing task! Way before this, the woman thought the snow too deep, too wet, and too taxing, but now she felt fearful of these foreign elements…and fearful of her stubborn macho-mate, and his reaction to *her* weakness.

Convinced the storm would pass, they paused beneath a yellow pine partaking of fine cheese and wine, while watching great snowdrifts press upon the periphery of their makeshift shelter. Domineering man expressed satisfaction with the first half of their American tour. Submissive Ms. meekly smiled, wishing she were facing the mundane dangers of Miami Beach's highly touted muggings of foreign tourists instead—on the second half of their great American adventure.

A CURIOUS phenomenon unfolded before kickoff, as Chelan citizen concern for hapless holiday lodge people reached epic proportions. It coincided with citywide power outages, which pulled the plug on several bar-scene Rose Bowl bashes—Signor Frog's included. It commenced with the snowmobile-powered arrival of Baker's Wenatchee-based parole officer, Ron Moore, in the company of drinking pal, Sheriff Paul Hilo. They complimented Thomas on his emergency readiness. They tasted the soup *du jour*. "Good to see that new generator's working fine," they hinted.

Baker nodded, knowing the real reason they'd braved the blizzard.

Hilo cleared his throat. "Gonna watch the game, aren't ya, Baker?"

"National Championship ya know—all the marbles!" Moore coaxed.

Baker invited them to stay, and they peeled back their parkas revealing every Washington Huskies' purple-paraphernalia they possessed.

Next came Councilman Barnes, who just happened to be twelve miles from home testing his new Arctic Cat with wife Martha on board in a blinding snowstorm. Neon and Pai's appearance marked the conclusion of this inclement immigration, adding six familiar faces to the pregame gathering whose *concerns* had all been quelled.

Nancy switched the television channel to CNN. The crowd squawked, demanding she return them to sunny Pasadena; then *Headline News* caught Sheriff Hilo's eye. "Holy shit!" he shouted.

The reporter, live from Montreal, pointed his mike to the steaming summit of the First China Bank building. The camera zoomed in closer. It looked like Mount Saint Helens after she blew her volcanic top.

"Christ's sake! Crank up the volume!" Hilo ordered. Everyone stared at the screen, listening to the nasal-voiced French reporter…

In a joint communiqué, provincial Quebecois leaders, longside the Prime Minister, declared all out war upon undocumented Asians in the commonwealth, citing last night's suspected drug-related carnage—which claimed the lives of at least 177 New Year's celebrants in a spectacular midnight explosion—as the proverbial last straw. Coming on the heels of growing Canadian resentment, this marks the end of Ottawa's long-standing love affair with liberal immigration policy...

"Long overdue," Wolf muttered inaudibly. "No one wants an aging mistress."

Such appalling domestic terrorism must not be allowed to take root in the commonwealth, the Prime Minister declared. Chinese community leaders also denounced the attack. In related news, CNN has learned that First China Bank officials have been under investigation for international money laundering for some time.

Wolf wanted to cheer for *all* the announcements, but bit his brown-necked beer bottle instead, noting the presence of Neon's China Doll.

The camera switched to a model-faced anchorwoman back in the studio, as CNN's news continued.

The Thai government made a stunning announcement today. Bangkok declared its troops had burned over two-thirds of this year's poppy crop, from which heroin is derived. The gesture was said to be a response to nearly one billion dollars in aid from...

Beer bubbles shot forth from Wolf's snout. "Yeah, right! Some trustworthy government officials are laughing their gold-plated asses off over that hoax. No one burns billions—in any form. Maybe a few million for the photo-op, but—" His remarks drew stern looks from Hilo and Moore. He smiled back, shrugging. "Enough with the comedy. Back to Pasadena!"

Sheriff Hilo shook his head, and expressed some concern about Seattle's Asian gangs spreading inland to Chelan. Martha Barnes concurred.

"Fear not, good citizens! If Asians wanna take over Chelan, they'll make like Japs in Hawaii, and buy the whole damn valley," Wolf growled. "Now, put the frickin' pregame show back on!"

Wolf's sarcastic remarks stirred even deeper suspicion inside Councilman Barnes.

IT WAS HALFTIME in Pasadena. The game was tied: 14 to 14. Wolf sniffed for the missing scent. Baker noticed too. Four o'clock, and no sign of the flaxen-haired fraulein. This brought the brothers to the bay window. It was still storming. They wistfully watched the sun-soaked marching band perform in Pasadena, flashed semi-serious smiles, then slowly shook their heads. "Naaa! They wouldn't—would they?" said the brothers.

Second half started. The brothers bent into the storm, and shuffled on snowshoes to Yeti Chalet. Michigan scored on the opening drive, taking a 21 to 14 lead.

The Bakers had knocked long enough on the chalet's door. "Anyone in there—*screwing*?" Bill screamed, as Thomas turned the knob. The German team was absent from the field of play. Skis and fanny packs were gone. No Nordic boots lay by the door.

"Arrogant assholes!" Thomas said, slamming the door to Yeti Chalet.

They found no humor in their discovery.

EIGHTEEN INCHES of new fluff had fallen. Temperatures plummeted. Gale winds whipped ice needles—billowing outerwear. Skis sank deeper with every step, adding weight from old, wet snow.

He had bowed to her threatened boycott of their sexual Olympics and started back long ago. Now, Macho-man felt fatigue, and dealt with doubt. Visibility dropped to nil. The trail sign he sought was a football field away—a fragile, crusty cornice only inches. His weight cracked the thin curve of snow-covered ice, casting him into a whirling white cascade! He tumbled toward a sharp tree snag, blurring bark, and jagged granite. *Snap!* Skis planted, popped, and catapulted Heinrich skyward...*Crack!* Bones snapped like stale peanut brittle. Macho-man screamed for his Mrs.

BACK AT the lodge—where game-fever prevailed—news of lost Germans was not well received. Washington scored. It was

21 to 17, Michigan. A reluctant rescue team was formed, and a game plan devised. Bakers on skis and a mechanized Neon would scour the north branch of the old logging road at the base of Bear Mountain. Hilo and Moore would motor south. Wolf and Barnes would run communications and serve as fresh recruits for any rescue. Hilo radioed Wenatchee to apprise them of the situation. They informed him the weather would break soon. *Soon enough? Before the fourth quarter?*

Nancy pecked Bill Baker's cheek, and slipped her lucky rabbit's foot in his pocket. Pai kissed Neon—deeply—with eyes closed tightly. Deli Twin Lynn, longed to give Thomas the same send-off, but merely wished him luck instead. The Englishman flipped his partner a flask of port. "Catch! Now, off with you lads! Tiz' a far better thing you do than—"

Wolf growled back at the limey.

"Terribly sorry about your American football," said the Englishman.

They didn't need to be reminded.

The television exploded with excitement: *And the Huskies stop the Wolverines on third and three at the 45 yard line! Michigan will punt the ball...after these commercial messages.*

It was time for the gang to grab the gloves, and hit the powdery trail.

IN SNOWY WOODS, beneath umbrellaed branches, Ancient Sitka Spruce instinctively protected puny humans below, spotted owls above, and raccoons inside, its friendly confines—as playful porpoise would protect a capsized driftnet crew, as mighty Humpbacks entertain Japanese tourists offshore Hawaiian coasts, e'en though ancestral harpoons be forever embedded in their *likewise* mammalian brains...

THE WOMAN was no longer submissive. Having dragged him beneath this tree, sliced his $2,000 ski-uniform to tie a tourniquet around his gaping thigh—while enduring his verbal abuse—she now served wine, cheese, and hope. "They will find us, Heinrich," she prophesied.

"Why say this lie? Stupid woman! We are not one of them. They will not leave their American football to search for us in such a storm."

The woman listened to her superior-no-longer German mate, recalling her father's protest of this marriage... *Gretta, you are young. Do not let your rebelliousness drive you to this Heinrich. Trust your Papa. Beneath his glitter there is crudeness and insensitivity which you will not find endearing...*

"They will wait." He chewed cheese loudly, mouth wide open. Wine spilled down his chin. "By then it will be too dark— too late."

The woman bit a frozen lip. Snowflakes fluttered around her face, freed by birds from above. She spread bread crumbs for them.

"Stupid bitch!" Heinrich shook his fists, scaring the winged scavengers to higher ground. "Better they should starve than us!" His rash movement earned him great pain—and the woman's wrath.

"Shut up! Shut up!" she screamed. Pent-up feelings took flight. She laughed. She cried. "I *am* stupid, for letting you play your macho games. Stupid for allowing this to happen! Your *endurance* on the trail is too much like your *endurance* beneath the eiderdown," she hissed.

He blinked rapidly, shook violently. Blood appeared in the corner of his mouth. Eyes closed. Heinrich grew still.

She feared for him. *She despised him!* She slapped him—hard. "Look at you. Stay awake, fool! You are ruining my holiday," she screamed hysterically.

Birds shuffled nervously above, knocking clumps of snow on the two lost souls.

He came around. "They will not find us," he mumbled.

Again she struck his cheek. "*Dummkopf!* You are delirious. We will make it. We will live!" She could not hold her tongue. "I should have listened to Papa," she cried.

He glared at her through thick, glassy eyes, grabbed the wine and shook his head, sweeping pine needles to and fro. "We will not last the night," he gurgled. "At least I will die happy."

The woman was afraid. Watching him fade, she almost regretted her words—almost. An eerie feeling came over her. Through misty mountain clouds of darkness she saw only fallen branches. Stiff, like fingers of the dead, they formed grotesque figures in the gloom: twisted, anguished, suffering emigrants overtaken by the same enemies which would soon reach out for her! Deep despair set in like thick fog. The woman wondered about God...wondered if he who created and protected all things— things like this magnificent valley—was watching. Would *they* be worthy of *His* grace as well? Cold fatigue called her name from outside her conifer cathedral. She closed her eyes and prayed...

SUN STREAMED in with warmth. Winds roared no more. She heard silence. Soft notes of native birds floated down from on high like an angel choir. Sparrows and finches searched for feed. A Canadian Jay landed on her boot, another on her shoulder. She broke their last bread. They shared *communion.* Something happened. A great release occurred. Some malignant hardness which hectic modern living had chained to her heart ascended...and was replaced by something soft as snow. The 'nightingale' tended to her mate. *"They will find us,"* she whispered to her flock. And then the woman listened for the *miracle* of rescuers.

BETWEEN THEM, Bakers and Neon canvassed five miles of white carpet, concluding they were far beyond the Germans' range. Occasionally, they received updates from Wolf-control: 'No word from Rescue Team Two. Temperatures were falling fast, and another snow-squall was sweeping through the Cascades en route to Chelan! Michigan had managed a 28 to 17 lead late in the game.'

For Rose Bowl and rescue, time was running out.

The south branch search saw two G-men spend the better part of an hour scanning an avalanche scene for signs of the Germans—in vain. With dusk descending, they too began to think the worse.

MEANWHILE the Baker Brothers stood in sweat-soaked ski wear awaiting the arrival of Neon's noisy snowmobile. Bathing in waning alpenglow, and leaning against a nearly buried sign, which marked the sole junction on the north branch road, Thomas licked chapped lips. "Hate like hell to quit on them," he panted, his breath shooting skyward in short, sharp bursts.

Brother Bill nodded, and scanned the steep slide area beside them.

The walkie-talkie crackled to life, transmitting a Wolf howl. "Huskies score! And its 28 to 23, Wolverines, with 6:45 remaining—skinny skiers! What's the word out there? Over."

"No score here," Thomas replied.

"Shoulda' seen the play! Our superior line allowed the halfback to take it student-body-right in their faces. Then..." There was static interference; then Wolf's gruff voice again. "Getting a call from Hilo. He and..."

Static.

"Will get back to you, Baker. Pronto," promised the pilot.

Thomas felt the trail sign's cold-steel-sting through his Gortex glove, and thought about the German guests' superiority complex; then Wolf's play-by-play of the game. Clouds rolled over Bear Mountain clutching treetops like octopus tentacles and inking out baby blue sunset skies.

The brothers locked eyes, and simultaneously slapped ski poles on snow encrusted steel, only to reveal the well-known warning *Do Not Enter! Extremely Dangerous!* sign. A skier's silhouette with an X over it emphasized the point for foreign tourists.

The radio blasted, breaking the brothers' telepathy.

"Baker, you read me?" called Wolf.

"Like a cheap paperback book. What's the word?"

"Sheriff ran into an avalanche at Slide Ridge. Says it's time for you kids to come home."

Silence.

Slide Ridge was too far! Baker had a hunch. Cheers rang out over the airwaves in the background of the Granite Falls Lodge command center.

"Pack it in, Writer Man," the pilot bellowed. "Bug out, Baker."

"Negatory, Wolfman. Whose got the ball?"

"Screw the game! This is real life. I told Hilo you'd try to pull this hero-shit. He told me to tell you he was *ordering* you three to return."

Baker snapped back. "I'm not a government employee. I'm a *free man*! Pass it on."

Neon arrived on the scene, announcing he was low on gas, and hadn't seen a thing.

Baker bit a slice of lip skin, spat into the air, and slapped the steel warning sign. "Whose got the ball, Wildman?"

"Michigan," Wolf replied. "But time's running out. Fans are heading for the exits."

Thomas Baker skated to the edge and studied the dangerous ice-slide there. It was a tree-covered nature tunnel, nearly a football field in length. A forty-five degree downer! Too much for Neon's snowmobile. An unearthly glow beckoned from below him as menacing black storm clouds gathered above, snatching day's last light. Thomas Baker took a deep breath. Then, right as he was handing his pack to Bill, a great commotion came over the radio.

"Michigan fumbled on the 45 yard line!" Wolf shouted.

"Whose got the ball now?" muttered the oldest Baker.

Thirty seconds of silence passed as the call was made. And then the pilot barked, "Huskies, Man! Huskies! But we need a *touchdown* to pull this one out. Baker? I think we—"

The walkie-talkie made a clicking sound when Thomas passed it to Bill.

"Baker? Baker? Damn it, Baker!" Wolf cried out over the airwaves. "Do you read me?" he asked in vain. "Over?"

THE WOMAN felt numb. She stopped shouting for help when winds returned, snatching precious silence from the forest. With parched throat and ice-laden eyelids, she watched darkness steal hope, second-guessed her decision to stay with the man beside her, and spread last bread.

Grateful birds again took flight, nabbing nourishment for the long, cold night.

The woman watched them, formed a frozen smile, listened...and fought fatigue. Wanting to give and receive warmth, she softly lay atop her mate. With sounds of appreciative avions serenading her...the faithful woman finally slept.

THOMAS BAKER GROUND sharp metal ski pole tips in deep snow, rocked rhythmically...and recalled the promise he'd made to his guests. *You're in good hands.* It was the same thing his greedy lawyer told him before his trial and sentencing. Memories marched through his mind. His pulse quickened. Snowfall began anew. *We need a touchdown to pull this one out...*and one hundred yards of ice away! If the Germans were prisoners of the storm somewhere below, soon he would know.

Swish! Colors blurred by. Ski-tips clicked. Snow crystals crunched beneath burning legs. Thirty seconds later, Thomas picked himself up at the edge of a ravine, and scanned groves of old growth trees. He saw nothing. "Hello-o! Anyone out there?" he cried. His shouts echoed an instant—unanswered— and were swiftly swept away on winter winds. The outlook grew as dim as the sky, and yet, some unnatural noise gnawed at his psyche, reminding him of youthful treks in California forests, of trailsnacks shared with feathered friends. *But it was dark. Birds should be silent in their shelters, bracing for the stormy night. Unless...*

Brother Bill's voice blasted through the tree tunnel. "Wolf says return! New storm front hitting."

Between wind gusts, birds clearly chattered loudly just below him. "Who's got the ball?" Thomas shouted to Bill.

"We do! Third and ten on their twenty! Looks tough—"

SO DID years of forced confinement in steel cages with human predators. So did an unwanted divorce, and the dream he was now living—*once upon a time.* Logical mind fought Leo Heart. Twenty yards away, the birds and Ancient Sitka Spruce beckoned him like spiritual messengers to descend the deep ravine. With every muscle rebelling, with anticipation pumping adrenaline through his pulsating veins—Thomas descended.

When Bill arrived, the woman was revived and Thomas was telling her about the birds which had brought him to her location. The brothers broke into matching smiles. They radioed the lodge to report the news.

"Yeah—yeah, Writer Man," Wolf's voice crackled with pride. "We never doubted you would—"

There was laughter on both ends of the walkie-talkie.

Wolf growled, and cleared his throat. "Team Two's on the way. Leave Neon at the top to mark the trail."

"Ten-four," Baker replied.

"Now, here's something *really* important. Just lay back and listen." Wolf put the mike next to the television speaker.

Fourth and goal at the five. Huskies break the huddle for what will be the final play in this epic battle for the National Championship. There's the snap. It's a bootleg right. Bledsoe breaks a tackle at the four! Bledsoe spins! He's tied up at the goal, but those legs keep churning. He refuses to quit. Pulling two men with him. Falling, falling...reaching out. Touchdown Huskies! Touchdown Huskies—as time expires! We won! We won! We won!

We won! We won! We won! Echoed the crowd from Pasadena...and Granite Falls Lodge.

IN SNOWY WOODS, beneath umbrellaed branches, three conscious celebrants danced in pine needles on popsicle-toes. Brothers embraced. The woman thanked them. Her kiss was wet with tears of gratitude. Thomas swallowed a lump in his throat. Pride swelled the chambers of his Lion Heart. Once again, lost love sang siren-like in his ear, causing *her ghost* to appear.

AS THIS *FOURSOME* DANCED, he pictured fans leaving stadiums whenever their teams were down with time running out—just to beat some traffic. Fair weather fans and fair weather friends. *Fair weather mates!* Fair weather lovers drinking their fill of life's champagne, soaking-up vacation sunshine, fondling strands of anniversary pearls, stroking that big diamond from the wedding band—long removed from the *promised* hand. When the storm came for *him*—where was *she? Going on with her life? Playing someone else's wife? Why was rescue so often the job of strangers? Why couldn't he forget her? He was so understanding, so he'd understood. He **never** understood! And so, he'd made his vow. Never Again.*

"Go away," the writer muttered.

Bill slapped his brother's back, and the rescue dance resumed.

Wonderfully noisy snowmobiles arrived. The shout rang out again. "We won! We won! We won!"

Thomas Baker showed elation, but inside he intermittently cursed and cried her name—*wishing she had stuck it out to share these victories.*

Chapter 11

Spring Expansion

THE JOVIAL redhead in tight-fitting jeans flagged the white Ford Ranger to halt, removed her orange hard-hat, and shook out her hair. "Morning Mr. Barnes. How you and Martha doing?" she asked, clipping her walkie-talkie to a trim waist, and walking to the Ford's window.

"Fine. How 'bout yourself?" said Barnes.

"Can't complain. Been working lots of overtime, but the money's good." She smiled. "Been asked out three times already today," she added proudly.

The councilman flashed a fatherly grin. "Only three?" Barnes laid his huge weathered hands on hers, and winked. "You're a beautiful young lady, Rita," he whispered.

Cars quickly lined up behind them. Her face grew flush. Someone honked their horn.

"How long a delay are we looking at this time?" asked Barnes.

"Trucks are averaging twenty minutes between loads," she replied over her shoulder, before walking off to inform the other drivers of the delay.

Barnes walked roadside and sat his big frame on a rock. Early spring's southwest Chinook wind ruffled his wispy white hair, sang a soft duet with the deep, wide river on the ridges above, and stirred the land to life. Below him, the mighty

Columbia ate its way through the Cascade's moody green foothills en route to the Pacific Ocean. Beside him, tender sage leaves and clusters of delicate buttercups sprouted from rejuvenated ground. Blossoms of bitterbrush and showy clumps of balsam-root painted streaks of yellow all the way to the swollen river bank, where colorful wood ducks nested in the reeds. Overhead, a red-tailed hawk circled round and round, catching wind currents...*watching something*...waiting for a moment of weakness and a meal. He rolled back flannel sleeves, plucked a shoot of western ryegrass, and stuck it between his teeth. Wildflowers were everywhere, long since awakened by winter's white retreat. Spring made him sentimental. He watched the river flow, and remembered his dear friend, Ken Warwick...*gone!* Gone too soon—like all these signs of spring would be when burning summer sun came calling.

Just last month, he'd lost another friend, when the elderly chief of the tiny Corral Creek Indian tribe's pickup slid off the shoulder of this very stretch of pavement into the swift, unforgiving currents of the Columbia. The chief had led the opposition to a destination resort/casino being built on tribal land along the shores of Lake Chelan. Already, articles in the Seattle papers reported a sudden change of position among tribal council members. The sheriff called *the chief's accident* brake failure. The councilman had doubts. Barnes raised binoculars to bushy eyebrows, and studied the scenery.

Twelve places back, the driver of the black Land Rover lowered his *Wall Street Journal*, squinted into the morning sun, and focused *his* binoculars—on Barnes.

Barnes watched construction barges up around the bend erecting enormous concrete supports with a super-crane beneath the Wenatchee Bridge. He thought about the sad shape Seattle and Tacoma's roads and bridges were in with no relief in sight, thought about the intense construction along scenic Highway 2 where trees were being cleared and the road widened, so streams of cars could race eastward from Vancouver, Bellingham, and Seattle. It was as if an asphalt carpet was being laid to Wenatchee—and Chelan. Then there was all that talk of massive airport expansion. The front-page photo of country planner Hank Hodge breaking ground with the governor at the site of Wenatchee's super outlet mall kept flashing before his eyes. Its construction could mean the death of every *mom and pop* store in downtown Wenatchee—and maybe Chelan. It was *WalMart-syndrome* times ten. It made him both angry and sad. A convoy of semis set off across the bridge with beds full of blasted stone. Black smoke belched from their chromed-steel stacks. Dynamite charges exploded in the distance. Dinosaur-size dozers chugged to life, chewing soil. Barnes despised these sounds.

Twelve places back, the driver in black sniffed the air for the sensuous scent of sulfur. The sound of explosives was music to the old soldier's ears.

Cars honked like angry geese. Rita called out the councilman's name. Vocal wood ducks took flight from river reeds below. Barnes bit his lip and slapped his thigh. *The war had begun!* He would have to expedite his investigation of Ming Yaht, and find a way to access Hodge's files. He would have to… The human herd parked behind his Ford grew angrier. Barnes ran to his truck, and rambled into the town of Wenatchee.

Gordon's Land Rover cruised west on scenic Highway 2, bound for Seattle. It made an unscheduled stop in the town of Cashmere at a pay phone booth.

HANK HODGE had been joking with the secretaries, enjoying the intoxication of his *two-cocktail lunch*. He had been— until he heard that deep, demanding voice on the secretary's telephone speaker box. He quickly retreated to the privacy of his office. "It's been a while," he said. "What can I do for you, sir?"

"It has been exactly thirteen days, ninety-six minutes and twenty-three seconds, Mr. Hodge, and you can *do* what is expected of you. Nothing more. Nothing less. My superiors are extremely concerned about meeting their timetable. They expect construction to begin in August on the distribution complex at Chelan Falls. I expect to see zoning approval and permits on my desk in Seattle ASAP! Do you foresee any problems with that?"

Hodge wound the curly phone cord around fat his finger. "No...not really. You see, those bankrupt trucking terminals and the vacant tract you've acquired are not in the jurisdiction of the City of Chelan. We won't be challenged on this phase."

"Do I detect some reservations in your voice? What does the City of Chelan have to do with our plans?" inquired Nicholas.

"Nothing, yet. But there's talk of annexation in the city council. And now you're expecting miracles for a thousand acres of waterfront property that *your superiors* don't even possess yet!"

"I assure you we will soon possess the estate, Mr. Hodge. Please continue."

Hodge hesitated, then responded. "I said the mall and the industrial complex would be easy to slip by these people. I said, if you gave me enough time we *might* push all three phases through."

"Might?" said Gordon with a threatening tone.

"Projects of this magnitude take years to pull off! There's state, county, and city officials to...win over. And this Indian gaming venture? That's federal! We don't want to attract that much attention. Do we? How in the world could your superiors hide their interests in a casino that size, pushed through a Native American tribe that small? I-I—"

"Forget the feds, fat man. We have obtained leverage with key political players. Continue."

"If we push too hard, we could endanger the entire program." Hank fumbled through his desk for stomach antacids. "These things take time! People need time to forget."

Forget what? Nicholas thought, as the human hawk's self-preservation alarm sounded deep inside him. "Time, Mr. Hodge," a composed Gordon said, "is the one commodity my superiors do not possess. Money—as you know—is their strong suit. That estate must be cleared for construction by next spring. Period."

"There's a surprisingly strong coalition being forged by local businessmen, environmental activists, and sports enthusiasts. These Lake Alliances and the City of Chelan are formulating a media campaign of their own. They're beginning to flex some muscle, Mr. Gordon." Knowing he'd slipped by saying his caller's name, Hank swallowed four Rolaids—unchewed. "You on your car phone?" the county planner inquired.

Gordon slammed a leather-gloved fist against phone booth glass, ground his gold crowns, and thought about the political scandal story he'd read that morning detailing how a Congressman's conspiratorial acts had been recorded off a cellular conversation. "Fortunately for you, Hodge, I am calling the old fashioned way... from a payphone!" Nick paused to regain his composure. "I believe we have demonstrated what *muscle* really is, Mr. Hodge. Too much is riding on the success of this venture—and *all* its phases. Never forget that, Mr. Small-town politician. Understand?"

Hank cleared his throat, and wiped his wet brow with a handkerchief. "I don't like being rushed, Gordon," Hodge declared.

"Your likes and dislikes are of little concern to me."

"Rumors are spreading around the lake. I think you've underestimated the locals' reactions. I think you're moving too damn fast. I th—"

"You are not being paid to think! Just perform the minuscule tasks required of you and your office."

Hank lowered window blinds, walked to the corner water cooler, and popped two Valiums. He wrapped the cord around his wrist and whispered, *"I never wanted to be part of this, Gordon!"*

"Part of what? You no-balls bastard," Nicholas bellowed.

"It's gone too far! All you said about old man Warwick, was every man had his price. You said he'd *agreed* to sell. That's the only reason I went ahead with the paperwork on that zoning variance. You also said *the corporation* never loses an acquisition bid."

"They don't, Mr. Hodge."

"But you didn't say shit abou—abou—" Hodge choked on the word.

"About what, Mr. Hodge?"

"M-murder!" Hank spat out.

Gordon glared into the phone booth's glass. "Listen closely...the death of the party in question was a tragic accident."

"What about the goddamn Indian?"

"Don't question that which does not involve you! You are not paid to question."

"But I am involved! "*You* listen! I don't think I can continue working with you people. I-I h-have a f-family, grandchildren, a-and I am a respected member of this community! I've lived here all my life and—"

"I know everything about you, my dear Hodge...and more. After all, I am the security chief for a multibillion dollar corporation. I have a file on *all* our employees."

"See here, sir! I work for the County of Chelan and the State of Washington. Not some slant-eyed sonuva—"

"Have you forgotten your former life so soon? The one without the cabin cruiser, Yacht Club slip, and tender young mistress?" Gordon paused for anticipated silence. "When you accepted that first manila envelope of Ben Franklin's, you came under *my* personal supervision. You, Mr. Hodge, will do *exactly* what we tell you to do. We've invested far too much to allow anyone or anything to stand in our way. Now, then, prepare Chelan Falls for an August ground breaking at the future distribution center. And get that estate zoned commercial. Pronto!"

"I'm warning you. Councilman Barnes will fight Phase Three to the bitter end. He's been asking a lot of disturbing questions. He even tried talking to my personal secretary."

"You are fortunate she is such a loyal mistress to an aging, bald-headed whiner like yourself." Sick laughter echoed inside Nick's phone booth. "Don't concern yourself with Barnes. Barnes is nothing."

"Barnes is the most respected member of Chelan's City council. He was a formidable corporate attorney before he retired to—"

"*Was*—is the key word there, Mr. Hodge. You just worry about getting your work done. I'll deal with the councilman. I'm going to be in Seattle all week. I expect to see your progress reports faxed to my office ASAP! Or...is *that* going to be a problem too?"

"N-no p-problem at all, Mr. Gordon," stammered the nervous planner.

"Good boy," said Nick.

Chapter 12

Wine Run

AS THE BEAVER descended to Lake Union, Baker savored sweeping aerial views of the Emerald City, Seattle, whose skyline signature—Space Needle—still managed to be architecturally cool some thirty years after its conception for the 1962 World's Fair. Thomas loved the pace of Chelan, but sometimes this city called him to come cruise her concrete jungle, experience street energy, hear her hustle, watch the waterfront flow, or stroll Pike Place Market and Pioneer Square. He loved Seattle all over, enjoyed every visit—even when *her* memory tormented him. Movie producers and tourists had recently found Seattle's magic, but Baker discovered it some thirteen years back—falling hopelessly in love with his ex-wife here.

THEY'D MET in Tahoe. She was a sweetheart with a snowburned face, and raccoon eyes—a ski lift operator at North Star Resort. He was the arcane owner of Lion's Share Antiques— a recently retired marijuana salesman who was peaceably laundering money and picking up local real estate. They hit it off, had chemistry, started getting close. He flew to Paris with a French dame from 'Frisco on an Art Deco buying trip, trying to avoid the inevitable union with the fox-fannied ski-lift-op. In France, he quickly found himself cursing her for wrecking his passion for multiple romance while staring out the window at the

Eiffel Tower—thinking of his Tahoe raccoon. He considered cutting his trip short, packing-up his purchases, and winging home with his tail between his legs.

Meanwhile, his Tahoe Raccoon's fur was ruffled. She'd hurt her back lifting someone's brats into the ski-chair, and craved a full-body massage. Her heart cried out for her playboy antique man—*the one fearing commitment,* the one screwing some French floozy in Paris! She went bonkers, punishing herself and a lucky carpenter during a three-day binge, snorting cocaine and screwing her way to oblivion.

Back in Paris, phone-fever prevailed as scores of his calls went unanswered. Baker grew nauseous during long Parisian nights. *Oo-la-las* lost their lusty luster. He called her best friend and weaseled the truth about his lost raccoon from her. Twenty-four hours later, she was waiting for his weary bod' at the Reno airport. "How was the carpenter, Norman? Did he hang your cabinets for you?" Thomas taunted.

"How was your French whore?" she fired back.

Anger melted to mush. She pried the suit bag from his grip. He slipped his arms around her waist, and whispered the words he'd refused to use during his entire adult life: *You know I love you.* It was the beginning of the end of an era.

They hung on like pitbulls in heat—hesitantly talking of co-habitation. Baker—deciding to test the waters—accepted the keys to an old associate's island home for that memorable April month on Bainbridge Island, Washington. Bainbridge was known as a bedroom community of Seattle. Lion and Raccoon did nothing to tarnish that image. They investigated the island, explored the Olympic Peninsula, repeatedly scoured Seattle, and reconnoitered every nook and cranny of each other—body and soul! Upon returning to Tahoe, she moved in her stuff to the disgruntlement of Baker's aging Irish Setter, Benjamin. They were the first couple wed inside the gondola above gorgeous Heavenly Valley Ski Resort on South Lake Tahoe's slopes…

AS WOLF'S BEAVER soared over Puget Sound, Baker watched the northwest corner of the United States break up into little island pieces before completely disappearing into Canadian waters. They banked sharply due east and began the final descent to Lake Union. Baker became entranced by mighty Mount Rainier, whose glittering sunlit snowcap, again reminded him of his sleek Tahoe snow princess in those days of yesteryear. *BAM!* They hit the water and bounced twice.

Thomas Baker slapped himself on the cheek.

"Need a barf bag, Baker?" asked Wolf.

Thomas shook his head. "Just thinking."

"About what?"

"About how I'm going to be late for my appointment."

"With the newspaper guy that Barnes turned you on to?"

Baker nodded.

When they hit the dock, Wolf tossed Thomas a set of keys, and waved. "Meet me at Lake Union Cafe for happy hour. There'll be lots of young coeds there shaking some firm young tail," the pilot said, winking twice. "Whatta' ya say, Writer Man? You ain't been laid since the twins moved to L.A."

Baker walked quickly, hoping to catch a cab. "See ya at five!" he shouted over his shoulder.

"Load your shit in the Beaver first!" Wolf screamed, as Baker broke into a run. "Lock it! And warn your little AA chef not to nag me about my drinking. Or he can walk back to Chelan."

THE SEATTLE PAPER'S editor picked FX McRory's for lunch—a place across from the King Dome decorated with lots of wood and sports memorabilia, and home to a hellacious selection of shellfish and beer. It was the restaurant he and Raccoon made their favorite oyster-stop during that fateful month and all subsequent visits to The Emerald City. With his ex on his mind, Baker struggled through his thoughts, but over-all, Thomas was well received by the receptive ears of the editor who had read plenty of his work. By the end of their business luncheon, they cemented an agreement. Baker would cover sensitive environmental issues east of the Cascades. Councilman Barnes' connections had bore fruit.

Afterward, the two men shook hands on the sidewalk out front where a cab's breaks screeched curbside. "Want a ride, Baker?" asked the editor.

"No thanks, Robby. I'd rather walk-off lunch, check out the street life. You understand."

"Keep my advice in mind, T. B. Lots of regional publishers are looking for work with Northwest themes and settings. Been lots of film crews up this way liking our low overhead, great scenery, and clean air." He ducked into the taxi.

"Don't have to sell me. *The Fabulous Baker Brothers* was a great Seattle flick. Of course, I was partial to the main characters. Then there was *Sleepless In Seattle*—sleeper of the summer of '93," Thomas snickered.

"Yeah! That's how they marketed it two months before release," Robby said, laughing loudly at the writer's joke.

"Guess that only goes to show you can take the movies out of Hollyweird, but you can't take Hollyweird out of the movies. Thanks for lunch, Robby," Thomas said. "Next time, I'll buy."

The editor's Nigerian cabby hit the gas.

"Send more wealthy clients to the lodge!" Thomas shouted as Robby disappeared.

"Will do, Baker," the editor promised.

Thomas untied his tie and stuffed it inside his charcoal sports coat. Across the street, The King Dome was dead. A cool breeze swung in off the Sound. His writer's eye filled the lot with Winnebagos, mini-vans, and every breed of tailgater under the sun—the autumn sun that shown for that last Seattle visit with *her!*

IT WAS AUTUMN 1985, game day. They were shuffling through the crowd to their gate, smelling barbecue aromas from tailgater's grills. Getting hungry. Listening to the trumpeting street musician—the one with cheeks so stretched-out, and brain so fried-out, and the face like Jackie Gleason's Frank Fontain. Thomas reached for a five-spot, and his host grabbed his hand. "Baker! The bum *lives* here. He's been playing that tune since they built the dome!" Thomas switched the five to a ten, stuffed it in the hat beside the homeless man, beside the worn old record album cover with that face—the street musician's face when his cheeks were rosy and those faded eyes twinkled with success from the features of a young Frank Fontain! The tired musician's eyes twinkled once again for an instant. Tears rolled down the burned-out trumpet player's stretched-out cheeks... before his horn blew, and the foursome shuffled on.

"Everyone's got to live somewhere," Thomas told his host. The band struck up a tune. Cool winds blew. A young Baker wrapped an Irish wool long-coat around his younger bride. Of course, San Francisco whipped the Seahawks' butts that day, but the beer was cold, the King Dogs warm, and his wife was the perfect female football fan. Baker regretted borrowing binoculars after that third beer and blatantly staring at the Sea Gals strutting the sidelines in those skimpy glitter-panties. Yeah, he regretted a lot of things...

APRIL WINDS whipped cool mist in off Elliot Bay. Baker buttoned up his coat, but sun broke through, burning his chilled cheeks. *Ah, Seattle! Cool-hot-misty, like love.* He'd seen faster cities, but like fast women—they only burned his passion for them too quickly. *Ah, Seattle! She was a lady he could romance over and over again. A sprawling, inviting spread, custom-made for a slow-hand lover like him.* He shook his head, smiled at ghosts of good times past, walked down First Street satchel in hand, studied worn facades of historical buildings, watched white cloud puffs roll over flat-top roofs...tickling crumbling parapets with salt-water fingers. *Were some things really worth the price of restoration?* he wondered. *Like lost love?* Jazz joints, antique shops, coffee stands, bus stops—all of Old Seattle sang songs of lost love in the reflective writer's ear. But this time tones were mellow, vibes were pleasing—like Tony Bennett's nineties comeback, like tenor saxophone solos...*like glorified afterglow.*

Standing beneath the dark Alaskan Way viaduct, Thomas scanned the Last Laugh comedy club's marquee and the international configuration of cabbies reading afternoon papers while waiting on fares. A frightfully too-skinny black hooker winked. The Bainbridge Ferry's horn blasted from Pier 52. Exhaust fumes erupted, and an armada of taxis set sail onto the asphalt sea.

BAKER RAN UP BACKSTAIRS to Pike Place Market, scrambling away from the haunting waterfront into a musty concrete stairwell where upper-middle-class-school-skippers puffed packs of heroin-laced cigarettes and pipes of crack cocaine, mesmerized by grungy guitar heroes—*awestruck by street life they knew nothing about!* The sad scene made him wonder how the naïve Chelan Deli Twins were faring down in Los Angeles.

The Market's main floor crowds flowed stall to stall. Tourists with taste and sincere city shoppers with money intermingled, and listened to first-team street musicians. An aging hipster had parallel parked his Kelly-green piano-on-wheels beside the entrance's bronze pig statue, and stood pounding the keys behind the butcher's stall. Three black guys in Goodwill suits sang *accapella* tunes...tap dancing by the vegetable vendors. The same blind Irish lass still ruled the sidewalk with cheery swaying smiles and her docile dulcimer, strumming soft notes from her native Emerald Island on the cobblestones of America's Emerald City—*Seattle.*

From famous Pike Place Seafood's corner stand, cleancut young-stud salesmen *white-rapped* hip routines in wardrobes marred by bloody fish stains—minus monster medallions and gold rope chains. *Deals on eels! Slabs and crabs! Tails and snails!* And such. A sultry miss in a polka dot shift bit the bait and pointed to a pyramid of fine silver salmon. The act ensued: one of the boys made a toss to the boss who slapped it on the scale, pointed to the big-faced dial, and got the nod from Miss Polka-dots. Her order was promptly wrapped in last night's Post, hurled over heads and handed to her. From an old brass purse came a worn five-dollar bill. From her flush young face came a priceless smile. She slipped her catch in a colorful cloth bag. Then, Miss Polkadots disappeared in the crowd, seeking the biggest bag of basil from an herb booth...*down the pike.*

From the old-fashioned news stand, *Read All About It*, the writer recorded this Norman Rockwell Americana scene, saluted the scruffy salesclerk wearing vintage twenties era suspenders, and strolled into dust-dotted street-sunshine to wait for Chef Fisher. A sidewalk salesgirl caught his eye...selling marvelous rice-paper watercolor greeting cards bearing messages of lasting love. *Like the last letters he'd received from his ex-wife in the joint.*

SHE'D NEVER BEEN much for writing, preferring the phone instead—as do most moderns—as he himself did before rediscovering the importance of the pen in prison, where he found both faith and purpose in the written word. Those first eleven months she wrote often...inside cards like these. Her words of love inspired her newly caged Lion, who hungered for his mate more than freedom, or family, or money. He would set them on his little metal convict locker, arrange them like an altar in Hell—and worship their love. Somewhere, they still existed. He looked down at a rainbow-colored fuel spill in the city street and remembered her final words of love: *Thomas—I am not whole without you in my bed! Thomas—When this is over, I'll pick you up like Kirk Douglas or Burt Lancaster in one of those old convict movies. We'll hit the first rest stop and make up for lost time! I promise. Thomas—this time will pass and no one and nothing will ever separate us again!* **Love forever, Raccoon.** The words rattled around Thomas's mind. Month twelve came. She stopped staying home for his collect-from-prison-calls. Thirteen. She stopped writing, changed the phone number; then refused to meet face-to-face. Her father— retired undercover cop, woman beater, bribe-taker, deserter of family—informed her it would be better this way—*in the long run.* Manly, moralistic daddy arranged for their no-contest divorce. She married that carpenter, Norman, and never wrote again. It wasn't that it ended, but how. *Nothing, and no one, ever hurt him so deeply.* Baker took a deep breath of diesel fumes...and exhaled.

A delivery truck's horn honked at the arriving chef's New Deli cabby. The writer rubbed rice paper greeting cards with sweaty fingertips, complimented the artist, and waved to Fish with a forlorn smile. "How'd your visit go, Gary?"

"Fine...just fine, my friend," Fish said with typical exuberance. Gary Fisher's spring sunburn glowed below his shaggy black hair. "Libby's growing leaps and bounds. I can't believe she'll be eight in May. I took her to Seattle Center. We rode the merry-go-round. How was your day, Thomas?" he inquired.

Fish looked happy. Baker decided not to ask about *his* ex-wife. "Great...just great. Always a pleasure to visit the Emerald City. Ready to shop for Easter goodies?" Thomas asked.

"I'm psyched! Let's do it," said the chef.

Together they sought cilantro, talked tomatoes, babbled with basil growers, and were lectured on the virtues of organic Buttercrunch lettuce. At first, Fish detected his friend's distant demeanor, but soon enough, Baker fed on public interaction, consumed market energy, and took to clowning around like his normal self. So Gary decided to let it go.

The owner of Pike and Western Wine Merchants knew the writer from the early days in Tahoe, and valued his friendship as much as his business. That's why he deliberated about passing on the news from his Tahoe store right up until their taxi arrived...and why he told him. "Tom, your ex-wife's been waitressing at Tahoe Keys Marina, hustling cocktails to horny old yachtsmen like me."

Baker shrugged, but struggled to slip his Visa card back inside its little plastic holder. "And?" he asked his old pal.

"She's been asking about you. She partied with one of my sales girls last weekend. Said she still loves you. Said she's getting a divorce from that construction guy. She's coming up here for a wine tasting in June. She wants to see you, Tom. Can't bring herself to ask."

When their cabby came to the door, the polite chef made himself scarce, and started loading wine cases.

Baker felt numb.

Time froze.

The taxi driver honked his horn.

The wine shop owner tucked a sales slip in the writer's sport coat, and wondered where *this* story would end, knowing how many years he had once waited to hear from her. "I thought you should know—author," he said, handing Thomas his change.

Baker nodded, and ducked out the door, mulling over options for dealing with the news. He felt sick inside. Only the meter ticking and tires clicking disturbed the silence during the long drive to Lake Union.

After they loaded the Beaver, Baker broke his silence by thanking Fish for his assistance. A college rowing team called out its cadence in the distance. Their oars' rhythmic repetition soothed Thomas's troubled soul. He wanted to row into a good hot lather himself, get high on the exercise rush—the solitude—and the challenge of nature. He needed to be out there casting eyes ashore from that clean, unique perspective of a man detached from his surroundings just far enough to assess them, and decide where next to go. But he'd settle for consuming several cocktails up the hill where he could forget about *her* and her damned divorce for a while.

Two men climbed 110 steps. Both looked back upon the waters and the day. They scanned Queen Anne Hill.

Hesitantly, Fish spoke. "I know you never talk much about her, but I see the expression on your face some days. Want to talk about it? I mean...did you ever experience a closure in your relationship? I mean, where you were and all. I—"

Baker was touched by Fish's concern, but vodka and tonics were only a motion away. He patted his friend's back. "Thanks Gare, but let it rest. Okay?"

Fish nodded.

The door flew open.

Mellow music combined with Cajun blackening and prime young womens' perfumes to overwhelm their senses! Across a sea of white linen tablecloths sat James Shawn Wolf sipping a cool one—surrounded by coeds—and waving.

"You're late, Baker! How'd shopping go?" Wolf said slapping his thigh.

Baker only nodded, bellied-up to the bar, and ordered the double he'd been longing for.

The chef served a cheery smile, stared at the empties in front of their pilot, and reached for the salted peanut dish with words about sobriety hanging from his lips.

Wolf tipped back a beer, took a gulp, and glared into Gary's eyes, hoping he had the sense to keep his AA remarks to himself. "How was your meeting?" he asked Thomas.

Baker tipped back an icy tumbler, stared straight on into the beveled mirror of the oak back bar, and said nothing.

"Okay," Wolf remarked, as he motioned for another Rainier beer.

The chef couldn't keep a lid on it. "Scuze me, James, but shouldn't you be slowing down? I mean, you are flying us back to Chelan in less than an hour. *Right?* I mean—"

Wolf was waiting for this. His eyes drew close. His upper lip curled, then twitched. He gnashed teeth.

The writer watched Wolf's reflection closely; then downed his double in record time.

The pilot half-growled: "I'm a grown, thirsty, beer-loving man. I don't have a problem with drinking—like *some people* seem to have. And—more importantly—no one is forcing you to fly back to Chelan in *my* Beaver. So, just drink your sody-pop quiet-like, and keep your speeches on sobriety and that damn river over in Egypt to your sanctimonious self! *Comprende'*—Gary?"

The young woman Wolf was working on rose to leave for the restroom. "I just love geography, Wolfy," she said. "What Egyptian River were you referring to?"

"*Dee Nile*, sweetheart. Dee Nile! It's a favorite waterway of our Mr. Fish here." Wolf laughed. Everyone within earshot laughed, but Baker. The pilot patted the off-duty waitress on the buns and sent her on her way to the powder room.

Fish forced a red-faced smile, blinked his eyes, and bobbed his head. Baker might actually benefit from a drink or two today, but Wolf's drinking worried him. Wolf intimidated the sensitive chef, surfaced pent-up anger and hidden insecurity—made him question his own thinking. He did not know if this was good or bad, and did not want to know today. All he wanted was to cherish the memory of his daughter Libby's smile that morning on the merry-go-round, and ponder the reason for his own ex-wife's coldness in the foyer of their fine Queen Anne home that afternoon. He pushed away his Pepsi, and kicked back his barstool. "Think I'll walk the docks until you two are ready," Gary declared, tugging theatrically on his belt loops with his thumbs. "I mean, someone has to watch the load. Right guys?"

The *load* remark brought smiles to the boys, who related the phrase to their old scamming days. "Give us half an hour," Baker whispered. The instant Fish swam out the door, Thomas ordered two more doubles.

Wolf growled playfully. "So, the luncheon went fine?"

"Uh huh," Baker gurgled.

"Then you musta' wasted another perfect day thinking about your ex," Wolf snarled.

Baker wiped his chin. "Does it show that much?"

"Sure it does. This is *Wolf* here—not Chef Recovery! Why in the hell do you let that cunt bother you still? Sometimes I just don't understand you, man."

"She's not a cunt. I'm the one who went off to prison."

"No shit, Sherlock? So? She sure as hell hung on when the champagne was flowing! Didn't she? She knew what you were about when she signed that lifetime membership. Didn't she?"

Baker banged back another. His liquor buzz begged him to side with Wolf's negativity toward his ex. He started on the other double; then pounded his fist on the bar. "Damn right she did!"

Wolf ordered another round. "Forget her! Get out your note pad, son. Let's play a round of the Writer-Man's game."

Instinctively, the writer reached for his pen.

Wolf dug right in. "After that Haitian fuck-up, I got into flying jumpers for a sports parachute club outta' De Land, Florida. That's just outside Daytona, Writer Man." Wolf witnessed that curious energy rising up in is friend. His strategy was working. "No. It wasn't just a parachute club. Everyone connected with that outfit was farming out to the *Agency*. Helping freedom's cause in South America this time," he laughed. "They were all tricksters! Monkey-biz tricksters, Baker."

Baker nodded, chewed the end of his pen, and reflected back to the *Roaring '70's.*

Nearby coeds came in closer, tilting perky tits toward their conversation. One plucked the pilot's leather bomber jacket off the seat back, and held it up admiringly. Wolf never flinched. It was his hunting jacket, specifically worn to attract the lusting curious eyes of all legal age female cocktailers. *Beaver Patrol* was emblazoned over his heart.

"What were the planes?" the writer requested.

"All jumpers flew Beechcraft D18's back then. They were perfect for lining up jumpers in," the pilot explained.

"Or stacking bales of pot?" added the author.

Wolf flicked his brows, and ran one hand dramatically through his wild salt and pepper mane. He shook his leg like a dog, wrinkled his snout, and sniffed the sensuous air around them.

Baker cracked a crooked smile, and took a normal sip off his drink.

The college girls giggled.

Wolf's intended prey whispered something to her pixie-haired pal.

The writer was curious. "Didn't you say you had an unwritten rule about hauling *shit* back to the States?"

Wolf pawed his playmate. "Damn right I did! I appreciated my freedom too much to play that smuggling game—even in those gravy days. Hell, Baker. I'm one of those idiots who fought for my country." He swigged some brew and belched. "Fought for *the Military Industrial Complex*—right or wrong! I hauled anything anywhere for my Uncle Sammy, but if it was Homeward bound to the good old U.S. of A. I didn't just take the shipper's word. I'd inspect preflight for weed or blow. All I ever found was dirty dollars in my return cargo crates." He rolled his eyes. "I could have made millions just like all the other kids...if only I'd overlooked my own personal vow—*voluntarily.*"

New arrivals flooded the female fox-pool. One stepped up. "'Scuse me,but are you the pilot?" she asked, with pursed lips and a poignant southern accent.

Wolf smiled devilishly, twitched his snout, and shook his head.

"But…Joanie here, says you're a damn good *pilot*," said the Georgia Peach. "And that you specialize in flying—*Beavers*. That true, Mr. Wolf?"

MING YAHT'S executive secretary pool frequented the Lake Union Cafe for its fine ambiance. They desired distance from downtown Seattle, and a place to relax. They desired good music, sweeping scenic views, food and drink—getting buzzed—and appreciating firm butts on young college boys! They carried on conversations in the far corner, where twenty-three year old Sharon debated forty-three year old Donna on the merits of young, wild men vs. older, experienced men.

Marla Decker almost died when the writer walked in—and she had been watching Thomas Baker ever since. Cindy Crane did a great impression of her Chinese boss. Marla feigned laughter and watched the man she'd met only once with pen in hand, girls gathered around him at the bar. She thought about the articles he'd written, and how she had collected them all. She thought about his humorous short story on his first kayak outing after his release from prison, thought about his novel—about his special way of expressing pain and passion, humor and anger. She watched, wondering, wanting to get closer, wanting to learn more—learn *all* about him. *How could a man write words like his in prison?* She remembered the funeral of Russ Warwick in Chelan, where she sensed some mystic warmth radiating deep within him—and the heat from that fire down below! Something had smoldered in her that day as well. Presently, she vowed to approach him; then sized-up the competition at the bar: *Formidable in appearance, but lacking in substance!* She produced an antique silver compact from her purse, and checked her lips.

"What do you think, Marla?" asked one of her co-workers.

"Sorry, Donna," Ms. Decker replied. "I was thinking about the mess I left on my desk this afternoon," she lied. "What were you saying?"

"We're deciding who's the sexiest boss down at Highrise Hell," Donna explained. "Sharon thinks it's Nick Gordon! What do you say to that?"

Marla's love-light dimmed upon mention of Nick Gordon's name. His cold piercing eyes and humorless persona gave her the creeps. He was so evasive, and Nicholas worked without a personal secretary, behind *closed*, locked doors most of the time. Nicholas rarely showed his face in Seattle. Maybe that was all part of being security chief for Ming Yaht. *Maybe not.* "Oh, he's okay, I guess," she answered conservatively, wary someone within their sacred ranks might be looking to score some brownie points with Old Nicky Boy.

"I can't stand the guy! He looks right through you," squeaked Robin Garth.

"Probably sees your panty lines," said Sharon.

"Very funny! He makes me nervous," scowled Robin, somewhat shaken. She studied their faces to see who agreed with her assessment of the admittedly athletic, but obviously mysterious Gordon.

"He's too much man for you, Hon," Sharon blurted out.

AT THE BAR, Baker dropped his pen and one of the girls bent to retrieve it.

Wolf howled, drawing the attention of the Ming Yaht secretaries.

"Now, there's a healthy specimen," Sharon said, squirming in her seat. "I wonder if he'd let me cut his hair?"

"Which hair?" Robin giggled.

Marla wanted to go to Thomas, preferring lean physique and intellect to macho beefcake. She wanted to, but a surge of college studs flowed onto the floor, eyeing the uptown ladies on their way to the bar. Marla plucked the red rose from their vase as an offering to Baker. She knocked back her cocktail, wiped her chin, and kicked out her chair like some gunslinger in an old spaghetti western.

When 276 pound Karl Krieg saw the pilot shouldering his mate of the month, bad blood began to boil.

The bubbly blond ignored the Neanderthal's arrival and hugged the happy pilot. "Take me for a Beaver ride, Wolfy," she teased. "Please..."

Karl Krieg and company kept right on coming. His teammates taunted the bulky tow-headed tailback for the National Champion Washington Huskies. "Looks like them old farts are fucking with your babe, big guy," one of them said.

Baker saw the kid's tense, stiff swagger in the back bar mirror, and tapped the pilot's knee.

Wolf micro-nodded, studied the extended steroid forehead approaching, and wondered if the kid was as stupid as he looked.

Krieg stopped right behind Wolf, planted both feet firmly, and placed his huge hands on broad hips. "Hey, *old man*. Go find some granny to impress with your fuckin' war stories," he commanded, tapping Wolf's shoulder.

The place grew quiet.

Wrong line, thought the writer, suddenly on standby for some unwelcome action. Baker's parole status came to mind, and how a barroom brawl could violate its conditions and send him back to a federal penitentiary. Thomas grew tense, hoped Wolf would show rare restraint, and hoped Wolf hadn't forgotten the feeling of having a parole violation hanging over his head.

Wolf turned to face the kid with one eye twitching like Clint Eastwood. "Go way, sonny," the wise old pilot said. "Go pump some iron. Or pop some steroids. Just get outta' my face...or I'll have to give *you* some flight instructions."

The cute coed snickered, secretly enjoying the ancient ritual she'd snared the aging Wolf into.

Krieg didn't snicker. His face turned radical red. Veins popped. Shoulders shook. He rolled his thick head around his even thicker neck.

Wolf's alert-mode clicked on. He casually requested his check.

Krieg, perceiving this inaction to be cowardice, brushed back his prematurely receding hairline, nodded cockily to his running buddies, and slapped Wolf's hunting jacket, laughing. "I didn't think you was a *stupid* Old Man," the big jock said.

Wolf growled, and glared into the reflective glass behind the bar.

Baker stepped down hard on his pal's boot.

Karl Krieg jerked his wayward waitress off her barstool by the waist of her tattered grunge-look jeans!

The girl grimaced. She spilled her drink.

Wolf and Baker stood to confront Krieg.

Karl picked the pilot for his sucker punch.

Pow!

Wolf fell back from the force of the blow, and found himself on the fine hardwood floors on all fours. His head spun. Steroid Boy started kicking him like a bad dog. The pilot ordered his parolee-pal to hit the exit, grabbed the kicking foot, and twisted Krieg to his knees in one quick motion! Wolf leaped up, and assumed a martial arts stance. "Let it rest! I'm warning you," he shouted. Both hands were ready for action.

Two letter sweaters lifted the tailback off his butt; then the threesome circled around Wolf making *kung-fu* sounds. One picked up a chair. Baker grabbed the other's arm, wanting to keep the odds right.

The bouncer grabbed a baseball bat, and readied himself to join the fight. The owner appeared from the kitchen, shook his head, and smiled. The owner hesitated, slipped the stun gun back in his apron, held back his bouncer; then watched and waited.

The chair-wielding wild boy went for Wolf, and caught a custom boot with his cheekbone. *Snap!* Krieg charged in and took a chokehold on the pilot.

Wolf growled, snatched the boy by his letter sweater, and yanked him forward for a full-on head butt. *Crunch!*

Karl Krieg crashed and burned. Blood spouted from the football hero's badly broken nose. Beaten, he cried-out in pain, "Enough, man! That's enough."

His two tough-guy friends turned tail and ran away.

The crowd reacted with applause. Wolf took a bow. Someone called 911. Soon a siren wailed from an arriving cop's cruiser top.

Secretaries scattered every which-way! Underaged coeds cried out in fear, and tucked fake ID inside padded bras.

Again Wolf waved the writer away. "Go on, Asshole! Get outta' here. Beat it. If I'm not there in ten—come bail me out!"

Baker refused to leave his wild friend for the capture.

The owner had seen enough. He rounded up the two rogues, whisked them through his kitchen—out the back door—and back into bright sunshine. "Still enjoy a good bar brawl I see. Eh James?" he said.

"No more than you," Wolf snorted, shaking his old friend's hand. The two men had been pals since Wolf's South Florida days. Both were ex-seals, both pilots. This was the guy who had turned Wolf on to Washington State, and *rescued* him from himself.

"Guess who showed his face in Vancouver last month?" Wolf's stocky friend said without thinking, as they caught their breath.

Wolf furrowed his bloodstained brow. "I give up. Who showed up, big guy?"

The bouncer called from the kitchen: "The cops are here, boss!"

The owner shook his head and said, "You two bums better beat it."

Baker led their downhill retreat.

Wolf whispered over his shoulder. "Who was in Vancouver? Tell me."

"Arturos Aquindo. I didn't see him myself, but—" His bouncer was waving frantically. The owner waved back. "Gotta' run, *amigo*. You owe me!" Wolf's pal said.

Years of suppressed emotions burst within Wolf: anger, hatred—*revenge*. Like a lanced boil on an inner lip, they left a bad taste in his mouth. He stumbled, nearly fell...spat out bile and blood. If James Shawn Wolf *owed* anyone, it was Arturos Aquindo! And his was no minor debt.

INSIDE THE CAFE, Marla's heart pounded beneath perky breasts. A policeman picked her for his report, and asked what had happened. "Oh, nothing serious, officer. I think the big kid at the bar just slipped and fell," was all that the secretary said.

FISH HAD HEARD all the commotion from the dock. He also saw Wolf's shiner as they jumped on top the plane's pontoon.

The Beaver bounced.

Fish offered the pilot his hand.

Wolf slapped it.

"I really hate to say this," Gary lied, "but I told you guys—especially you, James, about your drinking. And…"

The pilot begged Baker for permission to punch Fish.

The writer whispered in Wolf's good ear.

Wolf handed Thomas his wallet, and they tossed their coats through the floatplane's open cargo door.

Baker picked the puzzled chef's pocket, and pitched all their valuables into the Beaver.

They started for the fear-struck chef with hands out-stretched in a stranglehold position.

Fish back-pedaled, walking the pontoon plank. "Sorry guys," he exclaimed. "But this is serious shit! I mean, flying over a dangerous mountain range like the Cascades? Come on! You shouldn't have gotten sloshed! You shou—"

"Shut up—Gary!" they shouted, sweeping him off his sneakers. A second later, all three men splashed into the cool sobering spring waters of Lake Union—where upon they started laughing

Some angry college kids pointed down from the top of the steps—where upon *they* started shouting.

The boys dove into the Beaver like cold, wet dogs, and shoved off from the dock for Chelan.

IT WAS A QUIET FLIGHT BACK. Wolf silenced the chef by scaring him with aerial stunts every time he attempted to speak. Pilot and Writer had headaches—and plenty of personal thoughts—to nurse.

"Wolf no do good in the big city. Huh, Baker?" the pilot shouted, as the Cascades' green sea parted to reveal the promised-land. Below them, fishing boats flocked to shore ahead of the setting sun, and last-light painted golden glitter patches everywhere upon the surface of Lake Chelan.

Baker nodded—yielding to the noisy radial engine—and reclined in the comfort of his copilot seat. Seattle seemed worlds away. The security of his lodge was close by. He sighed.

With Bear Mountain behind him, Wolf relaxed and removed his headset. The Beaver's wings were over water, coming down easy over Mill Bay. "Let's have a beer. Huh, Fish?" he mused.

Thomas tapped the window glass. His face grew taut. "Take her up!" the writer screamed. *"Something's floating in Mill Bay."*

"Only driftwood," Wolf shouted. "This elevator's going down!"

Baker shook his head. "Take her up!"

Fish pressed his face against the glass. "You're still drunk! All I see is water," he said.

Baker grabbed the throttle, and glared into Wolf's eyes. "What I saw *wasn't* driftwood. Make another pass over Mill Bay. *Now!*"

Chapter 13

Genetic Driftwood

WOLF'S DRIFTWOOD had scales and fins. By Good Friday morning it was talk of the town. Chelan Alliance members gathered at Granite Falls Lodge; then hit the lake for a group cleanup effort. By noon, they had netted scores of floating salmon, trout, and a few stray bass, from the surface of Mill Bay—where a massive fish-kill had occurred.

This was not the first time the foursome of Bakers, Barnes, and guide Rick Graybill had come off the lake together with a record catch, nor was it the first time that a large crowd stood anticipating their appearance at the pier. But it was the first time they'd come in off their favorite body of water depressed.

Rick slowed their approach to shore, reflected on the ramifications of their find, and watched fellow professional fishing guide, Dave Rush, trolling the tree-line up-lake. Six weeks would see full-on fishing season in Chelan. Weekend warriors from Wenatchee to Seattle soon would flock to cabins, rent condos, and fill resorts with happy families. Perennial blossoms of *No Vacancy* signs would soothe valley business owners' winter-weary pocketbooks—but not if these waters were polluted. Whatever killed the fish would not kill Rick Graybill's livelihood. He was mobile. He could trailer his boat and business to Moses Lake and Potholes Reservoir—catch limits of walleye untill June. He and his clients could wrestle with sturgeon on the Columbia

River, and reap her salmon runs, too. But Rick was not selfish. He loved this blue lady, Chelan, and it's people. *Perhaps Barnes was right about keeping a lid on things?* He saw the young cub reporter pacing the pier, holding her notepad, and chewing on a pen. He recalled last autumn's small salmon catch, and felt a sickly twinge in his stomach.

Barnes watched the Bakers sift through slit stomachs of stiff salmon at the back of the boat, baffled by what they found. These fish showed signs of starvation, but their guts were bursting with bait such as minnows and Chelan's rare freshwater mysis shrimp.

To Thomas, Brother Bill's ominous expression negated the need for talk. Both avid anglers, they often dissected their catch's dinners to determine next choice of baits. Normally, this was a humorous endeavor. *Not today.*

Graybill cut power, halting the engine's horses. The boat coasted. The boys huddled in the cabin. The dock grew closer. "Well, Bill? What the hell caused this thing?" quizzed the guide.

"They all consumed a good variety from the food chain," Bill Baker noted. "The only thing in common among the dead fish's diet is the shrimp. You've seen eyes and skin on pesticide runoff kills before. There's no sign of that kind of pollution on any of these specimens, Rick."

Graybill lit a cigar, leaned on the wheel, and nodded. "Think it's pollution?"

Bill wiped his bloody hands on a smelly old towel, and shook his head. "I'm stumped. Ground water's my field, not fisheries. But I've never seen or heard of anything like this before."

Barnes watched the approaching shore through the windshield. He saw Sheriff Hilo talking to the Pakistani chemist, Ashwan Habib, beside the doctor's shiny new Mercedes Benz. He saw the *Chelan Mirror's* reporter pacing the dock. He looked to Bill Baker. "Like what? What do your instincts say caused this disaster?"

Bill drew a deep breath, and sighed. "Food's been in their digestive tracts over five days, yet they were unable to break it down. It's like all the enzymes—all the *oils*—were extracted from them somehow." He handed a ziplock baggie to Barnes. "Feel those fillets. The meat is bone dry! Ever seen salmon like that? My *instincts* say it's something man-made. Maybe a random dumping."

Barnes scratched his head as he watched Sheriff Hilo walk to the dock and talk to the reporter. Simultaneously, the Paki's Mercedes slowly drove away. "Should we issue a warning about eating fish from the lake, or not?" the councilman queried.

Bill felt six eyes' cold stare, knew what was at stake, heard only his heartbeat, and waves slapping at the hull. He swallowed hard. "It's not my call to make. The Department of Fisheries issues warnings like that. I can run some tests for toxicity, and we'll know something by tonight. But—"

"Do it," Barnes said, as they bumped the dock.

Sheriff Hilo grabbed their throw-rope, with the reporter hanging on his heels.

Barnes glared at his pals. "Let me handle this," he whispered. "If the tests dictate it, we'll do what's best. But for now..." Because he fancied himself a born-again environmentalist and a proponent of straight-talk, Barnes despised the position this decision put him in.

Thomas Baker saw himself reflected in the shiny black flats of the young journalist as she marched her faded jeans to the councilman and extended her hand.

"Councilman. Gentlemen. What exactly do we have here?" the reporter quizzed.

"Nothing certain, Molly," Barnes replied, offering her about as much eye contact as a scandalized politician.

Sheriff Hilo looked uptight. He wanted badly to take Barnes aside for a talk.

The boys in the boat felt a pinch of guilt below their belts as they silently weighed the situation. Chelan was one of the last lakes in the country labeled *pristine*. Overdevelopment and excessive logging grabbed the headlines week after week, but if something should happen to the water, and the news went public...all was lost. They gathered gear slowly, and tilted their soiled fishing caps down to the frames of their sunglasses.

"What's the story, Councilman?" Molly's eyes twinkled with energy. "The copy deadline for this week's *Mirror* is tomorrow. Come on, give me the scoop!"

Long ago, when he was spokesman for the timber industry, he'd learned to look reporters in the eye, and lie his ass off. Suddenly, it wasn't so easy. "Suspected pesticide runoff in Mill Bay," Barnes suggested with a forced, trusting smile.

The sheriff seemed relieved.

"Suspected?" Molly Parker probed.

"Suspected. Don't want to misquote me. Do you Molly?" said Barnes.

She shook her strawberry blond hair.

Sheriff Hilo looked nervous.

"Billy Baker is going to run some tests. You might want to add that, Molly," Barnes said, while packing his gear in a green duffel bag.

Hilo couldn't hold back. "It's standard procedure to send samples to the Department of Fisheries, Molly. Mention that."

She nodded as she wrote.

Sheriff Hilo studied salmon stacked upon the dock. "Oh, Molly. Why don't you stick this one on the back page of Section Two," he muttered, lighting a cigarette.

"By the classifieds?" she asked.

The sheriff blew smoke rings. "Would you? No sense getting folks all stirred up."

The pier was starting to stink. Thomas had work at the lodge. Bill wanted to get to the lab in Wenatchee. They slipped by the reporter en route to shore.

"Excuse me! Excuse me, Mr. Baker," Molly shouted, extending her index finger.

The brothers froze, and turned to face her.

"Could I please get a minute with you two?" she pleaded.

The sheriff stepped in. "They've both gave up most of their day already, Molly. Lord knows they are busy men. Why don't we just let 'em get on with their business?"

The *Mirror* reporter's pretty jaw dropped.

Barnes brushed by , waving. "See you later, Molly. Martha's waiting for me. We'll keep you posted."

The suspicious reporter wondered why the sheriff and the straight-shooting councilman had just fed her a line of bull. *"Will you?"* she whispered, as the fishing party walked briskly past her.

FROM THE HILL overlooking Mill Bay, Doctor Ashwan Habib held the cellular phone tightly inside the Benz, waiting for an answer in Seattle.

"Sir? Gordon?" he inquired.

"Yes, Doctor. How's the weather in sunny Chelan?" asked Nicholas Gordon.

"Not so sunny. Perhaps stormy. Sir, do you have friends at the Department of Fisheries?"

"Perhaps," a puzzled Gordon replied. "Why?"

The Pakistani chemist briefly contemplated his employers' rushed schedule and how it was cramping his perfectionist style...

Suddenly, Barnes' white Ford Ranger drove within sight.

"I'll explain later—on another line. Good day, sir," said the nervous doctor to Nicholas, as he tossed the car phone on the passenger seat. The Pakistani pressed the gas pedal to the floor. Then he and the Benz hightailed it for the foothills...far away from the mysterious fish kill in Mill Bay.

Chapter 14

The Alliance

MONDAY'S formal meeting at the lodge was dominated by Mill Bay's fishy dilemma. Barnes' suspicions ran deep. He sensed danger all around him, watched the sheriff in the back row taking notes beside the *Mirror* reporter and Baker—and wondered where things were headed. A spokesperson for Manson Bay's Horticultural Society surprised them, announcing that no sizable pesticide spraying had been recently undertaken by its members. That started heated debate and endless speculation.

At Barnes' request, Bill Baker gave his brief report: Good news! No toxins were found, but something killed the fish. Salmon samples were sent to the government lab in Seattle. Honest old Uncle Sam would enlighten the Alliance within two weeks time.

There were signs of relief all around the room.

Bill sat, satisfied with the strategy Barnes had suggested that morning. After years of employment by the federal government, he lost all faith in them—like his brother, like Wolf, like Barnes, but for different reasons. He recalled his and Russ Warwick's first assignment for the EPA on the Mescalero Indian Reservation near Ruidoso, New Mexico. Together, they compiled a whistle-blower-file on tainted tribal leaders and their own *dedicated superiors,* documented illegal dumping of radio active waste on reservation lands, and eventually exposed everyone involved. Russ was a real computer wizard. He was so happy then. So...*alive*. Their reward was exile. Exile and separation, handed down to them by pissed-off superiors who were directly involved in a high-level cover-up.

Bill wound up in Alaska working with Eskimos on ground water protection, met Nancy, and had a son.

Russ was never the same. He left the Environmental Protection Agency for Ming Yaht's corporate carrot, and settled in Seattle—disillusioned.

Destiny led Bill to his newly freed brother and Chelan.

BARNES PATTED Bill's back reassuringly, satisfied with placing his trust in the Bakers. He thought how his efforts to learn of Ming Yaht's Hong Kong origin kept coming up curiously empty. He hoped Bill's private chemist friend's findings would differ with the Department of Fisheries. They needed a break. Maybe Ming Yaht was not the perfect neighbor they portrayed themselves to be? Maybe they were behind the fish kill? *Maybe they were behind a lot of things.*

Barnes listened quietly to community concerns: the high-speed rail system from Vancouver to Seattle was now rumored running inland to Wenatchee and maybe to the shores of Chelan. The membership agreed that easy access was an undeniable economic temptation. The industrial park and commercial distribution center at Chelan Falls were becoming colossal—way beyond the original and deceptive proposal posted in the Public Notices section of the paper. It was noted that the new tax revenues Ming Yaht's ventures would generate could be put to good use in schools and parks. Alliance members were wondering about future ownership of the former Warwick estate, and concerned that the feds might approve a rumored waterfront casino on the adjacent strip of Corral Creek reservation land.

The forces of new financial-colonial-pioneers were closing in fast on the Evergreen State, and theirs was but a rag-tag, weaponless, militia with minimal might. Barnes' eco-friends throughout the Northwest were reeling—from islands in Puget

Sound, the San Juans, and Mount Rainier, to Columbia Gorge towns like White Salmon and Hood River. At every turn, big money was winning out over long-term environmental concerns and quality of life. It just took longer to wear down opposition in some places—depending on their degree of organization and the measure of their will. Barnes understood this all too well. Once he, too, was young and weak-of-mind, but age and experience had graced him with wisdom. How could these Baby Boomers and Generation X'ers appreciate Edens like Tahoe and Chelan—until they'd watched them die?

Barnes wished to disclose his suspicions, but lacked evidence. He pictured the armada of Seattle Security Systems trucks he'd seen parked in Ming Yaht's lab lot that morning. He had a mind for action, but there was need for speech. He rose to applause, and presented the 1996 agenda for the Chelan Alliance: #1) Draft and file an injunction by summer, freezing all commercial development in the Chelan Valley for one year, allowing time for independent environmental-impact studies and their full disclosure. #2) Rally valley voters to approve annexation of all lands within sight of the lake into the City of Chelan, or an incorporated Manson. #3) Fight for *Home Rule* status, which would effectively remove the valley's fate from county, state, or federal agencies. #4) Vow to oppose additional expanded high-speed rail and gambling initiatives, and join forces with like-minded state and national *green groups*. #5) Preserve the lake's *pristine* status at all cost, including stiffening residential and commercial ground water storage and filtration standards. Someone mentioned the future Warwick Memorial Nature Preserve proposed by the Englishman, Collins. Publicly, Barnes predicted it would come to pass. Privately—*he had his doubts.*

When he finished, not everyone applauded. So, he breathed a little trademark fire. "I've been having this reoccurring dream for months now," he announced. "Actually, it's a nightmare. There's this high-tech monorail winding around the lake filled with drunk depressed gamblers and their poor families to whom they've promised this great *outdoors experience.* The contraption unloads the whole kit and caboodle in the Stehekin Valley."

That got their attention! The sacred Stehekin Valley lay at the head of Lake Chelan, and wound through the Cascade Mountains to Cascade Pass. The milky Stehekin River flowed from rich high-mountain glaciers and serene snowfields, until it reached and fed Lake Chelan—this waterway's womb being where their rare salmon population spawned and was perpetuated. The tiny town of Stehekin was a step back in time. Seasonal visitation dated back over one hundred years. It was guardian of the gateway to one of America's last true wilderness areas, and had remained so because of its inaccessibility.

The councilman went on. "These passengers are so broke, they can only afford to eat at the new Stehekin McDonald's and head for home!"

There was laughter.

"You laugh now, but if we don't put some bite in our watchdog Alliance's bark, we'll all be crying someday. I swear. Think about it." He paced the floor, hands folded behind his back. "Monorails? McDonald's in Stehekin? Over my dead body," he promised, pounding the podium. "Don't kid yourselves. Tax revenues and service-sector jobs can *never* replace what we are fighting to preserve and pass on. We must not let Chelan become another Tahoe!"

BARNES WATCHED them leave, wondering who among them would report his intentions to the enemies of the valley. Later, in the driveway of the lodge, he watched headlights disappear around the bend, shook Baker's hand, and stared straight into the writer's eyes. "Tom…if anything should ever happen to me, I want you to assume the leadership of the Alliance," Barnes blurted, with a somber tone of voice.

His statement shattered the tranquillity of Thomas's night.

"Something wrong with your health?" Baker asked nervously.

Barnes nodded reluctantly. "Maybe," he mumbled. "Maybe not." He sat in his Ranger and started the engine. "Can I get your word on this?"

Baker nodded, paused, and said words used very sparingly by him since his prison divorce. *"I promise."*

Chapter 15

Mystery Faxes

NICHOLAS GORDON gazed across Elliot Bay's vast expanse to the islands of Bainbridge and Vashon, and beyond. Vision strayed north to Vancouver, origin of his last phone call from impatient employer, Po Lin. The clock upon his desk ticked loudly.

Less than one year remained until Hong Kong's reversion to the Peoples Republic of China, and already Beijing's operatives asserted control over the dimming British star of capitalism, threatening to advance China's takeover date. Communist troops continued to intimidate democratic Taiwan. Nervous Hong Kong citizens packed outdoor soccer stadiums demanding exit visas and British passports. Rioting was predicted. Media reports were being suppressed. Dissidents were disappearing. Vengeful attacks by angry *Sun Yee On* had resumed against Pos' promised ones awaiting the reward of deliverance. Then, there was Chelan—only relocation site of Ming Yaht's slant-eyed Moses which was seriously behind schedule.

Distant sailboats on the bay reminded Nick of his final days and fleeting friendship with father—desperately seeking to earn his son's love—*too little, too late.* The phone rang to life, bringing him back to the thirty-first floor of Ming Yaht's Seattle headquarters.

"Mr. Gordon?" the voice probed. "It's me, man with the plan."

"I know your voice," Nicholas replied. "Where the hell are my reports?"

"Patience, please. They're nearly complete. I'm drafting the Public Notice for the estate plat and taking steps for Multi-Family Residential, and T-A Tourist Accommodations zoning approval. All permits have been placed in the name of that Canadian corporation, just as you instructed." Hodge's voice wavered. He paused, praying for confirmation, painfully aware of the last time he'd asked about the status of the former Warwick estate.

Nick knew what Hodge wanted to hear. He enjoyed making people sweat, but it was time to inform his pawn of the move. "Stop worrying. Our bid will be accepted this afternoon," Gordon said.

Hodge sighed.

"Now, tell me about the distribution center, and the power diversion from Rocky Reach Dam. And don't ask for patience! In your case, that well has nearly ran dry."

Hank thought about the Alliance meeting report he had just reviewed. "There is opposition, but I believe we can count on an August groundbreaking at the Chelan Falls site."

"And the condo project? What do your *beliefs* say about that?"

Hodge swallowed hard, and wiped his forehead. Fearful of endangering Pos' steady flow of payola, he settled for deception, slammed his own door, and whispered. "Hold on, someone's entering my office. It's the mayor! Morning, Mr. Mayor," Hodge said to the water cooler.

At that moment, his curious secretary came looking for lunch, forcing Hodge to conclude his phone charade. "Yes, *councilman*. I'll fax you the information before you leave for lunch," Hank said to Nicholas.

Sensing Hodge's game, Gordon wrapped his hand around a steel grip exerciser, and squeezed off several reps, seething. "See that you do, fat man. And take the usual security precautions with any written material. Oh…and give my regards to *the mayor.*"

AT ONE O'CLOCK, Gordon was faxless in Seattle, steaming mad, and scheduled to meet with several greedy government representatives. He ground gold crowns and cursed Hodge's name during the long limo ride to his clandestine rendezvous.

THE SECRETARY PLEADED for champagne and caviar, promising promiscuity thereafter. The planner decided the faxes could wait. Nature took its course. They timed their return remarkably well, slipped through silent offices, closed window blinds and got down to business. The hairy potato-shaped planner was one pull on his heart-covered boxer shorts away from planting the flag pole when the ditzy dame depressed the retrieve button on the answering machine, filling the room with Gordon's deep, demanding voice. Hank's priorities immediately shifted. He shrunk back from the secretary, shuffled to his desk—shorts-on-knees—and sorted faxes. 1-2-3-4-5-6…7 pages! Everything seemed in order.

"What's wrong, Babe? You look like ya just saw a ghost," said Hank's personal secretary. "Who was that guy? Can't this wait till our—*lunch*—is done?"

Hodge attempted to concentrate on the closing text of his message to Gordon, but his secretary's able-bodied hands glided back to longing-loins, massaging.

"Why not just give it to me, my cuddly Walrus? I'll take it *all* down…type it up nice," she cooed, rubbing bare breasts on his blubbery behind. "Or is that some sort of *secret* document?"

Hodge managed to ring Nick's number, got an answering machine, and left a message confirming the pending transmission. Convinced no harm had been done, Hank's concentration shifted back to his lower-brain. He stood buck naked, happily feeding the fax machine, feeling the flicking mistress-tongue addressing the most sensitive document in the room. He moaned, delighted with the depth of her interest in her work and wondered if he could enter Gordon's fax numbers with one free hand, and hike up her pantyless skirt with the other. By the time page seven was fed and sent the Walrus' tusk was limp and spent.

ON FLOOR TWENTY-ONE of Ming Yaht's Seattle building, Marla Decker rested cramped fingers on worn computer keys. She dreamed of warm sunshine, cut-off shorts, and Cascade rivers swelled with snow melt—running wild with untamed white water! They were the best therapy known to a country girl trapped in a glass city cage. The brokers from Merrill Lynch had called to invite her on their annual spring kayak outing, but they were a boring group of guys. And the way they dressed. *Too G.Q.!* She had no desire to crush the tender egos of namby-pamby male corporate kayakers by outperforming them in the foam. But she did have desire—*desire which had simmered for a year now.*

She studied the smiling cover-couple on the *Outside* magazine atop her desk. *Where did they find these people?* she thought. What she wouldn't give for an outdoors-minded mate like that—with a brain. She had composed a singles ad for the *Seattle Weekly* once—requesting such a creature—but never mailed it. At thirty-three, this brunette had radiant beauty, but was far beyond the bar scene, where she only attracted one night flings and married men. Her worse fear was falling for some two-timing male deviant, and ending up like Donna in Accounting—a twice divorced, confirmed man-hater. Marla Jean Decker wasn't ready to give up men yet!

She had always sought solace in the mountains. Even now, the Cascades called her: *Come with kayak, invite adventure, recapture lost innocence. Visit your grandfather's cabin. It is time!* But this woman wanted more. She opened her drawer, paged through the scrapbook of Thomas's newspaper articles, pictured the writer at Lake Union Café, and recalled that feeling, that flutter. Just like she felt at the funeral. *Had he seen her? Had he sensed her arousal? Was it the liquor? Was he just another player? No!* **There was something there.**

THE FAX machine clicked to life. Papers appeared in the black plastic tray. Unexpected faxes! Mysterious, fateful faxes. Feminine curiosity attracted her to them. She drummed painted fingernails, skimmed forbidden pages until number seven topped the pile and the transmission ceased. The official state stationary caught her eye. Sentences were strange and crudely encrypted. She read the ending twice: *Assessment? CA can be divided, but Two B's (Councilman and Writer) are becoming dangerous obstacles. Please advise. Once again, congratulations on winning the land lottery. Hope you are pleased with progress this office has made on your behalf. Please respond at your earliest convenience.*

Sincerely, your humble Walrus.

This was either a mistake, or a bad joke. She found the cover letter and read it twice. Her brown eyes bulged. Her heartbeat hastened as she read...*Ming Yaht International, Seattle, Washington. Attention: Nicholas Gordon; Security Dept.* **Private and Confidential.** *File #CH-1997 Project Pristine Valley—page one of seven.* She swallowed hard and studied the sending party's area code numbers. They were Wenatchee based. Her mind raced. *Two B's? Writer?* She flipped frantically through the pages, then re-read number seven. Why would Baker be a *dangerous obstacle* to Ming Yaht's commercial ventures? she thought.

She experienced two emotions: feelings for the writer, and fear of creepy Nick Gordon. With these, a third emotion materialized—*paranoia!* She paced the floor reminding herself that she had pledged loyalty and confidentiality to the corporation when they recruited her from Merrill Lynch nearly four years ago. Maybe this fax was nothing, but she needed to know.

Marla Decker's normally steady fingers shook as she dialed Reception downstairs. "Robin? Hi! Fine. Is Nick Gordon in the building? No...nothing important. Would you ring me when he returns? Thanks, Robin," said Marla. She hung up the phone, and checked her watch—2:15 p.m. Gordon could return any minute, but she could count on Robin to warn her. She drew a deep breath, maneuvered the mouse, double clicked, and studied the menu on the monitor screen. *Let's see how good old Nicky Boy is at computers!*

*2:35 p.m....*Robin Garth vacated her receptionist post for the Womens Room.

2:36 p.m. Nicholas Gordon returned, raced for the elevator, and rode it to the thirty-first floor.

Nick's empty fax tray gave him fits! He pounded the desk-top and dialed Wenatchee.

The Chelan County Planner's secretary answered.

Nicholas heard Hodge in the background saying he wasn't in the office. Nick breathed deep, and summoned discipline. "Tell Mr. Hodge this call is concerning the faxes he sent to *Councilman Barnes*," Gordon said. While the secretary covered the receiver and passed on the message, Gordon squeezed his power-gripper repeatedly, and thought how ironic it was for Po Lin to have to rely on pitiful creatures like the planner.

Hodge's head spun from liquor and lust. He wiped his fore-head, cleared his throat, and took the call. "Hodge here. What can I do for you?"

"Where are my goddamn faxes?" Gordon blurted.

"I sent them hours ago! I—"

"Mind telling me where the fuck they are?" yelled the human hawk.

Hodge's secretary saw sweat, sensed fear, moved closer, and massaged his shoulders. Hank brushed her back, shook his head, and sent her out of the office on an errand. "I wouldn't lie to you, Gordon," the planner pleaded. "Believe me. I-I s-sent those faxes! If you want, I can retransmit the damn things right now."

"You kept the originals?" Nick screamed.

"Of course I..."

"You saved them? You imbecile! What other security pro-cedures did your fucking little penis tell you to forget today?"

"Want me to send them again?" Hodge asked meekly.

"Send nothing! Are you a religious man, Mr. Hodge?"

"I attend church with the Mrs. most Sundays. W-why d-do you ask?" stammered the Walrus.

"Because, I think you better start praying that I find those fucking faxes in one of our other offices. That is the only logical explanation I can think of for your latest fuck-up."

Hodge was shook. "I don't understand."

"Maybe, just maybe, you misdialed by one digit while Miss Bimbo was giving you a blow job! Right? Sit tight, save the originals, and don't leave your office until I get back to you. Understand?"

"B-but m-my wife is expecting m-me," Hank pleaded.

"Fuck your wife," Nick suggested. "That is, *if* you have another round left in that sawed-off shotgun of yours." Gordon slammed the phone, strode to the stairway, and started searching floor to floor for the missing faxes.

ON FLOOR TWENTY-ONE, Marla studied maps on the monitor screen: Mexico, Canada, Vancouver, Washington State, Chelan... There was Chinese script on her monitor, which she could not decipher. Her head spun. Frustration set in. She didn't even know what she was looking for. It was 2:50 p.m. and no call from Robin yet. Should she print out this Project Pristine Valley stuff, or settle for copying the mystery faxes?

GORDON FRISKED floors like a fox in the hen house! He scared Sue Ellen on twenty-six, surprised Margeaux on twenty-five, and entered twenty-four pumped up, red-faced— eying lovesick Sharon, and loosening his necktie.

When Sharon saw Nicholas enter her office, she felt faint, and figured this was the day for *them*. She made a lust-face.

Nick drew near, ogled her...desk, felt her...fax tray, and disappeared without remorse.

But he wasn't done yet!

MARLA PUNCHED the power button, and slipped fax pages into the feeder. A red light flickered. The copier warmed. She waited impatiently.

ON TWENTY-TWO, Nick Gordon got nasty while grilling Donna in Accounting. His own report was promised to Hong Kong that afternoon. His patience was wearing thin. He hit the stairs on the run, two minutes from Marla on twenty-one!

MARLA SNAPPED her fingers above the start button. The green light came on. The computerized copier spoke, *"Ready."* Suddenly, her phone rang. "Hello, Robin?" she said.

"No, Marla. It's Donna on twenty-two," she said, sounding extremely disturbed. "Seen any stray faxes down there today?"

Instant sickness struck Marla Decker. Her hands started shaking again. "No, Donna. Why?" she asked.

"Evidently, an important report destined for the icy fingers of our ponytailed security chief was sent to the wrong office by some male corporate genius. Or so he suspects."

"Who? Who suspects what, Donna?" Marla Decker felt hysteric.

"Gordon! Nick Gordon. He's on the rampage! He's looking floor to floor for those damn faxes. He just left here and—"

"Sorry, Donna. Gotta call on line one. Gotta run! Bye." Marla ran, heart racing, to retrieve the faxes.

The elevator door opened and Gordon stepped into the foyer of floor twenty-one.

Marla slid into her chair, flipped back her hair, cupped a hand over a silent phone, and bit a slice of skin from inside her cheek. "Mr. Gordon! Good afternoon. What a pleasant surprise. Can I help you?" she said cheerfully.

He stared coldly, and strolled directly to her fax tray where he fingered its contents, scrutinized them...then scrutinized her.

Her heart beat wildly. She hung up the phone, fidgeted, and flipped through her *Outside* magazine.

Nicholas Gordon smiled! His mirrored-steel blue eyes stared deep into Marla Decker's browns seeking any sign of deception. "Don't you *ever* check your fax tray, Miss Decker?" he said.

"I'm sorry, Mr. Gordon. Was there something in there?" She stood up, extending her hand. "Here, let me file those for you," she said casually.

She had one of those honest, innocent faces.

"That won't be necessary," Nick announced, as he noticed her magazine. "I hear you're quite an outdoors enthusiast."

She folded her hands, smiled sheepishly, and nodded.

"Thinking of taking some vacation days?"

"As a matter of fact, Mr. Gordon, I was. I've had an urge to find some whitewater and go paddling for a weekend. You see, my grandfather left me this cabin in the mountains…and the guys from Merrill Lynch invited me on their annual outing. And I—"

He was well aware of the cabin. *The invitation too.* "Perhaps you should take advantage of this warm spell, Decker. Go! Get some practice in," he commanded, slapping his faxes on her desk. "Then give those pantywaist stockbrokers a damn good lesson in kayaking."

She sighed, and smiled like a model in a toothpaste commercial. "That's exactly what I was thinking! Thanks. Yeah…I might just do that," Marla announced. "Gee, you must be a mind reader, Mr. Gordon."

Nick knocked his knuckles on her desk, and winked. "Good day, Miss Decker," he said. Then he walked off with a lilt in his step…whistling Dixie.

Chapter 16

Kayaks

CURIOUS EYES WATCHED Marla Decker emerge from her Pine Street duplex.

Honey sweetened coffee steamed into salty sunrise air as she packed her pickup truck with gear. A tiny calico cat pawed at her untied shoestrings, and batted the bottoms of her ragged gardening sweats each trip from the garage. She shouldered her kayak, secured it to the cap top, swept cobwebs from her hair, and headed inside cat-in-arms.

Watchful, caring, Georgette Kramer petted her black poodle, Bootsie, dug in a dresser, dusted the album, and ran weathered fingers over faded *fifties-photos* of a young couple kissing by an old canoe along the swollen banks of the Skagit River—reminiscing.

Morning sun briefly breached sea mist, cascaded through lacy sheers, and spilled over a Moroccan rug where Marla sat feeding her fish. The calico cat dove from the bed, rolled on its back, and mewed softly in quick broken bursts.

"Oh Punkin! I'll only be gone untill Sunday," Marla said.

The attention beggar mewed again.

She petted soft white tummy hair and rubbed the pink tender skin of her pet. "Things might not work out, Punkin," she explained. "He might not even be there."

Punkin purred, pawed her palm, bit it lightly, then licked every inch with her textured tongue. Marla had cravings much like her cat! She cradled the calico in her arms, and set off for the landlady's door. It swung open.

"Morning, Marla," those familiar green Irish eyes below that silverish curly hair greeted her.

"Morning, Georgette. I was just getting ready to—"

"I know," her landlady, and best friend, said. "Couldn't help but notice your rummaging 'round the garage so bright and early this mornin'." The perceptive senior citizen saw that a pretty flowered blouse had replaced Marla's coffee-stained sweatshirt. Expensive perfume scented the musty living room. "Mother Nature's called yer name. Hasn't she now? And you want me to watch yer little darlin'. Don't you?"

Marla nodded. "And feed—"

"And feed the fish," the landlady said, finishing her favorite tenant's sentence. They laughed, and passed the cat. "Just where is it you'll be headed to?" Georgette inquired.

Marla hesitated, just as she had with the girls from work at the Lake Union Cafe last night. "I think it's high-time I checked on grandfather's cabin—maybe stay till Sunday. Should I call you tomorrow evening?"

"No need. Mamma Kramer can handle yer domestic critters. Just you be mindful of the wild ones out there!"

The two women hugged. Marla petted Punkin, saw her own reflection in the hall tree mirror, and froze in place.

"Oh, don't worry your pretty little head none. You look fine," the widow Kramer pronounced with an encouraging wink.

"Thanks, Georgette," Marla sighed, before leaving with a skip in her step.

THE WIDOW WAVED a Punkin paw in the direction of the departing pickup truck. "We'll have a fine weekend, you and I," she promised the pet. Sea mist stole back the morning sun. She tightened the sash of her faded quilted robe—remembering. She was happy it was springtime in Seattle. She only wished it were the spring of '54, when she first met her handsome mill worker, George Herbert Kramer. The widow wiped mist from her Irish eyes, and offered the small calico cat some milk.

AS MARLA'S TOYOTA turned off I–5 and merged onto I–90, mellow morning traffic music was replaced by rowdier Bonnie Rait. She donned dark shades, tightened Croakies behind her head, and cruised east toward the sun soaked snow-capped Cascades. After Snoqualmie Pass, easy driving turned twisted and curved. Energy and confidence wore thin as mountain air.

It had been a sleepless night. Now, doubt debated her again. *What are you doing girl—stalking this writer? You're no ugly duckling. You have your independence. Why, Marla? Why?*

She rubbed tired eyes, opened a window, and replied. "I know what I want. I know when something's special. And, I'm not afraid to go for it!" She goosed the gas pedal. "I'm thirty-three! Not some flippy young groupie drooling over Seattle grunge musicians, or some drunken, macho-pilot! I'm tired of attending poetry readings at those little coffee shops alone. And what if this guy is in danger?"

She refueled at Easton, then cruise-controlled, reveling in the pastoral valley views that Kittitas County offered her. She crossed the Yakima River, bypassed Ellensburg, and headed due north into the rugged Wenatchee Mountains. Again, the road challenged her. Logging trucks raced around curves rocking her kayak. Just past Liberty, a female bear with cub dashed in front of her and lingered on the shoulder long enough for her to slow down and observe and appreciate their beauty. Off in the pines, Papa Bear's large shadow rose. Sow and cub responded and raced into the bush. The voice of doubt returned to Marla Decker. *What are you doing, girl?* She stepped on the gas. *"Following my instincts. Following my heart! I've just got to know,"* she said.

At Highway 2 she sat, blinker blinking, thinking about Grandfather's cabin, where she learned to love the outdoors in her tomboy youth. It had been three years since his death, and she hadn't gone back. Dare she take the drive through Levenworth past chalet-style shops with scallop facias, down that sacred, lonely logging road along the Icicle River? Maybe it was time.

In the windshield of her Toyota truck *he* appeared, the kindly old woodsman puffing that familiar pipe! His thumbs were tucked under wide red suspenders attached to woolly gray Nordic knickers. He was always the good and patient teacher to her. Couldn't keep her away from the woods when he was alive. *There'll always be time for another visit, my dear Marla.* She cherished his advice. *Look forward, child, not back. Remember, Marla, if you're following your heart, you can **never** be wrong.* A horn honked. Doubt died. "Thank you, Grandfather," she whispered before going forward.

Forty-five minutes later she crossed a tiny bridge into downtown Chelan, parked, stretched her legs, and walked upon the wooden Wild West sidewalks. Forever Neon, Lone Wolf Air, Campbell's Resort, Goochi's Restaurant, Signor Frog's Saloon—a vintage clothing store and bait shop! The place had style and class—kind of like some hip California town prior to the tourist-rush days. It grabbed her—kind of like the writer did.

THE WRITER dug the paddle deeper, worked each wave with sweat-stung eyes—stroked on—determined not to rest until he had sprinted further than the day before, and the day before that. He cherished gliding over this great blue body. She alone allowed him oneness with his world, and provided the ultimate freedom he'd spent years in prison pining for. When frail human love deserted him, it was *She* who filled those long lonely nights with wondrous dreams of unwavering loyalty, and a lifetime of days like today. From fall to May, lodge bookings were slow. Baker kept plenty busy though, filling the gap with family, fishing, landscaping, gardening, spring repairs, and rowing. It was also a time to write and reflect before tourists flooded the town. Displeased with progress on his latest novel, he dug the paddle deeper still.

When the sting became too much to bear, he paddled out of the windline and glided into Big Creek Cove, where waveless waters lay like glass. He splashed frigid liquid-blue relief on his hot, red face, and stretched cramped legs along-side his kayak. A carrot juice and a granola bar later, he gazed through clear, cool water, saw something strange, and strained to try and identify the white flash which had caught his eye.

Nearby, a bald eagle crashed the calm surface, thrashed about, snatched a fair-sized rainbow trout, and carried its catch to barren tree branches, pausing there to rest. The lines to a poem took shape inside him as Baker watched the bird soar to craggy peaks effortlessly with its catch's silver scales reflecting sunlight like some disco dance-floor sphere.

He soon forgot about the white flash below, and scolded himself. "When you're a writer? *Write!* When you're a rower? *Row!*" The rower dug his smooth, curved tool, deep into the blue body beneath him to begin the motion, recapture the rhythm, and attain the natural high once more.

MARLA SAW signs: Navaree Coulee Road, Lake Chelan State Park... She studied Baker's brochure, which she had gotten in town, reset her truck's odometer, and crept ahead on South Lakeshore Drive drinking-in refreshing scenery. Across the way, pleasure craft cruised Manson Bay, and luxurious condos dotted the peninsula of Wapato Point framed by fertile foothills and warmed by high-desert breezes. Small white digits clicked by upon the dashboard's instrument panel—1-2-3-tenths miles since passing the state park gates! Trees grew thicker, reminding her of the Icicle River area around her grandfather's cabin. She preferred an alpine climate.

At nine-tenths miles, her heartbeat quickened.

The zero rolled by, and the sequence started over. 1-2-3-4-tenths! There, off to the left: a tall totem pole, and cursive blue neon glass announcing; *Granite Falls Lodge.* And beside that, was a neon waterfall, where artificial whitewater glistened. Her heart fluttered. *This was the place.*

NANCY BAKER NOTICED the brunette bending low along the path, admiring emerging tulip blossoms and budding foxgloves. She watched her walk to the front porch, fondle the wicker love seat, and study stained-glass windows. She looked familiar. "Marla?" she inquired through the screen door. "How's the big city?"

Nancy's cheery smile was a comforting surprise. "Seattle's fine," Marla sighed. "Just a little too stressful, and a few months away from having all this sunshine! How are things here?"

"Good," said the Eskimo. "The tulips are beginning to bloom."

"They're beautiful! You've done wonders with the grounds, Nancy."

"Tell Thomas. He's the one with the green thumb."

The visitor's hazel eyes twinkled. "He likes gardening?"

Nancy nodded, then recalled the funeral, when Thomas became mesmerized by this one—after which, Bill labeled her a threat to his brother's bachelor vow: *She coulda' been a contender*, her husband had clowned. "Oh yes, Thomas says gardening and…" Keen Eskimo eyes spotted the kayak atop Marla's Toyota, "and *rowing* are the best therapy in the world."

Gold dust danced in the guest's eyes. "Is that where he is now? Out rowing?"

"Uh huh. Well, *kayaking*, actually. He goes out every day during these slow months," Nancy explained, stepping outside to join her guest.

"What a coincidence! That's what I came for," Marla said.

"That is quite a coincidence. Where you staying?"

The secretary shrugged. "You have any openings?"

"Uh huh…and I can give you great off season rates." The pretty Eskimo took her arm, determined to show her around and get a feel for her before interrupting Thomas's solitude.

Marla acquiesced, and saw humming birds buzz around brightly colored feeders, and macramé hammocks hung between behemoth cedars. Yeti Chalet caught her eye.

Nancy showed her the chalet's inside Jacuzzi. "This might come in handy if you plan on getting a lot of exercise."

Marla nodded. Mellow grounds, flower-filled meadows, her lovely Yoko Ono-faced hostess—each pleasant discovery erased any inclination she might have had to pitch a musty tent at the state park. The tour was over. The two women headed back to the lodge.

"You're Eskimo, aren't you, Nancy?"

"Uh huh. Born in Bethel, Alaska. Why do you ask, Marla?"

"Just curious about your totem pole, that's all. It's very interesting. I thought it might have some family meaning."

"That thing? It's just an eye-catcher. Thomas and Bill dreamed it up one night after drinking a pitcher of margaritas! One of the local Indian artists carved it out with a Huskavarna chainsaw."

The two ladies shared laughter.

"The entire place is an eye-catcher, Nancy."

"Tell Thomas that. Better yet, tell your big-city-boyfriends. Preferably the rich ones! We can always use more guests."

"I don't have a boyfriend," the secretary said sullenly. "But I'll be sure to tell some people. The place looks great!"

"Uh huh," Nancy noted, as they stood relaxing at the front desk. "We also have a really great chef," the Eskimo said. She booked the bubbly brunette into Yeti Chalet for the weekend and handed her the key. "I'll save the standard speech, and give you a hot-tip on *kayaking*."

"I'd appreciate that," Marla responded with a smile. "So...where's a good spot to put in?"

"I assume you're experienced?"

That question drew a nod and a blush.

"Uh huh," Nancy noted. "Then drive to where the pavement ends, and put in at Twenty-five Mile Creek." Her keen eyes scanned the mantle clock. "If you hurry, you might catch him out there somewhere between Big Creek Cove and Domke Falls."

They exchanged warm smiles.

Nancy handed Marla a map. "Need any help with your things?"

"No thanks, Nancy. You've helped me quite enough already. Oh, when is dinner?"

"Thomas will fill you in on all the details," she said with a wink. "Good luck."

BOTHERED BY the white flash, Baker returned to Big Creek Cove, and circled around until he saw it again, then he balanced the kayak with outstretched legs, and lowered his face to the surface.

A white ring wiggled below. He saw black letters on it, and a long rope restraining it, trailing off in the distance. He focused on the writing. He put his face so close to the surface that his eyelashes flicked water. *C-O-N-green algae...J-O*—a wave rolled in and slapped his face. He shook it off. Finally, the letters became legible—*Connie Joe.*

Baker couldn't believe it. By sheer happenstance, he had found the life-ring from Warwicks' boat, rising up buoy-like, marking the remains from a burned-out hull below—calling out to him! She hadn't disappeared in the blue abyss. She must have caught a ledge, then their bodies surfaced and the sheriff canceled the search, and closed the case: *Accidental Death.*

A bigger wave rolled in.

All kinds of thoughts flooded Baker's head. He felt sick, sensed danger, scanned the surface...and saw a strange black kayak barreling toward Big Creek Cove. Black, wet-suit-wearing arms churned water, closing the distance between him and them fast! Barnes' comments rattled his brain: *Warwicks death was no damn accident! Too good a boater. Too good a mechanic.*

The dark colored kayak closed in!

Thomas noted his position, and paddled away.

When he started off in the opposite direction, Marla Decker's heart sank. Surely he saw her coming on? Maybe he didn't want company. Her forearms burned. Her legs cramped.

Baker extended the distance between them.

Marla Decker decided to give new meaning to the term 'man-chaser', and several minutes of hot pursuit ensued.

At one point, she considered throwing in the towel, and wondered if faithful feminine intuition had finally failed her. But then she thought of her Grandfather: *Marla, my dear...follow your heart!* She waved her paddle in the air, and shouted his name across the water, "Baker! Baker!"

Thomas heard her cry, and strained to study his pursuer. Whoever she was, whatever this chase scene was about, he wrote off any connection to the wreckage of the *Connie Joe.*

She flipped up her Ray Ban sunglasses and coasted.

He studied his pursuer's profile, flashed back to the funeral, and quickly turned to set a course for the Seattle secretary.

Marla gave a sigh of relief, and rowed toward her writer.

They met halfway, dripping wet from the chase, locked paddles, and sealed their fate.

"Afternoon, Mr. Baker," she panted.

He smiled, while struggling to recall her name. "Good afternoon...Marla. What brings you to this neck of the woods?"

She had memorized these words. "Work's been hectic. I needed a break." She caught her breath. "Gave into the call of the wild for the weekend. Needed an exercise fix."

He nodded. "You're a weekend kayak warrior? Why did you choose Chelan?"

Sweet sweat ran down her flush cheeks as she considered a response. In wind and wave, her *Henderson Shorty* wetsuit served her well, but this cove was calm and sun-baked. She unzipped its turtleneck top to exposed some steamy soaked cleavage. "I was very impressed with what I saw here last fall, Mr. Baker." Again she paused to catch her breath. "Had an urge to return and do some exploring."

Thomas was twice impressed. The first time by her business look, her walk, talk, and class. This time, with her water skills, stamina, and again—undeniable chemistry! He was curious as to what other pleasant surprises the brunette would bring into this day.

She rested her paddle on his kayak, steadying herself.

"So...you picked the big lake for your first time out this spring. Sporting of you. How did you know it was me out there?" he asked, knowing only Nan could have sent her.

"Thought you might like some company, that's all." She splashed her face. "But if you want your solitude back, I'll understand. I wouldn't want to put a damper on your workout," she added, flashing pouty lips.

He was glad to see her, and could not hide it. "I don't know where you learned to handle a kayak like that, but I'm sure not worried about you putting a damper on *my* workout! How 'bout I show you around?" he suggested.

A shiver ran down her spine. She nodded her head, and flipped down her shades. Shapely legs squirmed inside her kayak shell. "I'd like that, Mr. Baker," she said. "I'd like that very much."

"Please. Call me Thomas," he said, before proceeding to show her his private world.

They hugged protective shoreline, paddling softly in synchronized harmony like aquatic ballet dancers honing their act.

Marla absorbed the beauty, captivated by his narration.

Thomas absorbed her. She had the kind of magic he'd given up hope of finding a long time ago, and the kind of beauty he only found in fiction...and nature.

They beached at Domke Falls. Marla peeled back her wet suit, exposing a well-filled, wet, tank top; then freed her frizzy locks from a ponytail.

They stood side by side, listening to surging waters, which were just out of sight. Light shafts penetrated forests to fertile fern-laden floors. Rhododendrons rose to spring's summons—budding. Birds nested on nearby branches, engaged in the mating game.

"How about some lunch, Thomas?" she asked.

"Lunch? I didn't bring much. I usually starve on these—"

She put a finger to his lips. "I did. Got a special place?"

He nodded. "Do you like natural hot springs?"

"Sounds great," she said, shouldering a full daypack she had stashed in her shell.

They walked beneath waterfalls to a series of clear, steamy pools, and stopped at one pearl gray in color.

She spread a clean white sheet on soft brown pine needles and lay a bounty, then herself, upon it. Perceiving hesitation, she held out her hand to him. "Aren't you just dying in that full-body wet suit?" she asked.

He unzipped, and slipped firm arms around her.

They kissed the kiss of a respectful gentleman to a classy lady. But, inside, both of them felt rising passion. "Let's get out of these and dig in," she suggested. "I'm starved. Aren't you?"

Thomas nodded. "Nature trips always make me hungry," he said. He helped her escape that skin-tight wetsuit; then shamelessly admired her matching Calvin Klein undergarments.

A breeze blew rainbow mist about them. They lay side by side.

She fed him strawberries from a ziplock baggie.

He fed her seedless grapes.

They talked a while, shared a skin of wine, tilted back their heads and aimed red streams at open mouths. A small squirrel stole their crackers. She sat up, and squealed with delight. Breasts danced briefly beneath thin cotton before she lay back down again.

He was touched by her sensitivity, and aroused to new heights by her sensuality. The woods were brighter when she smiled.

A tiny bead of red wine trickled down her succulent lower lip, and she sighed, sounding like she just let go of every care in the world.

"Thomas! I love it here," said the Emerald City lady.

"I can see that," he said, spellbound.

He was such pleasant company. So charming. She wanted him, but had questions. "Thomas...? Do you still smoke pot?"

He smiled—thinking how long it had been and how nice it might be in this setting with her now—then shook his head. "I *would* still smoke occasionally. I never had a problem with it." He pitched a pebble into a pool. "But, I can't."

"You can't?"

He nodded, knowing she'd read his novel and its jacket cover, which explained how he'd written it in prison, and what he was sentenced for. He bit his lip, and studied her. *She'd driven all this way just to hunt him down and share this time together.* He decided to be frank with her. "I've got my opinion about the legality of marijuana, but like a lot of other things, it doesn't matter what I think. It's the law." Thomas laughed. "I fought the law, and the law won."

He took a deep breath.

"For a long time, selling marijuana was my business; then laundering money was. I got busted, received a fifteen year sentence—because I wouldn't help the government collect more brownie-buttons for locking-up pot dealers—and served five years." He paused. "There's this little leash around my neck called parole. Know much about it?'

Marla shook her head. "No, not a thing. Tell me, Thomas."

"It can be tough, if you let it. The first two years I was drug tested regularly."

"And now?"

"I've been out nearly four years. I've got a relatively laid-back parole officer, and a spotless record. They should drop it completely this fall. One never knows about the feds though, Marla. And I'm sure the powers-that-be are not always pleased with the writings of Thomas Baker. But if they ever drug-tested me and I showed positive? They could ship me back behind the fence in a heartbeat. Nothing is worth that to me. Nothing! I could never leave all this behind."

"I used to smoke weed when I was in college," she admitted. Guess I just grew out of it one day." She admired his discipline. It only made her want him more.

"There was a time..." he continued, softer, "when I always carried a few good buds in my pack, in case I met a friendly face along the trail."

"Like mine?" she grinned.

"Exactly like yours," he replied, pecking her cheek.

She tossed a strawberry to the squirrels; then asked the sixty-thousand dollar question. "What was prison like?"

He drew some air, rested chin-on-knees, and released it.

She recoiled. "That's okay! We don't have to talk about it."

Ah, but they did. So he opened the skeleton closet door for her. "It's all right. It was nothing like television. Prison was a boring place, with lots of boring people. Lots of losers who thought they were winners. Lots of bottom-of-the-barrel predators always looking for prey. Lots of street punks without a clue about what counts in this world," he blurted. "There were a few good guys inside who got caught up in the madness, but getting close was dangerous, because people came and went. I kept to myself, and stayed away from clicks—wary of other people's nightmares. Then, almost twenty years after high school, I rediscovered my writing. I felt the system was stealing my life from me over something as harmless as pot. Writing kept me from getting bitter about all the violent people I watched walk out way before me. When I wrote, I took that time back. I was free. Freer than some people were on the outside," Thomas declared, tapping his chest.

"I'm one of those weirdos who needs meaning and purpose in my life. I found myself in there one day with neither, whining like a whipped pup over things I couldn't change. I remembered idealistic days from my hippie youth, when I thought there was no better legacy a person could leave behind than words which would last forever—maybe even serve to teach or inspire future generations." He drank some wine, and looked to azure skies. "Heavy shit. Huh, Marla?"

She shook her head, took the wine, and drank it. "Please go on about your writing," she said. "I find it fascinating."

"It started with poems and short stories that I typed down at work."

"What attracted you to novels?"

"I guess it's the same thing that makes me prefer oil painting to watercolors. Poems, watercolors—you finish them in a blink of an eye, and pat yourself on the back saying, 'Look what I've done!' All well and good, but novels—like making love, and fine red wines..."

The Seattle secretary smiled and shivered.

"...they take patience, creativity, discipline...and endurance."

The writer's innuendo did not fall upon deaf ears.

"But how could you concentrate that long in prison?" she asked.

"Perseverance," Thomas muttered. He let out a little laugh. "I wore ear plugs, and listened to NPR's classical music on a

Walkman to block out the noise. Nights, I took notes, wrote letters, captured thoughts, taped tattered pages on concrete walls, and edited till dawn. Even sacrificed my exercise time." His heart swelled with pride remembering those countless hours spent sweating in his underwear in a six-by-eight cell learning his craft by trial and error. "Writing soothed the pain of separation." His face *showed* pain. "It granted me strength from isolation." His fist was clenched, his forearm flexed. "When I wrote, I wasn't even there! I was *doing* the time instead of letting it do me. Long prison time is a terrible waste for tens of thousands of non-violent first-time offenders," he declared, rubbing his forehead. Baker's eyes briefly closed, then quickly opened. "Not many of them come out as lucky as I did," he added. His eyes were angry now. "But I guess luck's what you make of things."

"Is that why you wrote the first book?"

He exhaled, softened his tone, and relaxed. "I wrote that hoping to reach someone. Anyone."

"You reached me," she whispered. She kissed his lips, then changed the subject. "You mentioned you had a job. What did you do, make license plates?"

"No," he said. "I worked in the Chapel. I was a clerk."

"You?" she blurted. "In the Chapel?"

"Yeah, me. That shock you or something?"

"You just don't seem like the religious type, that's all."

"Oh, I've got religion all right," Thomas assured her. "I worship natural beauty." He stared at her, smiling. "Everyone inside has a job. Most inmates get stuck working for the Bureau of Prison's goldmine factory, UNICOR. Not me. My job afforded me a typewriter, a desk, and an indepth study of pseudo-religious zealots. My bosses were trapped between being cops and clergy, but they were good to me. They encouraged my writing. We've talked since."

She stirred moist earth with a stick, then rolled over onto her stomach. "It sounds so lonely! Did people stay in touch and support you?"

He sensed where she was headed. "Sure. My real friends wrote me. My family hung tight."

"Where do your parents live?" she asked.

Baker shook his head. "Heaven, I presume. They're both dead."

"I'm sorry," she said.

"Don't be," Baker answered. "They were good people. They lived good, productive lives."

She had to ask. "Ever married?"

Hurt returned to his face. He looked away, brushed it off, then stared deep into her brown eyes with serious intent, nodding very slowly. "She was young and pretty." He paused. "I couldn't have expected her to do my time with me. Life goes on. People are always popping in and out of it."

"Maybe," Marla said. "But we don't make that kind of commitment to everyone who pops in for a fling. Do we?" She felt his pain, and reached out for him.

"Listen, Marla. I'm a big boy now, a consenting adult. I'm not married anymore, and I'm not in any prison. I'm in a special place with a fantastic lady who I find extremely fascinating. I rarely think about prison since I walked through those open steel doors. Funny how we forget the bad."

"Do you still think about *her*?"

Thomas pulled back, put tongue to cheek, and twisted his rusty mustache hairs. He remembered how his narco father-in-law bragged about using his influence with the judge to get him the stiffest possible sentence. "I don't talk about it," he muttered.

"Maybe you should. It's important to—"

"See all this?" he gestured, arms spread wide. "This is what's important to me now. *This* is my life. I took a lot of things for granted once, Marla. Trust me. I'll never do that again." Thomas bit his lip, and slowly shook his head. "Can you believe that young people around here are leaving in droves for hell holes like L. A.?"

Marla shook her head; then took his hand. "They'll all come back some day."

They hugged, and kissed more passionately than before.

He ran fingers down her spine.

She shuddered with desire.

They embraced ever tighter with eyes closed, and her firm breasts pressed against his throbbing chest. They waded into warm waters of a picturesque pool, sat in silk-silt, and nuzzled.

Thomas leaned his neck on a fallen-tree pillow, and Marla leaned on him.

He reached for the wine and asked; "You all right?"

"It's wonderful," she cooed with both eyes closed. "It's all so wonderful!"

He slid an arm under her arched back, and uncorked the wine flask with his teeth.

She tilted her head, and stared into trusting eyes.

"Open your mouth," he whispered, already sending a nectar-stream which filled her quickly, cascaded to cleavage, and formed red saucy wine rings on oyster shell water.

The waiting was over.

She slipped the wineskin from his hand.

He slipped her tanktop over her head, and tossed it to shore.

She encouraged his hands to cradle her breasts. He bit her fingers slightly, catlike.

She moaned.

He sighed.

Ensuing eruptions shook hallowed ground, rippled pearly waters in special secret places, and spewed forth molten emotions which each of them had stashed in-waiting—awaiting a moment like this!

FOR THE LONGEST TIME they cuddled there, listening to cascading falls, and caressing.

She ran her fingers through his silver-blond hair.

He sat up, shook his head, and gazed down with wonderment. Mountain air smelled of lovemaking from their torrid tango. Her face was fresh. It made him flash back upon this day of surprise, opened his eyes, and stirred revelation: For as much as he'd loved his wife, she never provided him with such *total stimulation.*

He did not know whether to rejoice to the heavens above, or break camp, and hightail it for home!

"Penny for your thoughts," she said, rubbing his shoulder.

"Oh, I was just thinking about how nice a day it turned out to be. What were you thinking about?"

Her smile dimmed. She mulled over the message on the mystery faxes. "The same thing," she said, biting her nails, and wondering if he was reason enough to break her vow to the corporation. In one afternoon she'd learned so much about him—all to her liking. She pondered the pleasure of his touch. "Thomas, you know I work for Ming Yaht International in Seattle."

He nodded. "Same place Russ Warwick was employed by. Why?"

She shrugged, knees rocking, "It's a job. Pays good," she said, sounding apologetic. She paused...and Nick Gordon's piercing eyes suddenly materialized in their mineral pool! "Some faxes were mistakenly sent to my office this week," she blurted. "When I skimmed over them, I saw something disturbing."

"Like what?"

"I'm not sure," she stammered, recalling. "On the summary page of this report, the sender said his office thought a certain *writer* and a certain councilman were becoming *dangerous obstacles*. It was faxed from Wenatchee. Got any clue who these obstacles might be?"

"Have you read any of the articles I've written on development or old growth forest preservation?"

She nodded. "Some. I read that last one in the P.I. I must admit, I was impressed. I admire your courage, firing verbal volleys at big corporations like—"

"Exactly! So, I'm not surprised to hear Ming Yaht's allies label me and Barnes as opposition."

"That's obstacles, Thomas. *Dangerous obstacles.*"

He smiled. His smile distracted her. She liked his smile.

"Obstacle, opposition, optometrist, pediatrician..." Thomas clowned.

They shared a laugh.

"Was the Chelan Alliance mentioned anywhere in that report?" he asked.

She shrugged. "There were initials…CA."

Baker was curious. "What kind of stationary was this report on?"

"The Washington State seal was on the cover letter."

"Who signed it? Did you see a name?"

Marla shook her head, and rubbed the sockets around her eyes. Her knees rocked rhythmically.

Thomas realized he sounded like a cop, and stopped. "Forget it. Look…I appreciate your concern, but I'm sure there's nothing to it," he said softly. *Pop!* He pictured the life ring he had discovered below Big Creek Cove right before she appeared…and his entire body shook.

"Are you cold?" she asked.

He started to say no, but saw her lean his way, gave an impish grin, and winked one green eye.

She wrapped satin-white skin and a soft-linen sheet around him. "Here, let me warm you," she whispered.

IN THE PARKING LOT at Twenty-five Mile Creek State Park, the two paddlers worked like beavers to beat the dark. They secured kayaks, stowed gear, and silently reviewed the day: The paddle, the picnic, steamy therapeutic pools, and their even steamier passion play! Warm sun, that last run buck-naked through bone-chilling falls, laughing like children, sharing mean-ingful conversation, companionship…sensuality. That heavenly row back from Eden bathed in alpenglow and afterglow…

Thomas finished packing-up first, started his Chevy, and pulled alongside her. "You camping-out tonight, or what?"

"I was, until some nice Eskimo lady let me tour a local lodge."

He smiled. "What did you think of the place?"

"Oh, I liked it. Liked it a lot." She stretched a bungy cord to a hook. "Liked it so much…I booked a cozy little chalet for the entire weekend," she said. She hopped in her Toyota, hit the lights, and signaled her readiness by flicking her brights.

He shifted his Blazer into second gear, gazed into the rearview mirror, and shook his head slowly at her shapely silhouette...thinking: *Dangerous, Baker.* **Very dangerous.**

Chapter 17

Tests

NANCY WAITED patiently, twirling the strange gadget in her hand. She watched Thomas open Marla's door and help carry her gear. She allowed them their kiss, then called from the porch. "Thomas!"

"What's up, Nan? You look like a worried parent. Is Nathan okay?" Thomas inquired.

"Uh huh. Everything is fine. We were a little concerned, that's all," she said. "You haven't missed a weekend dinner in ages. Your chef was pretty disturbed." She studied the still-glowing guest. "I wasn't worried though. Hi, Marla! I see you found him."

Marla nodded, stared at the circular object with native designs and leather weavings which Nan was waving, and smiled.

Thomas frowned. "Why do you have that superstitious thing out tonight?" he asked. "Never mind. Explain your contraption to our guest, Nan. If you could be so kind."

"It's called a dream catcher, Marla," Nan explained. "It's one of those native things."

"What does it do?" asked Marla Decker.

"Filters out bad dreams. Lets in only good ones. I took a nap this afternoon in the hammock and had strange dreams about the valley."

"What kind of strange dreams, Nan?" Baker asked.

"Can't remember, Thomas. Anyway, after I got my dream catcher, all my dreams were wonderful. How was your day? Any good daydreams?"

"This whole day was a dream. Thomas is such a good host," the Seattle secretary sighed.

"Uh huh. He's why we have so many repeat bookings. The guests like to talk with the owner, Marla. He makes them laugh." She was embarrassing her brother-in-law, and enjoying it. "So, my dream catcher worked well for us today?"

"Very well," said Marla.

"How was dinner?" Thomas asked.

"It looked good, but I didn't eat," Nancy replied. "Bill's crazy chemist friend, Matt, drove in from Seattle to see one of the waitresses at Cosina del Lago. Matt phoned here just before dinner, and Bill left to join him right after that. Bill wanted us to head over there as soon as you two returned. He said to tell you that the test results are in."

AN HOUR LATER, their Mexican waiter cleared the remnants of mesquite-smoked chimichangas, stuffed leftovers into doggy bags, and served fresh margaritas. Neon was there with Pai. She and Marla bantered briefly in broken Chinese. Girl talk flowed freely across the table. The men behaved. The mood was light until Bill's comedic friend, Matt, turned semi-serious toward the tail-end of the meal.

The longhaired hipster sporting John Lennon specs said he'd never seen anything quite like the samples Bill Baker had sent him. Matt said they contained some man-made, gene-altered bacteria, which was most likely consumed by the mysis shrimp each aquatic victim had consumed. Apparently, this bacteria bandit managed to eat all the oils and enzymes in the salmon's digestive system—leaving them stuffed, but starved, before the fish expired. Once drunk, the congenial chemist dragged on.

"These...like, *Mutant Ninja Microbes,* were probably conceived at great expense for some profitable purpose by some pseudo-humanitarian," Matt slurred. "Which reminds me. Have you heard the latest study on the ill effects from milk copped from hormone injected dairy cows? *Udderly ridiculous!* Like those glow-in-the-dark veggies for romantic California cuisine that are lighting up L.A.!" He laughed like former Saturday morning kid's TV show host, Pee Wee Herman.

An anxious off-duty waitress tapped the chemist's shoulder. "Come on, Matt," she coaxed. "Let's dance."

The chemist rose quickly. "Like I said Billy-boy, these bad-ass bacteria have short life-spans in Chelan's cold water —probably because they were conceived in warmer, maybe saline solutions. But as long as no one goes around eating floating fish, you shouldn't have a health problem."

"What if people eat floating fish?" asked a serious Ho Pai.

The hip chemist removed his specs, leaned over the table looking worried, and whispered: "Then I suggest you be on the lookout for an outbreak...of constipation!"

They laughed.

The gorgeous girl gave Matt's tattered jeans a tug.

"It's probably an isolated dumping, Bill," concluded Matt. "But if you could get me a matching sample from the source, I'd love to help nail the bastards fooling around with Mother Nature like this."

The band struck up a tune, and the lab-tech-in-love disappeared downstairs with the wild waitress-in-waiting.

The small gathering of friends sat silently scanning the 180 degree view of gleaming waters and silhouetted mountains through the restaurant's windows. They bowed their heads in reverence.

"Who in their right mind would want to dump waste in a place like this?" Thomas whispered.

Not one of them could answer.

Bill Baker sipped his drink, watched his brother watching the brunette, and began to think about the Seattle secretary sitting beside Thomas. Marla Jean Decker liked poetry, played decent tennis, played fine mandolin music, and probably was good in bed. Bill Baker shook his head. He'd known all this a year ago. Now his loner brother knew it, too. Border music wafted from the lake-level lounge below them. He watched Marla and

Thomas bump and glow. He debated announcing the *other* test results, the *official government* ones, calling the kill a common fish disease—one he'd never heard of. He was worried, but why should they be tonight? He saw their smiles and listened to their laughter.

"Hey, Blood! Let's go downstairs for one more round, and groove-out on the tunes," Thomas suggested.

Bill Baker peered out to the moon-painted lake, raised his glass, silently pledged to protect her, and felt goose bumps on the back of his neck. "We go now, Blood Brother," Bill Baker said. "Round-um up squaws. Me pay-um check with EPA wampum. Ugh!"

The lower-level bar was hopping. They drank a final pitcher of margaritas, and danced. Across the room, a rowdier crew rocked the Casbah of Cosina del Lago.

Thomas heard a familiar howl. The band went on break. He watched Wolf working the local women, and decided it was time to go home. Thomas Baker was legally drunk and on parole. Wisely, he asked Marla to drive, and handed her his keys.

She was pleased that he trusted her, knowing most men were too macho to let a woman drive. "Just relax and enjoy the ride, Thomas," Marla said pecking his cheek.

Wolf walked over wagging his tail, just in time to hear her reply. The pilot was a good friend, but had a way of pushing things, *testing* people, and taking life to the limit—especially when he was drunk. He emitted a low throaty howl, followed with a gravely growl. "Yeah, *Thomas,* just lay back and enjoy the buzz. And let the lady do the driving." Again he howled. "My God! It's Writer Mon'...and he's a *couple.* Gotta hand it to ya, Tommy me boy. This broad drove all the way from the Emerald City just to break tacos with my buddy. Remember your *vow,* Baker."

Thomas Baker had enough. "We were just leaving, Wolfy," he announced.

"We were? This party going back to your place? Need a pet? Aren't you going to introduce me? Huh, Baker?"

The long forgotten jab of jealousy tagged Thomas on the chin. "Remember Marla...*James?* Tell our friend James good-bye, Marla."

"How could I forget?" The pilot's margarita eyes twinkled. "My pleasure ma'ammm," he muttered offering his hand.

Marla recalled the Seattle bar brawl at the Lake Union Café, and shook the pilot's paw reluctantly.

Wolf feigned a bite.

Baker, embarrassed by his drunken pal, cast a cold stare. "It's late. See ya round, Wolfy," Thomas said.

BACK AT THE LODGE, guests went to bed, and the Baker Brothers became engrossed in serious talk about lab tests. Marla and Nancy sat on the front porch and talked about Alaska, Seattle, and Chelan, until Nan retired.

Marla stayed awake, swinging on an old swing, counting shooting stars in a clear sky, and breathing fresh air. Seventeen hours earlier she was petting Punkin, feeling a sea breeze's nip, and debating the merits of making this trip. She'd done more, felt more, and enjoyed life more in a single day, than in an entire winter full of lonely city nights. *Was this, at long last, love?* she asked herself.

Once again she gazed at the brothers inside—who were talking in lowlight—and thought to say goodnight. She recalled their hurried departure from the bar, and wondered if she was just another guest at Granite Falls Lodge, or something more.

Coyotes yipped in distant darkness. Owls hooted in trees close by. Air turned chilly, fatigue weighed heavily upon her. She took one last look at the writer, and shuffled off alone to Yeti Chalet. Once inside, she soaked sore muscles in the warm Jacuzzi. Later, she grabbed her Grandfather's final gift—his fine old mandolin—and fingered it to life.

THE DARK FIGURE watched her—scantily clad, strumming. He contemplated intuitions, and started humming. While pondering his chances, he accidentally stirred pine branches.

She hadn't heard the wind blow, looked out the window, wondered about the legend of Big Foot, and lowered the volume of her tune. All she saw was half a Chelan moon. Shuffling feet on redwood decking caught her ear. She felt a surge of fear. Then came soft crooning. Marla Jean Decker started swooning.

Kindred spirits began to soar as *he* knocked upon her Chalet door. "Land Shark," he said.

She bolted the lock. Her legs began to rock. "Go way, Land Shark," she cried.

Again came the knock.

"Candy gram for Miss Decker."

"I don't like sweets," she giggled like a schoolgirl.

Once more the knock.

"Flowers for Marla Jean."

How could she resist? She opened her door.

They kissed.

Thomas held a wildflower mountain-meadow bouquet and a frosty magnum of Perrier Joet.

She invited him in.

He stayed…

Only heart strings were played.

SUNDAY CAME too soon, and went. Sunset was spent. Pink cloud plumes changed to shadowy curtains on a milky moon stage, and lingered in a first-star sky above the lodge. Marla had planned to leave that morning, but they played tennis instead. She thought to leave after the wonderful brunch, but sun was warm, water calm, and the lure of Domke Falls far too great.

At dusk, Bill and Nancy watched Thomas tie down her kayak, press her tight against the Toyota's door, and kiss her.

"They make good music together," Nancy noted.

"Yeah…it's kinda' scary," Bill blurted.

"Why is love scary, honey?" she asked her husband. "Are you unhappy with your life?"

He shook his head. "I just know Thomas. He's driven to make this lodge a success, and start that environmental consulting business with me, his brother. Remember *our* dream?"

"Uh huh. Do you think a dream will die simply because your brother opens his heart to love again?" she said, rubbing her husband's tense shoulders.

Bill relaxed, and soon regretted his remarks. "He could become a great writer, Nan. He has often said, '*lasting works are born of pain and solitude.*' That's why he succeeded in prison. He is still growing as a writer. He writes well because of pain—not love. Strange, isn't it?"

"Uh huh," Nan replied nodding, as Marla's Toyota disappeared, and Thomas tread his path towards home alone. "*Perhaps it's time for the pain to stop,*" she muttered.

FOR HOURS THOMAS TYPED like a man possessed, riding waves of passion and purpose he'd waited on forever to roll in. He stood to stretch, and checked the time again: *Midnight.* Marla was on his mind. It was her magic—their heat—which he'd just wove into a fictional romance scene bonding his main character to what had been a minor character until tonight. As always, it amazed him when his imaginary human creations took matters into their own hands and inevitably did the unexpected.

She'd left hours ago to cross the Cascades, and now he was concerned. He grabbed his phone, found her number, and stared out his window biting his nails—just like his main character had at the close of chapter sixteen—wondering if he'd just let something more than *another good woman* go…all for some foolish vow.

SHE HAD STARED at the phone for an hour, but it never rang. Nor had her answering machine offered any tender words. Mrs. Kramer had patiently awaited her return though, to hand her a plump, purring Punkin and a perceptive hug, before retiring. Now, Marla reclined on a Moroccan rug with her calico cat, and stared into the aquarium's fluorescent waters watching Alby the Albino Catfish, and Plecostomus the algae-eater, play.

Just this morning, she awoke on the other side of the mountains, in another world, in the arms of a gentle lover. Tomorrow, she would return to the corporate kingdom. Her world. *Or was it?* She was head over heels and sleepless in Seattle. She reached for the mandolin.

He dialed the number.

Marla Jean Decker's phone rang.

"Hello? Thomas!" she exclaimed.

"Yeah, it's me, Baker...your kayaking buddy. You all right, lady?"

"I'm fine. You?"

"Yeah, fine. I was just calling to see that you got home in one piece...that's all."

"That's sweet of you." She bit her lip, hesitated, then spoke. "Thomas? I really enjoyed spending the weekend with you."

He wanted to tell her the same thing, "Yeah, I really enjoyed showing you around," he said, reluctant to give-in to his emotions.

"Are you coming to Seattle anytime soon? I'd really like to return the favor." She massaged her kitty.

"I'm not sure, but I'd like that." He cleared his throat.

She coughed.

"You catching a cold?" he asked.

"No. You?"

"No. Listen Marla, I've got a few hours of typing to do, and a stack of papers to sort through. I'm way behind on my—" He turned off his computer for the evening.

"Me too. I've got tons of stuff to catch up on after skipping work Friday." She fed the fish.

"Well, I'm glad you made it home safely. Good night, Marla Decker."

"Goodnight, Thomas Baker," she sighed. "Thomas, wait!"

"Yeah? I'm here," he said. "What's on your mind?"

"On the drive home? I remembered the name that was signed at the end of that fax report I told you about. This may sound silly...but it was signed, *your humble Walrus.* Does that help any?"

"No. Not off hand, but I'll give it some thought. Good night, Marla Decker," he said.

"Goodnight, Thomas," she sighed.

Chapter 18

Questions

BARNES FOUND Thomas in the lodge garden's greenhouse thinning tomato starts and listening to National Public Radio news with the family dog, Spirit. Baker's face was streaked with black, his fingers smelled like manure. "Morning, farmer," greeted the councilman.

"Morning, Tim," said Thomas.

"What are we going to do when Newty and the Republicans try to take away the funding for our local public broadcasting station. Huh, Baker?"

"The same thing we'll do when they eliminate the environmental regulations so their special interest cronies can operate even cheaper at Mother Nature's expense—fight back."

Barnes nodded. "Atta boy, Baker," he said.

Baker turned the volume down, and dusted his dirty coveralls. "Oh well, I guess I'm just one of those privileged elitist liberals who prefers hearing the arts, education, and real news—as opposed to a *Rush* of hot air on my radio," he said. He sat on an old barn plank lined with peat cups, and motioned to Barnes to join him. "How was your trip to Bellingham, Tim?"

"Great! Got to see my grandson take his first steps," he said. "I heard the message you left on my answering machine. You sounded so serious. What's up, Tom?"

"Those lab test results came back last Friday," Thomas replied, while pressing moist soil around a spindly Willamette Red tomato start. "From *both* labs."

"What's the news?"

"Good and bad." Baker proceeded to brief him... "What if it's not an isolated incident, Tim? Got any ideas?" the writer asked.

Barnes was an idea man. *He had plenty of ideas.* What he needed was proof. "I think we should form a committee, canvas the community, see if we can get a lead, and try like hell to get to the bottom of this before tourist season rolls in."

"I agree," Baker replied. "But even if it was someone in the valley, getting a sample from the source will be like picking the lotto, Tim."

"Tom, how much stock does Bill put in this chemist friend of his?"

"He'd bet his left nut on the guy," Baker said. "Why?"

"That's what I was afraid of. Someone's ordered a cover-up, Tom. I've got a bad feeling about this. God, I hope I'm wrong." The councilman bit his lip. "Anything else?"

When Baker informed him of the life ring below Big Creek Cove, Barnes glared through dew-filled greenhouse glass with angry eyes. "We've got to find a way to raise the wreckage of the *Connie Joe*, check her fuel tanks, and determine the cause of that *accident*. Did you tell the sheriff about your discovery?"

Thomas sunk a metal garden claw into a pile of peat moss, and shook his head. "Hell no. I'm starting to think like you, councilman. Guess that's why I'm meeting with James Wolf tomorrow to—"

"Wolf! That psycho fly-boy? What do you expect to learn from him?"

"You'd be surprised. I've gotten pretty close to the guy. There's more to James than meets the eye. He's shared many secret stories with me. Old Wolf was a Navy seal, special forces in Nam, even helped mine Haiphong Harbor for Tricky Dick Nixon. The man knows a lot about explosives...and *sabotage*."

"Sabotage! Come on, Tom. You don't actually think he's—"

"No way. But, I do think he can devise a scheme to raise those fuel tanks. He's flown treasure hunters down in the Bahamas, helped salvage wrecks off the Florida coast, and sure as hell is capable of determining whether a metal fuel tank ex ploded—*or imploded.* Catch my drift?"

Barnes' eyes twinkled. "You just might have something there, Tom."

Baker's mind shifted to Marla and the misdialed faxes. "Listen Tim, there is one more thing I think you should know. It's kind of touchy...probably nothing."

"Oh my! You have been busy, haven't you?" remarked Barnes. "I thought you made a vow against butting heads with the government and risking your peaceful little life on this mountain?"

Baker frowned. "I did, but I don't think we're butting heads with the government per se. A friend of mine who is *involved* with a law firm in Seattle received an errant fax transmission destined for one of the partners' desk. It was an encrypted report assessing a series of development projects east of the Cascades."

"What kind of *projects?* Who's behind them?"

"Whoa there," Thomas blurted. Baker contemplated the sensitivity of Marla's position, and paused a minute. "Listen Tim, this guy's not well-versed on commercial real estate. And there's an attorney/client confidentiality issue here."

"Then why in the hell did this *lawyer* tell you any—"

"Because he's an old friend, Tim. And my name, and yours, were mentioned on the summary page." The writer proceeded to brief the councilman on the report's contents. "He was concerned and called me," Thomas explained, after filling Barnes in.

Barnes tugged his bushy brows and laughed. "I plan on being an obstacle until the day I die, Mr. baker. Looks like you better get used to it too."

"Yeah, but *dangerous obstacles?*" Thomas made a funny face. The dog barked. "I've never considered myself dangerous."

"You? A bloodthirsty ex-con like you? Why, of course you're dangerous," declared the councilman with tongue-in-cheek.

They laughed.

Barnes knew the writer's story, and shared Baker's opinion favoring the decriminalization of marijuana. The councilman—who had recently developed a case of glaucoma—occasionally smoked the forbidden herb medicinally himself for relief from painful inner eye pressure caused by the disease.

"So, your lawyer friend didn't see a corporate name, but this was sent on *official* stationary from Wenatchee?" Barnes quizzed.

Baker nodded and looked away.

"You're a bright young man, Tom. But sometimes you surprise me. Why in the hell would these developers and international corporations that want to *own* places like Chelan call you a dangerous obstacle?"

Baker shrugged.

"It's your pen, Tom," Barnes bellowed. "That's what they're afraid of. These vultures are masters at media manipulation. They'll promise the locals anything just to get one foot in the door. Then? *Bang*!" Barnes slapped their wooden seat. "They rape and plunder the countryside like Ghengis Khan! Guys like you can use words and passion to stir the apathetic hearts and souls of the masses into slamming the door in their greedy faces, and resisting their slick-talk and short-term fool's gold offers," insisted Barnes. "Believe me, Tom. You possess a very powerful gift."

The writer blushed. "And you? Why are you dangerous?" Baker asked.

"Because. I'm an insider, an insider who defected to the side of fairness, which is the side of their enemies. I know how they operate. I've seen their shell games, and their three-card monte dealers. Ain't proud to admit it, Tom, but I even played a dirty hand or two myself. They can't fool me. And I'm an honest politician. Trust me, Tom. Land sharks hate honest politicians. Tom, you need to exercise that pen of yours like your kayak paddle. Help wake up the *real* sleeping giant—the American

Public's consciousness! Now...what else did your friend say? Give me something. Who signed that summary page?"

The writer saw the councilman's wife waving to them from the lodge.

Barnes had appointments. It was time to go.

"He said it was signed, the 'Walrus'," Thomas replied. "That mean anything to you?"

Barnes scratched his head, called out to his wife, and started walking. "It might. I'll do some digging and get back with you, Tom," he said over his shoulder as he departed.

ANOTHER WEEK was concluding at Ming Yaht's Chelan Environmental Research Lab. Miss Ho Pai slipped her platinum security card in a slot, left the lab, entered the cleansing chamber, removed her lab-whites, washed, and waited in the employees' meditation lounge for Doctor Ashwan Habib.

Ever since the dinner at Cosina del Lago, Pai had harbored suspicions about their work and wanted to ask the good doctor some pointed questions. As a biochemist, she respected his knowledge. Habib was as skilled an instructor as she'd seen since her freshman year at Beijing. But as a man and coworker, she found him cool and calculating, money-hungry and humorless. She'd met other Pakistanis at Berkeley—all workaholics and overachievers, but none were as cold as Ashwan Habib.

The electric door opened, and the dark-skinned doctor appeared.

"Miss Ho. I must remind you that our entry system will be changing over to voice recognition next month," Habib said. "Nicholas has requested voice recordings from each of us. Your session will be two weeks from today."

"Yes, Doctor," Pai replied. She untied her ponytail, and shook her hair vigorously. "Since Mr. Gordon's arrival, our workplace is becoming a house of gadgets, doctor. Sometimes I feel like I'm working for NASA."

"Perhaps, but we are engaged in extremely sensitive research here, and corporate espionage has become a very lucrative occupation. You should surely know this to be true, Miss Ho. After all, your people are masters of the game. Take your Silkworm Missile technology for example, or that new line of fighter planes Beijing is pushing. Yes, yes, it is an extremely old story, Miss Ho. People like myself are bred, educated, and paid extremely generous amounts of money to conceive ideas. Then others, who are equally well paid, simply steal the end product, thus saving *their* employers millions—quite possibly billions—of dollars."

She meekly nodded, ignored the Pakistani's blatant nationalism, and recalled how often her father had reminded her—reminded *all* his students—that Chinese minds had invented gunpowder. "Doctor?" She took a deep breath.

"Yes, Miss Ho."

"Did you read about the fish-kill in Mill Bay a few weeks ago?" the lady scientist asked her mentor. She watched closely for his response.

He formed a puzzled face.

She feigned feminine innocence.

He coughed, looked away, and reached for an empty beaker on a small table, as if he had not heard her question.

"Did you hear about Mill Bay, Doctor Habib?" she persisted.

The beaker slipped from his grip, crashed to the floor, and shattered into a thousand shards of dagger-tipped glass. "Why do you ask?" he answered angrily.

She used her femininity and reacted fearfully. "So sorry to disturb you! I was curious about our work and..."

Habib's bronze forehead wrinkled. "Just what are you so curious about, young lady?"

"What happens to our experiments when they fail?"

Again he looked away—this time bending low—as if to assess the irreparable beaker. He was too Pakistani-proper to improvise lies, especially in response to a subordinate's queries.

Pai's suspicion grew.

"They are quite properly disposed of, Miss Ho," replied Habib.

"Then, it is not possible that something we create here should cause such a thing to occur?" she quizzed.

"Absolutely not," he snapped. "Our security and environmental protection procedures are fail-safe!" He snatched the in-house phone, and summoned maintenance. "Miss Ho. In the future, do not worry about things which do not involve you, or this corporation." The good doctor softened his tone. "I'm going to have some dinner, then return to my work. You are young and pretty. Haven't you better things to do, Miss Ho?"

She nodded nonchalantly, picked up her purse, and walked calmly toward the door. But in her worried heart she now knew...*Dr. Ashwan Habib was lying.*

Chapter 19

Heavy Road Work

BARNES WAITED days to play his hunch. Now he watched Wenatchee's County/City building's lot empty for lunch, and waited. He pondered Baker's mystery fax report, and Hank Hodge's recently acquired material possessions: A Lincoln Continental, an all-terrain Hummer vehicle, and a Lake Chelan cabin cruiser with a *Private Condominium Boat Slip* at the new and highly coveted Harris Marina. Then there was that custom golf cart which Hank regularly trailered over to the deluxe Desert Canyon golf resort. And what about all the times he'd seen Hank out to lunch looking shitfaced-goo-goo-eyed at his gaudy young secretary? All this, on a county planner's salary? *No way!*

The councilman clearly remembered the time he and Martha were seated behind them for dinner at The Quail, and heard Hank's young secretary call him *'my cuddly walrus'*. The fat man was moonlighting for Ming Yaht International, or at least playing *Mr. Fix-It.* And maybe…much, much, more.

Barnes' sources had informed him that Hodge was out in the field today with a Vancouver survey crew, so the councilman called Hank's secretary to arrange for a little lunch hour assistance.

The government employees' parking lot was nearly empty. The time had come for the councilman to make his move.

PENNY PENNINGTON chomped chewing gum, opened the records room door, and flicked on fluorescent lights. "What did ya say you was looking for, Councilman Barnes?" she asked, adjusting her wing-tipped glitter glasses.

"I need to take a peek at the big map and see what's on the old drawing board, Penny. Then I wanted to study Hank's file on Ming Yaht's Chelan industrial park expansion project."

"Piece of cake! That all you're after, councilman?"

Barnes crossed his fingers. "Actually, there is one other thing. Do you recall faxing a report to Seattle last week for Mr. Hodge?"

"Sure. I fax lots of stuff there. Could ya be more specific?"

"Oh…this one was seven pages long, and dealt with zoning issues concerning Chelan Falls and a large tract of waterfront property adjacent to some Corral Creek tribal lands. There was a Canadian firm involved, Penny. It was sent last week." He gave her his fatherly face, with eyes unblinking, thinking: *Come on! Be there.*

She fingered blond hair, leaned alabaster elbows on open files, and strained to recall the extracurricular afternoon in question. "Yeah, I remember. The old Walrus typed that one himself," she smirked. "Ya know, Hank's good ta' me, but sometimes he forgets to keep the records straight. Lucky he has me. Huh, councilman?" Smudged red lips smacked spearmint gum, as her baby blue eyes searched confidential files. "Didn't some guy with a real deep voice call for you about this report?"

"Might have," he said, somewhat confused. "Would you happen to have a copy?"

"Would I? Think I'm just another pretty face? I keep copies of *everything*. And one day, the old Walrus is gonna be awfully glad I do." She grabbed green file folders, handed stacks to Barnes, and bent low for more. Her ultra-short skirt climbed buns-high upon her cream-colored seamed stockings.

Suddenly, Barnes understood obese Hank's obsession with his svelte secretary, but the councilman rubbed his eyes and looked beyond those fleshy thighs to the skilled fingers scanning Hodge's files for him.

"Got it!" Penny shouted.

The phone rang.

She handed Barnes the goods. "Here ya are, councilman. That's everything on Ming Yaht and their affiliate, Maple Leaf, in Vancouver."

He wanted to kiss her.

The phone rang again, and Penny ran to answer it.

Barnes rubbed his hands together. Her timely exit left him alone in Hodge's records room—possibly with the key evidence he was after. *But for how long?*

"Councilman?" Penny shouted from her desk outside the door.

"Yes, Miss Pennington?" he answered, with heart pounding, and fingers nervously paging, praying she was not announcing the planner's premature return.

"Sorry, but I've got work out here. If you need anything, just yell."

"Will do, Penny. Mind if I use this copy machine?"

"Not at all, hon. I know how the government likes to waste paper. It's government property. Ain't it? We're government employees, you and me. Right? Copy your little heart out, councilman!" she shouted, laughing.

Barnes' knowledgeable eyes indulged in poorly encrypted papers, piecing together the painful picture Pos were painting of Twenty-first Century Chelan. The massive industrial park and distribution center reminded him of a tiny Wisconsin resort town which allowed Target Department stores to erect ones half the size. Four years later, they were filled with regret, and fight-ing the decision in court while their quality of life rapidly declined. As the millennium approached, retail giant, Walmart, was posing a similar threat to small communities in the U.S. and Canada. Suddenly, the heavy road and bridge work made perfect sense.

Barnes checked his watch, quickly skimmed further, and froze. Steady hands quivered. Sad, angry, eyes reviewed dated documents and recognized the plat of the former Warwick Estate, now deeded to Maple Leaf Limited, Vancouver, British Columbia—*AKA Ming Yaht International.*

There were studies and proposals predating Warwicks' death, and more: a condo city, sprawling ski resort, exclusive pro-am golf and racquet club, and a massive joint-venture waterfront casino on Corral Creek tribal land which would dwarf the existing Colville tribe's Mill Bay gaming enterprise. Barnes clenched his fists, cranked up the copier, sorted documents, and did the deed. On the thirtieth page of dozens, the Pitney Bowes D-640 died an untimely death. "Miss Pennington!" the councilman called out. "There's a problem with the copier. Could you give me a hand?"

THE BLACK LAND ROVER rounded the block a fourth time in fifteen minutes, hoping to see Hodge's Humm-V return to the county planner's reserved spot. Nicholas Gordon recognized the white Ford Ranger in the parking lot and felt compelled to see what *dangerous obstacle Barnes* was up to. He parked, slipped inside undetected wearing wrap-around Carrera shades and an old fishing hat, and noticed the records room open and the planner's office empty. Gordon stood still and overheard a conversation...

"Anything else ya wanna copy, councilman?" Penny asked.

"No. That ought to do me, Penny. I'm late for some appointments in Chelan," he said.

Gordon recognized that silky voice. It was the same one which had read the eulogy at Warwicks' funeral. Only now it was excited, eager to depart, and...*on to something!* Nick had no idea what action this situation was going to require, but he had never met Miss Pennington face-to-face, and decided to keep it that way.

FROM HIS CURBSIDE PERCH, Nick watched the sleepy little Columbia River city of Wenatchee's sidewalks bustle with noontime feet until a door swung open, revealing a noticeably relieved councilman carrying an unusually heavy double-wide briefcase stuffed with still-warm copies.

Barnes flung the luggage into the Ford's cab, locked the door, and started the pickup's engine.

Nick's Land Rover roared to life, ready for the cat-and-mouse game to begin. Suddenly, Gordon saw the red-faced county planner approaching fast in the rearview mirror. Hodge pulled curbside and blasted his horn behind him. Barnes zipped past him, and Gordon put the Rover on the councilman's tail. Moments later, Nick watched Hodge's Humm-V veering in and out of traffic behind him, creating a scene and attracting too much attention.

Nick grabbed his cellular phone and punched-in the Walrus' number. "Hodge?"

"Yes, Gordon. That you up ahead? I wasn't late, was I?"

"You're always late, you moron. Barnes just left your office with a shit-eating grin and a briefcase full of documents. What did you leave laying around?"

"Nothing! I swear. What are you gonna do?"

"My fucking job. You should try it sometime, Mr. Hodge."

"Say, you wouldn't..."

"Save it! Don't you worry about me."

"Wh-what a-b-bout our m-meeting, Mr. Gor—"

"Canceled! Go back and clean out your office, fat man."

THE COUNCILMAN cruised past Pizza Hut and Taco Bell. His stomach said stop, but his nerves said *go*. Soon there was no sign of Wenatchee's Commercial Row. He knew he'd hit the jackpot back at Hodge's office, and now believed he held the tip of an iceberg big enough to sink Ming Yaht's Titanic.

Six cars back, Nicholas Gordon wondered what the councilman's next move would be.

The councilman's Ford Ranger roamed the silent asphalt of Highway 97A. The mighty Columbia River meandered below him. Barnes was haunted by visions of the Warwick family's final moments, and the Po Prothers' plans for the valley's future.

Midway to Chelan—near the town of Entiat—the councilman parked beside twin phone booths in front of the Over The Hill Cafe. Barnes' hands shook as he entered the number for the Lodge at Granite Falls. The phone rang.

Nancy answered; then she had to retrieve Thomas from the lodge's garden.

Barnes tapped sweaty fingers on smudged glass.

Nicholas Gordon pulled his Land Rover onto the gravel shoulder, and raised its hood. He leaned over the warm engine, aimed a powerful parabolic mike at the twin phone booths, and listened.

"Yes Tim," Thomas Baker greeted the councilman. "What's the good word?"

Barnes felt claustrophobia and severe paranoia. He scanned cars in the cafe's parking lot. A friendly gas station attendant washing windows waved. "Tom? Listen closely."

His voice was tense.

"I was digging around this morning..." Barnes noticed the disabled Land Rover. He couldn't make the connection, but was instantly stricken with phone-a-phobia. "Tom, we need to talk."

"Go for it, big guy. I'm listening," said Baker.

"In person," he said pointedly.

Barnes' tone transmitted fear, and took Baker way back to his marijuana dealing days, when coded pay phone calls were a daily occurrence. "I read you loud and clear, councilman. Just say when and where, and I'll be there with bells," Baker replied.

"Good," Tim said, sounding relieved. "I found that bad apple tree, Baker. But I need some time to inspect the fruit. How about dinner at your place?"

"Sure. Where you calling from anyway?"

"Entiat. I'm at the Over the Hill Cafe en route back to my office. I was thinking about having some lunch."

"Good idea, Tim. Have a beer. Hell, have two. It'll help you unwind," the writer suggested.

"I'm not an afternoon drinker," the councilman insisted.

"Go on. It'll do you good. I'll see you tonight. Right?"

"Count on it. Thanks, Tom."

Barnes hung up, looked around, and saw the black Land Rover disappear toward Chelan. Somewhat relaxed, he walked through the swinging cafe doors, briefcase in hand...

Gordon circled back and parked beside the old brick building. He pretended to fill the radiator, and surveyed the scene. Barnes' call had determined the severity of the situation all too clearly. Nick peered through cafe windows with powerful pack-set binoculars, and saw Barnes nursing a beer and reading The Maple Leaf file. He saw road-workers in flannel shirts seated behind his subject, and recognized the redheaded female flagger. The Chelan County road crew's truck was conveniently parked beside him. He decided to pop its locks and hop inside for a little scavenger hunt.

BACK INSIDE the cafe, Barnes had been consumed by his reading, and had thought solely of returning to the privacy of his office to dictate his thoughts to his mini-recorder. He was certain he'd obtained enough ammunition to get an injunction against Ming Yaht—maybe even enough to initiate criminal proceedings.

Once he got back on the road, Barnes relaxed a little more. His two lunch beers had definitely calmed him for the last stretch to Chelan. He nearly nodded off watching big brown cattle graze lazily on grassy green foothills. A hawk's shadow shrouded his windshield for an instant, startling him. Seconds later, the councilman watched the big winged predator snatch a restless rabbit from scraggly roadside sagebrush in his rearview mirror. Timothy Alan Barnes watched cloud puffs swirl on foothills up around the bend, where a brightly-colored figure soon appeared, stop sign in hand.

The figure grew closer.

As the councilman's truck slowed to a crawl, Barnes thought little about the bulk and gender of the flagger signaling him to halt. He might have thought more, had two beers not mellowed him so. He might also have been curious about the absence of the regular county crew, and the presence of the black Land Rover on the road's shoulder. The councilman's truck stopped.

The too-tall flagger wearing the too-small orange county hard-hat quickly flew to the Ford's window, and tapped his talons on its glass.

Something wasn't right.

Tim rolled down the window. "Say, buddy. Where's the redhead today?"

"She went to lunch," the tall stranger replied, as he reached into his pocket for the chloroform cloth. *Evidently you were too busy snooping through our files to notice her,* thought Gordon.

Barnes saw his own reflection in the stranger's black wrap-around sunglasses. He looked down at the flagger's fancy boots, and noticed the expensive black business suit concealed beneath the bright orange county road crew vest. Suddenly, the councilman felt a pain in his chest.

The Hawk seized the moment, and the chloroform cloth made its way to the intended prey.

In the freeze-frame seconds which followed, Barnes saw Warwicks' burning faces flash before him, felt terror, and attempted to inch his hand toward the Ranger's gear shift. "So, tell me pal," the councilman said, as his left foot gently depressed the Ford's clutch pedal. "Just how long of a delay am I looking at this time?"

Like Po Lin, Gordon had a thing about eye contact. He removed his dark sunglasses, tossed them atop the white Ford's hood, and quickly covered the councilman's face.

Barnes tried to break free and slam the shifter into reverse.

Powerful, professional hands pinned his shoulders to the seat back, and pressed the chloroform cloth ever tighter.

The victim convulsed violently.

TEN SECONDS LATER, Timothy Alan Barnes had too much in common with the hapless roadside rabbit he'd seen earlier in the talons of the ravaging hawk.

NICHOLAS GORDON calmly removed his disguise, and answered the councilman's last question.

"Terribly sorry, old chap. But I'm afraid *your* delay, Mr. Barnes... *will be infinite.*"

Chapter 20

Evidence

IN THE BEGINNING, there was only a garage and an old work van, and any work was good work for the young Neonman. He bent glass for titty bars in Brewster, lit up watering holes in Wenatchee, and worked long nights on custom creations which soon became Northwest sensations. When Ming Yaht came to Chelan, they called upon him to create a pleasant work environment with soft, tasteful, backlighting. It was a big job, which led to others. He made big bucks off those mothers! Recently, there came a mysterious rash of failed neon glass. He, of course, was called upon to return and repair it all.

THE NEANDERTHAL security guard led Neon through the final sealed door to the employees' meditation lounge. *2:45 p.m.*....He was fifteen minutes early. The lounge was empty. He sat down his duffel bag, and began replacing defective lighting fixtures.

The guard got bored and returned to his post.

Perfect.

A buzzer sounded. A door swung open.

When the Neon-repairman heard her familiar flats shuffling toward him, he removed one sneaker and spoke softly into its sole. "Agent Pai? Agent Pai? This is agent Neon-Wan Kenobi—

" He held his nose and made crackling radio noises. "Do you read me? Over."

Ho Pai pulled a paper cup from the dispenser and placed it under the water cooler. "You are early," she whispered through her teeth, without looking at him.

"Mr. No Neck got me in quicker than you allowed for. Is that security dude the guy from the first James Bond movie?"

Pai scanned for the doctor nervously, then tossed water droplets on Neon.

"Hey!" he said. "Why you so—"

"Shhh!" she hissed, scowling. "This is very serious, Michael. Dr. Habib has yet to leave. We must be very careful. No one knows of our relationship. It is most important that we maintain this."

"We have a *relationship?*" Neon snickered to his sneaker.

She bit her paper cup.

"Okay! I'll just keep talking to my Nike here, while you continue the ventriloquist act with that cup. Listen, do you really think something they made here killed those fish?"

She filled her cup. "When Bill Baker's friend spoke of oils and enzymes being destroyed, at our dinner, I thought of our Oil Reclamation Project immediately. It involves bacteria genetically trained to consume fossil fuels. The doctor believes that once we perfect and clone the proper bacteria, it will replace detergents used on major oil spills like Alaska's Exxon Valdez. The corporation carelessly pushes Dr. Habib too hard to succeed, and yet they wish to show environmental green face to people of Washington State. This endangers our work. I could not speak of this to your friends, Michael. I am sworn to secrecy. This is why I speak little of this place, but this goes far beyond corporate loyalty."

Neon studied Pai's reflection in the water cooler's green glass, and noticed a marked transformation in her normally tranquil demeanor.

"My work could be threatening this valley I have come to love so deeply. I could not live with that." She emptied her cup and crushed it. "That is why I must know for certain."

"Are all Chinese women as crazy as you?" he asked, awestruck.

She quickly turned to face him. "Am I crazy to fight for a cause, Michael? Crazy to tarnish Hollywood's diminutive image of me and my peers? Would I make for better wife if I walked three steps behind you and every man?" She was shouting, and punctuating her remarks with broad sweeps of her hands. Then, she stopped, and whispered—articulately and determined. "I care. I feel. I think. I *love*, Michael! I loved a beautiful boy in Beijing. He show me how to open my mind, heart, soul! I was not a big part of Tiananmen Square's terror, but Tiananmen change me forever. I know this now."

Moisture filled her eyes.

"I can never walk away from fear...or love again, Michael."

"Anyone ever tell you how sexy you look in that white lab coat?" he whispered, with wet and admiring eyes.

The buzzer sounded.

Pai took long strides toward the Ladies Room and motioned Michael back to work.

Doctor Habib entered from the lab.

"Miss Ho?"

"Yes, Doctor?"

"I must leave at once for my appointment with our suppliers in Wenatchee. Please secure the new culture dishes and cleanup before you depart." He retrieved his sport coat from a rack, stopped to study the repairman hunched over faulty neon glass, and checked the time. "Do not forget, Miss Ho," he reminded her, before slipping his access card in the exit door's slot.

"Yes, Doctor," Pai said. Seconds later, she returned to the lab, where she collected a cross section of their last six months work, then set about covering her tracks.

THE NEXT TIME the buzzer rang, Neon felt relieved. "Agent Pai? Agent Pai? Neon-Wan Kenobi here. Congratulations on your stealthy—"

"Put your shoe on and get serious," Pai hissed. She was nervous. "Do you not realize what we do now is called corporate espionage?"

He nodded, and searched his duffel bag for the *special tubes.* "Yes, I do. Know what? I'm getting a rush from this! Maybe I'm in the wrong line of work. Say, we'd make a great international spy team. Don't you think?"

"You are too silly for such work. That is what I think." She cracked a smile.

He unscrewed the custom-made ends on cotton-lined glass tubes.

They placed *the evidence* inside.

"There. It is done," she sighed.

"You sure you won't get caught?" he asked for the hundredth time.

"I will be fine," she said confidently.

He tugged her coat, and stole a kiss. "Go on! Finish your work. I'll finish mine and have Mr. No Neck show me out. See you for dinner tonight. Right?"

She bit her lip, and nodded.

The secured door's buzzer sounded, and the lady scientist disappeared.

HO PAI had been gone for hours. The Pakistani waited at the front entry impatiently for the security guard—who folded his Playboy, and flushed the toilet.

"Evening, Doc," the thick framed guard said. "How many late nights in a row does this make for you?"

Ashwan Habib was tired. "Too many, Mr. Lee, but I prefer to work alone, and my project has a deadline." *You ungrateful moron,* he thought.

"Making much progress, Doc?"

Habib furrowed his brow. "Sir! I'll have you know that I am making great strides. Yes, yes. As a matter of fact, I am extremely close to a breakthrough which should preserve *all* of our positions here."

Mr. Lee smiled contentedly as the Pakistani penned his initials in Nicholas Gordon's new mandatory register. *Stay all night, Paki. I have a very good novel to read.*

THE PHONE'S unexpected ring broke Gordon's fixed gaze through the Octagon's glass in the Retreat's lofty summit. It sent him high-stepping down the silver spiral staircase, and left him panting. He heard excitement in the Pakistani's perpetually proper tone. "For God's sake, tell me you've done it, Habib."

"Sir? I wish that I could," came the dismal response.

Nick sensed fear. "Where are you calling from, Doctor?"

"The lab. I just completed comparison tests on our past experimental cultures. The organisms were inactive in culture codes CH-69 through J—"

"Please, doc," Nicholas said. "Just skip the chemistry lesson and get to the point of this call."

"Several of my cultures have been tampered with in a way which suggests that organism samples have been removed," he said.

"Are you certain?"

"Yes, yes. Quite, sir. I had them under my scope for hours. Their saline solutions have been diluted by approximately twenty-seven percent to mask the perpetrator's act. I decided it would be wise to contact you immediately, Mr. Gordon."

"An excellent decision, Doctor. Please inform our Mr. Lee that I will need to review the register and all security videotapes upon arrival. I'm on my way, Doctor. See you in twenty-five minutes."

GORDON ARRIVED gung ho, scrutinized the register, and quickly set about reviewing all security videos shot between 2:45 p.m. and 3:37 p.m.

The Pakistani admired Nick's machine-like approach and minimal emotions. Habib's bronze fingers brushed his black mustache hairs repeatedly as tapes rolled by their curious eyes in a tiny control room. Gordon stared intensely at the screen, uninspired by a single frame, until the employees' meditation lounge scene unfolded. "Is this the gentleman, Mr. Lee?" Nick inquired, pointing a pencil at Neon, who was apparently talking to his Nike sneaker beside the water cooler.

No Neck nodded. "That's him, boss. Same guy who installed the lighting four years ago. I checked. Did I screw up by letting him—"

Nick tapped the screen. Pai entered the picture, face to the water cooler, back to the camera, and stood there motionless for an extended period. Habib entered from the lab. Pai moved quickly toward the Ladies Room, and gave an obvious warning to the neon repairman. "There! There's our thief," Gordon declared. "And you walked right past him, Doctor."

The doc was stunned. "Sir, I'm a biochemist, not a bloody detective!" He tugged on his mustache again. "How could a simple repairman access the cultures?"

Nick fast-forwarded the tape to Pai's re-entry scene. The picture spoke volumes.

The Pakistani's fist struck the veiwing screen. "Why? The girl has a brilliant future ahead of her. For God's sake, man! Why would she betray the corporation like this? She's bloody well-paid for a woman."

Film continued to roll. Neon stole a kiss from the Paki's star pupil.

Nick punched the stop button. "Okay. Show's over. There's your answer, Doctor. It always boils down to love or money— sometimes both—when people betray." Gordon ejected the tape, slipped it in his pocket, and strolled to the exit. "Talk to you tomorrow, Doctor."

"Sir? What about the girl?"

"What about her, Doctor?"

"Should I let her go?"

Gordon's ponytail swished side to side. "First, I want to find out who she's working for, Ashwan. After that? We'll let the proper authorities deal with them both," he answered calmly. "And now, if you'll excuse me, I have another appointment to keep, Doctor. Good night."

NICHOLAS GORDON parked his Rover beside one of Campbell Resorts' guest cottages—over a block away—and walked to Forever Neon with his black bag of tricks. He stopped beneath Neon's balcony, and pointed his listening device between redwood boards toward the open sliding glass door above him. The sound of running water flooded his headset. He waited patiently.

The shower stopped running. Wine glasses clicked. Foreplay was conducted, and parlayed into passion. The subjects purred, panted, after glowed, and finally spoke.

"Today was a trip. I can't believe we did it," Neon sighed.

Miss Pai cooed contentedly. "Come on, Michael. Tell me where you took them when I was in the shower."

Nick Gordon held his breath below, straining to hear the kid answer. *Yeah, Mikey. Where is the evidence you just risked your ass for?*

Neon replied in an inaudible whisper.

Ho Pai giggled.

Gordon stomped his foot, and ground his gold crowns together.

Neon continued at normal volume. "Trust me. They'll be safer over there until Bill's friend gets back from his trip, Agent Pai." Neon tickled her feet.

Their laughter filled Gordon's ears. *Come on. Damn it! Give me more.*

"Then Bill, Tom, and Wolf will fly them to Seattle, and find out if they match up with the samples from Mill Bay," Neon concluded. "Come on, Miss White Crane Spreading Wings. Let's forget all this spy stuff and call it a night."

Nick had heard enough. He collapsed the mike and crammed it back inside the black nylon gym bag. A cool wind blew in off the lake. He buttoned his jacket, stared off toward Stormy Mountain, and started walking.

Along the way, he thought about his many years of mercenary work and his flawless record. He recalled his instinctual reluctance to accept Pos' offer, and return home to Washington State to handle this project. Nearly fifty years of robust living had boiled down to *this*.

Nick did not enjoy being overt and covert in such a small theater of operations. He did not appreciate having to depend on the likes of Hank Hodge, Ashwan Habib, and a host of others. He had survived financiers' crusades unscathed from Nam to Nicaragua, but now this Podunk place was starting to punch holes in his armor.

First came the Warwicks, then Montreal, the Corral Creek Tribal Chief, Councilman Barnes—and now this incident. Nick Gordon was nobody's fool. Too much exposure could make *him* expendable. Not quite the retirement he had envisioned. Perhaps it would be better to be a live expatriate, than a disposable pawn in Ming Yaht's deadly game? But no one left Po Lin's employment *alive*. Arturos Aquindo insured that policy. And Arturos was beginning to grate on Gordon. The Cuban was too flashy, too domineering, always talking about owning people.

Nobody owned Nick Gordon. The Hawk was too damn good to be owned.

For what seemed a lifetime, he'd been a spirited freelancer, fighting for the highest bidder. *Was he building his own death cage by staying here—like the one he'd freed his fellow hawks from in the Hong Kong market?*

Just last week, his *Sun Yee On* infiltrator had informed him of a tempting contract being offered by a vengeful Dragon Head. It was something to think about.

Nick undid his ponytail and looked to silhouetted Stormy Mountain in search of some metaphysical guidance. *Better to be a giant shadow on the distant horizon than play out Pos' security game plan?*

If only he could just *live* here…in Chelan.

Chapter 21

The Andros Affair

"Hey, Writer Man! I'm losing my concentration over here," Wolf announced. "I thought we were on a roll."

Thomas turned away from the window, and returned to his desk. He sat down, rubbed his eyes, and sighed.

The pilot patted him on the back. "Look, Baker. I realize you're bummed out. So am I. Crap! Councilman Barnes is missing in action, and my best friend is falling in love."

Baker scowled. "This Barnes thing is eating at me, man. I went to visit his wife, Martha, earlier today. She's a mess. Some dipshit doctor has her taking that damn Prozac like candy."

"Those happy valley quacks are just a bunch of legal drug pushers—brought to us by that wonderful pharmaceutical lobby in Washington, D. C.," Wolf said.

Baker managed a thin smile. "I can't stop thinking about that last phone call Barnes made to me from Entiat. He was definitely on to something big. I'm worried someone—"

"Save it! The sheriff is scouring the countryside for that white Ford Ranger."

Baker's eyes rolled back in his head.

"I know, I know. Now you think Hilo's on the take too. Maybe *you* should consider seeing the Prozac pusher-man," suggested the pilot.

Baker furrowed his brow.

"Listen, the best thing we can do is get on that plane tomorrow with those samples I've been sitting on, and deliver them to that loony-tunes chemist. Let's see where that leads us, then make plans to raise the *Connie Joe.*"

Baker nodded in agreement.

"Good boy. Annnnd now...back to our story! Aren't you excited? You're getting close to learning the secret of my mysterious deaf ear."

Baker fingered the computer keys. "Okay, hit it."

"It was 1978, and this was my fourth flight that year for the Colonel's crazy Cubans." Wolf winced.

The writer noticed, and italicized the word *Colonel's* in his text.

"They were operating off the Bahamas from Andros and Williams Islands. Williams is where the Cubans trained for the war that never was. Make note, Writer Man."

"The Bay of Pigs?"

Wolf lapped brew, and nodded. "That's where they discovered the drug trade, got hip to dealing arms, and mapped out the best staging areas—all under the guidance of their uncle, Uncle Sammy."

"Where did they fly arms to back then?"

"This group serviced Central and South America. This run, I was headed for a strip out on the peninsula near the Colombian-Venezuelan border called La Guajira." The pilot struck a match, took a two-second drag on a non-filter fag, exhaled, coughed, and continued. "Needed two interpreters on the ground to get me through this one."

"Two?" Thomas said.

"Yeah. English to Spanish, and Spanish to Indian."

"Indians? What were they like?"

Wolf's half-smoked cigarette met a half-drank beer, and hissed. "A fuckin' trip, Writer Man. A fuckin' trip. I landed that Beech D-18, and Indians spilled onto desert sand like red ants wearing loin-cloths and waving M-16s. Felt like I was in a scene from an old Tarzan flick."

"Were you stoned?"

"Oh, hell yes! I snarfed up two caps of blow about an hour before. Just finished listening to my Fleetwood Mac *Rumors* cassette. Owww! That Beech had one helluva stereo system, Baker."

"How did the coke affect your flying?"

Wolf laughed. "In the air? It's just more energy. But when you hit the ground? I guess you could compare it to driving cross-country with a good buzz on. You know? You're grooving along in your own little world, then you or your machine craves fuel, and you have to eject and interact with reality. Landing was always scary. I rarely knew the ground crew. The toot only made me a hair more paranoid than I would be naturally. So there I is—the only white cat in the middle of this tribe of diaper-clad Indians—with topless broads and naked babies dancing all around my plane like it was some damn altar. Shit! Even their chickens and goats were doin' the Texas Two-step. My interpreters told them to unload the crates and inspect the merchandise."

"What exactly was the *merchandise?*"

"The normal fare, grenade launchers, automatics and...ready for this?"

The writer nodded.

"Remember Clint Eastwood in *Dirty Harry?*" Wolf twitched one eye, Clint-like.

"Yeah, yeah. Make my day. What about him?"

"He made the Smith & Wesson Model 29, .44 Magnum, the most requested small arm in Latin America that year. By the time I finished refueling, and stood waiting for the payoff, there were hundreds of drunken Indians with .44's strapped to them thar' diapers shootin' up a storm and shouting: 'Clint Eastwood gun! Clint Eastwood gun! Make my day!'"

"You're kidding."

Wolf snarled. "I'll tell you when I'm kidding," my literary buddy.

"Sorry. What was the *payoff*, and what political group were those arms supposed to be for?"

Wolf snickered. "I suppose the heavier arms were eventually hauled overland to Nicaragua or staging areas in Costa Rica, but the .44s were from Toys 'R U.S.A. to pacify those green-thumbed natives."

"You saying the Indians were pot growers?"

Wolf belched, and twisted the top off another beer. "Yep. These injuns grew primo gold bud herb, then bartered for guns with the killer weed. This wasn't my first run to La Guajira, Baker. I dropped a ton on Andros in '77. The Cubans loved the shit so much that they made 'em promise them their whole next year's crop."

"So, let me get this straight. You flew herb back to Andros for a U.S. government agent?"

"Oh, hell yes! Why? You surprised? Told you I would give you shit that would rattle some cages, stuff only people involved knew about. That's what you wanted. Wasn't it?"

Thomas nodded, and reflected bitterly about his own past.

"Look, I share your feelings, Baker. I can see it on your face. We both did time for being peons in the great drug war, while guys like Colonel—" Wolf winced again. "Guys like these, brought in tons of weed and coke, buried megabucks, and later became political tough-on-crime Ollie North types backed by the goddamn religious right! And *they* never did a day in the slammer. Strange fuckin' country. Huh, Baker?"

Baker typed verbatim while voicing his bitterness. "I always knew customs agents took bribes to let loads slip in. Always suspected there were high-ranking U.S. government personnel involved. I heard the rumors, read articles in *Mother Jones* and *Playboy* quoting Senate testimony, but..."

"But what? What happened when *60 Minutes* finally had the balls to air the story on that CIA coke ring stung by the DEA last year? Nobody cared, pal. It's just not newsworthy. All that Ma and Pa Kettle out in Iowa care about is the O.J. trial, *The Bridges of Madison County*, and whether or not the local WalMart has enough Beanie-baby dolls in stock."

Baker pounded his desk. "We're real good at pointing the finger at foreign governments, but our screw-ups are always labeled *isolated incidents.* The American public is so damn gullible. Every day judges who know better, backed by politicians who *didn't inhale or take dirty money,* toss non-violent people in prison for decades over some marijuana. I can't help but think about Robert McNamara's recent book—in which he admits that he thought Vietnam was a senseless, unwinnable war, at the same time he was sending young people there to die—and wonder what remorseful government official will write a similar one on the drug war ten years from now. Damn it all, Wolf! Hearing this crap from you—a friend with firsthand knowledge—makes me so damn—"

"Chill out, Tommy! Let's get back to the story. Okay?"

Thomas nodded.

"Hey," Wolf said. "Am I really your friend?"

Baker smiled. "Hit it, hairball," replied the writer.

"Right. I was waiting for the payoff. After a couple hours, eighteen diaper dudes come truckin' up to my cargo doors humping these United States Marines duffel bags stuffed to the gills. I knew what came in bags like that, 'cause I'd seen them stacked in the warehouse on Williams Island. *That* cargo was definitely not in this kid's contract! I remember asking the head savage in the extra-extra large loin cloth: 'Hey. Where's the bales?'" Wolf wet his whistle and wiped it. "Never argue with a tribe of drunken injuns wearing Clint Eastwood guns, Baker."

"Why? What happened? What did they say?"

"No worry, gringo. Jus' do your *yob, Piloto.* That's beaner for pilot, Writer Man."

Baker frowned. "Yeah, I figured as much. So, how much cocaine did they load you down with?"

"Very good, Writer Man! They maxed me out. A long ton, easy. It was the first and last time I ever hauled *nose-candy.* I told my interpreter to tell them there was a mistake, and that I was going to take-off empty. Five minutes later? That Beech was surrounded by military vehicles! I was told they were filling the order my *superiors* had placed, and if I had a beef, I should take it up with them. That's exactly what I planned on doing, too. I didn't mind snorting a little rocket fuel now and then, but I'd made a vow not to transport that shit anywhere. Not even to offshore staging areas." Wolf looked away. "I guess the Colonel didn't think much of my vows."

"So, you took off to Andros loaded with cocaine for arms?"

Wolf knocked back his beer. "Affirmative. I was looking at head winds and a six-hour flight to a 5,000 foot grass strip smack dab in the middle of Andros. They called that little green baby, Hard Bargain, and it was one hell of a fitting name, Writer Man. Wolf just cranked up some energy music and cruised."

Wolf bobbed his head and banged out a beat on the side of Baker's monitor screen, while singing off-key. "*Running on empty! Running on...* Jackson Browne, Baker. Remember that one? *Running on...*"

Thomas covered his ears. "Nice, but don't give up your day job. *Comprende, Piloto?*"

Wolf frowned.

The writer typed, added color to his text, and fired questions. "Any radio contact?"

"Negatory. Standard procedure was to maintain radio silence until about sixty miles out, then reach down for the ground crew."

"Did you have a code to verify the ground crew?"

"No code. Voice recognition only, man," the pilot mumbled. Wolf's face lost its color.

The writer sensed revelation.

"The head agency honcho, who I met on the Haiti run, was supposed to be at Hard Bargain that night. Bastard!" Wolf muttered, choking up beer. "He was gonna pay me my fifty grand and brief me on some *changes,* but he was a no-show. His right-hand man was left in charge, took my call, and told me Arturos had an *appointment* in Miami. Years later, I heard it was really a three-day binge with an underage coke whore in Key West."

"Was it normal for him to supervise these off loadings?"

"In the early days it was, but eventually he got lazy and put his trust in certain underpaid employees. Big mistake. Because this particular ground crew had plotted to rip-off the dashing

Cuban colonel for several million bucks worth of blow, and stage a fiery crash scenario for yours truly."

Baker's eyes grew wide. His fingers flew across the keyboard.

"Here's some background info. First off, it wasn't unusual for pilots to touch down half-crocked or fatigued, and fuck up the landing—especially when flying overstuffed turkeys. Secondly, there are charred fuselages scattered all over islands like Andros which contain the ashes from many a fine smuggler's bones, and create a convincing cover-up for hits like these boys had in mind. Young Wolf encounters crosswinds. Wolf tired. Wolf stoned. Wolf come down hard at Hard Bargain. *Bam!*" The pilot slapped the wooden desktop. "Barbecued Wolf. And all the damn duffel bags burn to ash. A cryin' shame, Baker. The Colonel sheds tears for lost cash, and writes it off to the business-odds-Gods."

It was time to ask. "Tell me about this colonel, Wolf. Was he U.S. Military?"

"Nope. Patience, Baker. He was a Cuban-born CIA Station Chief. *Colonel A* was his code name, but like all the *Spook Shop's* honchos, Arturos did biz with the *real* colonels," Wolf snarled. "We'll get to him, I promise. Meanwhile, here's something else you can work in. There was a notorious band of thieves called the Black Pirates down that way. All us pilots knew about 'em. So did the boat captains."

Thomas's green eyes twinkled with curiosity. "What were they like?"

"What they were *really* like, was a bunch of cranked-up spades who ripped off amateur independents, then hauled their booty off to South Florida to sell for cash to the highest bidders. Sometimes they ripped the buyers for fun. Even sold dope to dirty Miami cops."

"Did they *look* like pirates? Give me some color here."

"You're the writer. Run with it. *Black Bohemians*, Baker. Can't get more colored than that! Can you? I think Black Pirates sounds cool. Shit, Baker. I want your book to sell. Remember? They did have these black cigarette boats." He lit a smoke.

"How about uniforms? Fatigues? Berets?"

"You know how blacks like hats. Sure. Dress them in fuckin' fatigues. Put little berets on those afros. Give'em a fuckin' flag and a symbol they all wear like swashbucklers on their belt buckles."

The writer's imagination ran wild with Black Pirates and the unfolding Andros affair. Words came fast and easy. Ten minutes later, Thomas leaned back, rested his eyes, and sighed. "So, how do Black Pirates fit in?"

"In a minute, Baker. I have to lift my leg. We've been at it three hours now. How 'bout a break?"

THEY WALKED to the edge of the grounds, and watched *The Lady of the Lake* passenger boat round the bend at Fields Point on her way to Stehekin.

Baker plucked a large pine cone from the grass and rolled it over the bank toward the water. "It's been a good session, Wolf."

"Good. I'm glad you're enjoying yourself. You know, it seems to me like you've been writing nonstop since that weekend Marla spent at the lodge. Hardly see ya anymore. What gives?"

Silence.

"Did I detect *Mr. Jealousy* maybe at the beaner restaurant the other night, Baker? Come on, she's getting under your skin. Isn't she?"

Thomas watched the pine cone bounce and roll en route to Chelan's crystal blue surface. It was his turn to respond to questioning. "Yeah, she's definitely getting under my skin," he said.

"I knew it! You're anti-love vow is in serious trouble. Huh?"

"Look, Jim. I..."

"Jim? *Moi...Jim?* Shit, Baker. This *is* serious!"

"Sorry I snapped at you that night. It actually bothered me a little afterward."

"No sweat. I bring out the animal in a lot of people. No hard feelings, Writer Man. Wolf has thick fur."

They extended closed fists, and banged them together top to bottom. It was one of those prison things they could never forget, called *Hitting the Rock,* and it signified agreement or unspoken understanding between two close friends.

Nathaniel Baker's yellow Chelan Valley school bus squeaked to a stop. The door swung open. The youngster charged the hill, high-fived the totem pole, and shouted, "Unca Tom! Unca Tom! Guess what? Teacher let us paint blue 'vironmental signs in town."

"What class was this, Nate? Graffiti 101?" Unca' Thomas inquired.

The bronze-skinned boy frowned, and pointed a paint stained finger. "Serious, Unca Tom. We made signs to teach tourists... *Keep Chelan Blue.*"

Unca' Tom ruffed Nathan's hair, then hugged his nephew. "That's great, Nate. Your mom's out back in the garden. Run and tell her the news." Baker's proud eyes misted-over as he spoke.

"Okay! Bye Unca' Tom. Bye-bye Mr. Woofy," the boy said.

The youngster scampered off like a coyote pup, with his Power Rangers lunch pail swinging from one hand. Wolf watched the writer's eye recording the picture.

"There goes a future environmentalist," said the pilot.

Thomas nodded.

"He's the boy you always wanted. Isn't he, Baker?"

"He's the reason we have a Chelan Alliance, too. I really wanted to have kids. Planned to," Thomas lamented. "Before all the shit hit the fan."

Two friends watched a wildflower sea swallow a puff of youthful wind-blown black hair in swaying sunglow, as Nathan disappeared.

"It's never too late you know," Wolf said.

"For what, kids?" Wolf's sentiment surprised Thomas.

"Kids, love. It's never too late for *anything,* Baker. When you gonna see Marla again?"

Baker shrugged. "It's not like she's the girl next door, you know. We live in separate worlds. She's used to slick CEOs and the competitive rush of the corporate crowd. It might as well be two thousand miles to Seattle, instead of two hundred. Maybe it's better like this."

"Listen to you! You must have seen another side of her to get so worked up. I've watched you and your part time romances for over three years now. No one's gotten to you yet. People do what they have to, to survive in their environments. You did it once in the joint. You told me you learned to act tough and keep quiet *inside* so you could focus on your writing, and regain your self-esteem. Remember? Wasn't that how you did your time?"

Thomas nodded. They started back for the lodge.

"Well? Maybe this dame is doing her time in the corporate maze of the Emerald City like a lost Dorothy in Oz, but that don't make her hard-boiled," Wolf said. "I've dated a few female CEOs in my day, pal. They may act tough inside their glass towers, but they melt like cotton candy in rain, in the arms of romantics like you."

Baker smiled, and opened the screen door. "Is that what life's all about, Mr. Woofy? Just doing time and marking days off calendars? Never rocking the boat? Never risking change?"

"Didn't used to be. Doesn't have to be." Wolf snatched a beer before they reached the writer's room. "Don't ya think I miss the old action days once in a while? Well, I do. I've even thought about smuggling cigarettes to the Canucks up north of the border…just for the rush of it, Writer Man."

Baker shook his head. "And I thought all you needed was young pussy and plenty of beer to keep yourself satisfied."

Wolf grimaced, growled, then grinned. "Ouch! Want some free advice, my friend? Make time to see Marla on her own turf. Take some ruby slippers. Maybe she's just waiting to be rescued from that glass prison of hers."

They sat back down. Baker read the screen. Wolf stared at the unopened beer, drooling.

"Okay, *Piloto*," Thomas said. "You were headed for a setup at a strip called Hard Bargain. Stop stalling, and give me a big finish for this scene."

"There was something in Carlos' radio voice that set me off from the git-go. But then he told me about the Colonel's *appointment* in Miami, and I got really paranoid—par for the course. Williams Island came into view, then Andros. It was twenty miles to Hard Bargain. I watched the Atlantic Ocean swallow the sun, flew over Fresh Creek, and thought about Carlos' voice. I checked out the action at the local marina, and searched for a sign. Then I spotted those black Scarabs moored in Hope Bay. Black Pirates' cigarette-boats, Baker! I was minutes from landing, and went on *alert-mode*. When the strip appeared, I decided to do a touch-n-go, and see what came out of the woodwork. If everything was kosher, I'd swing back around and explain myself. If not..."

"Explain touch-n-go."

"Normally, you cut the power on touch down, but on a touch-n-go, you keep the throttle halfback so you can pull up quick in case of an emergency. *Any* emergency. When that Beech hit that fuckin' grass...Black Pirates poured out that little pine forest! And Wolf had himself an emergency."

"Black Pirates?"

"Oh, hell yes! Hired by Carlos to do his dirty work."

"Packing weapons?"

Wolf nodded, and fingered the neck of his beer.

"Wearing fatigues, and little black berets?"

"Fuck yes! You got it. Cammy fatigues. Black berets with goddamn solid gold marijuana leaf pendants! And don't forget their matching belt buckles, and the lead spade wearing an eye patch and wavin' a fuckin' Black Pirates pennant. Shit, Baker. This was a trip."

"Where's Carlos at in this scenario?"

"In the middle of the fuckin' fairway, waving me in, giving me the okey-dokey. And off-right, I got the hit squad comin' on strong."

"What are you doing?"

"Full throttling the bitch. Getting lift, but the Black Pirates' M-16s are getting busy!"

Wolf's face grew wild. Nostrils flared. Beer bottle became throttle, and Writer's room the cockpit! Wolf was there...*back on Andros Island.*

And so was the writer.

"They stitched that Beech with lead, Writer Man! I couldn't gain altitude. Those .223 caliber rounds ate the fuck outta my gauges. One round burned through my forearm. Another plowed a fuckin' furrow above this ear." He bent back the ear in question, and displayed it to Baker. "Knocked me back in my seat!" Wolf's recliner rocked. "I took evasive action, turned away, kicked rudders with my feet. Climbing...but not fast enough! I was losing lots of blood, dazed and confused—like Led Zeppelin, Writer Man. I needed full throttle to get outta range, but my right arm was gone. I locked onto my bad right wrist with my left hand, and eased her forward..."

Wolf tilted back the brown beer bottle like a make-believe throttle. He was sweating heavily. Thomas was too.

"Want to take a break, Jim?" Baker asked. "Want a fresh beer?"

"Nope." James Shawn Wolf took a deep, long breath, exhaled, held up the forearm bearing the mark of the M-16 burned on the beast that fateful day back in 1978...massaged it with his thumb, and mumbled in funky pirate brogue, "Lucky for me, they had no silver bullets. Eh, 'me bucko? Arrrr!"

Baker nodded. He'd seen that scar a thousand times before, but had never bothered to ask how it got there.

"That day was the longest day of my life. It started twenty-four hours earlier from Fort Lauderdale's Executive Airport, loading crates of arms in a private, dummy-corporation/*Spook Shop*-owned hangar. I had jammed down hard, and spent minimal hours ground time. I was tired. Man, was I fuckin' tired. I was running out of fuel. Shit, Baker, running out of blood!" He laughed loudly. "I remember listening to Dan Fogleberg's *Fallen Angel,* fading in and out...in and out.

It was about one hundred sixty miles back to the Exec from Andros. I had a hangar there of my own, so I turned into a homing pigeon. Instinct, Baker. That's what kept me going.

Those last fifty miles were a blur." Wolf sucked air a moment. "When I dropped under radar for that last leg, I swear it was the only time I ever thought I wasn't gonna make it. I flew twenty feet off the Atlantic. Almost buzzed the beach. Pulled up to one hundred feet with both arms. Took her to one thousand so I'd look half-ass normal to the air controller's tower. Saw freaked-out faces on street people below. Saw cars cruising concrete, and a wild party at The Parrot Lounge. Or was it the Lauderdale Zoo Club?"

"I don't know. I wasn't there. Remember?" said the writer.

"The last thing *I* remember, was coming in on the final approach. I promised God all kinds of shit," Wolf said, breathing heavy. "If only I could make it back to my hangar before blacking out. It wasn't pretty, but I got that Beech to sit. The radio crackled commands. I couldn't comprehend, turned onto the wrong taxi way. Lights went out. The party was over."

The pilot relaxed, popped a warm beer, and sipped. "Needless to say, the controller got suspicious when he couldn't raise the Beech D-18 blocking the path of an outgoing Lear. They sent Airport Security out to see if I'd had a heart attack or something. Next morning? That fuckin' Barney Fife look-alike rent-a-cop had his smiling face on the cover of the *Miami Herald.*" Wolf chugged his beer.

"I woke up the following night in Broward General Hospital. Walls were white. Sheets were white. I actually believed there *was* a heaven, and *I* was in it. Had no idea how I got there though. So I yanked the IV out my arm, and assessed the situation. No cops in sight. *Allright.* Figured I musta' made it. Remembered those eighteen duffel bags! Figured I better split. Jumped up, and fell flat on my face in a shitload of pain. One of my legs was shackled to the damn bed. I let out a howl. The noise brought this nurse from hell in. She drooled over my naked ass until this DEA Agent stepped in saying, 'Looks like you're grounded Fly-Boy.'"

"Didn't you try to humor him with your wit and charm?" asked the writer.

"Nope. I asked how long I'd be grounded for. And he said, 'Quite a while, son. _Quite_ a while!'" The animation left Wolf's face. His body went limp as he sunk back in the recliner. "I'll take that fresh beer now, Baker."

"You certainly earned it," Thomas said, rising from his chair.

They walked outside and watched sunset over beautiful Lake Chelan, Washington, U. S. A.

The writer was wired, and couldn't cut the interview. "You sat quiet all through pretrial motions, convinced you'd never do a day?" Thomas inquired.

"That's right," replied the pilot. "I actually believed Arturos would pull some strings and fix the trial. They did send me a lawyer."

"Was he good? You never mentioned him before."

"Hell, I thought he was. He talked the talk, but I didn't know shit about law. Might say I was a virgin lamb in a wolves' den." He winked.

Thomas played a tiny, imaginary sympathy violin.

"In retrospect," noted the pilot. "I realized I had _two_ prosecutors. That little Jew-fuck scared me into a last-minute guilty plea. He told me if I went to trial, we'd not only lose, but we'd get hammered twice as hard for having the nerve to exercise my constitutional rights. Jew-boy figured his way, _we'd_ get six or eight years, and do two or three."

"How'd he figure that?"

"Said he was friends with the U.S. Attorney. Said there'd been this color photo of a ton of coke in the _Miami Herald,_ and an award given to some rent-a-cop by the mayor. John Q. Public craved blood. Someone decided that I had to pay. American justice, Baker. Kinda like the L.A. riots, Waco, Randy Weaver, and O.J. Simpson trial number one.

When the DEA debriefed me, they pushed hard for names and places. I lied my ass off. Pretended the head shot I took had given me partial amnesia. They pushed harder still. But my two _prosecutors_ made 'em back off suddenly. _Snap!_ Just like that. Like it was their job to insure my memory loss lasted until judgment day. They rushed the sentencing. I left the Honorable King's court with fifteen years hanging over my head, and that little pip-squeak, Jew-boy, sneaker-wearing, mouthpiece swearin' *we'd* file an appeal, and *we'd* never do more than one year." Wolf's lip curled and quivered. His canine teeth *tap-tapped.*

"Jew-boy said that right up until the steel slammed on that fuckin' cell door, and they chained *my* ass up like some rabid dog, and shipped *me* off on the diesel therapy circuit." Wolf spat bitterness. "This time, I landed on a real hard bargain, Atlanta's federal penitentiary. Right when Castro's castoffs arrived from Cuba's finest prisons and loony bins. Remember the *Marielitos?*"

The writer nodded. Now Wolf was rehashing old news. He had learned about the pilot's prison bit three years back, but not the details behind it. It was their common bond, and why they grew so close, so quickly. So Thomas listened patiently, awaiting the scene with the Lear, and what he *really* wanted to hear.

"There wasn't a month, a week, or a day, when I didn't expect someone from the Agency to spring old Mr. Woofy from that zoo. I thought they'd get His Honorableness to give me a B-2 number, and make me eligible for early release, but noooo! I waited five fuckin' years for the miracle day to dawn. Every mail call, I expected a legal letter with a get-outta-jail card. All I ever got was stroke magazines, and commissary money to buy cat food with. My mom died, and I was too damn dangerous to attend the funeral."

Baker watched Wolf dig up turf with the toe of his boot, and struggled to block out the memory of his own mother's passing while he was in prison down in Lexington, Kentucky.

"At least *I* didn't have a wife out there fucking around on me like *you* did, Baker. Had several bitches, though. They let me smell them all over, and even gave me head-jobs in the visiting room like D.C. Mayor Marion Barry supposedly got. But in the end? It was just me, the weight pile, and some dirty underwear bearing a sharp resemblance to Swiss cheese. I did have one good friend. You met him. The restaurant owner who saved our asses at Lake Union? He's the guy who picked me up when I got paroled in '84, and the pilot of that Lear jet we buzzed USP

Atlanta's rec-yard in half an hour after I hit the street! I hear they still talk about that little episode down Georgia way…"

Now, Writer! Ask him, thought Baker. "What became of Carlos and *The Colonel?*"

Glory faded from the pilot's tired face. Ghosts from past-life took its place. "Ask me about the ear thing. Okay? The ear wound got infected, and prison Medicare sucks. I lost my inner ear. Neat, huh?" He looked away and whistled. "That's why I tell all the babes I lost it in the war. It's the fuckin' truth. The great imaginary drug war! The international conspiracy our own damn Agencies created in Nam and keep alive for their own greedy-fuckin' selves."

"What about Carlos and the Colonel?" the writer pressed.

Wolf crammed hands in pockets, pissed. "Ask about getting my pilot's license back, or treasure hunting in the Bahamas. Ask how and why I ended up in the great Northwest flying that fuckin' Beaver! Ask about the first time I flew over Chelan…and fell in love for real. But don't ask about Carlos and the Colonel. Not tonight. All right?" The pilot's neck veins knotted up, and looked as if they might burst from beneath his skin. He was shaking and shouting.

Baker bit his lips, placed hands on hips, and decided to push his friend. "If not now, when?" he whispered. "What about those guys, Mr. Woofy?"

"You asshole, Baker! I tried like hell to block bitterness and cravings for revenge toward those guys. I had a nestegg stashed that kept me good and high between jobs, but it didn't last long. I would've flown smuggles if I wasn't on special parole." He threw a stone at some trees. "Know how hard it is to block-out some memories?"

Baker nodded, because he knew exactly how hard it was.

"From '86 to '88 I followed every lead, every rumor, hoping to find either one of those bastards. It was my Jekyll and Hyde era. Aged me ten years. Half of me wanted to find them both. Half hoped I never did."

The writer opened his mouth to ask.

Wolf spared him from the task, froze in place, and turned face-to-face. "You believe in karma, Thomas?"

"More than justice. Why?"

"Karma caught Carlos in the spring of '88...in a messy *accident* in the prop of a DC-3."

Baker's jaw dropped.

"Surprise, surprise," said the pilot.

Somewhere deep in those malamute-blue eyes, Thomas Baker saw rabid fire. For the first time in his association with the mysterious Mr. Wolf...*the writer was afraid to inquire further.*

Wolf lit a smoke and took a puff. "I never told you about some of the stuff I had to do in Nam..." Wolf drifted. The pilot's head turned. His cigarette ash grew long. His finger burned. Wolf felt no pain.

The writer drew a deep breath, and asked again. "And the Colonel?"

"Ah yes, the Colonel. When ant-head Nancy Reagan's *Just say no!* policy put the heat on South Florida, he kicked back, retired, and quickly got bored. Arturos wasn't content with the mere millions he had stashed. He wanted to make more cash, run more people, ruin more lives...be all that he could be! In '88, he crawled out from under a rock and ran for the Senate in South Florida, figuring the Cuban vote would insure a victory. A *friend* told me that Carlos admitted on his death bed that Arturos let me rot in Atlanta because I lost *his* load of coke." Wolf inhaled fresh cool air, and exhaled bad hot breath. "So, I stalked him."

"You what?"

"I stalked him, intent on getting the kill. Had it all set up for a campaign speech in West Palm Beach, two weeks before the general elect—"

Baker gave the cut sign "Maybe I shouldn't—"

"Shouldn't what? Don't tell me you support the 'don't ask, don't tell' policy, Baker! You asked. I'm telling. Relax. There's a happy ending. My buddy from Lake Union kept in touch with me, and got worried about his Wolf. Came down south for some fun-n-sun, and saved me from myself and hell just in the nick of time. Took me three thousand miles away for detox. Turned me on to the good life, clean air, and cigarette smuggling. For real, Writer Man. He bought me the Beaver, and I flew salmon from Alaska inbetween illegal cancer stick runs for cover," he sighed. "Good ol' 1989. It was a *verrr-ry* good year!"

"Okay, old Blue Eyes. But what happened with the election?"

"Funniest thing. Some photos of Arturos and a thirteen-year-old Fawn Hall look-alike hit the front page of the *Miami Herald.* John Q. Public was pissed. Colonel A was preachin' family values in the old dominion…had to pay his dues. Needless to say, he lost."

They laughed hard, and tapped their closed fists together.

"Pulled a Gary Hart on him," said Thomas. "Right on!"

Again, they tapped their fists top to bottom.

"Karma, dude," cried Wolf. "But I heard he shook off the defeat and rose above it all. The man lost his taste for politics and politicians. Couldn't *be* one, so he decided to help buy them, and own them. Colonel A followed the footsteps of other great Americans—Kissingers and such. He hired out to foreign nationals as a U.S. liaison." Wolf remembered his friend's report about Arturos showing up in Vancouver, and lied. "And I haven't thought of him since. End of story, Writer Man."

Baker opened the door. They bellied up to the Granite Falls Bar.

"I'm buyin'," the owner offered.

"No shit, Sherlock," hissed Wolf.

They downed a couple shots.

"Ever wish you would have done the patriotic thing, and hung Arturos out to dry when the DEA debriefed you? This guy had it coming, and you would have done the country a favor," said the writer.

The pilot grimaced. "A) I'm no snitch, and I wouldn't send anyone to the joint. B) We wouldn't be talking right now, 'cause I'd be planted in some pet cemetery, feeding fuckin' maggots!" Wolf responded. "Either that, or I'd be a fugitive."

Another shot went down hard in their bellies and burned.

"You *had* your ex-wife. I *had* the Colonel. May they both rest in peace and never cross our paths," Wolf bellowed, in his best pirate's brogue. "Wherever they may be—'me hearty Bucko. Arrr! Arrr!"

Once more they tapped fists.

"Amen, Brother Woofy," Thomas said.

The writer had a mind to drink some more with his wild friend, but Wolf had a wanton waitress to attend.

"Amen, Brother Thomas," Wolf whispered reverently. The pilot rose, winking one Clint Eastwood eye. "Be at the dock with that whiz-kid brother of yours at dawn, Writer Man," he added. "And ye best be ready to fly. Arrrrr."

Chapter 22

Burning Beaver

AT 11:30 P.M. lights faded above Forever Neon. And for day number three, Miss Pai's auto remained on the premises, as did she.

Next door at Lone Wolf Air, a wayward waitress with ratty hair crammed wrinkled tights and panties in a sequined purse, hit the lights, and—like a nurse done seeing a needy patient—*came* and went; her time well spent. The pickled pilot—well-exercised—puffed one last hit, and closed his eyes.

THE DARK FIGURE no longer had to hide. He parked his black Zodiac pontoon-side. Gloved hands quickly removed an inspection panel on the 1947 Dehavilland Beaver's engine cowling. A tiny techni-light, held tight by clenched teeth, concentrated a red ray on a soft copper supply line and some steel braided hose. Skilled fingers—which were boss—uncoiled a strand of jeweler's floss...*and went about their business.*

AS PASTEL DAWN'S watercolors washed a sleepy Chelan morning sky to denim blue, pilot Wolf conducted his preflight inspection. Everything checked true.

Neon and Pai conversed dockside with the Baker Brothers.

"You have great trust and confidence in your Seattle chemist friend?" the Chinese woman inquired for a second time.

Bill nodded. "Listen, Pai. We all understand the risk you took. And anyone who gives a damn about this lake would applaud your courage."

She blushed, then smiled.

"Only the five of us know how these cultures were *acquired*," Thomas added, placing a hand upon her shoulder. "And we promise it will stay that way. Because of your efforts, we will soon know—"

"Bullshit!" bellowed Wolf from the Beaver's cockpit. "We'll never know diddly-squat if we don't saddle up and get it on."

Pai made one last inspection of the customized Igloo cooler at her feet, and passed it on to Bill. "Here. This protect them from turbulence in tiny little airplane," she said.

"Turbulence, my ass," Wolf growled. "It's smooth and clear all the way to the Emerald City, Missy. And don't forget—these kids are flying with me."

The Bakers boarded. Cargo doors closed.

"Call us when you get back!" Neon shouted, hugging Pai.

The Beaver's radial engine sprang to life like scores of horses' hooves clattering over cobblestone streets. Oil quickly bathed and caressed its hundreds of moving parts, which were cold from a long night's rest. As she warmed, the trademark clattering subsided, and was replaced by the steady beat of a time-proven power plant.

Wolf routinely scanned the engine gauges: oil pressure—*fine*; fuel flow—*normal*; RPMs—*normal*; altimeter—*check*; instruments and gyros—*set for takeoff*. The pilot taxied into the lake. All control movements were normal. The pre-takeoff run-up was unremarkable.

"Loo-king good, kids! Perrr-fect morning for a mission," Wolf proclaimed.

The Beaver master ordered her engine up to takeoff power. The Dehavilland surged through the water. Pilot and plane became one. The Beaver was among the most durable floatplanes ever designed, and James Shawn Wolf respected her. Over the years, she had become an extension of his very being.

Soon the aircraft was racing over the smooth morning face of Lake Chelan, straining to break the adhesive bond between pontoons and water. *Swoosh!* They broke free—solid in the air. The Beaver accelerated toward now-tranquil Stormy Mountain, banked sharply, and faded to a speck of dust in the western sky, absorbed by a forest green sea.

FROM HIS vantagepoint at Lakeside Park, Nicholas Gordon watched the floatplane's departure through high-powered binoculars. When the Dehavilland Beaver cleared its first mountain peak and disappeared, Nick traded his binoculars for the morning paper, and prepared for the rest of his day.

THOMAS BAKER reclined in his plush copilot's seat.

Brother Bill cradled the cooler behind him, carefully considering some potential scenarios. "What if it is Ming Yaht?" he yelled up front.

Thomas thought a moment. "Can't go to the authorities with illegally obtained evidence. Only the feds play that—"

"Fuck the authorities!" Wolf shouted, wagging his middle finger. "Trust me. We have to tarnish these chinks' image. Chinese can't stand losing face. Image is everything to these slants."

Thomas Baker blocked-out Wolf's blanket condemnation of the Chinese people, and nodded in agreement with the plan.

"Don't you have an editor at the Seattle P.I. who will stand behind your copy?"

"Sure, Wolf. If I can verify my sources," answered the writer.

Bill tugged Tom's shoulder. "Ah, Tom?"

"Yeah, Bill."

"What about anonymous sources?"

Wolf's head bobbed responsively. "The kid's right, Baker! Journalists can have confidential informants, too. Just like the all-powerful feds. Here's your chance to flex that mighty *power of the pen* you've preached about since the day I met you."

"Hate to agree with him, Blood, but he just might have something there," Bill interjected.

"How 'bout this?" Wolf suggested. "Near Disaster in an Eden called Chelan. A tale of power plays, government corruption, greed...*and murder.*"

Eerie silence followed Wolf's remark. Everyone thought about Councilman Barnes. The pilot flew his plane. The brothers peered through windows. The village of Ardenvoir came into view beneath them, then quickly vanished in the trees.

Wolf broke the silence. "Will you take over the Alliance if he's gone?"

Thomas recalled his promise to the councilman and nodded reverently.

"There goes Writer Man vow number two," Wolf declared.

The Wenatchee National Forest spread green as far as their eyes could see. The rugged Wenatchee River emerged occasionally, carving cool, deep canyons, and roaring across rocky terrain, with angry white rapids foaming like rabid teeth taking big bites of Ponderosa Pine.

Lake Washington was nearly an hour away. Prolonged peace and quiet bored Wolf, even early in the day. The pilot stealthily pulled back the power. The Beaver declined quickly, like a theme park roller coaster.

"Hey! What gives?" Bill quizzed, gripping the cooler.

"He's just screwing around," Thomas assured his brother.

"Snitch!" Wolf complained, flicking Thomas's ear. "This trip ain't costing you two a goddamn dime. The least you can do is entertain me with some brother babble."

Thomas nodded.

"Hey, how 'bout that Neon?" Bill began.

The Beaver miraculously stabilized.

"Next thing you know, she'll be moving in with her Siamese cat," said Bill.

"He seems happy, though," Thomas remarked.

"Happiness...is a warm gun! Hap-py-nesss...is a warm gun, Baker boys," Wolf sang, Beatles like.

Another Cascade peak loomed before them. Their pilot gunned the engine, and the Beaver climbed higher.

"Hey, Wolfman. How come you never let any yetis shack up with you? Ever tried the marriage gig?" asked the younger Baker.

"Oh, hell no, Billy boy!" Wolf screamed. "Too much work. Too much compromising for this ol' dog. You know what I say. Don't ya, Writer Man?"

Thomas nodded.

Wolf howled. "Fuck that! In the beginning, they're attracted to our craziness. When we let 'em get close? They quit wearing those slinky dresses with red stiletto heels, and start slumming around the house in one-piece cat-print pajamas with a mud pack on their face, and their hair up in curlers. Then, they try to tame us. Bingo! The battle of the sexes starts, and life gets either very stressful, or very boring. Fuck that shit. Owwww! I gotta' give the kid's China Doll credit, though. It took guts for her to snatch those—"

The Beaver's engine coughed. Only Wolf could perceive the brief but disturbing pause in the radial engine's beat. The split-second cough broke his entranced stare at the mountainous terrain below, and turned the switch on his *alert* mode. His sharp eyes darted to the instrument panel. Oil pressure was dropping. *Bad gauge?* Wolf asked himself. *Hell no,* he answered, as the oil and cylinder head temperatures also started rising. These signs confirmed that he had not imagined the momentary burp of her engine. *Think fast!* the pilot thought, as the smile disappeared from his face. *What to do?* "Something's wrong, kids. We've got a problem," he announced to his passengers.

"Yeah, right. We ain't scared, Wolfboy," Bill scoffed.

"Save the act for the Comedy Club, *Piloto,*" Thomas remarked, but even as the words left his lips, he could sense that all the B.S. had ceased.

Wolf gave them a hard silencing look. "I'm not fuckin' around here," he said. "This is serious. Oh, shit!" He saw oil weeping from the top of the engine cowling, creeping over the windshield, and beginning to block their forward vision.

The Beaver banked sharply.

"What are you trying to do, man? Re-enact the Andros affair?" Thomas screamed.

"No way, asshole," Wolf replied.

"Then straighten up and fly right. Quit playin' a—"

Pffftt!

The engine belched again. The odor of burning oil coming off the overheating engine tainted the air inside the cockpit and irritated their eyes.

"Cut the bullshit, dude!" Bill Baker demanded.

Wolf glowered over his shoulder, coughing, blinking, and rubbing his eyes. "Think this is a fuckin' joke, kid? Just keep a good grip on that cooler, 'cause we're in for a rough ride."

Their pilot snapped into *command* mode. Playtime ceased, and the seasoned pro and all of his years of experience took control.

"Listen carefully," barked Wolf. "We're losing oil pressure, and this baby's gonna quit on me any minute. Baker, pop that window! Wolf needs another set of eyes. What's our location?"

"I see Merritt on the horizon," Thomas replied. "Fish Lake's about a mile off, right of Merritt. How about landing there?"

"No way!" Wolf snapped. "Too far. Where's the river?"

"The river?"

"Yeah. The fuckin' river. It widens out at the fork of the White Wenatchee. Find it!"

"It should be over the next peak," said Thomas.

"Keep me posted," commanded the pilot. "Now, tighten your seat belts and shoulder harnesses."

The brothers hesitated.

"Now!" Wolf ordered. "And empty your pockets too. Pens, keys. Anything sharp gets stashed in this pouch." Wolf tossed a padded bag to Thomas. "Bill, put that damn cooler between your legs!" Wolf bit a hole in his lip. His mind was racing, analyzing their options. "Oil is the lifeblood of any engine, brothers, and this bird is being bled dry."

The pilot carefully increased power, leery of how much the radial engine could give—without giving out. Landing in trees could cost them their lives. He preferred an old narrow logging road to that, but with all the green spring growth, none were visible. The Beaver slowly gained altitude. They cleared another peak.

Wolf knew he had to prolong the radial's life. He quickly reduced power just enough to keep flying, enriched the fuel mixture, and opened the engine cowl flaps—all necessary measures to help cool the hot engine and delay seizure. Another glance at the gauges: Oil temp—*buried solid in the red!* Oil pressure—*almost nil!*

"She's running rougher by the minute," Wolf shouted.

Engine failure imminent, Wolf thought. Hot oil fumes continued to filter into the cockpit. His fears now included the twin threats of fire and asphyxiation.

"Wolf! Over there," Thomas said. "Can you see it?"

Thick, honey-brown oil spread further up the windscreen.

"Wolf can't see shit," the pilot reported. A skillful yawing of the plane allowed him a glimpse out his side window. "Fuckin' A! That' she blows! Good work, Baker. That's the White Wenatchee. Now listen up. We'll both keep looking out these side windows, but as we near the water, you're the main man. When we start the final dive, give me the distance points between these pontoons and those trees, then call out the feet before water contact. Got that?"

"Got it," said the writer.

"Good," said the pilot. Wolf reduced the throttle to the minimum necessary manifold pressure required to keep flying, and put the plane in a gentle, powered dive, toward their only shot at surviving—a short but wide stretch of the White Wenatchee River. Andros, Haiti, and a hundred other missions flashed through his mind. He had to keep her running, avoid a fire, and get the hell out of the air as soon as possible.

Wolf continued his mental dialogue. *Westerly winds. Tight-ass spot. Land into the wind, stupid. Safer. Glide baby...glide! Maintain airspeed. Save enough for a landing flare. Fly the plane, hot shot!* Baker's eyes would be the crucial element in judging the landing flare. The plane drifted down. The pilot nudged the throttle. *Still responsive.* The river disappeared, and was replaced by waves of green. The tree-tops grew closer. "Whatta ya' see, Baker?" said the pilot.

"Jagged rocks, canyons, and white water," reported Thomas. "Wait! I see your wide stretch up ahead. Wolf! It's not *that* wide."

"Too bad, Writer Man. It's all we got. This is gonna be a Wolf special, no-shit, one-shot emergency landing."

"What can I do?" Bill asked.

"Thank God you're flying Lone Wolf Air, kid," answered the pilot.

"Wolf. Watch out! The trees are—"

"Tough titty, Tommy! No choice. When I clear this next hill, get ready to call out distances. Then we dive."

When they cleared the next ridge, Wolf yawed again to get a side-window glimpse of the final stretch. *The glide path looked good enough.* "Unlatch your door, Tom," Wolf said.

"What? Are you crazy?"

"Unlatch it! And be prepared to make a quick exit—just in case. And don't forget to unfasten your seat belts," the pilot said.

Wolf tweaked the throttle—as he had been doing all the way down—hoping the engine wouldn't seize on him. He would need some power during the last minute of flight to correct any miscalculations, and cushion the landing flare. *No response!* But she hadn't seized on him. She just quit. *Too hot.*

Wolf swallowed hard. His safety margin was gone. Now the windmilling propeller—no longer driven by the engine—was creating more drag and pulling the Beaver down. Their odds for survival had been substantially reduced. *Maintain airspeed. Fly. Fly the wing!* Airspeed quickly dwindled. Wolf pushed the yoke forward, converting precious altitude into airspeed—**and the wing flew!**

One small, forested ridge now separated them from the target, but without engine power, their glide path would carry them dangerously close to disaster. The Beaver quickly descended.

"Tree tops," Baker cried out. "Wolf! Too close to—"

The upper branches of a giant pine banged one pontoon.

"Wolf! Pull up," Baker screamed. "We're gonna hit—"

The stall warning horn began barking intermittently. They were running out of air, and losing lift. Wolf instinctively pushed the nose down further. "Brace yourselves!" he shouted.

The Baker Brothers panicked.

The modified glide trajectory forced Wolf to bury the Beaver in the rows of pines jutting up from the rocky ridge. Tree tops tickled, then scraped like squeaky chalk, across the underside of the plane.

Bill Baker wrapped his arms around the cooler of mutant bacteria, lowered his head, and prayed.

The Beaver sank deeper, snapping, bending, breaking branches as she bullied her way through the final resistance and miraculously broke free—five hundred feet above the White Wenatchee River! And not a moment too soon.

Wolf slammed the yoke forward, and regained airspeed and a modicum of control.

"Oh, God! Watch out," Baker screamed.

Wolf added full flaps, and began to slip the craft. The Beaver descended rapidly. Wolf's hands and feet moved instinctively. "Baker! Whatta ya' see?"

"Small fishing boats!"

"Any power lines?"

"No pow—"

Some cargo broke free and crashed to the floor. Crucial seconds passed.

"Showtime, Baker," Wolf shouted. "Start calling out the distance to the water."

Thomas saw tiny boats grow larger. Terror-struck faces turned skyward at the sight of the plummeting floatplane. "Three hundred feet," he called out.

Wolf slipped, banked, then lined up with the river and dropped as fast as he could.

"Two hundred feet!" Thomas shouted.

Through his side window, all Wolf could see was stands of pines and outcroppings of rock as the Beaver sank between two sharply rising slopes. He yawed right, then left, snatching his final look at the river below.

"One hundred feet, Wolf. We're coming down fast!" The writer watched fishermen frantically rowing for shore. A couple in a canoe paddled out of their path.

"Talk to me, Baker!"

'Seventey-five feet! When you gonna do it, James?"

"Patience, Writer Man." Wolf straightened the planeline with the flow of the river.

"Fifty feet!"

Seconds to impact.

"Thirty feet. Do it, James!"

*Just concentrate...*Wolf thought, with his white knuckles shaking.

"Twenty feet!"

"Pull up!" both brothers yelled.

"Timing, boys," Wolf said. *Now.* **Flare time!** Wolf summoned all his strength, tugged back the yoke, increased the pitch of the wing, and attempted to cushion their touch down.

The stall warning horn sounded the alarm.

Slap! Varroom!

The pontoons hit hard—too hard. The plane bounced high into the air.

Wolf held back the yoke—heart pounding—awaiting the second impact, and wishing he still had power remaining to prevent any fatal porpoising.

Whoosh!

Wolf held his breath, straining to keep the plane upright.

The Beaver shimmied and shook, dancing in broken water like a trophy Blue Marlin just introduced to an angler's hook. But the battle quickly ended...and much better than anticipated. The Beaver had landed. The big Dehavilland high-lift wing had saved the day.

Silence ensued as they drifted toward the edge of a swirling eddy.

Wolf exhaled a sigh of relief. He released his shoulder harness, cleared his throat, and took a bow.

The Baker Brothers applauded.

"Everybody okay?" the pilot inquired.

The passengers nodded.

Wolf wandered to the rear of the aircraft, rummaged through scattered gear, and tossed two worn canoe paddles at his passengers' feet.

The brothers gave him a puzzled look.

"What?" Wolf asked. "I just saved your asses! The least you two can do is row this beast to shore."

They emerged from the crippled craft like newsworthy astronauts, squinting in the early morning sun. Applause from nearby fishermen and the curious customers and employees of the White Wenatchee Resort Cafe reverberated across the water. Wolf walked to the front of the pontoon, bowed to the crowd, and began assessing damage.

Bakers stood by the door, paddles in hand, shell-shocked.

"Ahoy, Bakers!" the pilot called. "Roll up yer pant legs or strip to yer skivvies. Straddle those pontoons! Yer exercise nuts. Right? Yer rowers. Right?"

They nodded.

"Aye! So row. And see that buxom beauty servin' breakfast thar' ashore?"

"The foxy blond wearing the red tank top?" Bill questioned, as his paddle dug deep into the White Wenatchee River.

"Aye, Billy boy! Set a course for the wench. But ye best remember that ye be a married man. And, since yer brother's been bitten by the love bug, the big tittied broad's all mine. Arrr. Stroke! Stroke! Stroke!" Wolf called to his crew, right up until they struck a sandbar, and jerked to a halt.

The pilot dove in first. The Bakers quickly followed suit.

They walked the Beaver around the sandbar, and beached it by the big blond.

"Morning, Miss. Could ya bring me mates and I three cold brews?" Wolf inquired in an animated pirate brogue.

The waitress's face lit. She licked cherry lips, charmed by the daredevil pilot. "I'm sorry, sweetheart, but we can't serve alcoholic beverages before lunch," she said.

Wolf hung his head like a puppy, and pawed wet sand with his shoe. "I humbly beseech thee, lass. I don't often partake of the drink this early in the day. But ya see, she's been a rough one."

The cafe's customers tapped spoons on coffee cups. "Serve him! Serve him! Serve him," they chanted.

The blond shook her head, and smiled sensuously. "I'll wager that this resort's owner would think this morning's entertainment was worthy of bending the rules for. Have a seat," she sighed. "And I'll bring you those beers."

"Thank ye, lass," Wolf grinned.

The resort owner was a burly retired Navy pilot who'd spent seven years at Puget Sound's Whidbey Island Naval Station. The well-endowed waitress turned out to be his daughter.

After it cooled down, Wolf and the owner loosened the Zeus fasteners around the Beaver's cowling, and exposed the big radial engine. There was oil everywhere.

"Lucky there wasn't a fire," the owner remarked.

Wolf systematically checked every line and each connection. "Oil cap—tight. Dip stick—in place. Oil filter—fine," he declared. He wiped her down with a gas rag. Then he found them. Tiny cuts in two lines. *Too fresh, and too clean for anything but...*

"Bastard was good," the resort owner observed. "Sure doesn't look like a random act of vandalism to me."

"Nope. Definitely knew what he was doing," Wolf replied, as his sense of humor deserted him, and anger took its place. "Where's the nearest auto parts store?" Wolf asked the old pilot.

"There's a NAPA over in Merritt. Think you can fix her?"

"Oh, hell yes!" Wolf declared.

The big blond was giving Wolf hand signals from behind her daddy's back. She held up her key ring and pointed toward her car.

"Mind if I catch a ride into Merritt with your daughter?" asked Wolf.

The owner scratched his chin. "I guess that would be all right. Can you drive our guest into Merritt, Lisa?"

The daughter took off her apron. "Sure, Daddy," she said, handing it to him.

The Baker Brothers took a break from washing oil off the plane to watch their pilot at work. They shook their heads and snickered as Wolf and waitress disappeared into the woods.

"Say! Do you have any enemies?" the old pilot shouted to Wolf, just as his daughter revved the engine of her Trans Am.

"Evidently I do now," muttered Wolf.

BY THE TIME the repaired floatplane reached Bill's friend's private pier on Mercer Island, they were six hours late. His company's lab was closed until morning, so Matt invited the Beaver crew to spend the night at his place. After showers and cocktails, their host suggested they hit a club to hear some of Seattle's famous grunge music.

Since the accident, Wolf's *alert* mode had never quit ringing. He vetoed loud amplifiers and poor singing, and laid down the law. "Pick up the phone and call your favorite carry out, Mr. Chemistry, 'cause we're not letting these culture samples out of our sight. Business before pleasure, kids."

While they waited on their pizza delivery, Thomas watched powerboats cruise wakelessly past Matt's lakefront property at sunset. The morning's incident had reminded him of life's fragility. He felt a rush of insecurity—as close calls often stir inside a man—and looked to distant purple mountains, beyond which lay Chelan. His world was there, but tonight he was on Marla's side of the great divide. And it was too much to bear.

Thomas felt strangely alone. He paced the floor with hands in pockets, and stared at Matt's telephone.

Wolf watched the writer squirm until he had seen enough. He twitched one Clint Eastwood eye. "Go on, Baker," he said. You're excused from guard duty. Go to her, tough guy."

A HALF-HOUR LATER, Thomas exited a cab on Seattle's Capitol Hill with a single red rose in his hand. A petite gray-haired woman peered at him through pale pink sheers.

Georgette Kramer opened her screen door. "May I help you, young man?" she inquired from her side of the duplex.

Thomas Baker pulled a crumpled paper from his blue jeans pocket and presented it. "I was looking for Miss Marla Jean Decker," he said, showing the woman the directions Marla had given him.

Georgette's green eyes twinkled. "Would you be the gentleman from Chelan?"

"Yes, ma'am."

"Oh my. My Marla speaks highly of you dear! Never seen her so happy as—"

Marla Decker had heard enough. She opened the adjacent door and pretended to put the cat out. "Thomas! What a nice surprise. It's okay, Georgette. This is Thomas Baker, the gentleman I met in Chelan."

"Oh yes, the writer." The landlady smiled knowingly.

Marla ran her hand through her hair, and blushed.

Georgette watched Thomas lift and cradle the calico cat. "Our little Miss Punkin doesn't normally let strangers pet her, Mr. Baker. You should feel honored that she's taken a liking to you."

Baker winked at Marla. "Believe me, ma'am, I do."

"Goodnight Georgette," Marla hinted.

"Goodnight dear. Nice meeting you, Mr. Baker. By the way, I truly enjoy reading your articles. Marla saves them all, you know." Georgette grinned as she closed the door.

The twosome stepped inside.

"So Thomas, what brings you here?"

"Did I come at a bad time?" he asked, handing her the rose.

She rocked upon tiptoes, pressed pretty petals to her nose, and sighed. "You're welcome anytime. It's just that you look...tired."

He drew her near, and softly kissed her cheek.

"Something wrong? Did you have a bad day?" she whispered, rubbing his temple.

Thomas had craved her warm touch since landing on Lake Washington. He shook his head. "Just tired of business, that's all," he said. "How about allowing me to take you to dinner?"

Marla Decker was thrilled to see the writer again. She was melted by his touch, mesmerized by his golden jade eyes, and impressed by his easy, cultured manner. She thought of their weekend together—the magic of Domke Falls, and *kayaks*. "Dinner?" she said. "Sure. I'd like that." She wanted every moment he could give her. She'd planned an exercise run around Greenlake, but quickly changed that to an evening stroll to feed the ducks, and invited him along.

They drove her truck to the lake, then walked and talked along its path while tossing bread crumbs to the ducks. They sat on a small hill beneath the canopy of a fragrant Japanese Magnolia tree, and watched couples—first dates, newlyweds, young parents, and senior citizens—stroll hand in hand around the water's edge.

The spell was cast once more, and he at 44—resigned to bachelorhood—and she at 33—like she knew she would—fell softly as the shedding petals from delicate blossoms above. They rolled on grass bedding. It felt like first love, so simple and free. Ducks quit feeding just to watch them, and quacked approvingly.

Eventually, they picked themselves up and joined the parade of lovers on the path. In the warmth of Thomas's embrace, Marla professed her love for Seattle, and yet foretold of fast approaching days, when she'd have her fill of big city ways and the tolls they extracted from those who chose to dwell there.

He stroked her hair.

Together they gazed beyond Greenlake to the naturally beautiful snow-capped Olympic Mountains whose glacial blue pearlescent glow so greatly upstaged the made-up face of the elegant Emerald City.

Thomas sighed. Somewhere out there, the ghostly lights of Bainbridge Island's ferry sailed silently across Elliot Bay. He abruptly looked away recalling another day, another life, his ex-wife.

"How do you feel about Seattle, Thomas?" Marla asked, sensing his distance.

He swallowed the past and savored the present. "Oh, there are tons of good reasons to visit here," Baker replied. "There are endless lessons on the human condition, free to learn on every sidewalk, in every market stall, in every skyscraper's offices, down any dark alley. Seattle has every cultural and retail delight you could imagine. But there are even more reasons to do your living in quiet places, and feed on wide-open spaces, knowing full well that these curiosities are only hours away when you're ready for a refresher course—when you think there is something you've missed."

She tugged his sleeve.

He hugged his girl.

They gently kissed.

Marla loved his words. He was so open with her. Since their weekend together, he had sent her his work-in-progress, and requested her opinions. She'd sent him poetry. She was falling hard and fast for the writer from Granite Falls. In Chelan, they'd shared other passions. Tonight they shared philosophy and dreams. Having satisfied their cerebral hunger, they sought to slake another. Marla pointed to a red pagoda-styled restaurant.

Thomas shook his head, recalling the morning's near disaster and Wolf's suspicions. "I love Chinese, but not tonight," he said. "Do you like Japanese food?"

"*Hai! Thomas-san.* I love it," she exclaimed playfully.

He smiled. "There's a great place on Broadway I go to every chance I get. It's close to your house. We can drive back and walk from there. Trust me, you'll like it. It's called *Tobiko Row.*"

"I trust your taste, Thomas," she replied. "Let's go!"

HEADS TURNED when the couple entered *Tobiko Row.*

"*Thomas-san, Hai!*" shouted the owner, his wife, and the sushi chef.

Thomas and Marla sat at the sushi bar. They nibbled on crunchy seaweed-wrapped salmon skin rolls with bright orange flying-fish eggs sprinkled on top. They shared sips from a giant Sapporo draft beer, and fed each other fluffy morsels of tamago in wedding cake fashion. The owner brought them hot saki rice wine. Soft string music played in the background as the saki soaked in.

Baker thought of his discovery in Big Creek Cove on the day Marla had surprised him. He thought about her mysterious fax interception, the culture samples Pai had collected, and the morning's sabotage of Wolf's plane. He didn't wish to alarm her, or spoil their mood, but he was concerned about the direction in which things were headed. He watched her flirt with the silly sushi chef, then pour the chef some hot saki. He cleared his throat.

"Marla, just how well do you know the people you're working for?" Baker quizzed.

She rolled her eyes, and slapped her thigh. "Well, I'm not some corporate call girl, if that's what you're worried about."

Perhaps he'd mishandled the question, but he certainly loved the answer. "I'm sorry," he said. "I didn't mean it that way."

She scooted closer, and filled their porcelain cups from a warm flask. "Apology accepted. It's all right to ask. After all, you've answered all my questions." She found his apparent jealousy flattering. "For the record, I've traveled with the Pos only once, to the Warwick's funeral. And that's because I requested to come with them to Chelan to pay my respects. I was Russ's personal secretary. Remember?"

She squeezed Baker's hand, stared into his warm green eyes, and traveled back to the days preceding the Warwick family's tragic death.

Russ had been so nervous toward the end of summer. He took several impromptu trips to Canada, and displayed a growing sense of paranoia each time he returned home to Seattle. Then there was the time she stopped by Russ's place the week before his death, and encountered his jittery houseguest, Li Wong—a Chinese Canadian also employed by Ming Yaht. Three days later, Russ informed her that his Chinese visitor had died from food poisoning at his home in Vancouver. Her female intuition led her to believe that Russ wanted to share some deep, dark secret with her after Li Wong's death, but then he rushed off to Chelan that weekend. And they never spoke again.

Marla had wanted to mention all of this to Bill Baker at the funeral, but wasn't sure if it was only her imagination getting the best of her. "Why do you ask about my employers, Thomas?"

He was drunk on saki and her scent. She was lovely. He could see no reason to share all his suspicions with her, to put monsters under her bed, to mention the missing councilman and really scare her. Even if there was a war brewing, it wasn't her war.

"Ming Yaht may be violating some environmental regulations in Chelan," he told her. "We don't have any proof yet, though." He was starting to sound like a cop again, instead of a date. It was time to change the subject. He raised his saki cup high above his head, and offered an invitation to the owners and their sushi chef to drink with them.

They clicked cups. "*Compai!*" they shouted.

Marla swallowed hard. "Okay. Get out your notepad, Mr. Writer. Let's put some things to rest. I quit Merrill Lynch over three years ago when I heard they were hiring over at Ming Yaht's magnificent nouveau highrise hell. The only person down there I got close to was Russ. Otherwise, I have a drink with some of the girls on Thursdays, I type, I file, answer the phone, and send faxes. I enter information and do research on a computer. Thomas, it's a job! That's all. A damn good paying job that allows me to maintain my own identity, and independence from—"

"From us heathen men?" he asked.

She nodded.

They laughed.

The owner cut the elevator music, and made an announcement to the small crowd of regular patrons. "Hai! *Domo arigato*! Our Karaoke Night will start now. Feel free to step up to the mike and loosen your vocal cords. My wife and I spent this year's vacation money on this fancy new karaoke set-up. So please, don't be shy!"

While a well-sakied California-transplant businessman slurred the words to *San Francisco*, Thomas stealthily paid their tab and spoke to his owner friend. Moments later, he strolled up to the tiny stage, took the microphone from its stand, and announced in a saki-smooth voice, "This is a very old Nat King Cole tune, but like it's title, it is timeless. I'm singing this one for Marla...and it's called *L-O-V-E*."

The writer snapped his fingers, listened for the intro, and sang.

"**L**, is for the way you look at me. **O**, is for the only one I see. **V**, is ve-ry, ve-ry, x-tra or-din-ary. **E**, is even more than an-y-one that you adore. And..."

Several couples in the crowd kissed.

One Seattle secretary's eyes got misty.

When Thomas sat the mike down, everyone applauded. Goose bumps covered his arms as he walked toward the sushi bar. He felt like he'd just written a touching poem. It was something he had not done in years. He saw Marla's broad smile, and felt good. The world was right.

She saw yet another side of him, and liked it.

They called it a night.

LEMON-SCENTED CANDLES flickered. Light refracted from a beveled mirror found Thomas sinking into a clawfoot tub, soaking in a mineral bath, sipping herbal tea, and enjoying hot jazz broadcasting from her National Public Radio station. He almost feared how relaxed he felt here—or anywhere—with her.

A curious calico cat's head appeared at the bathroom door. Thomas coaxed her to the edge of the tub, and Punkin dipped a

trusting paw below the waterline in search of a playfully submerged finger.

The wood floors creaked. The skittish cat scampered away.

She'd been gone a while, but now his hostess crept into the
bathroom. Her hair was swept up, Geisha-girl style. She was
wearing a silk sable kimono with bright orange butterflies
embroidered upon it. Her extended arms held a large bath towel.

"Ready to dry now, honorable *Thomas-san*?" she asked
enticingly.

He rose slowly, bowed a hard, steaming wet body, and
stepped out of the tub. His lusting eyes locked on to her. He
was quickly aroused by her touch.

She tortured him briefly, breathing fiery breath in firm places,
before dropping the towel-drying act.

He lifted her, drew her near, and plunged his warm tongue
into her inner ear. "I love your butterflies," he whispered, while
admiring the inviting folds of silk around her familiar breasts.

A sultry *come take me* smile crossed her face.

He took her broad sash, and tugged it. Silk fell softly from
her shoulders. His eyes questioned but once. His lips answered
twice, slow and gentle.

"Butterflies are free to fly wherever they desire, *Thomas-san*,"
she whispered softly, as he pressed her flesh to the silk upon the
floor.

THE NIGHT was one long dream filled with silk and scent
—a briefly worn kimono, moist silk sheets, and fleshy treats.
There was the aroma of sandalwood incense interlaced with love
essence derived from sensual toil, and witch-hazel oil. There was
a mandolin tune. Then morning came too soon.

HE AWOKE to the feel of her warm breast and a calico cat
curled ontop of his chest. After making breakfast, she insisted
on driving him back to Mercer Island, where they both found it
hard to say goodbye, and return to their respective worlds.

James Shawn Wolf watched from Matt's window like the
curious widow, Georgette Kramer.

The couple kissed.

"I'll keep my eyes open for any interesting documents dealing with Chelan, *Thomas-san*," she promised, as her Toyota rolled away.

"Just be careful over there at Ming Yaht's Highrise Hell, Marla Jean Decker," was all that he could say.

Chapter 23

Antilon Lake

TRAVEL BROCHURES brag of Blue Chelan's three hundred days of sunshine a year and her miles of quality recreation cradled in the Eastern Cascade Mountains, but when May winds blow, even die-hard outdoors-persons seek calmer inland waters. When his Chinook salmon fishing guide, Dave Rush, canceled their trip due to high winds, John Greshem took a tip from his host at Granite Falls Lodge, and journeyed off the beaten path to the base of patriotic Fourth of July Mountain, and picturesque Antilon Lake.

The Greshem family appreciated Baker's advice. While winds whipped whitecaps on the big lake, tiny, isolated Antilon was calm and nice. It's waters teemed with fighting Eastern Brook trout and entertaining pan fish. Blessed by the absence of other human beings and the presence of abundant wildlife, the family had a near-perfect morning, and ate a picnic lunch.

Their sole source of frustration was the dozens of sub-surface tree-stump snags, which had claimed most of their tackle by midday. Around one, Little Johnny latched on to yet another one of these lifeless catches. Big John blew up, lost his cool, and became obsessed with salvaging a three-buck spinner bait. This endeavor led to the early cancellation of their Antilon family outing.

"Should I cut the line, Honey?" the wife called out across a narrow neck of water, to where her husband John fanned the air with a hand-tied fly, attempting to fish some shoreline reeds in peace.

Father watched son grapple with a bowed graphite rod, wishing the boy would work it free. But when his frustrated wife waved again, the good father reluctantly responded, and reeled in. "Wait for me! I'm coming around. We're not losing another dime to these damn tree stumps today," he declared.

Dad's waist-high waders hastily slopped through shallow water. Twice he slipped, cursed, and caught his balance on bankside brush, clutching his prized fly rod tightly. When he reached a teary-eyed John Junior, John Senior took control, tugged for ten minutes, and tried every technique taught him by *his* father. Still, he failed to free the artificial bait.

Dad nervously eyed the steep bank behind him and the small boy beside him. He did not want his kid to think *his* father was a quitter. Heroically, he released the button on the boy's reel, and started climbing. Freed fishing line spun out slinky-like below him. Broken chips of slick shale slid between his legs as he climbed.

Half way up he fell, cutting his hand in the process. With his boy's admiring eyes glued to his back, he secured the graphite pole in the bite of clenched teeth and crawled on, talking to himself. *"I love him, but he sure can be a pain in the ass!"* More shale slid beneath him and tumbled to the waters below. *"I'm getting too old for this crap."*

Greshem stopped for a moment to catch his breath, and noticed an indentation in the rocks around him. It alarmed him. It looked as though a steam shovel had scooped here, or something heavy had slid down the embankment sideways. Once ontop, he searched for tracks, but saw none. He stood panting, breathed pine-scented air, reeled in slack line, and regained tension. Confident that his new vantage point would help him prevail, he pulled skillfully from every conceivable angle—even employed his grandfather's patented *bow and arrow maneuver*—to no avail.

Eventually, Dad's luckless flustered, eyes followed the synthetic spider web strand of fishing line to the waterline and stared intensely, seeking the snag. Suddenly, a sunburst broke through partial cloud cover and shined like a beacon on the flashy spinner bait. A chill ran down big John's spine. He shook his head, blinked, and refocused, hoping—praying—he'd see a different picture. But once again he saw the gruesome, bloated cadaver trapped in the submerged pickup truck's cab! His son's fishing lure was attached to a corpse.

John Greshem felt sick. "Honey! Pack our things. We're going back to the lodge," he shouted.

She instinctively responded to the tension in his voice. "John? Are you all right?"

He nodded slowly. "Just pack up the stuff. Okay?"

"Dad! You promised we'd fish here all day," John Junior protested.

"Sorry, son. Something's come up," John Senior replied calmly.

"But Dad! You promised. *All day!* You said you liked it here. You said—"

"We're done fishing, Johnny," Dad said sternly. "Don't ask again."

"But what about my lure?" the son persisted.

The father slipped a bloody mesh fish-cleaning glove on his hand, wrapped the boy's line tightly around it, and cut it with his trusty Swiss Army knife. Then he quickly stumbled down the slick shale slope to retrieve his son and wife.

THOMAS BAKER had spent May's last Sunday hiking with his guests. He had his boots off, his feet elevated, and was reading rough draft manuscript when the phone rang. It was Paul Hilo.

"Tom?" quizzed the lawman's somber voice. "Can you meet me up at Antilon Lake? I think we found Barnes' truck."

THE TWENTY MILE drive was filled with flashbacks of Thomas's life in Chelan: He and Bill building the lodge with local carpenters, spending summer in a tent, taking showers at Lake Chelan State Park... He slowed as he drove past the state park's gate. The state park was where he met Barnes and his buddy Ken Warwick—at the dock, unloading a mess of silver salmon. Thomas lent the two kindly gentlemen a hand, helped set up their volleyball court for some reunion, and was instantly befriended. Brother Bill and family came to the affair—invited because of Bill's friendship with Russ Warwick—only to find Tom already there clowning around with the councilman's grandchildren. Tom, Tim, and Ken grew close, fishing, feasting, and hiking together. Often times they hit tennis balls together. And now? They were both gone. *Or were they?*

Baker motored slowly this Sunday, creeping past Sunnybank and Minneapolis Beach—two developments which Barnes helped shape. The Chevy Suburban stopped at Pat and Mike's Grocery to drink its fill of gasoline. Thomas watched Memorial Day weekend traffic clog the Knapp Coulee road en route to condo cities and the huge new Harris Marina. He took a place in line, crawled into town over Woodin Avenue Bridge, and peered down at crowds of contented pedestrians in beautiful Riverwalk Park. It was the first time in a long time that he'd passed by Forever Neon and Lone Wolf Air Service, and never even honked the horn.

At the North Shore's fifties-style Lakeview Drive In, cars were backed up three blocks deep waiting on the 'best burgers and fries in the Evergreen State.' Awkward young boys flaunted new-found muscles. Quickly maturing girls filled out floral bikinis. The teens all looked their coolest in their daddies' convertibles. They wore cheap sunglasses, and got silly in the sun dreaming of juicy burgers and tender warm buns—playing the dating game.

Beyond Lake Chelan Shores' red tile roofs, hot sands slow-broiled late afternoon sunbathers. Cosina del Lago's mesquite smoke-shack sent wordless advertising to condo decks, where weak-kneed weekenders wearing flip-flops waited impatiently for the dinner hour. The Shore Club courts were filled with athletic people wearing colorful summer fashions. If Thomas had an appetite, he'd surely have succumbed to the aroma of mesquite. He always carried his tennis racket behind his seat, but tennis was far from his thoughts this day.

At Wapato Lake Road he veered right off the Manson Highway, cruised past busy Mill Bay Casino, and sought solace in a vast expanse of roadside apple orchards. The Chevy Suburban slowly ascended the North Shore's three lakes region—Roses, Dry, and Wapato. In the early eighties, he'd nearly purchased waterfront property on Dry Lake for its arid climate and alpine view. Now, even small lakeside lots were bringing top dollar, but over-development had placed both Dry's peaceful ambiance and its water quality at risk.

Baker passed by Wapato Lake's campgrounds. They were crowded. Young boys in baseball caps proudly cleaned their catches. Stocked rainbows filled every frying pan. Plumes of trout smoke permeated the air. The senior campground owners saw the Suburban and waved, but Baker was in a daze and did not notice them.

Thomas turned onto dusty Lower Joe Creek Road for the last leg on the journey to Antilon. Fourth of July Mountain loomed large up ahead. A sparkling Lake Chelan stretched forever in his rearview mirror. The final ascent became soothing. Birds sang. Soft carpets of violets, buttercups, and yellow bells covered roadside gullies. In some ravines, scatterings of wild rose, elderberry, and mock orange materialized to anesthetize Thomas's impending gloom.

Two tiny horse farms' worn split-rail fences framed the final green mile of Upper Joe Creek Road, which ended abruptly at a closed Forest Service cattle gate. The Suburban stopped. Baker got out, raised the gate, and took a poetic mental photograph of the pastoral view.

Writer's eyes watched horsetails swishing flies. Two chestnut mares, one gallant white stallion, a darling dapple gray—each beast turned to look his way. Old man Rogers lay still as the dead, straw hat on head, swaying in the breeze between trees from a tattered hammock in the midst of his stock. A gaggle of grand kids stopped misbehaving and started waving Baker's way.

It was the highlight of his day. Thomas sighed, silently replied, and wondered if Barnes had been graced with such tranquillity before he became history...

RAISING THE WHITE FORD RANGER called for a big commercial wrecker out of Wenatchee. Sheriff Hilo stood behind the beast, inspecting chains and cable. He signaled Baker and shouted, "That's close enough! Wouldn't wanna fish two trucks from this pond."

Baker parked, drew a deep breath, and chewed his dry lips. He approached the scene slowly, nodding solemnly. "Afternoon, Sheriff. Well, what do you think?"

"Looks like he slid down this here ridge, Tom," suggested Hilo.

"Why you so sure it's him down there?"

Hilo dusted his ten-gallon hat, and adjusted his dark glasses. "I'm not, son, but we'll know for certain here directly." He held his hat high above his head, waved it at the driver, then ceremoniously dropped it like a checkered flag.

Black diesel smoke fouled fresh, mountain air. Chains snapped taut, and shot shale like shrapnel. The big wrecker's winch went to work. The white Ranger's hood rose from her watery grave. Windshield glass shattered. Water gushed forth, and rushed back into Antilon. A grotesquely bloated face appeared, came forward, fell back, grew closer...and clearer. It looked like a human pin cushion. It *looked* like councilman Barnes!

When the Ranger came to rest atop the ridge, Hilo watched the writer's reactions closely.

Thomas shook his head sadly, studied the limp-necked form behind the broken steering wheel, and fought nausea. Sadness turned to anger. He thought of his old friend's final phone call, and the fish kill samples that had fingered Ming Yaht. Suspect writer's eyes stared at the lawman.

Hilo put on his hat, produced a mini-cam, and proceeded to do a slow lap around the white Ford Ranger. He stopped at the driver's side door, zoomed in, and spoke loudly into the mike.

"Subject's neck is severely bruised—may have been broken on impact with the steering column."

"Subject?" said Thomas. "Christ's sake, Paul! He's not a fucking stranger."

The Sheriff walked calmly to the edge, and mini-cammed the slide area. "Can't honestly say I knew him that well, Tom. You two were close, though. Weren't you?"

Sheriff Hilo zoomed in on Baker.

"Was he depressed? Any problems at home? Enemies? What's the story, Mr. Writer?" The sheriff was shouting, playing bad-cop detective.

Baker didn't approve.

"Why this, Tom?"

"Why what? You calling *this* an accident too?"

Hilo nodded. "Unless the coroner tells me different, I am. Speaking of the devil..."

The coroner's ambulance appeared through the pines.

Baker shook his head in disbelief.

Detective Hilo dug deeper. "Why? You know something I don't—and should?"

Baker was disturbed. This entire scene reminded him of the day he was arrested so many years ago. "All I know is what I told you before," the writer mumbled.

"Refresh my memory."

"He called me from Entiat around noon. He was very excited about something..." Thomas hesitated.

Hilo took note.

Thomas Baker needed an ally badly. He was an author now, and a legitimate businessman. He hated lying, but he thought about their illegally obtained evidence, and the kind of money Ming Yaht could pay to buy pawns like Paul Hilo.

"Go on. You say he was excited? About what, Tom?" The mini-cam was still running. "You didn't mention this before. Did you, Tom? "

Baker blushed.

"Just what was he so damn excited about, Tom?"

Thomas moved in for a closer look at the corpse, and focused on the councilman's eyes. "Something we were working on for..." Baker cringed. Barnes' eyes had been eaten by crayfish! Some of the little bastards still clung to the dead man's fingers.

Thomas flung open the door. A final surge of lake-water filled his hiking boots. "You fucks! You fucks," he screamed, flicking crawdads from corpse to floor mats.

"Don't touch him," Hilo commanded, pulling Baker back, and slamming the door. "For Christ's sake! This is a potential crime scene."

"Is it?" Thomas said, rubbing his eye sockets raw.

"Real life is a helluva lot gorier than that fiction crap you people write. Ain't it?" Hilo remarked. He lit up a Marlboro, adjusted his cowboy hat, and offered a cancer stick to Baker—who accepted, and smoked for the first time since his prison days.

Together they stared across Antilon to trees, mountains, and sky beyond. Only heartbeats and wind-songs were heard as the coroner's crew removed the councilman's body.

"You think he died trying to save all of this, don't you?" Hilo asked, crushing rocks beneath the heels of his boots.

Baker nodded.

"Just what was it you two were working on, Tom?" Once again, he watched Baker hesitate to answer. "Well?"

"Barnes was working on an injunction to freeze future resort developments and other sensitive projects," said Thomas.

"Which projects?" Hilo quizzed, as he put the mini-cam back inside his cruiser.

Once again, Thomas considered all of Ming Yaht's millions. "I reckon we'll never know, sheriff," he said.

They finished their smokes, and the coroner's ambulance tailgate shut, shattering the silence.

"Well? What do we have, Paul?" asked the coroner.

Hilo spit the spent Marlboro from his lips, and crushed it beneath the toe of his Tony Lamas. "Not my call, Hoss. You're the fucking forensic expert. Get on it! Give me a call ASAP." He walked Baker to his Suburban. They shook hands. "Thanks for coming out, Tom. Going to be around the lodge tonight?"

Baker nodded numbly.

"I'll be in touch," said Sheriff Paul Hilo.

THOMAS PLAYED gracious host to his new guests during dinner, promising them their dream outdoors adventure week was neatly arranged, and would begin with Monday's three-day llama packing trip. When their host retired, he glued his green eyes to a baby-blue computer monitor screen, and his lips to a cold fifth of Finlandia vodka.

Bill Baker knew all about Barnes. Just like he knew his brother never drank alone. At 9:00 p.m., he finally knocked. "You all right, Tom? I hear the trout are biting heavy down at Twenty-five Mile Creek. They're averaging five pounds! How about a sunset excursion?" His strategy didn't work. Air was like quicksand in his brother's room.

"I'm on a run with the book, Bill," Thomas slurred between sips. "What say we hit 'em tomorrow night after all the tourists go back to work. Huh?"

Bill studied the empty monitor screen in front of his troubled big brother. "Yeah, Blood. Tomorrow," he whispered.

When the door shut, silence consumed Thomas. He thought about all the speeches Barnes had made to inspire the Chelan Alliance membership, thought of what Barnes said the last time they sat eye to eye in the greenhouse, after he told him about the faxes: *"It's your pen, Tom! That's what they're afraid of. These vultures are masters at media manipulation…"*

Baker hit the bottle hard, and heard more of Barnes voice: *"Guys like you can use words and passion to stir the apathetic hearts and souls of the masses."* Tim's words echoed all around the room. Tom's tears cascaded down his flush cheeks. Hairs rose on the back of his neck. His knees rocked. Ideas flowed. The writer's fingers sailed across the keyboard: *Near Disaster Sounds Environmental/Development Alarms in the Chelan Valley—By T. Baker. Special to The Seattle Post Intelligence: Since I began writing this column, a series of tragic events have unfolded in the pristine valley I chose to call home...* Thomas paused at keys, took a killer hit of vodka, and swallowed hard. *Through* **anonymous sources**, *this reporter has discovered...*

For an hour he typed like a man possessed, a man too busy to nurse the bottle. *Then a knock came on his door.*

"Not now, Bill! I'm jammin' on these keys," Thomas shouted.

Sheriff Hilo stuck his head into the writer's room. "Sorry to interrupt your work, Tom," Hilo said.

Baker slid back his seat, stood, felt a Finlandia Vodka rush, and surprise anticipation. "Any breaks?" he said with a slur.

Hilo sized up Tom's sobriety, and plucked a cinnamon toothpick from between his teeth. "Maybe. The coroner found traces of chloroform in Councilman Barnes' blood."

Baker's face lit. His eyes blinked. "And?"

"And it's got my curiosity going."

"How much?"

"Enough." Hilo capped the vodka bottle, pushed it back, and handed Baker his jacket. "Enough to keep the file open for a possible homicide."

Baker nearly smiled.

"Enough for me to ask you to stop treating me like the enemy, and try trusting me," said the sheriff.

They held a brief staring contest. Paul Hilo won.

"I thought you might want to ride out to the Barnes' place with me, break the news to Martha...talk about things."

Thomas took the jacket the sheriff was holding. He wanted to ask if he'd found any faxes in that doublewide briefcase he'd seen laying on the floor of the councilman's Ranger, but he didn't. "Let's go," Baker replied.

Hilo patted him on the back. "Try not to breath on her, Tom. All right?"

Chapter 24

Bombarder

PO LIN *was a very vengeful man. Nicholas Gordon didn't always agree with his employer's decisions and subsequent demands, but he never questioned them...*

Wolf warned Neon to be on guard, but they all agreed Pai should work her normal schedule. Time passed, and no one questioned her about the missing cultures from Ming Yaht's Chelan Research Lab. Inevitably, the inseparable couple forgot about this matter of fearing for their personal safety.

THEY RETURNED from dinner (at which he'd popped the question), made mad, passionate, premarital love, and slept soundly—more soundly than ever before. Excessive wine consumption called Neon to the bathroom around 3:00 a.m. He detected an odor. Even in his blissful semiconscious state, it alarmed him. The odor was familiar, but foreign to his upstairs apartment area. The odor was propane gas. He stumbled down to the workshop, and discovered that a valve had not been properly shut. Such carelessness was a first for him. He shook his head, tiptoed back upstairs, stood beside his bed—their bed—and watched her slumber.

Pai was the sleeping beauty who made his neon castle complete. He could have watched her until dawn, curled up in that fetal pose wearing nothing but a contented smile and the ring he'd placed on her finger from bent knees at their candlelight dinner. But then she stirred, and all he wanted was to be inside her again.

IT WAS A rainy Saturday morning. Ho Pai made breakfast for her future husband. They rented a movie for that evening, and spent the following hours in the workshop, finishing up a custom piece together. He was proud of her, proud of her courage, proud of her quick mastery of glass-tube bending. She was intelligent, funny, firm, and kind. He was grateful for her presence in his life, and told her so. They kissed often as they labored side-by-side. Eventually, they carried their fragile work to the bombarder area for the final process. They gently placed glass on a 4 x 8 table, and proceeded to attach electrodes to several dangling alligator clips suspended from half-inch copper clotheslines, which led beneath the table to the monster below. Neon called the bombarder, 'The Monster', for its character, just as he called his workshop, 'Frankenstein's Castle', because of the many strange lights and wires.

After glass is bent and shaped, after it is welded together, and electrodes are plugged in the open ends, it goes through the process of bombarding, where it is given life and color. Here glass is heated, impurities within it are pumped out, and neon or argon gas is pumped in. The actual bombarder is a large coil-filled transformer, like something perched on a telephone pole. It is big. It is heavy—and it is dangerous. When the beast gets turned on, she generates 100,000 volts—nearly 60 AMPS of electricity. Half an AMP can kill a person.

Neon stood on rubber matting with the black rubber-encased power-control joystick in his grip. He had thrown the breaker switch. The red light beamed off the back wall, warning them that the Monster was *alive* and well…*and warming to the task at hand.*

Pai protested one last time. "Michael. Do not treat me like a child. Please let me do this once—"

Neon shook his head emphatically, and imitated Humphrey Bogart. "Not on your life, Sweetheart. As long as I'm alive, you'll never be the one to press this red ceramic button. I told you what happened to my instructor one afternoon in class. Remember?"

She had worked with countless dangerous chemicals, and deadly equipment. The scientist/rebel in her was perturbed by his macho-male coddling of them. But the feminine side—recently rediscovered in his arms—could not hide the feelings his concern stirred deep within in her heart. Reluctantly, she acquiesced.

For all their experience, they still were awestruck when the red light shined, the transformer growled, the vacuum pump pulley *cluck-clucked,* and the beast came to life. Neon carefully extended his arm, and held the power control mechanism away from his body.

Pai slipped her arms around him, and pressed her body close to his.

He gently pecked her cheek; then pushed her back against the wall behind them. "No physical contact when I press this button," he reminded her. "Remember?"

The Monster was loud now. Neon was shouting.

She bit her lips, feigning fear. She bowed her head. "Yes, my teacher," she said.

He studied gas gauges, and fixed his gaze upon the bombarder's voltage meter. "Ready?" he asked.

Pai was holding her ring finger out, watching red rays reflect off the diamond, admiring it, and the man who had given it to her. "Yes, ready," she said.

Neon pressed the button.

A green light glowed bright beside the red one. The Monster roared. Glass warmed. The vacuum pump clucked and sucked air. Electricity surged. Michael smiled as their cocre-ation came to life. "Behold the power—of Neonman!" he shouted.

An artificial lightening bolt arced from the wall behind Ho Pai. It instinctively found her engagement ring, entered skin, burrowed through finger-bone, and metacarpal-waltzed its way right through her wrist! Bone marrow melted to marmalade. Her arms straightened out, grew stiff, then fell limp. Her body twitched and shook as the charge surged through her chest. *Snap!* It cracked her sternum.

She attempted to scream through clenched teeth—to no avail. She thrust both elbows into the wall freeing Michael's White Swan masterpiece from above. Her four seconds of hell ended when the White Swan fell, and the electric charge exited her right index finger like a deadly derringer bullet.

Crash!

Glass shattered. The teacher shut down The Monster.

Neon turned to see her succumb and slump to the floor. A wisp of smoke rose from her blackened fingertip. He watched her wide-open eyes cry out to his, then close. He heard her lips whisper, "Michael."

Time froze.

Michael's first thought was to raise her up and rush her to the hospital. He took her pulse—weak, but persistent. He put his ear to her breast—breathing was irregular. He was worried about moving her.

He retrieved his cordless phone, and lay down beside her on the cool floor. He cradled her head in his warm lap, ran his fingers through her long black hair, calmly dialed 911, and waited for what seemed like an eternity.

As crucial seconds ticked away, all Neon could wonder was... *why?*

He screamed her name, ***"Pai!"*** It echoed off the wall above where they laid, and for the first time in more years than he could recall, the Neonman prayed.

IT WAS AFTER midnight in the Emergency Room of Lake Chelan Community Hospital when his friends dragged Neon home. Miss Pai was in a coma, lucky to be alive, and her condition was difficult to diagnose. What she needed was rest, undisturbed rest. Neon needed answers—answers to questions which were eating his insides out.

Nancy Baker returned to the lodge, where the baby sitter was logging overtime, watching Nathan. Bill, Tom, and Wolf stayed with Neon.

"I can't believe this happened," Neon snapped, standing in the center of his workshop, and trying to hide his feelings.

"Shit happens, Mikey. It's not your fault," Wolf consoled him.

"I'm supposed to know my stuff. Shit! I do know my stuff," Neon declared. He bolted to the bombarder table, and checked The Monster below it. He traced wires up the back wall to large ceramic insulators at the end of the copper clothes-line. He pounced atop the table, and kicked off their work.

Poof! It exploded in a puff of gas on the tile floor.

The artist's eye examined every nook and cranny above him, below him, beside him. "Move, Bill!" Michael shouted uncharacteristically, waving his best friend off the black rubber insulator mat.

"Bastards!" Neon cursed, jumping to the floor. He knelt at the wall where Pai had stood at his request, and found a bolt protruding there—a shiny new bolt, whose blackened tip smelled of burned flesh and singed hair. "I should have noticed." He head-butted the wall. "See these copper strands running from this bolt to the ceiling, then over to those insulators?"

His friends nodded.

Neon pounded the wall. "I should've noticed. Someone did this because of those goddamn cultures!" His eyes rolled back in his head, then Michael *Neon* Johnson went off like a rocket. He whirled around, kicking tables, splintering wood, and ripping out wires. He grabbed an expensive tube of European glass off the rack, raised it like a battle sword, and swung it toward The Monster's breaker box.

Kaboom!

The Beaver pilot intervened. Wolf's grip surprised Neon, and prevented him from drawing another glass sword. Wolf stared hard into the kid's hate-filled eyes.

Neon challenged Wolf's restraint. His right forearm rocked and twitched. He formed a fist with his free left hand.

Bill Baker grabbed hold of it.

Neon grated his teeth intensely.

Three pairs of caring eyes focused on their friend until his hatred subsided, and the Neonman drowned in an overdue flood of emotion.

"It wasn't an accident! Ming Yaht did this because of those damn samples. I knew it. I told her. Shit," he sobbed. "This was probably meant for me." His proud chin dropped to his chest. Strong arms fell limp at his sides. "I'll never—"

"Never what?" Wolf snarled. "Don't pull one of those *I'll never bend glass again* routines on me! You're the fuck who bragged how proud you were of her. It was you who said she wanted to do this for all of us. For Chelan! She's a fighter, Mikey. You should feel lucky."

"Yeah, a fighter," Neon laughed. "And look where it got her!" He reached for the glass again.

Wolf grabbed him, shouting, "There's better ways to vent that anger, Mikey. Get a grip, man."

Neon broke down, sobbing. "But I-I-I love her."

"No shit, Sherlock," Wolf said, releasing his grip.

"Don't you think we know that?" Bill whispered.

Neon buried his face in his hands atop the bombarder table, and wept. "We were going to get married."

His three best friends hadn't known. No one knew. They shared silence, sorrow...and anger.

"What's this *were* shit?" Wolf asked, extending a closed fist and inviting the gang to huddle. Slowly, but surely, all fists came front and center, and four good men *hit the rock* of friendship.

"Let's get those bastards!" they shouted in concert.

Wolf went to his place, and brought back two cases of beer. In the hours which followed, the foursome assessed everything that had occurred in and around Chelan prior to Pai's electrocution. The list was extensive. It all appeared to start with the sinking of the *Connie Joe,* and the not-so-coincidental arrival of one Nicholas Gordon on the scene.

Neon told them about the suspicious propane gas leak.

Wolf saw similarities in his Beaver's sabotage. "The guy is good, but he definitely leaves a signature. He likes to rig the odds twice. He cut two of my engine lines just deep enough to enable me to fly out of safe landing range. He rigged your contraption downstairs as the main attack, Neon…but left the gas on too, hoping you'd space out and light up one of those burners you use." The pilot tilted back his beer. "Yeah, the guy's real good. And the guy—" Wolf belched. *Is Nick Gordon.*

"Gordon?" Neon questioned.

Wolf cupped his good ear. "Is there an echo in here?"

"Are you serious?" Thomas asked.

"As a heart attack," Wolf growled. "I had a feeling about him the minute he stepped off that McKinnon Goose for the funeral."

Bill whispered something to Thomas.

"My guess is that Ming Yaht wanted Warwick's land for some long-range project like—"

"Like what, Wolf?" Neon slurred between sips.

"Like whatever Barnes was on to," Wolf said. "Right, Writer Man?"

Thomas nodded.

Wolf tossed his bottle, which just missed the trashcan.

Neon jumped up off the carpet and ran to the window— *again.*

"Would you please stop staring out the window every time you hear a noise, Mikey! It's three o'clock in the fuckin' morning. No one's watching us now."

"How do you know?" Neon asked.

"I know," answered Wolf.

"How?"

"Because I scouted the perimeter again the last time you nodded off. That's why. And because this Gordon-fuck knows *I'm* here with you kids." Wolf shook his head, and muttered aloud; "He probably knows more about me than any of you people ever will."

"What do you mean by that?" Thomas quizzed.

"Nothing. Drop it," Wolf snapped back.

"How can we get these bastards?" Neon asked.

"It's up to us to do something," Bill pressed.

"I've been working on one hell of an article for the Seattle paper." Thomas cleared his throat. "If I just had a little more ammo, it could really rock Ming Yaht's—"

"What's your source...anonymous?" Wolf ribbed.

The writer nodded.

"That's good, Tommy, really good. But what we need now is physical evidence, and inside information." Wolf glared suggestively. Neon and Bill stared at Thomas too. "Talk about an *inside connection*...your main-squeeze works for them."

"Think she'd help?" Neon asked, his eyes glowing.

Thomas pictured Pai lying unconscious in that hospital bed. Thoughts of Marla ran through his head. "I didn't want to get her involved. I didn't—"

"You never did say who told you about those faxes," Wolf said with penetrating eyes that made their point. "The ones you told Barnes about."

Thomas tossed his empty bottle on the floor. "Don't ask me to put her in harm's way." He looked to Wolf.

"There is no other way, Writer Man. We need a fuckin' break."

Thomas sweated through the silence which followed. These were his friends, and Ming Yaht's headquarters probably did hold the key to many unsolved mysteries. If so, they would need his brother's skills too. He hadn't felt so uneasy since his divorce— since the day they hauled his butt off to prison! He was about to get tangled up in some risky business, probably bump heads with elements of the government. And, he might be getting two people he cared about involved as well. He could not promise Marla's help, but he would ask.

Thomas Baker nodded reluctantly.

They all talked until dawn, eventually deciding on a course of action. The crucial city council meeting was set for July third. Notices had appeared in the *Chelan Mirror*. John Q. Public needed to see the faces behind the Ming Yaht Corporation, so both Po Brothers were scheduled to attend.

Thomas targeted the meeting as their D-Day for action. He hinted that he might come up with a surprise ally who could present some new and damning evidence, or at least help bluff the big shots from Ming Yaht. The writer would handle the media himself. His main concern was that he still had a lodge to run.

Bill quickly relieved that weight by announcing that he would take two weeks vacation time from the Environmental Protection Agency.

Wolf volunteered his Lake Union Cafe friend's assistance.

They agreed to save the raising of the *Connie Joe* for last, after exhausting all other leads.

"One more thing," Wolf added. "I've flown over this gaudy Asian retreat that Pos built up-lake over a hundred times. It's got my curiosity going. If I can learn a little about the place, I'd like to take an unescorted tour of—"

Neon slapped the table. "I know all about it." He swallowed hard. "I've been inside it, and I can describe the security system to a T," he slurred through clenched teeth. "But you guys have to swear to keep what I'm about to tell you a secret."

Neon's request needed no reply.

Neon proceeded to tell them about his greatest work—a moving martial arts scene constructed in a glass octagon atop an opulent pagoda-style palace located a couple miles past Twenty-five Mile Creek. It was a work for which he was paid eighty-thousand dollars cash money by a Latino male with cold dark eyes who told him in no uncertain terms to keep his mouth shut. "I figured it was drug money," Neon explained. "But I needed it to expand my business."

The kid had said a mouthful. Wolf heard whistles blow and bells ring following Neon's revelation. They held out their fists once again and did that prison-born male-bonding thing. Their plans were extensive. Upon the rock of friendship, they made a pact to take the offensive.

And then? They passed out, one by one, in the early Chelan morning sun.

Chapter 25

Offensive

ON SUNDAY NIGHT Baker called the Capitol Hill duplex of Marla Decker, uneasy with the decision to enlist her services, and uncertain about the security of his own phone lines. "Marla?"

"Thomas! Good to hear your voiced," she said. She had not heard from him in over a week, and was worried. "I missed your call last Sunday night," she said. It was the first time since their kayak weekend that he had neglected her. "How's the book coming along? Figure out the ending yet? Do we—*they* live happily ever after?"

"I don't know how it ends yet. Haven't worked on it all week. The lodge is booked, and I've got my hands full playing host."

"Punkin misses you," Marla purred. "She likes the way you rub her belly." When the writer did not reply to her sexual innuendo, Marla Jean Decker knew something was wrong. "Thomas, you don't sound well."

"I'm not, Marla. We need to talk."

Not those four words! She nearly dropped the phone. She felt sick. What had she done to scare him away? "I'm listening," she said.

Wolf suggested he take every precaution. Even so, it was difficult for him to ask her to do this. "Remember that sushi bar?"

"How could I forget? I'm saving it for an encore appearance with—"

"Have you been there since our date?" Baker quizzed.

'No," she sighed.

"I want you to go there. Now."

"Thomas? It's Sunday night. They close at ten."

"Do you trust me?"

"Yes, of course."

"Then call a cab and go. I'll meet you there in fifteen minutes." The pay phone operator demanded more money. Thomas hung up.

Many frightening thoughts flooded Marla Decker's head. She had been dressed for bed. *Why hadn't he said he was in Seattle?* She squirmed into some tight blue jeans, and grabbed her purse.

Fifteen minutes later, the manager of *Tobiko Row* handed Marla the phone. "Thomas? Are you in trouble?" she asked. "What's with all this spy stuff? Where are you? You're scaring me!"

"I'm sorry," Baker said. "I'm calling from the Lake Chelan Yacht Club's pay phone. I didn't want to say anything sensitive on the lodge's line."

"Why?" she inquired.

"I'm a dangerous obstacle. Remember?" He paused, preparing himself to ask for her help, and probably put her at risk. "Marla—"

But she had news of her own, and needed to get it off her mind. "Wait! Something crossed my desk Friday that I think you'll find interesting."

"What?" asked the writer,

"Documentation on land acquisitions around Chelan. Thomas, I think one of them is Warwicks' estate! I think our subsidiary in Vancouver won the bidding to purchase their property from state probate court."

Baker swallowed hard, and nervously scanned the Yacht Club parking lot for Nicholas Gordon's black Land Rover.

"There's more," Marla whispered, cupping the phone. A tall male customer with a small ponytail entered *Tobiko Row*. She eyed the man suspiciously.

The congenial owner smiled, and bowed to the feminine-faced Asian.

Marla sighed, and resumed her telephone conversation. "I think Russ kept a secret file on his computer. He was so paranoid those weeks before the accident. Thomas, I think he was bringing a whistleblower diskette to your brother."

"Why, Marla? Why do you think that?"

"After Russ died, Gordon went over his workstation with a fine-tooth comb. Couldn't find a thing."

Baker couldn't believe his ears. "Can you?"

"I've tried. Russ was a computer wizard. I'm not. But he once said your brother, Bill, was just as good. Thomas, I want to help. If there's even a chance the proof you need is in our computer, I..."

Thomas decided she needed to know how deep the shit was getting. "Does Gordon suspect you of snooping?" he asked.

The phone made a strange clicking noise. Their mechanical operator called for coins.

"I don't think so. He spends all his time in Chelan these days. You don't think I'm in any danger. Do you?"

She needed to know. "Marla, listen..." He fed the phone and informed her of the facts. He told her about Barnes, the Indian Chief, the sabotage of the Beaver, matching samples, Pai's *accident*, and his intention to publish a damning article before Ming Yaht's big July third public spectacle in Chelan. "Still want to help?" he asked.

"Damn right I do!" she answered. "I could use a little excitement in my life. Heck, I can always find a new job. Need a co-author, Thomas?"

"*Please deposit one dollar and twenty-five cents for overtime charges,*" the robotic phone-voice requested. Baker only had a buck-fifty remaining.

"Marla, how unusual would it be for three government officials to show up for a tour of your corporate headquarters Thursday afternoon?"

"What kind of government officials?"

"I don't know yet," he said between quarters.

"Uh huh. Thursday, you say? Gordon won't be around. I guess it wouldn't be unusual at all. Especially if these three officials were with some department, like Immigration and Naturalization Service?"

Baker's Seattle secretary continued to amaze him. They made arrangements to meet Wednesday evening, before the mechanical money-grabber called for coins again.

WEDNESDAY MORNING, guests at Granite Falls Lodge went horseback riding with a local outfitter. Thursday was set aside for golf and tennis with Shores Club pros. On Wednesday evening, the Baker Brothers dined with Marla Decker at Il Bistro restaurant below Seattle's Pike Place Market—without the company of their pilot friend.

Wolf and his pal from Lake Union flew out to Whidbey Island to dine with an old Agency buddy—and do some digging.

THURSDAY MORNING, 7:30 a.m. Marla Decker drove to work. 11:00 a.m. A long gray limo parked in front of 1604 Pine Street on Capital Hill. James Shawn Wolf emerged, and strutted to the door in a snappy ensemble carrying an overstuffed suit bag.

When Georgette Kramer grew suspicious of the longhaired stranger, Thomas told her he was a celebrity from Hollyweird. "What gives with the limo?" Thomas inquired, once Wolf stepped inside Marla's home.

"Classy. Huh, Baker?" replied the pilot. "This baby's on loan from my restaurant buddy." Wolf unzipped the luggage.

Baker stared out the window. The driver tipped his cap and waved.

"Relax. It's a prop, Writer Man. Just like this shit," he added, plopping down two official U.S. Immigration officers' outfits, and two pairs of spit-shined dress black shoes.

"How come you get to wear the silk Armani suit and the three hundred dollar pair of Bally loafers?" Bill asked.

"Because I'm the CIA Special Operations guy who is coordinating this investigation of illegal Asians with gang affiliations—in tandem with our Canadian brothers, of course." Wolf cleared his throat, then smirked. "And you two are just deadweight beat-walkers. Green-card inspectors is all you are. That's how come. Got it?"

The brothers nodded, and changed into their costumes.

"What did you learn on Whidbey Island?" Thomas asked.

Wolf unbuttoned his jacket, loosened his tie, and mulled over the scuttlebutt he had scraped off a human cog in the Intelligence community's rumor mill. Arturos Aquindo was alive and well, and working for the Ming Yaht Corporation in an *official* capacity as their international liaison. Colonel A was suspected of using his Agency contacts to dispense millions in offshore bribe money as pavement on the inroads which would insure the success of Po Lin's *Era of New Direction*. The establishment of immigrant labor sweatshops from Mexico to Canada—which would produce low cost counterfeit merchandise for overseas export and domestic retail sales in Ming Yaht's super malls—was high on the agenda. Only rapidly growing legions of American and Mainland Chinese prison laborers would be able to financially compete with the Pos' expansive work force. Corporate infiltrators were poised and ready to pirate the West's forbidden technology, and use the Pos' ancient network to place it in the jaws of any number of emerging Asian Tigers.

If his writer pal could break this story, it would make Thomas Baker a journalistic superstar overnight...*or put him six feet underground.* **Maybe both.** Wolf rolled his neck, reached inside his suit coat, and straightened the leather strap on his shoulder holster.

When Thomas saw the butt of Wolf's big Smith & Wesson, he nearly shit his pants. He started to protest, but the pilot pointed to his pistol, patted it, and mouthed the word p-r-o-p.

Bill repeated his brother's question. "What did you learn on Whidbey Island, Wolf?"

"I learned this is big, boys. We're talking billions invested in the Northwest and Canada. BCCI-style banking. State Department and Immigration people on the take from here to Hong Kong. They've been setting this thing up for years. It all evolves around Hong Kong reverting back to China in 1997. Ming Yaht don't mind doing business with the commies, but they don't want them guaranteeing their bank deposits. Chinks have been flooding Canada for years. Now they've established a beachhead in the Pacific Northwest. And according to my sources, we ain't seen nothin' yet!"

"I thought Congress was drafting strong anti-immigration legislation and setting strict quotas?" Thomas said.

Wolf nodded. "Yeah, Tom. That's how the headlines read for the benefit of Mr. and Mrs. Joe Blow. But behind closed doors, where they smoke those *really* big Havanas, the price for guaranteed citizenship and a share of those *strict quotas* in the *meiguo* just got tempting enough to enlist an entire army of extra-greedy government officials."

"What's the *meiguo*?" Bill asked.

"It means *beautiful country* in chink, Bill. And it's the reward the old triads—Hong Kong's version of the mafia—are offering faithful members for their years of service in the heroin trade. Canada is slamming the door on them 'cause they're sick of triad turf wars like that Montreal Mount Saint Helens blast we saw on t.v. on New Year's Day. The Canadians are also on the verge of discovering what happens when an ethnic group that makes up a small percentage of the population controls a large portion of a nation's wealth. We're gonna see a lot of the same crap down here before it's all settled, 'cause the yellow tide is coming. Surf's up, kids! Evidently, even the most ruthless Hong Kong capitalists don't like the kind of music being played off Beijing's infamous *human rights* record."

Thomas shook his head, and tied his shoes. "Old drug money? Triads trying to launder their way to the promised land? Small world. Huh pal?"

The pilot nodded. "History repeats itself," mumbled Wolf. "Like the roaring twenties and Al Capone. Like the present day drug wars. Without prohibition, how could the rich ever get richer? Think about it, Baker."

"So, the path to the *meiguo* is paved with washed greenbacks, and all the rats are abandoning the good ship Hong Kong?"

"You got it, Writer Man. And they're bringing all their dirty laundry with 'em too. Not to mention their roulette tables. They are obviously in a hurry to finish building their nests in the *meiguo*. And any obstacles are being dealt with by a series of neat, explainable accidents."

Thomas swallowed hard.

"I hear they've got an *army* of Nick Gordons north of the border," Wolf added, while slipping a pearl handled derringer into an ankle holster.

A shiver ran down Baker's spine. *More than one Nick Gordon?* He started second-guessing himself. "Wolf...we can't stop this thing."

Wolf tossed two INS agent's hats on the couch. "No, but we can sure keep them the hell outta' Chelan! If we can catch some more of their hurried, stupid, sloppy mistakes, that is. Put those hats on, and I'll have the limo take us to lunch—on you of course, Baker."

Georgette Kramer was conveniently clipping geraniums when the boys walked by. Her green eyes bulged at the sight of their outfits.

Wolf blew her a kiss, and whisked the Bakers into the limo. "These fine young men are my movie extras, Ma'am. We're shooting a scene in the city this afternoon," Wolf shouted.

Thomas smiled, waved, and slunk down in the big back seat.

Georgette Kramer relaxed, and canceled her yard work performance for the day.

THE GREY STRETCH limo glided to a stop in front of Ming Yaht's glass towers. Three officials emerged from it, and adjusted their ties in mirror-like tinted glass windows on a windswept Emerald City sidewalk. Huge banners hung from a marble facade: *Ming Yaht: An environmentally conscious corporation, working to bring prosperity to the great Northwest! Ming Yaht: Watch us grow! Ming Yaht: Working to insure a bright tomorrow!*

Bill Baker flipped the bird. "Bull shit! Working to get richer at your expense," he muttered. His reddish-blond mop was held dark and fast by a ton of mousse beneath his cap. Tortoise-shell Ray Ban sunglasses rested on the bridge of his nose. "Think anyone will recognize me from the last time I visited Russ here?"

Thomas shook his head. "I can't. Not in that outfit."

Wolf led the way—briefcase in hand—and they marched right up to Reception.

Robin Garth greeted them warmly. "Good afternoon. May I help you?"

Bill had met Robin before. Somewhat alarmed, he turned away, scanned the huge glass atrium, and saw a massive Asian security guard coming toward them with Sharon Riker.

Wolf slapped genuine CIA-ID on the solid marble desk, and explained their mission.

Robin smiled. "Oh, yeah. Marla said your people phoned up to Records. Take the elevator to the twenty-first floor. And have a nice day."

It was almost too easy.

As they cruised across the floor, Sharon and the security guard stared coolly, studied their costumes, and closed in for questions and answers. "Excuse me, but do you gentlemen have an appointment?" Sharon asked.

Silence.

"Lady asked you a question. Better have an answer," the gorilla guard said. He zeroed in on the INS patches on the Bakers' khaki-green sleeves, swallowed hard, and shrunk back.

Sharon Riker pressed on. "Mr. Gordon doesn't approve of unescorted tours of—"

Wolf flashed his ID. "Here's my appointment, pinhead," he snarled at the tough-guy guard. "And since you insist on playing Q and A, I've got a question for you. Are you a naturalized American Citizen, mister?"

Thomas Baker's heart nearly popped out of his chest.

The big Asian guard bit his tongue.

Elevator doors opened, and the three pretenders disappeared.

On the way to the twenty-first floor, Wolf straightened his tie and did his Rodney Dangerfield routine to relax his friends. "Tough neighborhood! I get no respect," mused the pilot.

"That's because you're nuts, Wolfy," Baker said.

Marla smiled when they entered her office. "Anything wrong, officers?"

"No ma'am. Just here to raid your computer," Thomas replied. He wanted to kiss her, but there was work to do.

"Have any trouble getting up here?" she inquired. When Bill mentioned Sharon and the guard, Marla frowned. "She's got the hots for Nick Gordon. All the secretaries are getting sick of her humping his leg. Say, nice outfits, guys."

Wolf took a bow, wandered around, sniffed things out, and took a stance by the door. "Let's get down to business. Bill? Show us your stuff."

Bill quizzed Marla on the computer system, sat down at the workstation, slapped keys, retrieved information, and started reviewing it. "Hey, Blood! I think we better invest in this Ming Yaht high-speed rail stock. Mmm...Asian Satellite Telecom looks tempting too."

Wolf growled.

Bill got serious. "Marla, you think Russ was keeping a private record on—"

"Russ Warwick kept a record of everything, Bill." She leaned on Thomas, remembering. "He spent plenty of late nights at that keyboard. His wife, Angy, actually thought we were having an affair, until she found out it was that IBM. Believe me, I've tried everything to access his file. Maybe you can crack it. You two worked together. Right?"

Bill nodded, queried the hard drive via Norton Utilities, and determined how much data had been stored in each of Warwick's subdirectories—immediately noticing an alarming contradiction. "I knew it! There's hidden directories here, folks. He's used way more space than one directory holds. This unit has an older DOS version installed which prevents use of all disk space on a single directory, and—"

Thomas tapped Bill's shoulder, and cleared his throat. "Ah, Bill?"

"Yeah, Blood. What?"

"Just speak-a-da'-English and proceed!"

Bill punched more keys.

Wolf paced impatiently.

The minutes passed slowly by.

Bill flashed back over the early days at the EPA with Russ, when they teamed up to blow the whistle on a nuclear waste disposal scam on New Mexico's Mescalero Indian Reservation. It was the last time that they worked together.

Wolf cleared his throat, and glared at the whiz kid. "Well?"

"All I need to do is guess the password to his hidden directories," Bill pronounced, while playing the computer keyboard like a baby grand piano. "Come on, Russ! What were you thinking?" During that *hot* New Mexico summer, they hid their radioactive dirt under the code heading, *Black Cloud*. "Bingo!" Bill blurted.

"Bingo what?" Wolf asked.

"The motherload," Bill said. "That's what."

They sighed collectively.

Bill studied the monitor screen and continued. "When Russ and I worked together in New Mexico, we had a Sun Workstation tied into a digital mainframe. We used two file codes back then. One for our worthless superiors to snoop into, and one to catalogue the environmental violations they were taking bribes to overlook."

A somber expression swept over the features of William Virgil Baker as the Black Cloud II File revealed itself to him. "You always were too damn wordy, Russ," Bill muttered, rubbing misting eyes as his cohorts congregated around the monitor screen. ***Greetings Willy V!! Congratulations! If you found this, then my paranoia paid off, and at least you know I didn't sell out to the corporate world...***

It only took Willy V. twenty-five minutes to access the treasure trove of information his fallen friend had hidden; but it would take hours—maybe days—to absorb it all.

There were megabytes on maps depicting Ming Yaht's operations and proposed resort communities north of the border. There were blueprints for industrial parks of monstrous proportions, and floor plans for scores of city-sized super malls. Proposed high-speed rail routes crisscrossed Canada with high-tech tentacles that stretched down from Vancouver to Seattle, and inland through sensitive Cascade Mountain passes—all the way to Chelan.

There was an index of *Phases,* and mention made of *The Ten Year Plan.* Po Lin's *Era of New Direction* was frequently referred to, as were several encrypted banking and immigration contacts. A file on a Ming Yaht subsidiary's condo-city in Victoria, British Columbia, documented how its massive filtration plant had pumped untreated waste into the harbor there. A flow chart showed ocean currents carrying the raw sewage south via Puget Sound—*to Seattle.*

Then came the Chelan file, stored under the heading *Operation Pristine Valleys-CH-97.* It featured topographical maps marked with red X's and white O's. Bill Baker made mental note of the foothills above Mill Bay with all their football play-book markings; then fast-forwarded to Chelan Falls, where the proposed industrial park and super mall distribution center sprawled for ten square miles along the Chelan River.

There was more. Ming Yaht's camouflaged land acquisitions from Wenatchee to Chelan were extensive. Huge tracts of road frontage were targeted for purchase alongside proposed high-speed rail-routes. All Pacific Northwest Native American lands were enlarged and dissected. Details on casino gambling goals in the U.S. and Canada were listed in lengthy footnotes, as were the names of several of the offshore shell corporations involved with native American tribes.

Bill fast-forwarded again. An overview of Warwick's one thousand acre lakefront estate appeared, and a clear picture emerged of its intended destiny: A compact, self-contained, condo-city with a shared-access community beach which would eventually be independent of Chelan-proper, and be annexed by a proposed Lin City. Adjacent Corral Creek tribal land would be the site of a massive casino.

"You folks catching this shit? Or am I rolling the tape too fast?" Bill said, after whipping through hours of scandalous info, in less than forty-five minutes.

Everyone nodded.

Bill put the last entry in Russ's *Black Cloud II* File on the monitor screen.

Marla squeezed Thomas's hand tightly.

Wolf stood stern-faced, staring at the words, and slowly read the last writings of Russell Warwick.

Entry. October 17, 1995: My good Chinese friend and fellow environmentalist, Li Wong, spent the entire weekend with Angy and I. Li was born in Hong Kong. His father grew up in extreme poverty in Kowloon's infamous 'walled city.' Li's father's only chance of rising above that squalor, was to become a 'triad member'. (That's the Chinese version of the mob, Willy V! Still with me?) Li's old man helped pack shipping containers at Hong Kong Harbor filled with China white. (Heroin!) He became head of the dock workers and got very close to one Mr. Po Lin. Evidently, too close! Li's father drowned last week in Vancouver's Frazier River. He was a world class swimmer. Li was heartsick...so he decided to visit his American friend (AKA, me!). Li's the guy who fed me most of the megabytes you just reviewed, Bill. Last night, Li Wong died from food poisoning at his home in Vancouver. (What's wrong with this picture?) I'm getting strange vibes, partner. No one to talk with who understands this kind of stuff...and I can trust. Or...want to endanger. Marla, my secretary, is a sweetheart, and sharp, but I'm too much the gentleman to involve a lady. It's time to tell, Willy V. This far outweighs any corporate loyalty! Here's my plan: I'm coming to Chelan with all this on disk. I know the risk is high, but you're my guy, Willy V! Just you and me again, old friend. Tried and true. Are you ready...for Black Cloud II? (Oh yes, if I should fall victim to 'an accident' along the way, I've planted a message in Marla's computer to contact you ASAP and talk to you about all my late hours on this keyboard.) Over and out, Good buddy!

   Your friend forever, Russ.

Bill shook his head, stood, and walked to the windows. "You wordy wildman," he whispered. He did not want the others to see him crying.

Marla couldn't hold back her tears.

"It wasn't just the land," Bill sighed. "Russ *was* going to blow the whistle on these shits! They must have been on to him. Maybe they found out why he was transferred from the Mescalero Reservation assignment." Bill Baker regained his composure, and confronted the secretary. "Marla! You said you saw a document that officially transferred the Warwick estate to some Vancouver corporation?"

She nodded nervously.

"Was it called *Hongcouver Ventures?*"

Again, she nodded. "How did you know?"

"It's all right here," Bill said patting the monitor. "No doubt the actual purchase was made by their front trust, Maple Leaf Limited. Tom, didn't your Englishman, Jimmy, turn in a generous bid?"

Thomas nodded.

"But the bid was rigged by Ming Yaht," Wolf barked, while studying his watch. "Better make a printout of that crap so we can get the hell out of here, Billy Boy. We're really pushing our luck by hanging around here. We can always sift through the dirt back home."

"Negatory, Wolfman. You're a great field general, but your technical skills suck," Bill blurted. "If I make a print-out on this monitored corporate gear, there could be a record of it, and that might endanger our girl, Marla, here."

"Screw that idea," Thomas exclaimed.

Marla pecked his cheek, and put on a brave face. "I'll be all right. They don't suspect me. No one even knows that I'm dating you, Thomas. I mean, it's not like they can just go around killing everyone."

Wolf-eyes stared straight through her.

"Is it?" she asked sheepishly.

Wolf shook his hair, and paced impatiently. "We definitely need this evidence, but make no mistake about it kids—these guys do play rough."

Thomas wrapped his arms around Marla.

Bill whipped out his computer paraphernalia and waved it in the air proudly like a custom condom. "Not to worry. Chill out, folks. I, your wild and crazy computer wizard, came prepared to practice safe computer sex! I will now proceed to record the entire Black Cloud II file in a matter of minutes, and take it back to Chelan in my pocket for our reviewing pleasure."

Thomas tapped Bill's shoulder. "Will that goon, Gordon, know we've made a copy of this stuff?"

"Of what stuff? Ol' Nicky Boy doesn't know the file even exists! You think I wasted all these years of training? Not only will he still not know it exists, but I'll leave it stashed safely just in case we decide to send the good guys here on a scavenger hunt for *admissible* evidence."

"Wake up, kid! There are no good guys when the money gets this big," Wolf bellowed. "Hear me now, but believe me later...they've all been bought and sold."

The phone rang.

It was Robin Garth at the Reception desk. Marla Decker recalled that fateful day when the mystery faxes found her tray, and remembered the fear she felt when Gordon searched for them floor to floor! Fortunately for them, Nick Gordon was in Chelan.

"Marla? Everything ship-shape up there?" Robin quizzed.

"Sure, Robin. Why? What gives?"

"Donna just came back from lunch. She says another limo full of big wigs pulled in behind that gray stretch out front. Maybe they'll stop by your office too? You sure do seem to be one popular lady today. I'm not sure what's going on, but I thought you'd want to know."

"Thanks, Robin. Gotta' run."

"I figured."

"Talk to you later," said Marla. She hung up the phone, and turned to Wolf. "We've got a problem. Another limo just parked behind yours. No telling who's in it." She was shaking and biting her lips.

"Wrap it up, Bill! It's time to hit the road," Wolf barked.

"Did you get enough?" Thomas's asked, as his green eyes bounced from Bill to Marla.

"Got it all! Let's boogie," Bill said.

Thomas looked longingly into Marla's eyes; and in that moment, he questioned what she was, or had become in his life. *A lover? A sexual playmate?* They were not committed. She had her life. He had his own.

Wolf tapped his watch.

Thomas gave Marla a kiss and a hug. "You going to be all right?" he asked.

She bit her tongue, and acted tough. "You gentlemen need an escort to the lobby?"

"You've done enough already," Thomas Baker said, starting for the door. He stopped in his tracks. They waved goodbye. An uneasy feeling grew inside him.

"By the way…you look good in a uniform, Thomas," she said cheerfully. "Call me," she whispered. She wanted to say *I love you,* or at least mouth the words.

And so did he.

ELEVATOR DOORS opened wide. They hit the first floor walking fast for the front exit of Ming Yaht' Seattle corporate headquarters. Singsong-speak of Asian voices echoed in the cavernous atrium. A walkie-talkie crackled in the distance.

Wolf's keen eyes caught a glimpse of the crowd gathered at the receptionist's desk. *Oh shit! They're on to us,* he thought. There were eight suits. Several of them wore standard security-detail headsets. Six of them were stocky Asians with hands tucked inside open jackets. *Probably packing heat!* One looked Latino. The slim one in the center wore a silk suit with a *power*-red tie, looked clean-cut, bright-eyed twenty-something, and acted like some brash young hotshot issuing commands in Cantonese. The Chinese pretty boy was too high profile to be working security. *Someone important*! Wolf's *alert* mode kicked in.

"What's up?" Bill whispered, midway to the exit.

"Nothing. Keep walking," Wolf said.

The Nick Gordon-loving secretary, Sharon Riker, entered the picture to talk with the Latino man. The hauntingly familiar Latino listened intensely, took the regular security guard aside, slapped his face and cursed him in perfect Cantonese.

"That's them!" Sharon shouted, pointing toward the escaping masqueraders.

Wolf's *alert* mode ran wild. *Fight, or flight?*

The Latino leader broke for the front doors.

The six stocky Asians closed in protectively around the slender pretty boy with the face of a young Po Lin.

Wolf walked even faster, with one eye on the encroaching Latino, and an uneasy feeling inside. "Follow me. Look official! Stay close! And whatever you do, don't stop," Wolf advised his troops.

The Cuban called out to them. "You there—"

Wolf struggled to ignore him.

"You men," cried the Cuban. "*Stop!*" Something about the one Sharon had told him was with CIA Special Operations stuck in his Caribbean craw. Arturos quickly closed the distance between them, determined to take a closer look.

Wolf heard the Latino's voice loud and clear. It echoed in Ming Yaht's atrium, and filled his one good ear. He'd heard that voice before. "Go around me! Get to the limo," he ordered, shoving the Baker Brothers toward the door.

The Cuban kept talking.

"Keep walking! Don't look back," Wolf told the brothers, as he reached for the butt of his Smith & Wesson, and sized up all of the others. A vengeful voice from the past reminded him: *It's never too late.* He flashed back to Haiti, Andros, Atlanta's federal prison—and south Florida's senate race of 1988.

Arturos Aquindo found himself strangely drawn to that same year, recalling his political demise due to a media-manipulated scandal. Finally, he recognized the face. "*Ai, Carumba! Es El Lobo,*" he shouted with a sick smile. The Latino felt for the pearl handle of his .45 Sig Sauer automatic pistol, completely forgetting where he was...and *who* he was supposed to be guarding.

Time froze. Two mortal enemies stared coldly at their pasts, minds racing.

Thomas Baker's hand fell hard on Wolf's shoulder.

The slim Po Lin prototype took control. He shouted commands across the atrium with a stilted English accent that made him sound like a caricature of a spoiled princeling. "Neau, Colonel! This nawt propa time, nor place. Show some klahss." He straightened his red power tie. "Let them pass."

Arturos Aquindo shrugged, and responded with a nod. "Pompous little slant-eyed ass," he muttered under his breath. "Lin's little *Puta* thinks he's God."

BAKER PULLED Wolf through the exit doors, out of the movie scene. And the three spies from Chelan sped off...*in their waiting limousine.*

Chapter 26

Site Inspection

THE BLACK CLOUD II FILE took days to study, but provided dozens of leads. It directed Bill Baker to Chelan's North Shore, where days of driving around pinpointing Russ Warwick's mapped-out locations were beginning to bear fruit.

This day had been spent reviewing Union Valley view parcels off rough, dusty roads like Ridge, Castle Rock, and Blue Grouse, which ranged from 100 to 1000 acres in area. Similar sized acquisitions appeared throughout the North Shore's isolated up-country view ridges in places like Puritan Gulch, Swanson Creek, and Cooper Gulch. They were land tracts no other investors would touch for lack of county road systems, power, precious water, and no *known* development plans on county planning charts for the foreseeable future. Bill Baker saw these as an integral part of the Pos' plan to place thousands of extended family members on country ranches—for which they could charge a king's ransom to retiring triad mobsters accustomed to Hong Kong real estate prices. What Bill did not foresee, were the rural labor sweatshops these *feudal lords* intended to establish on their spacious ranches.

Bill also figured color-coded map areas indicated Ming Yaht had located large drinking water aquifers trapped in granite pockets beneath these tracts, thus further guaranteeing their development potential. He also assumed they possessed the new ultra-sound technology he heard was being tested for such purposes.

Two pieces of the real estate puzzle bothered Bill. Both of these were non-view parcels. One was just off of Boyd, above Cooley Road, where Building Department records showed a new home had been constructed. The other was a 2,200 acre spread in the Washington Creek-Highland Bench region—totally barren, thirty minutes from the lake, and suddenly starting to look like CIA Headquarters. He did a drive-by yesterday. The big spread's recent high-security fence fetish reminded him of Mescalero dumpsites down in New Mexico, and made him wonder if some of Hanford's honchos had found faceless middlemen to manage the stashing of their little nuclear nightmares. All of this he told his brother, Thomas, as they toured Chelan's North shore together.

"So, that's it, Blood. The industrial park was phase one. It was a way for them to get their foot in the door, make a small, visible investment, and show what good tenants they were, with their green-minded Environmental Research Lab at the center of things. They did the same thing in British Columbia back in the mid-eighties. Now they own most of Vancouver, and shit from their condo-cities' toilets is threatening ecosystems in Puget Sound and the Straits of Juan De Fuca. And people wonder why the cod don't come back to Bainbridge Island's Agate Pass, and salmon catches are down in Seattle's Elliot Bay."

Thomas barely nodded.

"So, I'm thinking the markings I saw on Russ's map of this Cooley Road parcel are the key," Bill continued. "I'm thinking all those X's were drill sites where they tested both their new fresh water aquifer-finding sonar's accuracy, and this oil-eating bacteria in some type of controlled underground saline settings. Maybe they employed these new fracture-drilling techniques that cracked the rock barrier between their fresh water and test sites? Maybe that's how the bug got to the lake—through underground springs."

Bill wheeled off Cooley onto a county road and unfolded a map. He watched his brother brooding from the corner of one eye, and kept the other on the road. "Glad you decided to come along today, big brother."

Thomas twisted his mustache hairs in silence.

"Yeah, Bill. I'm really psyched about finding the source of the fish kill in Mill Bay," Bill said to himself sarcastically.

Thomas still did not respond.

Bill slapped the dash. "Okay, what's up? This morning you were raring to go. Now, you're acting like a zombie."

"Remember that phone call just before we left the lodge?"

Bill dropped the map. His face drew taut. "Did someone else die?"

Thomas sucked air, sighed, and shook his head. "No, more like reincarnation. That call was from Ann. She's..."

The truck swerved off onto the shoulder of the road.

"You're shitting me! *She* called you after all these years?"

Thomas nodded, and tapped the window glass. "She's coming to Seattle this weekend for some wine tasting thing, and wants to meet me at the Westin."

Bill braked hard, and stopped the truck. "You told her no. Right?"

Thomas removed his sunglasses, and rubbed his temples. "Her marriage is falling apart, Bill. She sounded like a nervous wreck. She'd been up all night."

"So what! She wants to come dig up the marital grave, and screw up your life? You're nuts! Prison did warp your mind." Bill noted Tom's pained eyes, and pondered his own past.

He and Nancy had briefly separated when Tom was in prison. He recalled what his brother said then: "No one's an expert on love, Blood. I'm in here and can't do a damn thing about my marriage, but you're out there! To hell with what all the experts are saying about statistics and cultural differences. Listen to your heart, Bro! Look at your son..." Thomas was the only one who did not tell him to get a divorce. It was the best advice he never got.

"I've gotta' go, Bro. I just need to look her in the eye and see. I-I...just got to know if there's anything left inside us," Thomas stammered. "We spent all those years to—"

"What about Marla?" Bill said. "You love her. Don't you?"

Silence.

"Just tell me you'll cover for me Friday and Saturday. I'm scheduled to take some guests on an overnight kayak tour to Domke Falls."

Bill put the truck back in gear. "Okay, you're covered. But what about Wolf's little raiding party on Gordon's fortress of solitude?"

"He'll handle it," Thomas said. "Fish can help him out."

Bill made a face, knowing how much Wolf despised the chef.

"Look, Bill, I'm on parole. Remember? I've already impersonated an INS officer! Isn't that enough?" he asked.

His younger brother looked away.

"I'm going to take the rough draft of that article with me to Seattle, and convince the *Post Intelligencer* to print the final draft in next Friday's edition," Thomas said. "Maybe I can drum up some national attention, and attract some out of town eco-troops to Chelan for the showdown. Plus, if someone is watching us...*I'll* be the decoy on the day Wolf does his thing."

Bill scratched his chin. "Ah, Tom?"

"Yeah, Bill."

"If we attract these *out of towners*, let's not allow them to wear camouflage fatigues, carry assault weapons, or call themselves the Chelan Alliance Militia. I'd hate like hell to see Granite Falls go the way of Ruby Ridge."

Thomas frowned. "Very funny, but seriously, Bill..." He cleared his throat. "As far as Wolf is concerned, the decoy idea and my newspaper article are the only reasons I'm making this trip." Thomas sighed, temporarily at peace with his decision to see his ex-wife. "Let's keep my little reunion with Ann between us. All right?"

Bill stepped on the gas pedal. "What reunion?"

Thomas smiled, and slipped his sunglasses back on. "Cool! Now, let's do these damn drill site inspections, Blood."

AS TRUCK TIRES tread over unnamed rocky roads, the brothers discussed strategies for the all-important July third city council meeting, and the amazing recovery of Neon's fiancee, Miss Ho Pai. They talked about their mysterious friend, Wolf. Thomas revealed some of the things he'd learned about the floatplane pilot's past.

"So, Wolf thinks that Latino who confronted us in Seattle is some retired CIA honcho?" Bill asked.

Thomas nodded. "It's a long story. Evidently, the guy's a ghost from his sordid past, who sold out to the Hong Kong triads. But I've got a feeling it goes way deeper than Wolf's willing to say."

Bill slapped the wheel. The truck lurched to a stop in front of a closed cattle-gate "*This* is what you should be writing about!"

"What?" asked Thomas.

"Chelan! You've been looking for a story, and its happening all around us," Bill announced. They got out, slammed their doors, and checked the gate. An old Ford truck came barreling out of nowhere, slid to a halt behind them, and nearly nudged their bumper.

"You dudes lost?" two bearded longhaired men in overalls shouted out their windows.

Thomas stared at steer manure, blood meal, peat cups, and other growing paraphernalia in the pickup's bed. There was a Grateful Dead sticker on their door. The nearest agricultural area was miles away—in the opposite direction.

The hostile driver laid on the horn. "Hey! You deaf? Move that thing?" the driver commanded.

The hip Baker Brothers knew exactly what was going on. They gave each other the eye. "Chill out!" Bill suggested as they approached the Ford. "We're not the feds. We work for the EPA. Got a tip there's hazardous waste being stored out this way."

"We wouldn't know about that. Most folks out this way mind their own business," the big biker passenger said.

"I hear ya," Thomas said. "My partner and I got no beef with what grows from Mother Earth, though." He smiled. "We're not *crop inspectors*, or po-leece. We're environmentalists. And if we don't find the deep-well drilling site we were tipped about, two things are gonna happen."

The big strangers scratched their chins, whispered suspiciously, then grinned.

Thomas wondered if *they* had Clint Eastwood guns.

"What two things?" they asked.

"First, the lake is going to get polluted, and the salmon population will die off," Thomas said. "Then, after we tell our boss we failed to find the site where all the waste is being stored, a fucking army of real feds is going to sweep through here and stick their noses in everyone's businesses! Probably go on a major land grab. Right, Bill?"

Bill nodded. "They'll go after your guns, your pets…*and* your pot.*"

The suspected marijuana growers told a little tale about a two hundred acre parcel down the road that had been visited by a well-drilling truck out of Pateros over fifty times in the last two years. The Baker Brothers, finding this information extremely interesting, thanked the two avid fishermen for enlightening them, and wished them luck with their crops.

The brothers followed the growers' directions, and soon found themselves boxed in by two sides of brush and barbed wire, and an electronic gate with *No Trespassing* and a Maple Leaf Land Brokers sign posted on it. There was no car in what appeared to be the driveway, which led to a circle of shrubs. They slipped under the gate for a closer look, walked right up to a new southwestern style ranch house, knocked on the door, and looked in the windows.

The house was well furnished. It had a Far-Eastern flair. A large carved elephant stood in a corner. An ornate slot machine sat beside a small wet bar. The one-armed bandit was adorned with dragons, large cats baring teeth, Chinese script, and in English: *Hungry Tiger*.

The driveway continued on to a stand of pines where a large pole barn had been constructed. The pole barn was locked, but the brothers peered through a crack in the door and saw stacks of crates with Chinese and Pakistani labels on them. They fought off a growing sense of paranoia, and followed a dirt path behind the building into a deserted apple orchard. Bill walked briskly between the apple trees, and scanned the soil surface. Thomas stayed on the path.

"What are we looking for?" Thomas inquired.

"Steel or flush concrete surface mounts marking the locations of their capped-off experimental sites," Bill panted. "You watch that side of the orchard, and keep your ears open for any approaching vehicles."

Thomas nodded, and walked slowly, scanning the soil and listening for cars. Bill increased his speed, zigzagging between apple trees. Hot sun baked them. Their hearts beat like scat-singers. Silence overwhelmed them. Thomas thought about Marla, the Westin's wine tasting, and the meeting with his ex-wife.

"Over here!" Bill shouted from up ahead.

THEY WERE in a clearing, taking pictures of scores of capped-off drill sites, when the noise alerted them. When the sound of the approaching auto's engine grew too close for comfort, they scampered for the front gate, hearts galloping, bodies sweating, briers grabbing them with thorny fingers as they stumbled through thickets to avoid being seen.

The silver Mercedes motored straight for the pole barn.

The brothers emerged from the brush, back of the house, and broke for the front gate.

Ashwan Habib hit the brakes, looked over his shoulder, and confirmed the intruder sighting from his rearview mirror. Tires spun, dust flew, and the Mercedes did a doughnut in the dirt.

The Bakers dove under the gate, and rolled to their rig.

Bill fumbled for his keys.

The silver Mercedes quickly closed the distance between them.

Thomas saw the driver grab a flashy chrome revolver.

The foreigner screamed at the top of his lungs, "Sirs! Stop! You there! Do not force me to shoot."

The electronic gate swung open.

Bill revved the engine, ground gears, and slammed his shifter into reverse. Spinning tires spit rocks at the Mercedes' windshield.

"Jehovah's Witness! Sorry to disturb you, sir," Thomas screamed out his window.

"Brace yourself!" Bill shouted, as the truck sped off backwards.

Ashwan Habib shook his head, and laid his weapon on the Mercedes' dash. The doctor decided not to pursue them. Perhaps the Paki was the perfect frontman for Ming Yaht's drill site safe house—a well-paid professional with no wife and no social life. But Ashwan was not a cold-blooded killer.

The bronze-skinned doctor could only watch while the intruders disappeared in a cloud of dust. He briefly considered calling Gordon on the cellular phone. And then he pondered why he ever left his employer in Karachi, declined lucrative offers to perform chemical weapons research in Baghdad and Tehran, and instead, came to work for Ming Yaht in Chelan.

Chapter 27

Retreat Raid

THE OLD YELLOW Volkswagen van coughed and shimmied up the steep grade of Coyote Hill as Chef Gary Fisher coaxed and coddled his hippie-relic driving machine. Neon leaned forward suggestively from behind Fish and snickered.

"Christ's sake, Fish!" Wolf cursed. "Don't Baker pay you enough to buy a decent set of wheels?"

"Laugh if you must, gentlemen. But the Yellow Submarine here has taken me from Mexico City to Maine and back. And it will surely see us safely to our mystery man's fortress of solitude as well."

"Sure, Fish," Neon said, winking at Wolf. "Whatever you say."

Wolf wanted to ask Fish how many engines the wonder-van had blown, but decided not to rile the boy. With Thomas peddling his Chelan story to the newspaper in Seattle, and Bill playing kayak-camping instructor with lodge guests, Wolf needed the chef for a road sentry—even though Marla had informed them that Gordon was in Seattle until Monday.

They made Coyote Hill, motored off pavement through thick stands of pine with strands of barbed wire strung between them, came within sight of the retreat's front gate, and stopped. Wolf unrolled a cloth, checked the tools he'd selected for the raid, and stashed them in his daypack and pockets.

Gary saw wire snips, lockpicks, field glasses, and mystery gadgets. And then the gun! The chef's jaw dropped. "Where did you get all that stuff?"

"From a Cracker Jack box!" Wolf snapped. "They're mine, Gary. Relax. Don't make me regret allowing you to play with us grownups." Wolf tossed the chef a walkie-talkie. "Now, go park off the side of the pavement just before this turnoff and wait for my call. Don't act like your usual nerd self. All right? Act like you're picking mushrooms or something."

"Act? Act? The morels are out there, James," Fish assured him.

Wolf growled. "Just don't you go *out there* too fuckin' far, mister space cadet. Stay within sight of the road, and get your ass on that radio if Gordon's Land Rover or any other vehicle comes rolling down Coyote Hill. Got that?"

Gary Fisher nodded. "Got it."

Wolf shouldered his pack, slammed the sliding door shut, and slipped beneath the barbed wire perimeter of the corporate retreat, with Neon close behind him.

"Good luck," Fish offered, as the forest swallowed them.

"Fuck luck! Just follow my orders," Wolf growled, as he loped off toward Pos' pagoda.

THOMAS WAS LATE—stuck in traffic, trying to stay focused on his luncheon engagement, and hoping he would convince his editor to risk his job for what would be an extremely controversial scoop. His Suburban crawled among compact cars down First Street past Schmicks and McCormicks restaurant, and parked curbside on Marion, a couple blocks away from the popular meeting place.

Baker fed the parking meter.

The 12:05 ferry from Bainbridge Island blasted its horn at Pier 52.

Thomas fought mixed emotions, and debated the merits of meeting his ex-wife at the Westin. He could sense her presence in The Emerald City—just as he sensed Marla was near. He erased both women's faces from his mind's eye, and jogged off to Schmicks, rehearsing his lines for the editor.

RED TIP OF HAVANA cigar glowed, sending green-gray snakes slithering to the clean white ceiling of Gordon's thirty-first floor, downtown Seattle office. Nick couldn't stand the Noriega-faced Cuban's smoke any more than watching another rerun of the Ming Yaht security video. Gordon studied the barrel-chested Arturos Aquindo beside him—shirt undone, gold rope shining off his wrinkly neck, gut protruding, wing-tip shoes on desk, hands adorned with diamond rings, wrist wrapped by a platinum Rolex...*Puke!* Nicholas Gordon had seen enough tape to cancel his Seattle weekend and rush back to Chelan. He shut off the VCR, and raised the blinds. "That's them all right, Arty. What did you say they told Sharon that day they showed up down here?"

"This *Agent* Wolf used the old intimidation routine. Said he was here to investigate undocumented Asians suspected of gang affiliations." The Cuban crushed the cigar between his teeth, seething at having mentioned his old nemesis' name.

Nick's study of the Colonel continued.

"Very creative of him. Wouldn't you say, Nicholas?"

Nick ground gold crowns. "Very stupid. That's what I say. So, what's our next move?"

"I'm not sure..." Arturos Aquindo lied. He wanted Wolf liquidated, and he wanted Gordon to do the deed. It was simply a matter of when and where. He wondered, how many more miles did this over-the-hill mercenary have left in him? "This public meeting in Chelan is only ten days away. Hopefully, it's too late for them to stick a monkeywrench in that. In the mean time, I'll study damage control scenarios. Your main concern should be sitting on the Chelan nest." He took a long pull on his stogie. "You know what they say, Nicholas. *While the cat's away, the mice will play.*" The Colonel exhaled a thick puff of smoke.

Nick perceived an attitude problem in the self-appointed Colonel, and was becoming increasingly paranoid. The human hawk sensed a power play underway. The contract that he had been contacted about came to mind. *They* hadn't been disturbed by the two hundred people he sent to hell on New Years. *And why should they?* he thought. *They all multiplied like rabbits.* It was the billions lost because of Po Lin's strategic move to burn Golden Triangle poppy fields that had really pissed off the ruling Hong Kong *Sun Yee On* hierarchy.

Nick recalled the astute advice of his Special Forces instructor all those years ago—a *real* colonel. *Never underestimate your opposition, Gordon. Is that clear? Perfectly clear, sir.* It was the opposition, which was becoming unclear to Nick. And both sides in his current predicament were severely underestimating him.

"Nicholas! Did you hear what I said?"

Nick nodded. "Loud and clear. You know, Arty...I really think you've been spending too much time around the chinks in Hong Kong. You're starting to sound a lot like the old man with your goddamn proverbial sayings."

Arturos detected signs of insubordination. "Speaking of the Great Po, the *old man* is taking Canada by storm, Nicholas. He's making personal appearances at all the work sites." Aquindo knocked ashes from his cigar onto Gordon's clean floor. "Paving the yellow brick road for his people. Fortunately for you, my friend, he's saved Chelan for the last stop on his North American tour."

"Fortunately?" Nick quizzed. The hawk had never worried about his relationship with Po. *Should he be worried now?*

The cunning Cuban nodded. "Lin has personally conveyed his displeasure with your progress in Chelan to me and—"

Gordon's concern grew. "Really," Nick said calmly. "And what did you tell him?"

Arturos stood, turned his back to Gordon, and poured two stiff drinks. "I told him I had faith in you. I said we'd have this little chat and get our priorities straight." The Colonel sipped his scotch. "Nicholas, I think you should deal with this writer, Baker, immediately."

"Just what do you suggest I do? This isn't South Africa, or some two-bit dime store novel, Arty. There's been way too many *accidents* for a town that size already."

Arturos nodded. "You're right, Nick. Our options are limited. The guy's had too much media exposure to risk liquidation."

"Agreed," Gordon said coolly.

"I've reviewed his file myself, Nick. The man's an ex-con. He's still on parole. Perhaps your local contact could arrange to have him violated?"

"Are you suggesting we let the feds handle him?"

"Precisely. A dirty urine specimen, and a well-placed news release would discredit him as a worthless druggie, and send his ass back to the pen like the threat to society he is!" They clicked glasses and laughed robustly. "We have to remove the writer from the public eye before this decisive meeting on the third. Oh, yes. Evidently, this Baker fellow has another weakness. Your girl, Sharon, thinks he's become romantically involved with a Miss Decker down on floor twenty-one."

Nick punched buttons on the phone bank, downed his drink, and strained to speak into the speaker box with a pleasant tone of voice. "Good morning, Sharon. Could you locate Marla Decker and have her report to my office? She doesn't seem to be at her station."

"Marla took the day off, Mr. Gordon," Sharon Riker replied. "She went to a wine tasting at the Westin Hotel. Should I leave a message on her home phone for you?"

"No, that won't be necessary, Sharon. I'm heading back to Chelan immediately. It wasn't important anyway. Have a nice day." Gordon grabbed his briefcase, and knocked back his scotch. "What about this Wolf, Arty? Why haven't you provided me with a file on him?" he asked the Cuban.

"Ah, *Agent* Wolf. He could prove to be an interesting challenge for you, Nicholas." Aquindo avoided the question, then enjoyed watching Gordon grimace for a moment. "We'll play that one by ear, *amigo*." He poured himself another drink, and offered Nick one as well.

Gordon turned it down. "I've got a two hour drive ahead of me, Arty." Nick shook Arturos' sweaty hand, and broke for the door.

"Keep me posted," said the Cuban.

"Will do. *Adios...amigo*," replied Gordon.

When the door closed, Arturos Aquindo popped his briefcase, paged through Nick's file, and punched the proper code numbers on the face of his scrambler box. The number in Vancouver rang. It was time for him to give his *real* assessment of Project Pristine Valley-CH-97 to the Great Po.

WOLF AND NEON had combed the corporate retreat twice, and came up empty-handed. They'd gone through the garage, and been to the boathouse. They even broke the arm off a bronze Buddha in the center of the koi pond, hoping to find some secret mechanism which would reveal the stash they sought. They ascended the spiral staircase again, and stood side by side in the center of the glass octagon. Wolf shook his head. Their patience grew thin. Neon fixed his eyes on the full-wall artwork he'd inadvertently installed for their adversaries. It was still his greatest work to date, but the longer he studied it, the angrier he got.

Wolf eyed the weapons wall opposite the life-sized glass-light-warriors. He studied swords and metal stars, straining to think like Nick the merciless mercenary might—hoping to find a clue. When none came, he cursed the warrior wall, plucked a staff, and employed it in a *kata* movement across the matted floor.

The walkie-talkie blurted from his belt, and Wolf froze in place.

"Agent Fish to raiding party! Agent Fish to raiding party!"

Wolf dropped the staff he was holding. "You see something out there, Gary? Over."

"Yeah, James. I seez da' biggest morel mushroom I eva' did see! How's hunting in your neck of the woods?"

"No luck, dumb fuck," Wolf growled. "And this ain't no game! Don't bother us again without a damn good reason. I'm trying to think here. Over."

"Touchy, aren't we? Over."

"Grrr! Unless there's an emergency, don't call us. We'll call you. Got that, *Agent Fish*? Over."

"Loud and clear, *Mon Capitain*! Over." The contented chef switched off the device and strolled deeper-still into the morel-filled forest surrounding him.

Neon had decided they might never prove it, but Nick Gordon had to be the guy behind Ming Yaht's Chelan mayhem. Accordingly, he tore a tube-flesh leg from his glass creation.

Wolf scratched his chin as the kid waved the tube above his head, waiting for approval. The pilot rubbed his palms together, strutted to the weapons wall, and pulled upon the jeweled handle of an ancient warlord's sword. After freeing the blade from its affixed silver sheath, he faced his angry young friend and bowed in salutation.

Neon returned the gesture and sliced air with glass.

Wolf sized up the slender colored tube. "*Shazzam!*" he shouted.

Steel shattered glass. A puff of trapped neon gas escaped its prison.

Neon's jaw dropped. He pointed to the weapons wall behind Wolf, which was parting like the Red Sea.

The pilot jumped high into the air, and landed in a combat-ready position—only to face the stash they had been looking for.

They had been looking for a wall safe, but they were thinking too small for the Pos. The removal of the jewel-handled sword had revealed a secret walk-in closet. Inside its climate-controlled environs, jade statues, ivory tusks, and rhino horns sat beside cases of vintage wines, and several priceless paintings. The entire back wall was a safe! But the corkboard beside it was what really caught their eyes. Upon it hung a collection of newspaper clippings—all proud trophies from the private war of Nicholas Gordon.

Accidental Explosion Suspected in Boat Sinking on Lake Chelan. CHELAN MIRROR, OCTOBER 23, 1995.

Asian Turf Wars Come to Quebec as First China Bank Building Blows its Top! MONTREAL GAZETTE, January 1, 1996.

Corral Creek Tribal Chief's Death Due to Brake Failure. CHELAN MIRROR, March 15, 1995.

There were more.

Neon read in horror over Wolf's shoulder. "Those murdering bastards!"

"Don't be so surprised, kid. Who'd you think was behind this shit?"

"Like you knew all along, Mr. Action-Adventure?" Neon snapped.

Wolf ignored him, and sat his pack on the floor beside the safe.

"Think this guy wired my shop?" Neon asked.

Wolf shrugged, and removed something wrapped in brown paper from his pack. "Most assuredly," he muttered, as he molded light-gray putty around the safe's dial.

Wolf ordered Neon from the room, lit a short fuse, and ran. Seconds later the big steel safe blew open. They returned when the smoke cleared, and saw marble shelves laden with treasure. There were stacks of currency—Greenbacks, British Sterling, Japanese Yen, German Marks, Canadian Dollars. There were gold and platinum bars, and plastic tubes packed with gold coins—Chinese Pandas, Maple Leafs, American Eagles, South African Krugerands. They found four passports—U.S., Canadian, Macau, Irish—each with an officially stamped photo of Nicholas Gordon, but not one showed that name. Below the shelves, a file drawer beckoned. Wolf grabbed the handle warily and slowly pulled...

THE BLACK LAND ROVER rolled over Coyote Hill. Fish heard the engine's roar, and soon saw Gordon stop roadside, right beside the Yellow Submarine. The chef nearly swallowed his tongue when Nick strode into the woods and called-out for the van's driver. Fish removed the walkie-talkie from his belt. His heart raced wildly as he depressed the *talk* button.

Gordon kept coming. He bent back some tree branches and saw Gary.

The frightened chef tossed the two-way radio behind his back where it landed in some ferns.

Crack!

FILES GALORE filled Gordon's secret safe. Most of them were coded. All of them had photos. Wolf whipped through them, searching for familiar faces. Some had *position terminated* stamped across ID pictures. Russ Warwick was among those unfortunate former Ming Yaht employees. There were files on the Pos, with Chinese script and figures. One extensive file stirred Wolf's animal blood. It listed secret Senate testimony targeting one Arturo Aquindo as a major co-conspirator in the BCCI banking scandal. There was more. The words *cover up* appeared often.

Wolf's unchecked growl echoed in the closet-sized enclosure. He snapped the folder shut. *Evidently, Nick saw **everyone** as a potential enemy. Gordon was collecting insurance policies, carrying heavy baggage...and battling some ghosts of his own.*

"Who was that guy?" Neon quizzed.

"Never mind, Kid," Wolf mumbled, closing the Cuban's file, and opening the next batch.

These files contained close-up photographs of the good ship *Connie Joe* and the Warwick family, Granite Falls Lodge and the Bakers, Lone Wolf Air's building and Beaver and pilot, Forever Neon...and Ming Yaht's entire secretarial pool. An enlargement of Marla Decker caught their eyes, as did a series of shots from the Chelan Biotech Research Lab, featuring Neon and Pai in action. A file on his fiancee gave Neon fits. He snatched it from Wolf's hand, and stormed out of the secret room screaming obscenities.

Wolf would have taken the file back from Neon, had he not noticed the large black nylon gym bag at the bottom of the safe.

The Beaver pilot carefully unzipped the black bag... *"Yes!"* he whispered.

The first thing Wolf discovered was the remote control detonator, then a collapsible parabolic listening-device, and a pen-tech light. There were C-4 plastic explosive cakes, a container of chloroform, and some folded cheesecloth, too. He tried on Nick's night vision goggles. "Nice," he muttered. He fingered fine, sharp jeweler's floss, which Gordon had used to sabotage his floatplane's engine lines.

Suddenly, Wolf's walkie-talkie crackled to life with the voice of the sentry chef.

"James? Neon? Can you hear me? Damn this thing!"

The chef never cursed. His voice sounded tense. Wolf heard tapping sounds and static. He depressed the *talk* button on his two-way radio. "Gary? Fish! Do you read me? Over."

"James Wolf! That you? Listen, I just—"

"Thought I told you not to use this damn thing unless—"

"He's on his way. Get the hell out of...now!"

The transmission was weak and broken.

"Fish?" said Wolf. "Could you repeat? Who's on the way? Over."

"Gordon! Gordon just quizzed me five minutes ago. Over."

"Don't fuck with me, dipshit. Why did you wait so long to call? Over," asked Wolf.

"It happened too quick! Didn't want Gordon to s...walk-ie-talkie...Tossed it in...batteries popped out and...Fuck your macho shit. Just get the hell out! Are you deaf, or what? He'll be there any second now. Run for it!"

Old one-ear Wolf heard perfectly. "Check your watch, Gary. In five minutes have the van along the fence. Come all the way to the gate, turn around, and start driving back toward paved road slowly. Don't worry, we'll find you. Just be ready to haul ass. Got it? Over."

"Got it. Good luck! Over," Fish exclaimed.

"Fuck luck. Just be there. Over and out."

Wolf drew his revolver, checked the hollow-point bullets in its chamber, and snapped it back in his shoulder holster. He stuffed Gordon's dirty tricks bag with selected items, and bolted from the stash room with his daypack hanging over one shoulder.

Neon was transforming his martial arts creation into shattered rubble in the center of the glass octagon.

Wolf grabbed him. "Forget that, kid. We're outta here!"

"No, wait. I'm not—"

"Wait my ass!" Wolf slapped his friend's face. "Move out! Gordon's on his way here."

"Gordon?" The glazed look left Neon's eyes. "Sorry, man. I just couldn't let those bastards keep my work after—"

Wolf slapped the kid's back. "I understand. You know, you've made this an interesting crime scene. Maybe Gordon will think it was just an isolated act of mindless vandalism? Naaah!"

Neon smiled, and high-fived his comrade.

"Let's haul ass," Wolf commanded.

And the two raiders flew down the silver spiral staircase.

GORDON HAD just cleared the gate, when two figures flashed across the drive and dashed into the thick woods like wild jackrabbits. Instinctively, he dove from his Rover and flew through the forest like a hungry hawk.

Wolf heard a door slam shut, and loped even faster toward the rendezvous spot. He concentrated his canine vision for a flash of the rescue van. He strained to hear the sickly sounds of the Volkswagen's engine.

A horn honked.

Wolf whistled. "Run, kid! Run," he ordered Neon.

Fish skidded to a halt and flung open his sliding door. "James! Someone's coming in the woods behind you. Look out!"

"Here, catch!" Wolf screamed, tossing the heavy gym bag to the weak-armed chef. The barbed wire web was spun thick between tall trees where the Yellow Submarine had surfaced. Wolf produced a pair of wire cutters and quickly went to work.

Snip. Snip.

Two tightly stretched strands snapped. Their metal thorns cut Wolf's hide and face. "Fuck," he cursed, as he pushed the slimmer Neon through the gap in the fencing.

The kid's clothes ripped, and Neon fell.

Nicholas Gordon popped into the clearing right behind them.

Snip!

Another strand of wire snapped.

Gordon reached for his gun.

Wolf hit the ground and rolled. He tossed his wheelman his daypack, leaped into the van, and felt for his holstered gun. *They didn't need a firefight.* "Floor this bitch, Gary," blurted the pilot.

Fish hit the gas.

The retreat raiders rolled to the rear of the bus.

Nick Gordon aimed uncharacteristically high and fired twice, before choking on their dust.

"DID I DO GOOD?" the chef asked above a stressed-out Volkswagon van engine.

"Do you have my luggage, Gary?" Wolf inquired.

Fish patted the bag and pack on the seat next to him. "Sure do. They certainly are heavy. What's in 'em...rocks?"

A smile creased Wolf's bleeding face. "Pieces of the puzzle, man. Just pieces of this damn puzzle," the pilot muttered.

"So, I did good. Eh, *Mon Capitain*?"

Wolf crawled up behind the driver's seat, snatched Gordon's black bag, and patted his wheelman on the back. "You're damn right you did, *Chefman*. You done good today. *Real good.*"

Wolf howled.

The Yellow Submarine filled with victory cheers.

Three blocks back, the hawk ground his gold crowns as the corporate retreat raider's laughter found his ears.

Chapter 28

Reunion

THOMAS SCANNED tables in the Westin's Palm Court, seeking the face which had lured him to this place. Most men would not have attended this reunion, but then, he prided himself on not being like most men. Ann's second marriage had failed. He had spent a large portion of his life with her. They had history, albeit scarred. In his mind, he owed her this much. And so, he scanned the colorful sea of sun dresses and sport coats in the Westin's glass enclosure for lost love.

Stay calm! The voice of reason told her as she tapped painted nails atop her table. *I come all this way dressed to kill and he's late! He'll be late to his own funeral,* said another voice.

Ann fondled the pearl necklace he'd given her for their final anniversary, felt a nervous neck rash coming on, and dabbed it with a damp cloth napkin. She saw him at the hostess station. He was wearing the charcoal sport coat she'd given him for their last Christmas together. She started hyperventilating. Ann took one more peek in her tiny compact's mirror, puckered red lips model-like, gave her hair a pat, and oh so slowly…she stood.

Thomas watched a golden shaft of sunlight fall upon her broad shoulders, and thought, *God, she still looks good!* Then he thought about the way she let her father influence his prison sentencing, and how she'd kept her distance all these years. Out of nowhere, a powerful wave of bitterness swept over him. He shook it off, donned his warmest smile, and went to her with open arms. "How's my big girl?" he asked.

Their pulses raced. Their lips met. They embraced.

MARLA JEAN DECKER. emerged from the Palm Court's powder room in a cheerful mood. She was glad she had convinced Mrs. Kramer to attend the afternoon session of this wine tasting with her. She was feeling slightly giddy from the grape as she sauntered toward Georgette. She was feeling good about her life—until she saw a gorgeous blond locking lips with her man from Granite Falls!

The impact of the picture was earth shattering. She dropped her purse, and felt a pain in her heart. She watched the scene for a moment—only to be sure—then turned away, unable to take any more. *Men!* she thought to herself. *He'd been so damn open with her. Men!* He'd never so much as hinted of another woman, but this was another woman—a woman he had journeyed all the way from his sacred Chelan just to heavy-pet in public. *So...the romantic writer was just another player? Men!*

"Marla? Marla, dear. Are you all right?" Georgette inquired as she picked the fallen purse off of the floor.

Part of her wanted to confront him. She rubbed her temples and decided to go quickly, before Georgette noticed them, or Thomas saw her. "I'm not feeling very well, Georgette," Marla Decker said.

"Let's get you home then," the kindly landlady replied.

FOR THOMAS and Ann, the wine tasting scene went surprisingly well. They talked of old times and memorable travels from his outlaw era. They laughed and relaxed. Ann's low self-esteem was bolstered by the attention he gave her. He suggested they break away and enjoy the remainder of the day. Ann agreed. Their optimism grew. For Thomas, the time had come to act out a scene he had written and edited a thousand times with countless endings. He drove his Chevy to Pier 52, and they boarded the Bainbridge Island ferry.

On the upper deck they stood amid tourists listening to live dulcimer music, and holding hands. A rare pod of killer whales swam by. Ann leaned over the rail to watch them, with his strong arms wrapped tightly around her slender waist. Her flaxen hair flowed freely. Puget Sound's salty breath lifted her floral sun dress, exposing shapely legs and thighs. He wanted badly to undress her—*with more than just his eyes.*

Eagle Harbor's guardian, Wing Point, welcomed Thomas and Ann back to the set of Island *déjà vu*. The ferryboat captain slammed powerful engines into reverse. Time stood still for these two former lovers. And as the steel mass beneath them glided like a sleek seabird to the waiting dock at Winslow, they both began to wonder just what it was they were looking for.

They took a quick tour, only to find that so much had changed. They saw the yuppie McDonald's, and a large shopping complex with an enormous Safeway supermarket. They drove by the beach house where they spent that romantic April—only to discover that someone had covered its rustic wood exterior with gaudy vinyl siding.

Thomas parked the truck, and he and Ann walked down Main Street. Every shop, each restaurant, represented a memory. They sat in front of the picturesque white wooden church where he had proposed. A rare crop of native middle-class children offered them free kittens from a cardboard box. Affluent transplanted California adolescents cruising for tourist girls flattered Ann with wolf whistles.

They meandered to the waterfront. He peered longingly through the windows of Eagle Harbor Book Café, and remembered when he used to shun such intellectual meccas. Ann admired a neighboring jewelry shop's display. They went to Harbour Public House for wine and hors d'oeuvres on the outdoor deck, and watched sailboats returning from Puget Sound. Thomas sought the elusive combination of scent and emotion, which had once captured him body and soul. Ann remembered all the good times she had conveniently forgotten.

"Bainbridge used to be such a diamond in the rough," he said, pointing toward scores of new buildings peeking through forests of white sailing masts with only an occasional green tree.

"Looks like she's gone through a lot of changes," Ann said.

"Too many," he remarked sadly. "Too much polish. She's starting to lose her luster."

"Am I?" Ann asked half-hearted. She perceived the return of her neck rash, and nervously reached out for his hand.

He shook his head, and pecked her cheek. "Come on. Let's take a nature break," he whispered.

He drove to Fort Ward Park, backed up to a rocky bank overlooking Rich Passage, and dropped the tailgate. They sat in silent reverence watching seabirds feed at sunset. He wanted her so badly he could taste her! But she would have to come to him.

Ann slowly massaged his shoulders, then slipped trembling fingers beneath his shirt. She closed her eyes tightly, dismissed the demon she'd created to justify her desertion, and in the waning light she saw the tear-streaked face of the man she fell in love with in her rebellious youth.

He hadn't cried, since the day she left him. A stubborn voice commanded him to resist her touch. He swallowed hard, remembering his bachelor code: *Nothing lasts forever.* And then he shuddered as he recalled the day she'd said those very words to him in a lonely prison visiting room when the going got tough, foreshadowing what was to come.

Her nails dug deeper. For years now she had secretly longed for the old excitement she had yet to experience with anyone but him. She had been feeling old. *She needed to feel young and desired!* She unzipped her dress.

He unbuttoned his shirt.

The Berlin Wall between them came tumbling down. They fell back in the bed of his Chevy and made passionate love. She received all his affection, and more importantly...*his forgiveness.* In his familiar arms, she purred softly and securely.

Thomas held her tenderly, trying to forget the other man she ran to so quickly in his time of need. He thought of Marla as well. Far below, a huge car ferry ran Rich Passage en route to

Bremerton, and sent hypnotic waves crashing over smooth rock shores. Sensible skippers fell in line behind the brute, riding the ferry's wake to safe moorage at Poulsbo's Liberty Bay. Soft pastels painted slack tide waters. Dusk descended. A reflective writer breathed salty air from the sea, and drank life's bittersweet poetry.

ON THE JOURNEY back to the Emerald City, Thomas and Ann found second wind. They drove to Jazz Alley for music and drinks, and ended up in the Westin's lounge. Ann got a little tipsy, but maintained her best behavior—like a blind date content with the luck of the draw. Even when their waitress spilled Grand Marnier on her dress, Ann showed rare restraint. "That's okay. Don't worry about it," she said politely.

Thomas was impressed, but suspected her Hungarian temper was boiling behind those big brown eyes. Especially after their awkward waitress returned, and he tipped her, then winked.

Ann merely shook her head, and directed his attention to a full-wall mirror. "We always were an impressive-looking couple," she said.

Thomas nodded. "So tell me what happened with you and the carpenter."

She bit her lip. "I caught him fucking some young slut divorcee in our own bed."

He struggled to contain his smile. He kind of felt sorry for her, but thought of karma too. "So, good old Norman turned out to be quite the handyman?"

She dipped her napkin in soda water and rubbed hard at the stain on her dress.

Thomas noticed a drunk ogling Ann from across the room and remembered how jealous he used to get. *He wasn't jealous now.* He had a brief affair when they were married. The affair was good. It was the guilt that nearly killed him. She never knew for sure. *Screw affairs!* Adultery definitely didn't belong in the home like good old Normy thought. But the writer recognized lust for the primal instinct that it was. Anyway, adultery was so much easier to forgive, than say…*desertion.*

They ordered more liquor. It was the most Thomas had drunk in years. His head spun. He was reminded of their final free-world nights together when excessive drinking and wild sex relieved the pressure of his trial, numbed emotions, and soothed the painful thought of their impending separation.

"Why were you so late this afternoon, Thomas?" She had been dying to ask him this question.

"I had a business luncheon with a newspaper editor."

She eyed him suspiciously. "Oh? How did it go?"

"Very well. I represent an environmentalist group in Chelan and—"

"You?" She laughed and ruffled his hair. "My green-eyed rebel without a cause...*involved?*"

"That's right." He pulled away, stung by her remark. "I've always enjoyed the great outdoors. Remember? I thought it was time I got involved with something worthwhile." A familiar tune played over the sound system. Thomas mouthed the words.

"Do you still get up and sing those stupid old songs to lounge lizards in piano bars?" Ann asked with a sultry smile.

He was tempted to ask if she ever read his novel, or if she still only indulged in fashion magazines featuring glamorous accessories and original stories like '*How to Keep Your Man.*' Instead, he stared at her with devilish eyes, and said, "Not lately. Why don't we finish these drinks...*in bed.*"

ONE MINUTE after the door closed they were naked in the sack. Ann lay on her stomach, lit a cigarette, and handed him some lotion. She sipped Grand Marnier coyly from the nightstand, and covered the telephone with her lacy panties.

Thomas straddled her, began massaging, and became aroused. He recalled her negative remark about his improv singing in public places, and pressed himself firmly into the small of her back.

"Ow! Ease up," she squealed.

He took her cigarette and crushed it.

She flipped over, assumed a luring pose, and licked her pearls. With one wet finger she fondled herself, and moaned, "Come on, Lion." She had dieted for weeks for this moment. She was five pounds from her wedding weight. "Come on down," she coaxed.

This was their old game. Get good and drunk and play sexual warriors. It sustained their marriage for years, and would have continued to, had he been there. But was this *all* that he had missed? He grabbed her wrists and pinned her to the bed.

A poem took shape in his weary head:

Why does man's power and pride
leave the room, when perfume fills the air...
and sleek thighs spread before hungry eyes
*to reveal that wonder '***down there?***'*
Magical beads of moisture call from the oyster—the cherrystone—
to the bone.
Men may have all the power and money...
But women got the honey!
Why resist?

Thomas took a dive to the hive...and kissssed.

This was a big part of what Ann had missed. Wanting to gain the upper hand, she grabbed him by the hair.

He came up for air, downed her drink, and whispered softly. "You know, Annie...I understand what you did. I really do." He pushed her head down onto the pillow and bit her nipple. "But how you did it sucked!"

She bucked.

He tantalized the edge of her desire, then abruptly pulled away to say: "Even my old high school girlfriends kept in touch when I was locked up in that place!"

Confusion and guilt swept over her face. Sexual prowess she relied upon fell prey to the angry lion. "People very close to me convinced me to let it go, Thomas."

His body drew tighter. "That's bullshit, Ann. It was *your* decision!" He wanted to ask her how her dear old dirty-cop dad was doing, but the time had come for some serious screwing. For a second he considered shattering her world by walking away, but the liquor in his belly wouldn't let him. This time, Ann would not forget him.

"But Thomas, I-I…"

"*Shhhh!*" he uttered as he lunged for the peace, the long sought, oh-so-soothing release.

"Thomassss…" she shuddered.

MARLA JEAN DECKER snapped her book shut. She was too disturbed to read. She walked to the refrigerator for the hundredth time and studied its contents. Too confused for food. She kicked the frig-door shut. All she hungered for were answers about a certain writer. *Who was the blond? Was he just using her? Once a con…always a con? Where was he now?*

She picked up the latest note he had written her and tore it into little pieces. *How could she have been such a fool?* Men! She paced the floor. *Men!* She had risked her job for him. ***Men!***

She checked her phone to make certain it was working. She turned on her radio and tried listening to some jazz. She lay on the floor with her cat and stared into her aquarium. Soothing bubbles rose from fancy colored gravel. Her favorite fish fluttered up to the glass to greet her. But the longer she looked at the aquamarine background, the more it reminded her of Baker and Lake Chelan.

She eyed her phone and drew her calico cat close to her breast. *"Men,"* she said meekly.

Marla Decker had never felt so alone, but there was nothing she could do.

She could not even rest.

BACK AT THE WESTIN, Thomas was being reminded that Ann was a natural in the sack, or as some would say…a nymphomaniac. Beneath sweat-soaked sheets their rhythm was hot and fast. The bed rocked.

The neighbors banged on the wall.

Ann's raccoon claws demanded more from her writer cat.

The phone call changed all that.

Thomas glanced at the clock radio. 2:45 a.m.! When the phone rang again, he noticed the red message light blinking beneath Ann's lacy panties. His fever broke. "Answer it," he said.

Another climax was so close. "Dear God! Let it ring," she suggested, pulling him down. "Nothing can be that important."

Thomas remembered telling his brother to call him if anything went wrong with Wolf's raid on Ming Yaht's corporate retreat. His heart skipped a beat. He lifted the receiver and handed it to Ann.

She furrowed her brow, and punched his arm. "Hello?" she answered, panting.

"Hello, Ann. Sorry to disturb you, but I left a message with the front desk for my brother to call me. Is he there?"

"Yes," she sighed, handing Thomas the phone. She watched his face, and felt him withdraw, as Bill informed him of the afternoon raid and all the things Wolf had found.

Thomas listened intently. The photo files were extremely unnerving—especially the one on Marla. He wondered what these latest discoveries might mean for all of them...

"Are you there?" Bill asked after a minute of silence.

Thomas swallowed hard. "Yeah, Bill. I hear you."

"So how's the reunion going? Or can't you say right now?"

"Uh huh. I see, but why aren't you out camping with that kayak club from Baltimore?"

"Stormy Mountain lived up to her name. It rained like hell here this morning. The lake was rough. We had high winds, hail, and...*hey!* Did I interrupt your porking scene, or—"

"Yeah, Bill. You did good. So what's the forecast look like?"

"Cloudy, real cloudy. I'm starting to wonder what we've gotten ourselves into."

"Me too. What's Wolf say?"

"He asked me if you'd be back tomorrow. Says he wants to talk about raising the *Connie Joe*. I guess I'll take those city slickers out on the lake at sunrise and..." Bill hesitated. "Are you gonna spend the weekend with Ann?"

Thomas cleared his throat. "I don't know. Go ahead and take them out if the weather breaks, Bill. Let me think things over tonight."

"Listen, Tom. Maybe you better have a talk with Marla."

"Maybe. Be careful out there tomorrow, Blood. Keep your eyes open and stay close to shore. Thanks for calling. Good night." The call snatched Thomas from fantasy and brought him back to reality. He sat up on the edge of the bed and rubbed his temples.

Ann saw a major mood swing in his sober face. She ran manicured nails down his spine.

He shook his head and pulled away.

She pushed her luscious breasts together and licked them, recalling how it used to turn him on. She reached for him, and she touched.

He felt. He watched. He remembered for a moment...then tried to forget. Ann was lovely in the flesh, but the overwhelming scent of sex—even her skilled hands' caress—could not revive his affection, or alter his direction.

She sensed she was losing him—after finally finding him again. "What's wrong, honey? Why did Bill call here?" she said with pouty lips.

"Problems at the lodge," he lied, looking away.

She suspected more. "Can't they wait? I planned on spending the entire weekend together. Thomas, it's been so long."

"Too damn long," he said, watching her light a cigarette. He hated women smoking. It was the only thing he had asked her to give up for him when they were together. "When did you start that nasty habit again?" he scowled.

She nervously snuffed it out in the ashtray, and turned on the radio. "Norman didn't care," she muttered. "*He* smoked too."

"Fuck Norman!" Thomas shouted, jumping off the bed. He tossed her cigarettes against the wall, switched her radio station from rock to oldies, and walked over to the window. The mellower music soothed him. His thoughts shifted to Marla and her attractions to music, art, the environmental movement, the outdoors, and writing. He considered his feelings for the Emerald City secretary; then looked back at Ann biting her lips and pulling wet sheets over chilled breasts. Sure, Ann was still as sensual as ever, but what they had in common now ended there. He'd always been able to attract sensual women, even ones with supple young skin like the tender Chelan Deli Twin. But if he was going to fall again…*he wanted it all.*

Ann was worried. Once they had been lovers—soul mates— sharing everything, but no more. She'd closed that door with silence when he needed her the most, hoping love would die, and he would disappear. And now? She finally realized that she had succeeded.

Thomas closed his eyes, and imagined hearing songbirds by the soothing waters of Domke Falls. He envisioned Marla's fresh face, and felt their kiss amid a rainbowed mist. He recalled their synchronized kayaking, the hot spring pool, and her stay at Yeti Chalet. He remembered a romantic couple walking at Green Lake, drinking warm saki, and making *real love* on a black silk kimono with bright orange butterflies. Thomas Baker sighed.

Love was such a strange thing. Baker did not know what tomorrow would bring. But he believed that both he and Ann had been correct in saying *'nothing lasts forever.'* And as for love the second time around? Maybe there were exceptions, but at this moment he could say beyond a doubt that it tasted sweeter when it was new and unscarred.

She felt compelled to break the ice. "Why can't Bill take care of things in Chelan until Sunday?"

"It's not as simple as that, Annie. I'm involved with this environmental group. They need me."

"I need you," she declared. They were difficult words for her to say.

"Do you? Do you really?" He watched tears form in her big brown eyes, and started to feel guilty.

"Thomas, it's not like you to-to—"

"To what? Walk out on you? Get involved? What? Things change, Annie."

"Obviously!" she screamed, shaking her head. She began to hyperventilate. Pulsating veins protruded from her neck. "All you used to care about was your precious marijuana money! You managed it. You laundered it with fancy bookkeeping, and by buying real estate, an-and antiques from that faggot Englishman! I'll bet you were screwing that redheaded accountant of yours, too. You-you—"

"Shut up! You're drunk. That's not true," he said through clenched teeth. "I cared about you more than you'll ever know." Her harsh words hurt him. He charged the bed and shook her. "What was I supposed to do with the fucking money, keep it buried in the ground? I did my best to make you happy, to take care of you."

She nodded repeatedly and punched her pillow. "And your best was good, Thomas. Too damn good! I woke up one day and all that was gone. *You* were gone," she sobbed. "What was I supposed to do? Be a martyr? Wait five years in an empty bed?" She shook convulsively. "What would you have done?"

He lowered his face to hers, and said quietly, "Kept in touch. Shared your life."

"What life?" She laughed bitterly. "You were as good as dead."

He grabbed her by the chin.

She pulled free, flailed the air wildly with both arms and screamed, "All right! I was a selfish bitch! I'm not as strong as you are. It's not a perfect world. Is that what you want to hear?"

"What was I to you?" he asked, reaching for the six grand string of pearls glistening around her pretty goose neck. "Just some young sugar daddy?"

Ann tore the pearl necklace free and tossed it in his face. "You asshole! I didn't love you for the money." Her tears fell freely. She drew her knees to her breasts and cried. "You didn't know the pain!"

Thomas stepped back and shook his head. He took several deep breaths, and paced the carpet. He raced back to her bedside and pounded his fist on the nightstand. "Don't tell me about pain, Annie! I'm not some macho asshole. Believe me, baby. *I...**know...**pain.*" He fought back tears.

Ann was trembling.

Thomas heard Barbara Streisand's voice on the clock radio. He cherished the lady crooner. Ann did not. He turned up the volume, walked to the window, and tugged at the drapes. The Emerald City landscape was captivating. The legendary singer's song was so apropos. The words were penetrating.

Two former lovers listened intently. *"A writer takes his pen, to write the words again—that all in love is fair! All in love is fair..."*

Thomas turned away from the window, craving the last word. "Remember me however you want, Ann. But don't say I never loved you." He pointed a finger at her. "And don't blame it on the money, either. Money has to be managed just as sure as people have to have dreams and goals. Yes, I made it. And perhaps, for a time, I was imprisoned by the power of gold. Let's just admit it gave us security and was a necessary evil which we both enjoyed." He picked his silk Victoria's Secret brand boxer shorts off the floor and slipped them on. "And I...no, we paid dearly for it. *End* of story."

She opened her mouth to speak, but he walked over and put his finger to her lips.

"As for Bill's call and my life, let me tell you a little bedtime story." He lowered his voice to a whisper. "Once upon a time in a dark and lonely place, a Lion had nothing but a dream about living in a pristine valley and watching it grow. Now that I've been lucky enough to live the dream, I've made a commitment to help preserve it."

He kissed the tears from her face. "You know me, Annie. I don't make many commitments. But by God, when I do? At least *I* stick with them...no matter what the price."

Thomas pecked her cheek, walked into the bathroom, and closed the door behind him. Barbara Streisand sang the tune: *"A Writer takes his pen, to write the words again. That all in love is fair..."*

Baker echoed the words in front of the bathroom mirror.

THE TALL DARK figure slipped through the duplex's open window and stealthily made his way to the unsuspecting woman. A calico cat's eyes caught the intruder's silhouette. The small, but loyal, feline bounded to the floor—back arched, claws extended—and sounded the alarm with a shrill hiss.

Pow!

The killer's kick propelled little Miss Punkin across the room.

Thud!

Marla Decker awoke to the sickening sound of her kitty's last mew. She attempted to scream, but powerful, gloved hands quickly grabbed her lovely neck. She struggled briefly, knocking over the bedroom lamp. Her hazel eyes bulged. Her lips gasped for air.

"Falling in love with the writer from Chelan was a fatal mistake, Miss Decker," he told her, as he tightened his death grip.

She twisted and turned in his grasp.

"I'm afraid I've been ordered to terminate your position with the corporation," he whispered.

Her eyes closed. Her lifeless body twitched.

Nicholas Gordon took no pleasure from the postmortem rape which followed. It was strictly good business. His crime scene needed a motive. He wrapped Marla's corpse in the black silk kimono, and laid it gently on the cold floor.

And then, the hawk took flight.

THOMAS AWOKE in a cold sweat and a dark hotel room. His heart was pounding as hard as his hung-over head. He scanned the floor for a black kimono or a bloody cat, and found neither. He jumped out of bed and drew back the drapes. Dawn's first light seeped through the sheers.

Seattle slept soundly, but the mountains were wide-awake. Soft pinks painted glacial peaks and valleys in his easterly Cascades view. Baker sighed. Mountains had always been good to him, providing mental and physical relief and never refusing to welcome him, regardless of their mood. In them, he staked his future, and placed his sacred trust. From a far horizon, they called out to him, just as they always had. Only now, they called him to come home.

He watched Ann sleeping as he gathered his clothes. He used to take such comfort from watching her sleep in that fetal repose when they were man and wife, but now he only felt sorry for her. He shook her gently.

"Annie, I've got to leave," Thomas said. "There's someone else I—"

"I know," she muttered in her morning voice, not wanting to wake to this day. "She must be very special."

Thomas nodded. "Listen, if you ever need me…"

"Thomas, I need you now," she murmured with puffy eyes blinking and a neck rash rising from beneath the bed sheets.

He kissed her cheek. "You need someone, but it's not me. Someone else needs me more. Don't sell yourself short, Ann," he said, rising from the bed to dress. "It's not you, or what you had to do to survive. It's all just timing, honey. That's all. We had our time together and now it's gone."

She grabbed his hand. "But you said you'd always love me!"

"And I will. I will, Annie," he whispered, wiping tears from her cheeks. "Will you be okay?"

She bit her lip and nodded. "I'm a big girl, and don't you ever forget it." She forced a smile.

He walked to the door and turned the handle. "How could I?" he said, with one foot in the hall.

"Thomas? Can I call you sometime?" she asked.

"Anytime," he answered without looking back, before closing the door behind him.

THE MOUNTAINS had also called to Marla Decker at dawn. By six o'clock she had secured the last bungy cord around her kayak, and was talking to the calico cat who had been mewing at her feet for nearly an hour.

"Oh, all right, Punkin! You can tag along to Grandfather's cabin, but only because you're a girl. Listen and learn: *Men suck and love stinks!*" She picked up her pet by the scruff of its neck and sat her on the seat of her truck. "No men allowed from here on out. Got that, Punkin?"

The cat mewed twice, then purred.

Marla made one more trip to the house to talk to Georgette Kramer.

THOMAS MOTORED from the Westin Hotel into morning sea mist, which enshrouded the Emerald City. His heart told him to run to Marla, but reason said it was too early in the day for rushing fate. He parked by Pike Place Market, and walked along the waterfront. He went to Starbucks for coffee, and stopped at Three Girls Bakery for fresh goodies-to-go. He bought some flowers, and paid a kid to take a bouquet up to Ann's room at the Westin.

The writer stood at the end of the market scanning Puget Sound for the incoming Bainbridge Island ferry. He heard its horn crowing like a steel rooster boasting to the still slumbering metropolis. He saw bright yellow sunshine unseal the gray envelope surrounding Elliot Bay. Shopkeepers who'd been sweeping sidewalks opened their doors for business and slapped on Saturday smiles. Cool concrete steamed beneath an onslaught of curious tourists' feet.

A new day began in earnest—not just for Seattle, Washington, but for Thomas Baker too. He exhaled a sigh of relief. It was time, time to go forth firm and fast—undaunted. For at last he'd heard that horn blow from his past, and was not haunted.

GEORGETTE KRAMER watched the writer strutting toward her porch. The fact that he was grinning and carrying a pretty bunch of gladiolus only fueled her curiosity. She opened the screen door so quickly that it startled him.

"Good morning, Georgette! Is Marla up yet?"

There was no time for small talk. "Listen, Mr. Baker. I don't know what's going on between you and the girl, but..." Georgette bit her lip, and wrung wrinkled hands nervously.

The Nick Gordon nightmare—which Thomas had awoke to—engulfed him. "What's wrong with Marla? Is she all right?"

"I wish I knew," the old woman whispered, studying the suitor's face. Her poodle barked at her feet. She considered Marla's mysterious parting words: *"Don't tell anybody where I'm going. All right? Promise me you won't, Georgette."* Georgette Kramer had promised, but Irish instinct and wisdom born of age overruled that vow. "She's gone to the Icicle River cabin to be alone, Mr. Baker. She's probably only half way down the alley toward Broadway Street."

She pointed toward his Chevy with a shaking finger. "If you drive that thing fast enough, you might just catch her."

Thomas kissed her cheek and ran.

"Hurry, Mr. Baker. Hurry now! She loves you," the landlady shouted.

The squealing tires of Thomas's Chevy painted Pine Street's pavement black.

"I love her too!" Thomas shouted back.

WHEN SHE saw him blocking the alley ahead of her at Broadway, Marla slammed the stick shift into reverse and sped off backwards. Her flight was abruptly canceled when an elderly couple in a vintage Lincoln Continental emerged from a garage right behind her. A worn bungy cord snapped. Her kayak slid sideways.

Baker's Chevy stalled. Cars honked and skidded. Traffic quickly backed up on Broadway. A husky man on a motorcycle gave Baker the finger. Thomas returned the gesture, and ran down the alley to his girl's truck, flowers in hand.

An angry biker pursued him.

Marla shook her fists and banged the steering wheel. "Ooo—weee! *Men!* Of all the nerve. Can you believe this, Punkin?" she asked the skittish cat beside her.

Thomas reached for her door.

She depressed the lock, and rolled up the window. "Go away," she said.

He tapped the glass. "Marla! Marla, what's wrong?"

"I saw you with that blond bimbo at the Westin. *That's* what's wrong," she snapped, scowling. "Now please—just go away."

His heart sank. "That was my ex-wife, Ann," he explained.

"You said you hadn't seen her in years. Liar!" She cranked up the volume on her radio, and covered her eyes with her fingers.

A Harley Davidson motor cycle's front tire rolled over Baker's foot. Its leather-clad driver dismounted and reached for the writer's shoulder. "Hey, buddy…"

A slender gay neighbor who'd been bagging his trash recognized the biker and ran toward him. "Oscar! Is that you?" he exclaimed.

Thomas jumped on Marla's hood and pounded her windshield until she looked. He pointed to his heart and mouthed three words; *I - LOVE - YOU.*

The biker pulled Baker's leg.

Thomas grabbed the wiper blades.

The big man tugged harder. "Get off the lady's truck, asshole," he ordered.

Marla watched—horrified—as Baker got body slammed in the dirt. She opened her door and screamed, "Thomas!"

The people in the Lincoln behind her dialed 911 on their car phone.

Baker picked himself up, and poked his attacker's chest.

The biker cracked his knuckles, and lunged for the writer.

The slender gay neighbor grabbed the would-be hero's arm. "For Christ's sake, Oscar—let him be! It's just a lover's quarrel." He pinched some familiar rear end. "No one ever stuck their nose in *our affairs*," he said. "Remember?"

Marla stood with hands on hips. "So, you say you love me?" she said coldly. "Why didn't you call me? And where did you sleep last night? Well? Come on, Thomas. Tell me another lie."

"I never lied to you," he said. "I hadn't seen Ann in years. She called me last week and asked me to meet her." His eyes moistened as he turned his attention to Marla. "Her marriage fell apart."

"Big deal!" Marla replied.

"Marla, she needed me. And I needed answers to some questions," he said, moving towards her and her truck.

"Oh? And just what did you learn?" she asked, backpedaling.

He gently leaned towards her until she sat behind the steering wheel pressed against her seat. "I learned a lot," he said, pecking her cheek, and placing a bunch of crumpled gladiolus on her lap. He kissed her lips.

"Why are you here?" she asked, struggling to resist him.

"I came to rescue you from Oz, and take you to the other side of the mountains. I came to take you home with me to Chelan."

She pushed him away. "Why? Because you think I need you, too? Let's get something straight, Baker. I've lived happily by myself for some time now and—"

He kissed her again. "Uh, huh. Go on."

"And I don't need any men in my life, thank you please! And another thing—"

"*Shhh!*" he hissed before gently biting her lips. "Forget what you need. What do you want? Do you want to be together?"

She fidgeted beneath his weight. "Thomas, I—I just don't know. I—"

He kissed her neck, and whispered, "Do you believe in fate?"

Her breathing got heavy. Her knees rocked. She nodded, and searched for sincerity in his warm green eyes.

He stroked her hair. "And do you agree that timing is everything in life?"

Her lips quivered. Goose bumps spread across her skin. She broke a weak smiled. "Yes," she answered.

He slipped his hands under her thighs. "Then believe me, Marla Jean Decker. You and I were meant to be together. And this, sweet lady, is *our* time."

Marla's heart melted. "I love you, Thomas," she sighed.

He lifted her off the seat, then they stood there in the alley entwined in a passionate embrace.

The Lincoln's horn blew. A bicycle cop and a curious crowd from off Broadway clapped their hands approvingly. Marla's gay neighbor led the would-be-hero biker back to his place by the hand. "My God, Oscar. It shouldn't have taken an emergency to bring you back to me! How 'bout some yogurt and croissants?"

"How about a beer?" the biker asked.

"What now, Thomas?" Marla quizzed.

Baker petted her cat. "How long did you pack for?"

"Only until Monday," Marla replied. "Why?"

The cat licked his hand. "That will never do," Thomas said. "Let's swing by your place and get your things."

"What about work?"

"You just came down with the flu, Decker. You'll be calling in sick from Chelan first thing Monday morning," he said, while securing her kayak atop her truck.

"How long do you expect my *illness* to last?" she asked.

He laughed. "Don't get me wrong, but I hope it's a long one."

She rocked on her toes while a calico cat's mew pierced another hole in Thomas Baker's heart.

"Yes, Punkin, you're welcome too," he said, as a hot sun climbed high in the Pacific Northwest sky. "Come on, Decker. If we hurry, we can still paddle up to Domke Falls this afternoon."

Chapter 29

Countdown

THE LAST WEEKEND in June was busy with visitors from around the country and the world enjoying Lake Chelan and numerous activities in the valley. The colorful U.S. National Paragliding Championships were being launched off Chelan Butte. A Bach Music Festival, mountain bike and motocross races, and the Western Jubilee Rodeo were also scheduled. There was even a circus for the kids.

James Shawn Wolf worked dawn to dusk shuttling passengers from Seattle, and giving tourists a bird's-eye view of the valley. He flew over Ming Yaht's fancy pagoda twice, only to find the merciless Gordon peacefully meditating near the water's edge. Once, Nick even waved at the passing pilot! Wolf decided to stick with his plan, and save their final act for the hectic Fourth of July weekend when there would be plenty of witnesses in Big Creek Cove.

Michael Johnson's *Forever Neon* gallery was packed with delighted customers, and brightened by the glowing smile of the rapidly recovering Miss Ho Pai. Amazed doctors now predicted her imminent departure from the wheelchair in which she was presently confined.

The Granite Falls family kept busy as well. Marla was warmly welcomed at the lodge, especially when she rolled up her sleeves and helped with everything from kayaking instruction to gardening chores. Not once did Thomas regret bringing her back with him; for even with an escalating atmosphere of confrontation all around them, he'd never slept better.

MONDAY began with a strange request. Parole officer Ron Moore summoned Baker to his office for a UA. (Urine analysis, or drug test.) After many years of clean living—let alone watching Washington win the Rose Bowl together, and teaming up in the New Year's Day rescue—it seemed out of line to the writer. Still, Thomas took the drive to Wenatchee, and made the required appearance.

"Sorry, Tom," Mr. Moore said, handing Baker a glass jar and pointing to the open door of the Mens Room. "But I'm just doing my job."

It had been well over a year since he'd been asked for a UA, and Thomas took offense. *Someone must not agree with my politics*, he thought. "Who pulled my name out of the magician's hat?" he asked angrily, as Ron witnessed him pissing into the container beside the toilet, by watching his private parts in the reflection of a mirror. This was one of those indignities the writer thought had died with his desperado past. Through the bathroom mirror, he watched Moore leaning on the doorframe, biting his fingernails. When he saw the P.O. smirk, Baker felt bitterness, and reacted by deliberately missing the target.

"Believe me, Tom. It's only a random testing," Ron explained. "The feds shot me a list of names, and yours was on it."

When the P.O. took possession of the wet, warm container, his shamefaced expression reminded the writer of all the paid-to-lie employees he'd been exposed to during his stay with the Bureau of Prisons.

The P.O. wiped the sample clean, and walked his parolee to the door. "Sorry for the inconvenience, but I'm just another underpaid peon in the federal bureaucracy following orders." He patted Baker on the back. "Don't work too hard, Tom."

Thomas froze in the doorway. Moore's rash of apologies bothered him, but that wasn't all. "Aren't you forgetting something, Ron?" he asked, producing a pen from his pocket.

Moore's face turned red. "I'll be damned! Must be getting senile," he said. He sealed the sample as required by policy, and pointed to the tamper-proof label bearing an identification number. "Sign here, Tom."

While Baker signed, Marla, who'd been waiting in the hall, stuck her head in the office. "Ready to go, Thomas?" she asked.

Moore ogled the brunette as he slipped Baker's UA sample into a special shipping bag. "Speaking of going places. Are you folks going to the big Chelan City Council meeting on the third?"

"Sure are! Wouldn't miss it for the world," Marla replied.

"Why do you ask?" Baker quizzed suspiciously.

The P.O.'s phone rang. Ron Moore shrugged his shoulders. "No particular reason," he replied. The phone rang again. "Guess I gotta run. See you two Monday. Nice meeting you, Miss Decker."

During the drive home, it occurred to Thomas that he'd never introduced Marla to his parole officer. *Only Nick Gordon could have given Ron Moore her name.*

ON TUESDAY, a prominent attorney from Montana checked into the lodge and joined the Chelan Alliance team. The former colleague and friend of the deceased Councilman Barnes reviewed evidence and options *in-confidence*, and fine-tuned a motion to the court for an injunction freezing all Chelan Valley development for one year. They drafted a petition to city and county planners demanding detailed Environmental Impact Statements from all potential developers holding land in the area, and circulated it via Chelan Alliance members and like-minded business owners.

ON WEDNESDAY, Riverwalk Bookstore owner, Libby Manthey, held a *petition signing* for frightened small business owners and concerned senior citizens. Sheriff Paul Hilo paid a surprise visit to the lodge, and had a private meeting with the resident writer. Between chores, Bill Baker burned up telephone lines rallying environmental friends to the Chelan battlefront. Marla made flyers for distribution around the valley, and faxed some media friends of hers in Seattle. Nancy Baker scrambled to find housing for the anticipated scores of protesters, and helped keep the lodge afloat. Little Nathaniel Baker played with the family Labrador retriever, Spirit, and enjoyed being a kid on summer vacation.

BY THURSDAY night, Granite Falls became an environmental stronghold. Two busloads of *green* activists pitched blue dome tents in the meadow beside Yeti Chalet. A group of touring English naturalists arrived with Thomas's partner Jimmy Collins, and jumped into the fray with trademark British enthusiasm. The Brits made posters promoting a *Warwick Memorial Nature Preserve,* and brewed bottomless pots of extremely strong tea.

FRIDAY AFTERNOON, Thomas's newspaper article hit the stands, and instantly became the talk of the Evergreen State. Around dinnertime, a National Public Radio crew—good friends of Marla's—established residency in the lodge's meadow, and began interviewing locals on both sides of the issues. Having recently covered a heated Senate hearing on the Endangered Species Act in the state capital, Olympia (a hearing which was dominated by vote-hungry republicans) the crew's impassioned station manager decided to extend her expose' series on the topic to one more segment... ***Chelan:*** *Struggling to Preserve a Pristine Lake and Small Town Life in a Rapidly Growing Resort Community.*

As the sun set, a large crowd gathered at Granite Falls. Solemn faces glowed around crackling campfires, while ancient trees stood guard. Upon the deck of Granite Falls Lodge, a guitar and a mandolin played perfect harmony. People sang old protest songs.

Spirits soared to the starry heavens above. The scene reminded the writer of Woodstock. There was peace...*and love.* Later, the NPR crew set some speakers on top of their equipment van and played soft, soothing jazz for the gracious crowd.

Campfires faded. Weary travelers swapped stories, and retired to friendly sleeping bags. But in the green forest, the concert continued...*Curious coyotes with rhythm be-bopped on granite boulders nearby. Wise owls scat-hooted with renewed hope for humanity. Even 'bears in the wood' were jivin', high-fivin', and gettin' high.*

IN THE SUMMIT high atop Ming Yaht's Hongcouver Harbor House Building, the Brothers Po and Arturos Aquindo sat motionless before the interactive telecommunications screen viewing a political puppet show. It was quite a show. Even the Vancouver-born keynote speaker was firmly tucked in the Pos' hip pocket. Since the inception of Lin's *Era of New Direction*, Canada's parliamentary power base had shifted west—an uncomfortable distance away from Ottawa. The Pos' bankroll made this possible by backing scores of sympathetic Canadian politicians. And now, as 1997 drew near—like most wellmeaning public servants—these players had to dance to the tune of their puppeteer.

In accordance with the New Year's pact with their *Sun Yee On* rivals, Ming Yaht had received payment for and initiated simultaneous withdrawals from all its Hong Kong and eastern Canadian interests. But even as this civil action was being carried out, *Sun Yee On's* foot soldiers were being rooted out and rounded up throughout Canada by Ming Yaht's indebted political allies—who also stood to benefit from an apparent show of force against illegal immigration. Meanwhile, Ming Yaht consolidated its stranglehold on the west coast, and anti-Asian rhetoric continued to subside, as the Montreal Massacre quickly faded from the public's short memory.

Po Lin had many irons in the international fire. He assured Taipei that he would continue to transact with them upon completion of his North American move. At the same time, he also promised Mainland China that Ming Yaht would collar all its young rogues so that no more *unauthorized* nuclear material or weapons of mass destruction would be smuggled to Iran, Iraq,

North Korea, or Pakistan through ancient triad networks. Lastly, Po Lin vowed to use his well-oiled *guanxi machine* to sway Western public opinion, and help preserve China's precious *Most Favored Nation* status. In return, Beijing would allow Ming Yaht International—once safely relocated in North America—to serve as the main conduit to its vast emerging marketplace.

Like most Hong Kong capitalists were discovering—albeit too late—the Pos could not live beneath the evil parent's roof, nor abide by its ever-changing House Rules. But doing business together? Now that was an entirely different story. For if Lucifer himself had a buck to spend, Po Lin would surely take it!

The Dragon Head rubbed his palms in a circular motion, lost in thought. Perhaps Beijing would ruin the former British colony by dismantling all signs of democracy? Already, Hong Kong's liberal media was shaking in their boots. But maybe the spineless Americans and their European allies would not allow this to occur? Regardless of what became of Hong Kong, Ming Yaht would continue to prosper. So thought Po Lin.

Brother Jing directed his sibling toward the giant tele-communication screen.

Lin's dark eyes leaped to attention as the keynote speaker made his opening remarks. When their marionettes spoke, *Ming Yaht's leaders listened.*

"I am the Prime Minister of less than 30 million individuals. By law, I cannot dictate policy to the provincial leaders of this great nation. How then, can I expect to tell the Premier of China how to govern his 1.2 billion people? I cannot." The Caucasian's face grew ghastly white as he read the text on his Tele-Prompter screen. Beneath hot stage lighting, his blue blood began to boil. Canada's head of state clenched his fist, then grimaced like a kid drinking castor oil.

In Ming Yaht's communication center, Po Lin tapped his front teeth, and twitched his nose. "Come on...say it," he hissed.

"This government now believes that nagging Beijing about its human rights record is not in our best interests, nor the best interests of those oppressed in China. Our policy should not, and will not, be altered month to month in knee-jerk response to each new Polaroid snapshot we receive from Beijing's

labor camps. Frankly, we can ill-afford to close the door to the world's biggest marketplace. We simply must face the reality that Canada's trading opportunities in Asia are a key element of our economic recovery." The Canadian Prime Minister cleared his throat.

Po Lin flexed his forearms, and furrowed his brow.

"*Let me reiterate. This does not mean we will ignore human rights violations in China...*" The politician paused again and sipped nervously from a glass.

Po Lin shook his fist. "*Gwai Lo*! Go ahead. Cover your proper white English ass," the Dragon Head exclaimed in a rare display of emotion.

"*Nor do we condone the detention of foreign nationals who choose to disagree with Beijing's policies!*" the Prime Minister proclaimed, pounding the podium.

The live audience responded with scattered applause.

"This guy has been watching President Clinton too much," Po Jing remarked, mockingly pounding his armrest, in the Summit's communication center.

"*Another consideration in this decision is the disproportionate economic power enjoyed by our largest trading partners, the Americans. It is wonderful to have an enormous client like the United States, but we must not settle for only one. Experience has taught us that this practice leaves our nation in a weak and vulnerable business posture, which is simply unacceptable!*" The Prime Minister repeated his podium-pounding move. Applause erupted everywhere, led by all the Prime Minister's men. A rousing round of cheers rose from an audience of voters who were ripe for some America-bashing, and ready to sell their very souls to stimulate the sagging Canadian economy.

On the forty-seventh floor of Ming Yaht's Harbor House Building, Po Lin could barely contain his elation. He sprang from his seat and strolled to the window, acutely aware that the best was yet to come.

Arturos Aquindo watched his boss closely. He saw a helicopter's lights in the distance, and thought about the rumors he had heard. The Latino dropped his cigar and raised his hand, intending to suggest that Lin step away from the glass.

Po Jing grabbed the Cuban's wrist. "Let him savor the moment," Jing whispered.

Great Po took a deep breath. His dark eyes scanned the evening sky. Canada was his, and it made him high. In the background, the Prime Minister spoke *his* words like soothing music in glass elevators. Far below, sparks flew as the world's finest steel workers labored long into the night beneath powerful spotlights to meet the deadline for Jing's latest vision—*the New Monte Carlo*: a two million square foot waterfront casino and convention center, which would serve as the flagship for scores of similar Ming Yaht ventures.

All the pieces were coming together. His corporate heir had received the finest education Europe could offer, gained business experience with his father's Asian interests, and ultimately, came of age. The migration of his minions was in full swing. Within months, he would be a ruler in exile, a ruler to be reckoned with—the Dali Lama of North America! Lin had come a long way since his childhood in the ghastly walled city of Kowloon. Not even Brother Jing's clairvoyance could have predicted such a life. The sky was the limit…and perhaps it too awaited the Great Po's arrival. Only tiny Chelan was yet to be annexed.

The closing portion of the Prime Minister's speech caught the Dragon Head's ear. It was the part he most wanted to hear, and he rushed back to his seat to listen.

"Canada's interest in China has quite literally swelled in the last ten years due to our increased immigrant Asian population. Nowhere is this more evident than in my birthplace, Vancouver, where many of the one million plus Chinese, who have legitimately entered our country, reside. An influential number of these naturalized citizens—especially those evacuating Hong Kong due to British abandonment—have immigrated with high moral standards, hard to match work ethics, and valued investment capital and expertise which have helped keep Vancouver's head above stormy economic waters in recent years. Let me assure you, these law-abiding Asian members of our diverse community are actively working with my government to rid our cities of the gangs and drugs which wrongly stereotype them. With their help, I intend to form the nucleus of a potentially lucrative network of trans-Pacific

*trading relationships which should raise **all** Canadians' standard of living to unfathomable heights."*

After their marionette closed his act with some obscure Christian blessing, Ming Yaht's giant viewing screen went blank. The Brothers Po rejoiced, the Colonel popped the cork on a vintage bottle of champagne, and together they toasted the victory. This private party lasted but a moment, before Po Lin clapped his hands.

The barrel chested, pizza-faced, Arturos slicked back his greasy, black mop, and buttoned up his silk shirt. He centered his gold chain, sucked in his gut, and stood at attention.

Great Po groomed his pencil-thin mustache, and combed his thinning silver hair. The Dragon Head polished the ruby in his ring, while Brother Jing retied his tie for him. Then, Lin snapped his fingers, and the threesome formed a high-tech receiving line. The interactive system came back to life, and within seconds scores of congratulatory communications from around the globe filled the giant screen. Po Lin flashed his alabaster smile and thanked them, one and all.

THE LAST RESPONDENT wore a wrinkled, oversized dinner jacket, a too-obvious toupee, and dark sunglasses. His identity was poorly disguised. There was bright red lipstick on his unbuttoned white collar where his tie should have been. He seemed a bit tipsy.

Po Lin shook his head, then glared at Arturos Aquindo.

The Colonel swallowed hard. "Good evening, Robert," he greeted the caller, wondering why in the hell this crucial contact was employing Po's personal telecom system so close to his appearance before the Senate Ethics Committee—especially in light of his apparent condition.

"Evening Colonel, Misters Pos. Please accept my heartfelt congratulations," the pickled politician slurred. A scantily clad dark-skinned girl leaned into the picture. The Senator pushed her away. "Sorry to disturb your victory party, but I..." The Senator cleared his throat. "**We** have a little problem down here."

Arturos bit hard on his slimy unlit Havana.

Po Jing grimaced beside him.

Po Lin stared stern-faced at the drunken politician. "Please remove your glasses and describe this problem," the triad Dragon Head ordered the United States Senator.

Inflated egos collided. A brief staring contest ensued.

Reluctantly, the representative from the Evergreen State complied. The removal of his glasses revealed dark bags beneath his eyes—bags big enough to pack a power-lunch in. "There was some extremely negative press in the Seattle newspaper this afternoon, Lin." The Senator produced the paper in question and fanned his face with it.

Po Lin snapped his fingers angrily.

Arturos pushed enlargement buttons on the arm of his captain's chair. Newsprint filled the screen. "Hold the god-damned article out in front of you, Bobby! And for Christ's sake, quit shaking," the Cuban strongman commanded.

The column came into focus. The title was foreboding. **Near Disaster in An Eden Called Chelan Sounds Environmental Alarms**—*special to the Post by T. Baker.* Arturos nervously rubbed his temples, then polished off the bottle of warm champagne. *"Carumba! Es el escritor!"* the Latino exclaimed.

Brother Jing donned his cheater specs, and leaned forward. Po Lin's black pupils ping-ponged across the page. The Hongcouver brain trust silently digested the raw meat of Baker's yellow journalism. Several minutes went by.

The Senator—on the verge of dozing off—decided to break the ice. "Mr. Po, may I speak frankly?"

Lin responded with a slight nod. "Please do, Senator."

"This Baker fellow is a skilled adversary, Lin. He skirts the *yellow peril* issue that your opponents are publicizing down in California. But because of the way he rails against unrestrained foreign investment, this is bound to sway a large, nasty racial element…maybe even some of our unemployed loggers who'll be torn between begging for work, and waving the fucking flag. He's already got the ecology nuts firmly in his camp. Perhaps you should have hired this guy as a lobbyist."

A young lady laughed in the background.

The Senator smirked. "We Americans have a saying for this, Lin: *Shit Happens!* Just what do you suggest I do, sir?"

Po furrowed his brow, seething. "I do not give suggestions, Senator," he hissed. "I give orders!"

Brother Jing whispered in his ear. Lin shook his head, and tossed his champagne flute towards the screen. He jumped up, and paced the floor. Great Po stewed but a moment, then pointed at the politician, and barked out commands. "You will contact the newspaper tomorrow morning and tell them to print a retraction based on erroneous information, or be bought out on Monday! You will make a prime time speech echoing the Canadian Prime Minister's sentiments on China policy and legitimate immigration. Do this Sunday." Po Lin cracked his knuckles. "And...you can cancel all of your appointments for Monday, and plan on making an appearance with us in Chelan."

The Senator wiped his brow with his sleeve. "That's a big wish list, Lin. I'm not certain I can deliv—"

"You look happy tonight, Robert," the Dragon Head interrupted. "I like to see older men so happy. In fact, I fail to understand why your constituency scorns your well-publicized womanizing...when I applaud it!" Lin clapped his hands. His comrades followed suit.

The Senator swallowed hard. "Different strokes for different folks, I guess."

"Agreed," said Po Lin as a pleased smile crossed his face. "My people have a saying befitting of this occasion: *'Happy Customers Always Pay Their Bills—especially if they do not wish to give up their iron rice bowls.'*"

What had been a minor headache for the Senator suddenly increased tenfold. He devoured four Advil, popped a Valium, and rued the day his too-detailed diary and certain compromising photos fell into the hands of one Arturos Aquindo. He cleared his throat. "I believe I see your point, Mr. Po."

The pretty black girl popped back into the picture and plopped on the Senator's lap. "Come on, Bobby," she said. "It's time for some affirmative action. You promised!"

Po Lin quickly backed away from the young woman's view. He pointed to Arturos, and snapped his fingers again.

"I see you're up to your old tricks again. Eh, *amigo*?" the Cuban remarked with his gravelly voice.

"Everyone's got a vice, Arty," said the Senator. "Booze, sex, money...power." The Senator lifted the girl off his lap, and disappeared from view. "By the way, Arty. Could you send me another box of those Havanas? I'm having a helluva time getting good cigars with this damn Castro embargo crap! And don't worry, Colonel. I'll take care of things down here," he moaned from the floor.

"See that you do," the Cuban commanded.

"Who were those creeps, Bobby?" the girl asked her Senator between acts.

"Just two chinks, and a spic, sugar. Nobody important," the Senator answered.

THE SEATTLE newspaper article angered Po Lin, and initiated a lengthy, heated damage control session inside the Hongcouver Summit. Arturos had placed all the cards he intended to show to Lin on the table, and now paced the carpet—unlit Havana between his teeth—awaiting the Dragon Head's decision.

The Summit was dark. Po Lin sat in a meditative pose, eyes serenely closed, listening to Beethoven's *Moonlight Sonata*.

Brother Jing concluded his consultation with the stars, lit two candles, and spoke. "The unusual ability of this gang to evade the hawk has imbued them with heroic dimensions." Jing lit many sticks of jasmine incense and placed them in the golden grip of an ancient Chinese warlord statue. The seer handed one glowing stick to Arturos, another to his brother.

Lin's eyes blinked rapidly, as if he'd just been awakened from a deep trance. "What did you see, my brother?" he whispered.

Jing's weary eyes rolled back in his head. Jasmine scented smoke-snakes coiled around his haggard cheeks. "I saw a carefully collected box of colored marbles spilling into the middle of a wide street, and rolling in every direction." Jing's leather sandals shuffled over the carpet toward his brother. His long wrinkled fingers came to rest upon the bright gold dragon on the back of Lin's silk robe. "I saw a bloodied bird of prey peering through a cage of steel at his captors. I saw—"

"Enough! Enough," Lin shouted, quickly rising. "We are too close. In no way must we allow this rebellion to spread unchecked. The ultimate goal must be achieved." Po peeled back one silken sleeve and stared at the Dragon Head tattoo. His nostrils flared. His black pupils beamed barbarously at Arturos Aquindo. "Mr. Baker and his associates have earned themselves a very powerful...and vengeful enemy."

"I understand perfectly," the gravel-voiced Cuban replied. "They had guts, boss. But rest assured, the writer's fate will be worse than death." The Colonel coughed, and held the incense away from him. "What about Gordon's exposure?"

Great Po's proud shoulders sagged. The fire left his eyes. His face looked old and sad. "Over the years, I have grown fond of my hawk. And yet, common sense tells us there must be losers as well as winners." Ming Yaht's mighty leader recalled a painful day in his Hong Kong youth when he decided to put his prized hunting dog to sleep. He turned his back to the Cuban and swallowed hard.

"Believe me, Lin. It's the only solution," said Arturos.

Great Po sighed. "The good of many, outweighs the sacrifice of few," he said, nodding. "Make it so, my Latin friend. Make it so."

Po cinched his golden sash, then pressed some buttons. The *Moonlight Sonata* was replaced by loud, boisterous martial music. Po pushed more buttons. One floor below them, cameras in elegant suites projected crisp *lu, tou,* and *guai* images of fresh young concubines to the Summit's giant screen. The maidens preened and cooed like caged canaries. Great Po made his selections, and clapped his hands.

Attendants lit ornately carved phallic candles, and prepared the ritual chamber. The aroma of sacred oils filled the air. Glass elevator doors opened wide. Security escorts stepped inside first.

And then, an uncommonly large *tantra troupe* entered the dragon's lair.

Chapter 30

Raising Connie Joe

SUNDAY AFTERNOON saw Lone Wolf Air's final flight of the busy Fourth of July weekend. Blue Chelan and its environs had become a symphonic sea of humanity. Every campsite was filled. Every condo, cabin, tennis court, putting green—even every neighborly Native American slot machine—was occupied. A mesquite cloud hovered over *Cosina del Lago*. Lakeview Drive-In's serving window attended to love-hungry teens. Tourists handed their sacred vacation money to happy valley business owners. The Chamber of Commerce was satisfied. Water skiers were water-skiing. Hang gliders were gliding. Fisher folk were fishing. All the lake's trout were in hiding.

Sun set. Solar winds died. Dusk's calm settled in around the 1947 Dehavilland Beaver anchored in Big Creek Cove. On board the floatplane, gear was being gathered. The pilot handed out beers, and plopped in his seat. "You're one hell of a diver, lady," Wolf said between slurps. "That rocky ledge that caught the *Connie Joe* is a long haul in cold water when you're not packing oxygen."

Marla nodded reflectively. "My grandfather used to call me his little mermaid," she said.

Bill Baker grinned. "You should feel honored. Wolf is stingy with his compliments, Marla."

"And that was a strong one, especially coming from a former Navy Seal," the pilot replied, poking his chest.

"Thanks," Marla said with a curious smile. "Why can't you dive anymore, Mr. Wolf?"

Wolf pulled back his hair, exposing a nasty scar. "Lost this inner ear in the war," he explained, lighting up a cigarette. "Wolf has no equilibrium." He slowly took in a big hit of nicotine, then blew it out the window. "Ya know, I sure screwed up when I estimated how long this mission was gonna take."

"Shit happens dude," Bill said.

"We wouldn't even be here without your help pal," Thomas suggested, while massaging Marla's tired shoulders.

"True," Wolf said, snuffing-out his smoke. "Oh well, kids. At least we're close, damn close. We'll just have to get back here bright and early, finish freeing that fuel tank from the hull..." He started a slow upward gesture with his hand. "...and raise that bitch to the surface nice n' easy." *Slap!* He struck his thigh to emphasize the point, spilling his beer in the process. "Shit!" The pilot popped another brew and slammed down half. "It's either that, or we can rush, and risk losing our most admissible piece of evidence to the bottom of Lake Chelan."

Thomas shook his head. "At least that bastard, Gordon, hasn't noticed us."

Wolf rapped his worn knuckles on the wooden dashboard. A big pleasure boat cruised nearby. The pilot instinctively switched on his running lights to alert other boaters to their presence in Big Creek Cove.

Bill gulped the last of his beer and crushed the can. "The city council meeting is scheduled for two o'clock tomorrow. Are we gonna be ready?"

"I think so, Blood," Thomas replied. "But we'd better call it a day and get some rest." He tapped Wolf on the back. "Driver! Oh, James? Could you take this water limo—"

"Shhh!" Wolf snapped. "Listen." He put his one good ear to the open window of the plane.

The crew congregated at the cargo door with butterfly stomachs.

Coyotes serenaded ashore. Soft music from some mountain cabin wafted across Big Creek Cove. "You're losing it, Wolfman," Bill concluded. "There's nothing out there."

The pilot cut the lights, pushed past them, and stood on the plane's pontoon. He scanned a resplendent Northwest sky until something caught his eye on the distant horizon. He saw a lunar aura appear between two jagged peaks. His arm hairs stood on end. His alert mode clicked on as Stormy Mountain slowly gave birth to a bright, full yellow moon.

Wolf cupped his good ear. "Hear that?" he asked the others.

Across a stellar sea, they watched a white bird sail. And with it rose a second moon—the one on the Goose's tail! No one said a word. The encroaching high-pitched whine of Ming Yaht's corporate seaplane said it all.

Wolf cranked up the Beaver's radial engine and set a beeline for the liquid moon runway, *sans* running lights.

THE BOLD CREW was back on site at dawn. Thomas's surprise ally, Sheriff Paul Hilo, arrived shortly thereafter and anchored his boat beside the Beaver. By ten, they had unbolted the fuel tank and began raising it with a hand winch affixed to the floatplane's wing. Around noon, with the precious catch precariously suspended a few feet below them, a speeding jet boat's wake caused a panic aboard the plane.

The Bakers quickly dove in, hoping to stabilize the swaying mass of steel. Marla helped Wolf steady the winch ropes on the plane's wing.

"Goddamn yahoos!" Hilo yelled, shaking his fist. "That's it," he hissed. Hilo tossed his ten-gallon hat on the floor, stripped down to his skivvies, and traded the mini-cam he'd been holding for an underwater 35 millimeter camera. "I'm going in," he announced.

"Without a wet suit?" Wolf asked.

The silver-haired sheriff nodded affirmatively.

"But, it's cold down there," Marla protested. "I'd hate to see—"

"See what?" Hilo said, sucking in his beer gut. "Don't you worry about me, young lady! I'm pretty fit for fifty-something." He sat his dark sunglasses on the seat, and climbed up on the stern. "I want to see this with my own two eyes, and take some pictures—just in case."

The pilot eyed the lawman suspiciously. "In case what?" Wolf growled.

"Who the hell knows, fly boy? Like the younger generation says nowadays, shit happens. Geronimo!" Hilo shouted as he jumped into Lake Chelan. The sheriff swam beneath the splintered steel cylinder the Bakers were steadying. What he saw sickened him. His camera clicked away capturing all the signs of a substantial external explosion, which made the *Connie Joe* a prime suspect for sabotage—just like Councilman Barnes had said!

Thomas pointed to the ghostly wavering life ring, the charred hull below, and the dark blue abyss beyond the rocky ledge on which it rested.

Hilo struggled to hold his breath. A shiver ran down his spine. The abyss reminded him of how deep he'd be involved, *if he made the wrong decision.* The sheriff cleared his lungs, turned away from darkness, and swam toward the light of day.

A minute later, Paul Hilo stood in his boat thinking about the appointment he had with Baker's parole officer and two U.S. Marshall's, before the big event. He dried off with a beach towel and checked the time.

The Beaver's crew watched his face, and waited.

"It's twelve-forty-five, people. I've got to head on back. I have some official business to attend to in town."

"And...?" Thomas prodded, while he drifted in the water beside his brother.

Hilo slowly adjusted his hat and sunglasses. "And, I suggest you people finish securing that extremely valuable piece of evidence and get your behinds to this meeting."

Thomas smiled and put his hand on his brother's shoulder. "Hey, Bill?"

"Yeah, Tom."

"I want you to go back with Hilo."

Bill slapped the water. "No way! We're blood. You stay, I stay. You're gonna need my help raising—"

Thomas cut him off. "I've got Marla and Hairball here," he said, gesturing toward Wolf, who bared his teeth and growled. "You're the family environmental specialist. Get your wife and son and go rally the green troops. And tell our fancy Montana lawyer the game plan, too."

Bill made a face like a whipped pup.

"Go! Go hold down the fort until we get back," Thomas demanded. He shoved Bill toward Hilo's boat, and the sheriff helped him aboard.

The younger Baker looked back toward his brother and chewed the inside of his cheek. "What about that wild man, Gordon?" he asked.

"Are you kidding? He's Ming Yaht's main man in Chelan! Don't worry about your big brother," Wolf shouted. "You can bet your ass that Gordon will be at that meeting glaring at you with those sinister eyes. He's probably there already."

Bill bit his lip.

Thomas tread water. The writer felt a rush of emotion, and raised a clenched fist above the blue liquid engulfing him. "I'm counting on you, Blood," he whispered. "Do it!"

Bill bent down and extended his fist as well.

Two close brothers tapped fists.

"Now go," Thomas insisted. " Take off, hoser! Go rattle those slick developers' cages with a healthy dose of that environmental impact stuff. Go on. Beat it!"

Hilo hit the ignition, and gunned the Evinrude outboard.

Thomas watched his brother wave from the back of the speeding boat. He watched Bill's face fade into a sparkling sunlit wake, and heard his wish for them echo across the glistening lake: "Good Luck!"

"Fuck luck," Wolf grumbled. "Go-fight-win! Let's get to work, Baker. I don't wanna miss the look on Gordon's face when he sees this fuel tank."

NICHOLAS GORDON lowered high-powered binoculars from his face, rubbed a furrowed brow, and reclined behind the wheel of his black Land Rover. He listened to Mother Nature gargle rocks in the mouth of Big Creek, thought about the crossroads he had reached, and begrudgingly acknowledged the fact that he had come to love Chelan as much as his adversaries. It disturbed him that Arturos's advance-security team had spotted the Beaver before him. It disturbed him that Wolf had discovered the listening device in the floatplane several days ago as well. Smoke from his Cuban passenger's cigar fowled the air he breathed. He started the engine, shifted into 4H, and stepped on the gas.

Many things disturbed the human hawk as they motored back to the corporate retreat. Po Lin had projected an eerie coldness toward him at last night's dinner. Nick recalled the Asian brothers' reactions when they ascended the spiral staircase to the glass octagon, and found their custom neon artwork had been destroyed. He remembered the way Lin looked at him when he explained that *young vandals* had penetrated their high-security sanctuary while he was away in Seattle. Nick slapped his steering wheel. *Screw the Pos,* he thought.

The sight of Wolf in Big Creek Cove made his Latin blood sizzle. Arturos Aquindo knew all about the *Connie Joe*. It was all so convenient. His pawn was already in position. Gordon would *do* Wolf and company. The pawn would *do* Po Lin's hawk. Arturos Aquindo could see the headlines now: **Crazed Corporate Employee Responsible for Area Murders.** Ahhh— sweet revenge! And no loose ends. "Sorry to ask you to work in broad daylight, *amigo*," Arturos said to Gordon. "I realize that you prefer the night, but they know too much."

Nick nodded.

The Colonel checked his platinum Rolex. "The motorcade will arrive in town in approximately one hour. The Pos will be secured inside the city council chambers shortly thereafter."

Nick's foot slipped off the gas pedal. "It's only a thirty minute drive, Arty. Why so long?"

The Cuban looked away, and coughed. "Lin scheduled an appearance at the launch site for this U.S. Paragliding event, Nick. Evidently, an old and trusted associate's son has entered the competition, and the old man promised to wish him well."

Security people scrutinized Gordon's Land Rover before allowing it to pass through the corporate retreat's front gate. Arturos got out at the pagoda and slapped the Rover's hood with his palm. "*Adios, amigo.* We'll be expecting you," the Cuban said.

Nick yawned nonchalantly, and drove off toward the boathouse. "*Sure you will, you filthy Judas spic,*" Gordon muttered, while simultaneously brushing cigar ashes off his seat.

The time for indecision had passed. Nick did not need Po Jing's gift of clairvoyance to read the cards now. It was clear that fate was forcing him to play his hand today. There was no way around it. The Hawk had work to do.

And so, the Pos would attend their precious meeting with their Hong Kong bodyguards and their Cuban Colonel. And he would pilot the black Zodiac one more time.

THE PARKING LOT outside City Center was a sight to see. Politicians paraded around shaking hands. Environmental protesters piled off of two old buses, and unfurled three large banners: **Lake Chelan, Keep it Pristine & Blue; No Tahoes in the Pacific Northwest;** *and* **Just Say NO to Ming Yaht's Industrial Park Expansion!** A British contingent carried posters promoting a Warwick Memorial Nature Preserve.

Several loaded pickup trucks pulled into the lot. Their human cargo—big men wearing baseball caps bearing logos of chain saw companies—jumped into the fray, and accused the environmentalists of destroying their jobs.

A National Public Radio reporter completed an interview with an unemployed logger's wife; then spoke to her listeners. "*Overall, residents of the Chelan Valley appear to be more worried about overdevelopment's effects than ethnic diversity. There is, however, a nasty undercurrent which is clearly visible in some of the local citizens' bumper stickers. The one in front of me reads, 'Lake Chelan: Don't let* **Them** *taint* **Our** *Water Yellow'. Here's another, which appeared in Friday's*

Seattle Post-Intelligencer article: 'No Chinese Beverly Hills in Washington State.' And lastly, there is one which reads, 'Will the Last American to Leave Lake Chelan Please Bring the Flag.'"

Sheriff Paul Hilo was there with boots polished, and his official uniform neatly pressed. Paul had traded his worn ten-gallon hat for a jet-black Stetson, and stood chewing on a toothpick and watching for Ming Yaht's motorcade. It was supposed to be his day off, but the Pos needed extra security people, and Paul Hilo needed money.

Ron Moore arrived, and immediately walked over to a black Lincoln parked in the back of the lot. Baker's parole officer pawed at the automobile's door handle. A tinted window opened an inch, and greenish-gray smoke slithered out. "Is that you, Hank?" Moore asked.

"Just call me Santa Claus," Hodge bragged between puffs on *his* Cuban cigar. "Hop inside my office, Ronnie. And close the door behind you." As soon as his passenger was seated, the plump county planner popped twin locks on a blue eel skin briefcase, and sat it on Ron's lap.

Ron Moore swallowed hard. His heart beat faster. His eyes grew big as silver dollars. He fanned smoke from the Walrus' cigar, coughed, and lowered the power window further still.

Sheriff Hilo watched the Lincoln closely from across the lot.

"Don't get all choked up on me Ronnie," Hank said. "See that plain white government van over there?"

Moore nodded. He saw two stocky men in navy blue windbreakers wearing dark sunglasses. The van's driver dangled a shiny set of stainless steel handcuffs outside his window. The passenger waved at Hodge. "So, your man Gordon and his billionaire buddies even have United States Marshalls on their payroll?" the parole officer asked.

"That's right, Ronnie. And they're ready to transport that smart-ass parolee of yours back to prison, as soon as you sign the paperwork. Are you ready to make some easy money?"

Moore bit his lip, and scanned the parking lot.

Sheriff Paul Hilo started heading toward them, panning the crowd with his mini-cam as he walked. Hilo aimed its zoom lens at the Lincoln for a moment; then stopped, stuck a Marlboro between his teeth and lit it.

Ron Moore nodded, and looked the Walrus in the eye. "You know Hank," he said in an abnormally loud tone. "I've given this offer of yours a lot of thought."

"And?" said Hodge.

"And I don't like looking in the mirror since we had our little talk about Mr. Baker," confessed the parole officer.

"Too bad," Hodge grunted, handing the P.O. a sealed glass container filled with someone else's dirty urine. He ran one fat finger across the crisp contents of the blue eel skin briefcase. "Twenty-five grand is an assload of green, Ronnie. More than enough to help you feel good about your work. Don't you agree?"

Moore leaned back and eyed the money. "What exactly do you want?"

Hodge pounded the dashboard. "You know damn well what I want. I want this writer Baker's goddamn ass picked up the minute—no, the second—he sets foot on the lot! My people want to see him in handcuffs, waist chains, leg-irons—the whole nine yards. Our Seattle TV crew will be waiting with a pre-rehearsed…"

The fat man's voice faded into little more than background noise. The P.O. shook his head, held the doctored drug test by the open window, and watched Sheriff Hilo's movements intently.

Tiny beads of sweat formed on the back of Hodge's neck. "Ronnie, listen. You sent out a piss test. It came back dirty. End of story."

"Yes, sir. It sure did come back showing drug use. Came back straight from your people's dirty lab in Seattle, just like them damn fish kill tests," Moore shouted, before slamming the briefcase full of bribe money shut.

"Calm down," Hank replied. "It's only business, Ronnie."

"Not my kinda business. I can't do it, Hank. Not to Thomas Baker, and not to this valley." The P.O. depressed the door handle beside him.

The Walrus grabbed his passenger's knee. "You can't do what? For God's sake, Ronnie! I know damn well you need the cash. My people know how many bookies have your name on their collection lists. Be real. You're up to your eyeballs in gambling debts." Hodge reopened the briefcase. "I wouldn't want to see you lose your cabin on the lake. Believe me, property is gonna get pretty damn costly around these parts when the Siamese cat's let out of the bag."

Moore kicked open his door.

Hodge tightened his grip. "Ronnie! You haven't done anything illegal."

"You're damn right I haven't," Moore shouted as he swung the sample marked *T. Baker* like a pendulum above the parking lot. "And I don't plan to either."

Hodge lunged across the seat spilling twenty-five grand in the process. "What the hell are you doing?"

"The right thing," Ron said confidently. Then the federal parole officer tossed the doctored drug test on the hot pavement, freeing stinking yellow liquid from shattered glass—and a ton of guilt from his own chest.

An enraged Hank Hodge went for Moore's throat. "You chicken shit! You just caused my people a world of embarrassment. Th-th-this c-could c-c-cost us all a fucking fortune."

"Is that a fact?" Moore said calmly, as he pushed the planner away. "That may well be, but I just saved *my people* something that even Pos' billions can't buy."

Sheriff Hilo stuck his mini-cam lens inside the Lincoln. "Surprise! Smile, Hank Baby. You're on candid camera," announced the sheriff. Hilo zoomed in on the white froth around Hodge's lips; then he spit a spent Marlboro on the dirty piss-stained money, and filmed that. "Just for the record, Hank? I hope the vote at this council meeting costs your people their greedy yellow asses!"

Ron Moore slid out of the car, and high-fived his friend Paul Hilo. The P.O. removed his tiny body mike and beeper-sized transmitter, then leaned back toward the sweaty, red-faced planner. "You're gonna need an assload of green pal—for legal fees!"

"And forget about that country club membership you just bought," Hilo suggested. "You're a conservative Republican. Right, Hank? Maybe your friends can get you into some kind of *Club Fed.*"

Hodge shook uncontrollably. "G-gentlement! P-paul...R-r-Ronnie? Be reasonable. Let's not make any rash decisions."

"*We* didn't," Hilo said.

"You make me sick," Moore added, slamming the door in Hodge's face. "You've lost it, Hank. Get a grip. And don't ever call me *Ronnie* again, you old walrus!"

As county planner Hank Hodge watched the two lawmen disappear into the crowd, every bone in his obese body advised him to fire-up the Lincoln and head for the hills. And had he not been completely blocked in, he might have done just that. His awkward hands trembled as he scrambled to collect the scattered bribe money. His weak heart murmured fearfully at the thought of explaining the bungled arrest of Thomas Baker to an angry Nick Gordon.

Crowd noise increased. Horns honked. Onlookers cheered and booed as three black limousines rolled by them, and pulled right up to the building. An entourage of lawyers, security people, and retired politicians-turned-lobbyists unloaded first, then the Po Brothers emerged. Lin brushed the lapel of his conservative Western-style suit, waved and flashed his alabaster smile.

Protesters surged forward. An aggressive news reporter pushed past Arturos Aquindo, and stuck his microphone in Lin's face. "Mr. Po! Mr. Po," the reporter pleaded. "Is it true that Ming Yaht International has contributed over one million dollars toward the passage of gambling Initiative 651, which will appear on the November ballot?"

The great Po Lin's smile quickly faded.

"No comment," Po Jing hissed through clenched teeth.

The gutsy reporter tried again. "Mr. Po! Isn't it true that plans have been submitted to the National Indian Gaming

Commission for a multimillion-dollar joint venture between one of your Vancouver subsidiaries and the Corral Creek tribal council? And—*Ugh!*"

Arturos Aquindo gave the hard-nosed reporter a persuasive shove. "The man said 'NO COMMENT'! Are you deaf, *amigo*?" The Cuban flailed the air above his head. A small army of security people got busy. Doors opened, and the Asian enclave moved out.

Hank Hodge combed what little hair he had, and exited the Lincoln. He took one long last look at the entourage, and uttered a sigh of relief. "No Nick Gordon," he muttered. "Thank God." Hank Hodge gathered his composure, fell in line, and shuffled through the entrance to the Chelan City Council Chambers.

THE SLENDER CHINAMAN gazing at the scores of colorful hang gliders at the top of Chelan Butte could hardly believe his good fortune. For weeks he had lived in squalor aboard the snakehead's freighter with hundreds of other illegals. Yesterday he strolled the golden streets of America's Emerald City, browsing its waterfront market and spending greenbacks in its shops. Today he walked the *meiguo* heartland's unspoiled soil, breathed its fresh air, and felt its warm sun.

The sight of all the happy Americans rising into azure skies to ride spectacular thermal winds reminded him of his amateur flights back in Mainland China. Wen Wei Chen remembered when his father—a staunch communist—beat him with a stick for sneaking away from the fields to fly a wealthy friend's glider. Wen watched as a dust devil ripped across the top of the promontory causing havoc for the hang-glider pilots gathered there. Wen Wei smiled. How apropos, thought he, that what had been a child's hobby in his homeland, would prove to be such a treasured asset to the great and powerful Dragon Head, Po Lin.

Wen took a deep breath. He was ready to live the American dream. He had a Seattle Supersonics jersey on his back, Air Jordan sneakers on his feet, and a fine American cigarette between his teeth—just like the *Marlboro Man* on those giant billboards back in Beijing. The nightmare fate had chosen for him was finally over. He was brave and loyal, young and strong, certain of a bright and shining future in *The Beautiful Country*!

The slender Chinaman inspected his special aircraft again. He ran his fingers over the leading edge of the smooth wooden push propeller looking for nicks, then attached his lanyard and other accessories. He puffed his Marlboro, took another look at the map, and tucked it in the waistband of his tiger-striped pants. He strapped on his harness, and started the tiny two-cycle engine. The normally noisy motor was much quieter than he'd expected—a result of a custom-engineered muffler system. For this flight, no expense had been spared.

Wen Wei Chen took a final draw on his cigarette and tossed it. A tall, blond, freckle-faced California girl in a well-filled tank top waved at him, and he, in turn, waved back. Wen Wei Chen bit his lip, increased the throttle, and launched from the parking lot of Chelan Butte—in the direction of Big Creek Cove.

WHEN JAMES SHAWN WOLF saw the black Zodiac hugging the shadowy shoreline, hairs stood erect on the back of his neck. The rubber boat looked vaguely familiar, but he could not recall where he had seen it. Wolf studied the occupant of the craft: a reclining adult male wearing a black vest and hat, with a fishing rod propped up on the motor mount, and monofilament line trailing behind him. *Probably trolling for silver salmon, or trout,* thought Wolf. *Stupid tourist.*

"Hey, piloto!" Thomas shouted the second his head popped above the water. He pounded his fist on the rusty steel cylinder in his grasp. "Let's get this baby in the hold and get to that city council meeting."

Marla surfaced beside Baker. She was holding the life ring from the *Connie Joe,* which she'd just cut free.

Wolf dismissed the fisherman and directed his attention to the fuel tank. "Make sure those straps are good and tight, Writer Man," Wolf commanded. "We don't wanna lose this catch."

Marla nodded in agreement.

Thomas tugged the straps and smiled. "Fish on! Reel her in, Mister Wolfy," Baker said.

THE FISHERMAN in the black Zodiac saw a pack of paragliders swing out over the water a couple of miles away. He pulled his vest up to his nape, toyed with the Honda engine's throttle, and waited for Wolf to be fully distracted. "Now! *Showtime*," the hawk whispered.

Nicolas Gordon gunned the silenced Honda outboard engine, blew a crater in Lake Chelan and set a collision course for the 1947 Dehavilland Beaver.

THE MEETING wasn't going very well. The vast majority of environmentalists had been kept out, paid Po supporters comprised most of the audience, and the stage was lined with the corporation's entourage. The mayor and concerned city council members—torn between progress and preservation—struggled to stay neutral, and made notes. After nearly an hour of hearing proponents pound home the theme of *jobs, job, jobs*, even several Chelan Alliance members appeared to be leaning toward Ming Yaht's expanded presence in the valley, and the money it would generate for the community.

Po Jing jabbed his silver pointer with Ross Perot precision at detailed charts and graphs depicting a misleading picture of their plans for Chelan—condo cities and mega-casinos went unmentioned. Arturos Aquindo stood behind Hank Hodge watching the Walrus sweat, keeping an eye on the crowd, and wondering about the outcomes of the assignments in Big Creek Cove.

At the conclusion of Ming Yaht's presentation, an aging ex-governor, and several captains of industry who stood to benefit from impending progress, flanked Po Lin fielding concerned citizens' questions. They encountered some hecklers, but the Ming Yaht team's retorts were quick-witted and sharp-tongued.

BILL BAKER had arrived early, sat patiently, and listened closely. Now he fidgeted in his steel folding chair, chin on fist, elbow-on-knee, while the white-haired Montana lawyer seated beside him counseled him. Bill's wife Nancy and son, Nathan, were also beside him. Neon and Pai were there as well, but his brother, Thomas, and Wolf, were noticeably absent. And this worried him. What's more, there was no Kenneth Warwick, and no Councilman Barnes, to lead their counter attack to Ming Yaht's claims.

Bill Baker was not an accomplished speaker, but he was a well-informed one. He swallowed hard, slapped his thigh, and stood to begin their counter-offensive with a full barrage of environmental impact questions. "My name is William Virgil Baker," he began. "I am employed by the Environmental Protection Agency's Region Ten, but I want to speak as a private citizen today, if I may."

"Please proceed, Mr. Baker," said the chairperson.

Bill cleared his throat. "Mr. Po, isn't it true that Ming Yaht's British Columbia developments have greatly contributed to an impending ecological disaster in the Strait of Juan de Fuca and Puget Sound?"

Omnipotent Po Lin's black pupils ping-ponged back and forth across his pawns like a maestro's baton, until they came to rest on the broad shoulders of one of the corporation's attorneys.

The large, silver-haired, athletic-looking gentleman from a big Seattle firm wiped his brow, and wished he were with his friends at the Bainbridge Island Raquet Club playing doubles tennis, instead of playing mouthpiece for the Po Brothers. But then, he grabbed the microphone, blocked out his conscience, and did his job. "Young man, I believe you're confusing Ming Yaht International with another, Canadian firm."

The Montana lawyer took off his cowboy hat, unbuttoned his buckskin jacket, and stood beside Bill Baker. The two men conferred briefly; then Bill introduced his new friend.

"This is Zane Spencer from Flathead Lake, Montana," Bill said. "Zane represents the Chelan Alliance in this matter. And Mr. Spencer would like to respond to that last remark."

The chairperson nodded.

The wily lawyer produced a stack of papers from a worn leather saddlebag, and fanned his wrinkled face with them. "Mr. Po, I'm no jackass, and neither are some of the people you're attempting to railroad here today." Zane pointed a steady finger at the documents he was holding. "Ladies and gentlemen," he said, with a country singer's twang. "Just for starters, my clients intend to prove that Ming Yaht International and numerous other shell companies with piss-poor environmental histories are in fact, one and the same."

Po Lin glowered at Arturos Aquindo.

A hush fell over the crowd.

The Cuban recalled the day Wolf and company paid a visit to the corporation's Seattle headquarters, and wondered how much information they had managed to access.

The crowd murmured.

FROM BELOW the waterline of Big Creek Cove, Thomas Baker heard the high-pitched hum of the oncoming Honda outboard's propeller, but he ignored this omen, and continued to guide the steel cylinder in his grasp toward the floatplane's pontoon.

Wolf and Marla leaned down from the floatplane's cargo door, and grabbed the fuel tank with gloved hands. "We've got it!" Marla shouted.

Thomas surfaced.

Wolf looked up and saw the oncoming black Zodiac, but both of the pilot's hands were occupied. The mercenary's impeccable timing had caught him off guard. *Think fast Wolf,* he thought. To him, there was only one answer. *Kill or be killed.* The pilot bypassed alert mode, let go of the tank, and reached beneath a seat cushion for his Clint Eastwood gun.

The heavy, metal fuel tank swung out of Marla's grip and clipped Baker's forehead.

Gordon cut his engine, flipped up his glasses, and pointed a weapon at the crew. The rubber boat's bow slammed into the Beaver's metal pontoon.

"Good afternoon, Mr. Baker, Mr. Wolf. Please place your hands on top of your heads. Ah, Miss Decker! What an unpleasant surprise it is to find you here. I see you've recovered from the illness which required you to take a leave of absence," Nick announced, from behind the barrel of a .45 Sig Sauer with a very big silencer.

A slightly dazed Thomas Baker obediently reached for the sky, and started treading water.

Wolf stared coldly into Gordon's blue eyes. His nose twitched. His brows involuntarily flicked. The pilot felt the butt of his .44 magnum, slipped his finger over its trigger, and shoved Marla away from him.

Pop!

Gordon fired first.

Hot lead penetrated Wolf's thick hide. The pilot dove forward, bounced off the pontoon, and disappeared below the waterline.

Thomas dropped his hands, and prepared to dive.

Nick stuck his silencer in the back of Baker's neck. "Keep those hands up! And don't worry about your friend. He's tough enough to survive that wound."

Marla scampered to the rear of the Beaver, where she tossed aside tarps and packs, ropes and pulleys, until she found what she was looking for.

The Hawk glanced at the shoreline, quickly scanned the skies, and then waited patiently for the pilot to surface. "Oh, Miss Decker. Come out, come out, wherever you are," Nick called.

Marla bit her nails, and studied the contents of Wolf's emergency kit. "I don't work for you anymore, Mr. Gordon," she said, stalling.

Wolf popped up, gasping for air, and put a death grip on the pontoon. Blood flowed freely from his shattered forearm, and formed a dark red slick on the aquamarine water.

Gordon patted the pilot on the back. "Atta boy, Wolf! I knew you wouldn't disappoint me. You've been such a brilliant adversary so far," Nick sighed. "Maybe in another life we could have been allies."

"Fuck you, Gordon," Wolf growled.

Nick shook his head, and frowned. "Miss Decker? Come out at once or I'll be forced to shoot the writer next."

Marla tucked the flare gun she had found underneath her, and scooted for the doorway.

"Mr. Baker, please help your wounded friend aboard the floatplane," Nick said.

The pilot shook his head. Thomas hesitated.

"Do it. Now!" Nick ordered.

THE SLENDER CHINAMAN pushed the control bar forward, and the power glider ascended. As he flew over the final ridge, he sited his quarry between two towering, green pines—dead center in the patch of blue water below. Wen Wei Chen's pulse raced. He twisted his suspended body, banked sharply, and positioned his aircraft, stealthily keeping his back to the sun. The choppy afternoon air concerned him, but all he could do was take a deep breath, and focus on the assignment. *"For the dream,"* he whispered with one fist clenched.

Wen Wei Chen drew the silenced 9 millimeter Mac-10 from its clip holster, pulled back the glider's control bar, and commenced his descent into Big Creek Cove—quietly as a bird.

WHILE BAKER and Wolf climbed aboard, the Hawk maneuvered himself into the optimum position. He secured the Zodiac alongside the pontoon, and stood holding the floatplane's wing, looking out across the lake. There wasn't another boat within a mile. For as far as his eyes could see, skies were clear blue and empty. He heard no engine's noise. The only thing exposed to the predator-bird was his back. *Perfect,* he thought. "Much better," Nick said, once they were all inside the Beaver. "Now that I have everyone's attention, I—"

Marla's shoulder dipped slightly as she slipped the loaded flare gun under Thomas. Instinctively, she covered her suspicious body movement by handing some folded gauze to Wolf.

"Hold it. Don't move! Don't do anything stupid. Damn it! Don't make me hurt you," Nick yelled. The crew raised their hands, and Nick lowered his voice to a conciliatory tone. "Just listen to me. There's already been enough killing in Chelan. You amateur detectives stumbled across a billion-dollar operation that has been in the works for a decade, and forced my employers to arrange several nasty accidents. As of this morning, *your* accident was scheduled to be next."

The pilot pressed Marla's compress to his wound. "Was?" Wolf asked, sounding confused.

Nick nodded. "That's the way the script was written, folks."

"Weak-assed plot, Nick. No one would ever buy it," Baker blurted.

Gordon grinned. "I agree. It is at best, a well-worn plot. But you're the professional writer, Mr. Baker. And as you probably already know, truth is stranger than fiction. At any rate, I've done a last-minute rewrite. You see, it seems I have had a significant change of heart regarding my present employment."

Baker did not understand what was going on. His heart beat wildly. He felt the flare gun beneath his buttocks. He glared at Gordon, envisioned all of Nick's defenseless victims, and tried to get his courage up.

Wolf attempted to rattle the Hawk's cage. "I've known plenty of men like you, Nick," said the pilot. "You're the best in places like 'Nam and Nicaragua, but you're out of your element here."

"Is that so? Save it," replied Nick, wondering if his survival instinct had alarmed him prematurely about his pending predicament. "You're an interesting man, Mr.....*Wolf.* I must say, I admire your courage. And because you made it your business to find out everything about me, I, in turn, made it mine to find out everything about you."

Wolf's mind reeled. He pressed the gauze tighter to his wound, and wondered just how much Nick really knew about him.

Gordon continued. "Life's such a charade. Isn't it, Wolf? By the way, do your new friends know about your dark little secret?" Nick noted Baker's puzzled expression. "Evidently not," he said.

James Shawn Wolf started sweating bullets.

"You know, Mr. Wolf. We have a lot in common. More than you realize. Like you, I came here running from my past. And, like you, I also made the crucial mistake of getting attached, and learning to care again." Gordon saw the pilot's eyes look skyward, and paused to adjust his vest. "But then, I must admit...there is a certain *magic* to this valley."

Wolf gestured to Baker, then spoke. "Ya know, Nick. I'm an old dog like you. But I sure as hell learned something new from this crazy writer. At some point in life, a man has to take a stand, regardless of his situation, or he's no man at all. You're a good soldier, Nick. But you're fighting for the wrong side." Wolf paused. The pilot had lost a lot of blood, and the afternoon sun was so bright and warm. He blinked—unsure of what he had seen—and the winged vision was gone. "I know your employer very well, Nick. Trust me, even you are expendable to him."

Gordon kept his weapon aimed at them, pulled his K-bar knife from an ankle sheath, and raised its blade above him.

Baker bit his lip. He saw sunlight glisten off the mercenary's big blade, and wondered what Nick's next move would be.

"You know I'm right. Don't you, Nick?" Wolf said.

"As a matter of fact, James, I do. That's why I took it upon myself to cancel *your* accident. And why we're still talking." Nick swung his knife, and cut the straps supporting the fuel tank from the *Connie Joe.*

The splintered steel cylinder quickly sank into the deep blue water below.

The writer had often wondered what it took to make men kill. Revenge? Jealousy? Fear? When Thomas Baker saw the power glider pop out of the blinding sun and another weapon being pointed at him, *he* was ready to kill.

The dark shadow from the glider's wing fell upon the Beaver. The slender Chinaman steadied his automatic weapon.

Gordon looked up.

Baker raised the flare gun and screamed as he fired it, "This is for Warwicks and Barnes, you bastard!"

The flare exploded inside the rubber raft, and Gordon fell backward. Hot sulfur stuck and burned on his exposed facial skin. Fuel from the Zodiac's five-gallon gas tank burst into flames. Black smoke billowed skyward from the Zodiac as Nicholas Gordon dove into the water.

The Chinaman pulled the trigger on the 9 millimeter Mac-10 automatic.

Crack-pow-pow-pow-pow-pow-pow!

Bullets zipped down all around them.

Ping-ping-ping!

Several shots penetrated the pontoon.

"Hit the deck!" Wolf screamed.

Baker covered Marla with his body.

The airborne assassin sailed over them, and banked his aircraft for a second pass.

"Everyone all right?" the Beaver pilot asked.

Baker pointed to the flaming Zodiac.

"Get back in!" Wolf commanded. He pounced on the pontoon, and kicked the rubber boat away.

Within seconds, it exploded.

The glider pilot swung back around.

Wolf grabbed the frame of the cargo door. Baker scrambled to the opening, and reached out for his friend. They heard the shrill sound of fingernails scratching on the pontoon and froze...as Gordon's burned face appeared from beneath the waves!

The airborne assassin descended once again.

Wolf gazed deep into the Hawk's mirrored steel blue eyes, leaned back...and extended his hand. *Two* killers' bloodstained fingertips touched.

This one tough American, thought Wen Wei Chen, as he aimed the Mac-10 at Gordon's broad back, squeezed the trigger, and fired.

Crack-pow-pow-pow-pow--thud! Thud! Thud! Ping-ping-ping!

"Ughh!" Gordon cried out in pain.

Nick's weight was just too much for the injured pilot.

"Let go. Save yourself," Nick whispered to the confused pilot, right before he jerked his hand free of Wolf's grip.

The pilot, the writer, and the daring Miss Decker, all watched Nick disappear into the blue abyss.

Finally relieved of one world

The Hawk relaxed with wings unfurled.

***This** is how it had to end.*

Now Blue Chelan would be his friend—

his resting place on Mother Earth—

until the moment of rebirth.

The spiraling Hawk's eyes

saw golden sunshafts and bright blue summer skies.

His big body shuddered.

"Liberation! Reincarnation," he uttered.

And with these thoughts, ***'Nicholas Gordon'*** *blacked out, let go...*
and followed the path of the Connie Joe.

The Chinaman crammed a fresh 30-round magazine into the warm automatic weapon, and pulled back the powerglider's control bar.

Wolf pointed at the bullet-riddled pontoon. "We're taking on too much water. Time to fly!" he announced. He scurried to the cockpit, and cranked up the Beaver's radial engine.

Wen Wei Chen fired his gun again.

Crack-pow-pow-pow-ping-ping-ping-ping!

Bullets pierced the Beaver's fuselage. Wolf gave her full power. "Hug the floor! And hang onnnn—" the pilot shouted. *And the floatplane surged forward.*

Chapter 31

The Decision

INSIDE THE CHELAN City Council Chamber, Po Lin responded personally to a racial slur from an irate taxpayer. "It is true many of my people will come to Chelan in years ahead, but they—"

"How many?" a heckler yelled.

Ming Yaht's head man cleared his throat before continuing his response. "But these *yellow devils* some needlessly fear will not fit popular cinematic stereotypes envisioned. One need only look north to the Chinese community in Vancouver to alleviate such concern." Po Lin smiled impudently, scanned the crowd boldly, and pointed a crooked finger at the Beijing-born Miss Ho Pai. "This lovely young woman makes a perfect example of people who will come and benefit, not burden, your community."

"Obnoxious bastard!" Neon screamed as he leaped from his seat, and lunged for Po Lin.

Bill Baker grabbed his enraged friend's leg, and watched hopelessly as a security guard's kick cracked one of Neon's ribs.

Arturos Aquindo tackled Neon, applied a Half-Nelson, and dragged him down the aisle toward the exit.

Neon struggled to break free and cursed the Cuban.

Ho Pai, still weak from her accident, attempted to stand, and fell. "Michael!" she cried as she hit the floor.

"Pai!" Neon called out to her, as the Cuban tightened his hold on him.

Po Lin himself quickly approached her and offered his hand.

Pai attempted to scratch Lin's face. And when he blocked her, she tore the gold cufflink from his sleeve. Her nails drew blood beneath the great Po Lin's Dragon Head Tattoo. She spat on Lin and cursed him in his native tongue, *"Luimang!"* she hissed.

Po Lin instinctively raised his hand to slap her.

Pai shook her fist tauntingly. *"Liumang!* Go on, hit me. Show people your true face, *Luimang* Po! You care nothing for your people. You seek only more power."

Young Nathaniel Baker closed his eyes and clung to his mother's side. "Mom, I'm scared," he cried.

Po Lin saw astonished looks in the crowd. He heard people whispering, lowered his hand, and backed away.

Bill Baker helped Pai into her chair.

The brave Chinese woman covered her eyes with dark glasses, took three deep breaths, and pointed to the Dragon Head. *"You* do this to me, *Luimang* Po! Please tell these people why."

A bright red Po took a clean white handkerchief, wiped spit off his face, and returned to his seat without remorse.

Hank Hodge turned up the volume on the microphone, and took the floor. "For God's sake, people! This is getting out of hand. We're not talking about welfare recipients coming to the valley. These immigrants will contribute. Chelan will never become another California."

A rumble arose from the back of the room. Sounds of Neon struggling to escape the grip of Arturos Aquindo could be heard.

Hank Hodge continued. "My friends, ours is a nation of immigrants. We must never forget that fact. And don't kid yourselves abou—"

Bam!

The chamber's door blew open behind a surge of human force.

Every head turned toward the disturbance.

Po's security men scrambled to the area.

Arturos Aquindo's jaw dropped when he saw the Beaver's Crew enter the building behind Sheriff Paul Hilo.

The crowd roared.

The threesome looked like the famous rag-tag fife and drug corps in the painting which embodied the spirit of the American Revolution. Wolf, bleeding badly through makeshift bandaging; Marla, draped in the Beaver's Fourth of July dress flag, shivering, wet, and angry; the writer Thomas Baker's head-wound bleeding, his arms wrapped around his friends...and upon Baker's shoulder hung the life ring from the good ship *Connie Joe*.

The Cuban locked eyes with the pilot, loosened his hold on Neon, and slowly reached beneath his coat for his gun holster.

"Release him, Colonel A," Wolf snarled. "It's over."

Arturos fingered the butt of his weapon and seethed. "They say a cat has nine lives, but how many does a Wolf have, *amigo?*"

Security members with itchy trigger-fingers encircled the intruders and muttered among themselves in rapid-fire singsong Cantonese.

Sheriff Paul Hilo pointed his service revolver at the Cuban, and echoed Wolf's request, "Release the kid, now! Or I swear, I'll book you for assault."

The crowd collectively held their breath.

Great Po clapped his hands in front of the microphone.

Arturos Aquindo grimaced, set Neon free, and ordered his security team to back off. "You just made the biggest mistake of your miserable little life, sheriff," he said.

Hilo spit a splintered toothpick from between his teeth and smiled. "Believe me, *amigo*, this is no mistake," said the sheriff with a stern look.

The Cuban's fingers clicked like castanets. His security team responded by marching to the front of the room. Arturos combed his slick black hair, and stuck his pockmarked face in front of Wolf's. "It's never over until it's over, *Senor Lobo*. Don't ever forget that," he whispered with a sinister smile.

The pilot poked the Colonel's chest. "Fuck you, Arty."

The Cuban nodded. "It's a small world, *Piloto*. We will finish this later," Arturos promised, as he walked backward toward the Dragon Head. "And next time, you'll stay dead."

A stream of parking lot protesters surged toward the doors, propelling the Beaver Crew within a couple feet of the speaker's platform. The Council chambers quickly filled beyond capacity. Environmentalist posters fanned stagnant air. Chelan Alliance members chanted slogans. Sentiment shifted.

"Mr. Baker! What is the m-meaning of this outburst?" Hank Hodge yelled into the mike. "I'll have you know that I still have the floor."

A big logger fanned the air with a bloody Spotted Owl, which was fastened to a stick.

The crowd booed. Baker raised his hand.

The chairperson pounded her gavel.

Hodge continued. "There's a myth that this is merely a resort community, a retirees' Mecca, a goddamn artists' *Shangri-La!* Truth is, many residents never set foot in Lake Chelan. They just live here. Well, those regular kinds of guys and gals, and their children, are going to need real jobs." The county planner gestured toward the Pos. "Here sits Chelan's assurance of prosperity in the Twenty-first Century. Ming Yaht's *Greenfield Development* proposals have already been approved throughout Canada."

"Approved by whom, Mr. Hodge? Corrupt government officials with enough bribe money in their offshore bank accounts to anesthetize their consciences?" Thomas Baker interrupted.

Hodge shook his head. "What in the world is wrong with economic stimulus backed by foreign investment? It's not like a bunch of Martians are going to take over the valley and skin us alive!" Hodge snickered nervously. "You head a group who claims to want to save Chelan. Am I right, Mr. Baker?"

Thomas nodded.

"Mind telling us what you want to save it from?"

The fatigued writer took a deep breath, and began his response. "Not everyone is afflicted with greenback fever, Mr.

Hodge.   Some of us see this white-knight-in-shining-armor scenario for the Trojan Horse it really is." Thomas distinctly pointed to each and every member of the Pos' entourage. "These people are treating this entire affair like some damn Wall Street corporate takeover."

The crowd murmured behind him.

The Montana lawyer made his way to the chairperson and officially presented their petition.

Thomas Baker continued."This is not Hong Kong, Hong-couver, or New York!   And Chelan is not just another commodity to be bought and sold. Chelan is a sensitive, unique environment, that affords us a rare and rapidly vanishing way of life." Thomas turned toward the audience and looked at their faces. "I don't know about the rest of you, but some of us are here to talk about prevention. Because the last thing in the world that some of us want to do is attend one of these meetings ten years from now to debate ways of getting Lake Chelan off the Endangered Species List."

The environmentalist majority applauded loudly.

Hodge glanced toward Po Lin.

The Dragon Head glared back.

The county planner decided to go for broke. "Mr. Baker, if you and your Alliance were so damn worried about the quality of life deteriorating in this valley, then why did you allow the land around Ming Yaht's proposed industrial park to be zoned commercial back in 1989?"

The writer's mind went blank. He pictured a tiny one-man prison cell, fought a pain in his stomach, and carefully considered a response. "One good reason is because people like you are so talented at slipping projects like these through the system, Hank. You simply disguise the true scope and—"

"Funny thing, ain't it, Mr. Baker? We zone areas like this commercial and—presto! Commercial developments spring right up out of the ground." Hodge grabbed the mike from the stand and walked toward the writer. "Mr. Baker, it's been rumored that you have ulterior motives behind your opposition to Ming Yaht's expansion in the Chelan valley. Motives like half interest in a resort on the former Warwick estate backed by a British corporation. But that's an entirely different matter than the one we're attempting to address here today."

A hush fell over the crowd. They listened to every word.

"Mr. Baker, isn't the real reason you didn't oppose these county planning decisions back in 1989, because you were in federal prison for drug dealing?"

Thomas Baker lowered his head and bit his lip. He listened for a moment while Marla whispered in his ear, and then he raised his voice in anger. "First of all, Mr. Hodge, rumors are a dime a dozen. There are rumors that a certain overweight county planner—who is, coincidentally, blatantly pro-development—has a nice cabin cruiser, and a fancy new Lincoln that he paid for in cash."

"Are you accusing me of impropriety, Mr. Baker?"

Thomas nodded. "If the shoe fits? Wear it."

Arturos Aquindo gave the writer a menacing glare.

Thomas Baker didn't even blink. "I submit to this council that there have been numerous improprieties which have helped forge Ming Yaht's emergence to the forefront of development in Washington State and Canada."

City council members who had been discussing the Chelan Alliance's petition, leaned forward and listened intently.

Thomas took a step toward Hodge, and leaned close to the mike. "And as for my past, Mr. Hodge. I don't advertise it, but unlike most hypocritical lawyers, politicians, and businessmen, who broke out of the pack with dirty money—at least I don't deny having one! I grew up grooving in the sixties, rock 'n' rolled right through the seventies without regret, and would have managed to mellow out in the eighties without the help of the United States Justice Department, thank you please. And yes, I smoked—and inhaled—a little pot along the way."

The *inhale* remark drew scattered laughter from the crowd.

Wolf emitted a muted howl. "Sic-'em, Writer Man! Sic-'em."

"Nice try, Hodge," Thomas said confidently. "But we're not here to blame the world's problems on marijuana, or praise the government for locking up thousands of nonviolent people for growing or selling it, while simultaneously letting corporate America literally get away with mur—"

"Do you condone the use of drugs, Mr. Baker?" Hodge asked.

Baker shook his head. "Do you condone conspiring to sell out your own people, let alone, being a party to murder?"

Po Lin pounded on the table in front of him.

"I will not allow you t-to use this m-meeting as a f-f-forum for your sensationalist innuendoes, Mr. Baker," the shaken planner screamed. Hodge pointed the microphone toward Thomas. "Look at him, people! He's starting to believe all that pulp fiction crud he writes. He probably still s-s-smokes p-p—"

The writer motioned for the planner's microphone.

Hodge pulled it close to his chest.

Pos' security men moved a step closer.

Thomas Baker took the *Connie Joe's* life ring off his shoulder and shoved it against the Walrus' protruding gut. "Like the Warwicks and Councilman Barnes, I more than paid my dues, pal," Thomas whispered, just loud enough to be heard over the sound system. "But believe me, Hank...*your* time's coming."

Hank Hodge's well-tanned face turned ghostly white.

The crowd went crazy.

The chairperson's gavel struck wood repeatedly.

The *Connie Joe's* life ring fell to the floor, and Hank desperately clung to the mike shouting, "Listen to me, people! We need more than just this lake and some damn mountains. We need the jobs that—"

Sheriff Paul Hilo fought his way front and center, and snatched the mike from Hodge. "Let him speak, you old bag of wind!" Hilo commanded, as he thrust the mike in Baker's hand.

Concerned city council members feverishly fingered paperwork, then paused, huddled and conferred. Again, the chairperson's gavel struck wood. "Mr. Baker, you have the floor," she announced.

Television cameras took aim. Reporters put pens to notepads.

The perceptive county planner skillfully faded from the limelight.

Thomas Baker plucked the life ring from the floor, and raised it like a fallen battle flag. He recalled his promise to Councilman Barnes, took a deep breath, and began. "This is *our* community. And this debate is not about immigration, or China bashing. It's about complete disregard for the welfare of this valley we call home. It's about abusive power, and greed. About careless deep well drilling, secret casino proposals, and large land acquisitions at *any* cost—including murder!"

Marla and Wolf took a stand beside Thomas.

The Po Brothers rose from their seats of honor.

The room got so quiet that when the reporter for the *Chelan Mirror* dropped her pen, practically everyone heard it hit the floor.

For Arturos Aquindo, the scene was hauntingly familiar. The air smelled of scandal. It reminded him of his own failed Florida senate race back in 1988.

Thomas raised his voice another notch. "This is about fish kills in these sacred, pristine waters, and altered tests from government labs which covered up the real cause. It's about bribed public officials putting their wallets above the public's trust they were sworn to uphold. It's an old story folks, destined to be one more classic example of big business interests winning out over proper zoning procedures and environmental regulations—*if* we let them win."

Environmentalists waved posters. "No way! No way! No way," they chanted.

Bill Baker stepped up with his family. Chef Fisher squeezed through the crowd with several Chelan Alliance members and Ron Moore's help to join his friends in a show of solidarity. They all locked arms with the gallant Beaver Crew, and listened to Thomas Baker speak from his heart.

"Ladies and gentlemen," Thomas said. "The Chelan Alliance does not oppose smart, green, inevitable growth in this valley. You all watch the news, so you know what can happen to special places when they are mismanaged. Just look at our overcrowded

National Parks, like the Grand Canyon. And look at the way Lake Tahoe's water quality and wetlands have declined. Look at how the Pacific Northwest's salmon fishery has gone to hell. Why? Mismanagement. That, and poor planning. Ming Yaht's expanded industrial park would house an enclosed commercial distribution center the size of 20 football fields under one roof.

The crowd rumbled. Even loggers looked surprised.

Thomas nodded. "That's right. Independent studies show that it would service approximately two semi tractor trailers per minute, twenty-four hours a day. The associated lighting and activity would snarl traffic, steal the stars from our night sky, and be incompatible with the tranquillity our valley offers countless tourists every year." He turned toward the Pos and pointed. "But these *good tenants* chose not to give you all the facts in their mandatory Public Notice, which was unethically prepared and presented by County Planner Henry *Hank* Hodge."

Working class men and women looked angrily at their county planner.

The Walrus envisioned himself on a hangman's gallows in the hands of a bloodthirsty lynch mob. He could feel Po Lin's beady little eyes burning a hole through his tense, sweaty skin. Hank Hodge swallowed hard as he watched the writer approach the speaker's platform...*and the noose got tighter!*

Thomas slipped the microphone back in its stand and sat the life ring on the lectern. "If we allow this? Then, I ask you—what next? A segregated condo-city where a nature sanctuary had been proposed? A Pacific Northwest playground where wealthy Hong Kong immigrants gamble and play golf—while your kids carry their clubs, and your grandma sweeps beneath their slot machines for minimum wage? Would Mr. Po and his gang have floating crap tables on these pristine waters, and monorails outfitted with video poker machines going to Stehekin?" Thomas lowered his voice. "None of us oppose extending the tourist season. None of us objects to Native Americans establishing one environmentally compatible casino on their land here; nor should we. Lord knows *they* deserve that much, or more. But we must not let outside business interests monopolize the resources of this valley. What we are talking about is losing control of our own destiny!" Once more, the writer turned toward the Pos. "Honorable guests, I beseech you to answer this question. How many bowls of rice can two wealthy brothers eat?"

An enraged Po Lin took a great leap forward, and elbowed the writer from the microphone. "What we offer is good for people of Chelan and state of Wash—"

"Bullshit!" shouted Bill Baker, as he moved toward his brother.

"Bullshit!" echoed Marla, Wolf, and Chef Gary Fisher, as they too edged closer to Thomas.

Pos' security men formed a circle around them. A conflict seemed imminent.

Po Lin raised his hands, and snapped off a command in his native tongue. The security men relaxed, and the Great Po continued. "Ming Yaht has been a good tenant in Chelan valley! Do not judge us by—"

Vociferous discontent, and verbal assaults from the crowd, quickly dissolved what little feigned humility Po Lin had managed to muster. His face grew red with anger. He flailed the air with a clenched fist.

"This why America becoming a third-rate country," Lin said belligerently. "You *people* fail to seize opportunity when placed before you. Others beg for what we offer you! In Canada, they welcome us with open arms. *We* can go anywhere."

"Then, go," Wolf snarled.

"Go to hell!" Neon shouted, as he helped Pai to stand beside the others.

A restless crowd glared at Po Lin's scornful face.

A television crew's camera zoomed in on Lin's raised fist. They filmed the gold Dragon Head ring with its five carat ruby shimmering beneath the bright lights. They filmed Po Lin's forearm, from which his clean dress shirtsleeve—torn by Ho Pai's fingernails—had fallen to his elbow. They zoomed in closer and captured the blood-streaked ink image.

"Ask him about the Dragon tattoo," Ho Pai screamed.

Po Lin lowered his fist, pulled down his shirtsleeve, and moved in front of the lectern. He extended both arms, palms upturned, and flashed his alabaster smile. "If you trust in us?" he shouted. "Then future hold good things for the people of Chelan."

Thomas snatched the life ring from the lectern. "Good things come to those who wait, Lin," he prophesied. "Believe me, I know."

Crowd noise increased.

Po Lin quickly turned to face the writer.

Thomas raised the life ring. "Quiet, please. Please listen," he pleaded. "For years we were graced by the presence of Councilman Barnes' wisdom in this chamber. Good men like Ken Warwick and Tim Barnes gave their lives to prevent the exploitation of this valley by men like these."

The angry crowd moved in closer.

The Pos' entourage prepared to abandon ship. Attorneys stuffed their briefcases. Arturos Aquindo—concerned about deteriorating security conditions—radioed his parking lot team, and told them to have the limousines ready.

But the writer wasn't done yet. "Mr. Po, could you please explain what that tattoo on your arm stands for?" he asked.

Po Lin clapped his hands and hissed.

Arturos charged the lectern.

"I see," Thomas said. "Could you explain the term *triad* to the good people of Chelan?"

The Latino's hand fell hard on Thomas's shoulder. "That's enough," Arturos bellowed.

Wolf shoved past Po Lin, and grabbed the Cuban's arm.

Sheriff Paul Hilo moved in behind Wolf. "Let him finish talking," Hilo yelled.

Thomas leaned into the mike. "Perhaps we should ask the Po Brothers about the Warwicks' accident, and how a corporation controlled by them had its substantially lower bid for the Warwick estate accepted over one submitted by Mr. Jimmy Collins."

Po Jing gestured to his brother that it was time to back off.

Po Lin brushed past Thomas, and projected a deadly stare.

But the writer wasn't done yet. Baker held the life ring to his face like the scope on a rifle, and sized up Po Lin. Suddenly the head honcho from Hong Kong didn't look so big. "Po!" Thomas shouted from between the words *Connie* and *Joe* on the life ring. "I've got one last question that's been asked of so many, too many, great leaders throughout history, who became blinded by greed or power. Just what *do* you know, Mr. Po? And *when* did you know it?"

Po Lin had had enough. He lunged for Thomas.

Thomas tossed the *Connie Joe's* life ring at Lin's face.

Po Lin caught it in midair. The sleeve covering his tattoo slipped down again.

Protesters rushed the stage. Several scuffles broke out.

Arturos grabbed Wolf's throat.

The chairperson's gavel hammered the table repeatedly.

Sheriff Paul Hilo fired a single shot into the ceiling.

The crowd stilled. The combatants separated. The Pos and their entourage congregated on one half of the stage. Chelan City Council members huddled on the other half. Security people and Baker's backers stood close enough to smell each other's breath.

The Chelan City Council President gave her permed gray hair a pat, gathered her paperwork, and walked to the speaker's platform. She adjusted the microphone, and cleared her throat. "Can't say that I recall attending a livelier council session," she began, hoping to defuse the crisis. "Councilman Barnes was revered by this institution," she said, tapping a chewed pencil tip on the cherry wood lectern. "That is why we have the utmost respect for the Chelan Alliance, which has submitted this petition to the Council." She held up the document and the attached pages with hundreds of valley citizens' signatures upon them.

Protesters for and against Ming Yaht's expansion moved forward.

Baker and his friends pleaded for quiet.

The distinguished speaker slipped on a thick pair of eyeglasses, flipped through her notebook, and glanced toward her colleagues, who then nodded. The Chelan City Council President swallowed hard, then read the decision. "In light of today's developments, various documents which have been presented, and this moving display of public concern, the City of Chelan, as the lead agency, which is fully intent on annexing the areas in question, has determined that Ming Yaht International's proposal is in fact, likely to have an adverse effect on the local environment. Therefore, an Environmental Impact Statement *will* be required."

Pos' lawyers protested loudly behind her. Lin cursed in Chinese. Environmentalists jeered them. Unemployed loggers booed.

The Chelan City Council President lowered her glasses to the bridge of her nose, and addressed the angry parties. "Ladies and gentlemen, be reasonable," she said. "*This* is our decision. No one is going to die over a one-year delay while proper studies are conducted. Well? Are they?"

No one replied.

The feisty council president pounded her gavel on the lectern. "All right, then. Everyone is invited to comment on the scope of the Environmental Impact Statement through proper procedures. *This* meeting…is adjourned!"

Chelan Alliance members rejoiced. They flooded the stage, and gave the rag-tag Beaver Crew a rousing round of heartfelt applause. With friends, family, and Marla beside him sharing the moment, Thomas Baker shed tears of joy unashamedly, and savored the apparent victory.

Even the mysterious Mr. Wolf was visibly moved.

Po Lin shook his head, straightened his tie, and ordered that a path be cleared to the exit. "Pathetic," the Great One grumbled to his brother. "We will, of course, appeal this decision."

"Of course," Po Jing replied.

Arturos Aquindo radioed the parking lot team, pushed aside an aggressive reporter, and signaled for the Pos to follow him.

A worried Hank Hodge grabbed Po Lin's wrist. "W-w-wait! Mr. P-Po," Hank stammered. "I can fix all of this! Llisten to—"

Po Lin elbowed the obese planner. If looks could kill, the Walrus would have died right then. The Dragon Head's bodyguards blocked back boisterous citizens, and Ming Yaht's entourage moved out.

The stammering Walrus continued to babble. "M-Mr. P-P-Po. These p-people will b-beg for you to come back!" The county planner clung to Po Lin's tattered coattails all the way to the parking lot—with Paul Hilo right behind him nipping at his heels. Once outside, Hodge quickly plopped behind the wheel of his Lincoln.

"Baker's right, Hank," Sheriff Hilo said, slipping a fresh cinnamon flavored toothpick between his teeth. "This is one nice automobile you have here."

The Walrus cringed, turned his key and cranked on the engine.

Paul Hilo tipped back his black Stetson hat. "Listen, Hank. How'd you like to spend the Fourth of July in one of my cells?"

"J-j-jail?" the nervous planner questioned.

Hilo nodded.

"W-w-why are you asking me this, Paul?" whined the planner."

"You know why, Hank. It's called *protective custody*. If you're smart, and decide to cooperate with this investigation, you'll be in danger of—"

The Pos' long black limo pulled alongside them. A tinted window glass was lowered…and the pockmarked face of Arturos Aquindo glared at the confused county planner.

Hank Hodge slammed his door, and the Lincoln sped away.

Paul Hilo spit his toothpick on the Cuban's silk suit, and leaned inside the limo.

Ming Yaht's Seattle lawyer gestured to Arturos, indicating it was best to remain silent, then came down hard on the small town lawman. "My clients are foreign nationals sheriff," the attorney said. "You have no right to impede their—"

"Piss off!" Hilo shouted, peering past the mouthpiece into powerful Po Lin's beady black pupils.

"We break no laws, sheriff," Po Jing said.

Hilo sighed. He didn't have enough to detain them, and they obviously knew it. "You and your brother are free to go at this time, but I suggest you stay around a week or—"

"So sorry sheriff," said a smiling Po Lin. "Have business commitment in Hongcouver July fifth. We leave when pilot completes maintenance on airoplane...tomorrow evening."

The Cuban tapped the sheriff's shoulder.

The limo's window closed tightly.

The limousine's driver revved his engine.

Paul Hilo nodded, lit a mashed Marlboro, and rapped his knuckles on the door twice.

Tires squealed. A puff of dust rose from the hot pavement *...and the Pos' long cool limo motored away, to Ming Yaht's corporate retreat.*

Chapter 32

Plenty of Fireworks

EACH YEAR thousands of visitors and residents drive or boat to Manson, *Village by the Bay*, to watch the spectacular fireworks display explode over Lake Chelan's sparkling waters and celebrate America's independence. The 1996 edition promised to be the best show ever, and this was true for a myriad of reasons.

Sunset sky painted soft pastel smiles on pleased passengers as the *Lady of the Lake* lay anchor in Manson Bay. In a brief moment of solitude, Thomas Baker stood on the massive ferryboat's upper deck, reflecting back upon what had already been an eventful day.

THE SUNNY *morning after* was filled with love and laughter as summer breezed back into the Bakers' lives. Bill and Tom jogged the old logging road at dawn to begin the holiday. Following breakfast, the expanded Granite Falls family organized entertainment and games for friends, guests, and some of the local children. Bill and Nathan won the three-legged race; Pai and Marla flew a thirty-foot Chinese dragon kite; and the Englishman, Jimmy Collins, was crowned the reigning king (or queen) of Lawn Croquet.

During an all-American dinner buffet prepared by Chef Gary Fisher and the ladies, Miss Ho Pai and Michael *Neon* Johnson set their wedding date for August in the wildflower meadow behind Yeti Chalet. Immediately following their surprise announcement, speculation on the marriage of Thomas and Marla ran wild. Granite Falls Bookie, James Shawn Wolf, set the odds at four to one against Baker taking the official paper plunge. Betting was heavy.

After the holiday feast, the Bakers led a caravan into the city, where everyone enjoyed the antique automobile parade, arts and crafts booths, and entertaining street fair activities. The *Lady of the Lake* was the last stop on the lodge hosts' guided tour. Thomas had promised his guests the best seats in the house for the fireworks display, and *The Lady* would fulfill that promise.

JUST AS they were leaving the dock, an open-air Jeep bearing California plates and crammed full of luggage sounded its horn from the parking lot. Thomas and Wolf couldn't believe their eyes. It was the Deli Twins, coming home from Southern California like Dorothy and Toto returning from Oz. Wolf waved to the sunburned girls, and ordered the captain to reverse the engines.

"Wait for us! You were right. L.A. sucks," the twins shouted to amused passengers.

As the three last-minute arrivals boarded the big ferryboat, Wolf, who had reluctantly agreed to attend this lovers cruise with the gang, had a sudden change of heart. "My how you've grown, Little Red Lyla," Wolf growled in a deep and sexy voice, as he drooled over her familiar breasts.

"Yeah, yeah. Sure, sure," Lyla said, swishing the hem of her low-cut sundress. "But did ya miss me, ya big bad Wolf?"

The wounded Wolf bobbed his head emphatically, and fell to his knees courting sympathy sex.

Lovely Lynn did not return alone, she was accompanied by a handsome UCLA Bruin. Unable to express her attachment for home in words, she elected to *show* the young man the magic of Chelan. After meeting Marla, Lynn introduced her boyfriend to Thomas.

"Lynn's told me all about you, Mr. Baker," the college kid said sheepishly.

Thomas shook his hand. 'Oh, really? I hope it was all good."

"It was, sir," the UCLA sophomore snickered. "Rest assured. Lynn tells me you're some kind of writer."

Thomas smiled. "I try."

"I'm a poet myself. Perhaps we could rap about the muse a little later?"

Thomas nodded. "Great. I'll look forward to it," he said.

When *The Lady* set sail, a glowing Lynn cornered Thomas alone and leaned close to him on the rail. "I learned a lot from you, Thomas," she whispered, pecking his cheek. "Thanks."

The Writer was deeply touched.

PRESENTLY, *The Lady's* anchor found bottom in Manson Bay and night sky's star-dancers took the stage above. In nearby Lynn's young eyes, Thomas still perceived some kind of love for him, but the heat of her passion had subsided. Lynn had found someone her age, and brought him home to where her heart resided—*Chelan.*

Thomas Baker was relieved.

HANK HODGE'S cabin cruiser bashed the starboard side of a classic *Chris-Craft* yacht packed with prominent Emerald City attorneys as it sped away from the dock at Harris Marina.

"You moron! Your fat ass is mine! I'll sue you for every penny you've got," the firm's senior partner promised, while shaking a fist dripping dry vermouth from a spilled martini.

"Hank, wait. Honey, honey, wait! You left without me!' shouted the large potato-shaped woman wearing the tiny bathing suit, who had spent the majority of her life reminding her husband of such gravely important things.

Hank gunned the big outboard engine. Expensive hair replacement plugs blew away from his wrinkly forehead. Their voices faded. He gave them all the finger, guzzled his last gulp of Jack Daniels, donated the empty bottle to his wake, and watched the city of Chelan, his wife—his entire world—disappear into the hazy dusk behind him.

ON BOARD their luxurious corporate seaplane, the Brothers Po talked about their revised timetable in soft-toned Cantonese. Lin cut cabin lights, reclined in his plush seat, and looked to their pagoda-style retreat, fondly remembering his white hawk. The Dragon Head had not mentioned him since making his decision, and would probably never mention him again, but Nick's liquidation had pierced a needle-sized hole in his hardened heart.

"Do you anticipate any legal ramifications for the corporation resulting from this debacle?" Po Jing inquired.

The first burst of color exploded on the far horizon, briefly illuminating the Dragon Head's troubled reflection in the bullet-proof window. Po Lin signaled for the pilots to pull away from the dock. "The Cuban assured me everything would be resolved," Lin replied.

The second pyrotechnic spider spread its vibrant, phosphorous legs above the far end of the valley, as the customized white McKinnon Goose taxied into the calm, cobalt, lake.

Jing saw a look on his fearless brother's face that he had not seen in many years. "Does the American's elimination bother you?"

Lin shrugged, then lied. "Has smart business ever bothered me?"

Jing shook his head, and changed the subject. "How is the boy?"

His brother smiled. "Soon he will be ready to assume his rightful place in the corporation and complete the last leg of his journey, safely by my side." Lin rubbed the sockets of his eyes. "The Americans are a peculiar race. Are they not, Jing?"

The seer nodded.

"We built their railroads with the sweat of our labor when this nation was little more than a sniveling infant. Today, we back satellite communications technology, which will lead them down the information highway, straight into the Twenty-first

Century. We even manufactured the fireworks they employ to celebrate their Independence Day." Lin slapped the seat back in front of him. "Fools!" he hissed. "It is they who will suffer from this apparent victory."

Twin turbo engines roared. Ming Yaht's white bird surged through dark waters, broke free of the bond, and soared off toward Stormy Mountain.

Lin leaned back on his headrest. "Oh, well. There are other pristine valleys," he sighed.

Po Jing, vexed by the apparent failure of his vision, peered intensely into the vast, fast-moving stellar sea; then made a plea. "Have faith in my visions, Lin. This dream is not dead," the seer said. "Chelan will yet be ours, for it is written in the stars."

LAKE CHELAN meanders through the deepest gorge in North America to its headwaters at Stehekin and the scenic North Cascades National Park. Over fifty-five miles long, blue Chelan offers boaters countless private places in which to do their thing. But on this night, nearly every craft afloat lay anchor in Manson Bay enjoying the fireworks display.

HANK HODGE'S cabin cruiser was there, drifting aimlessly in the dark, less than one hundred yards from the *Lady of the Lake*, and less than one hundred feet from the Po Brothers' corporate yacht—which was captained by one Arturos Aquindo.

It had been well over an hour now since the delirious county planner pondered such gruesome things as Walla Walla State Prison, Nick Gordon's nasty temper, or Po Lin's deadly glare. Hank had guzzled plenty of whiskey though, and was known to get mean and stupid when he drank to such extremes—which was exactly why he chose to be alone for this fateful voyage. This way, there was no one to be mean to...*but himself.*

Thirty minutes after swallowing his secretary's monthly prescription of Valium, Hank sank back in his captain's chair—entranced by man-made nebulas in the heavens above—and flashed back upon his past...*his marriage, the big move to Wenatchee with his svelte young bride, raising the girls, and landing the county planner's job.* Life was challenging back then, when everything had to be earned and he had goals to keep him going in the right direction. But now, it was old and boring—*just like him.*

MING YAHT'S WHITE BIRD banked toward patriotic Fourth of July Mountain, where Councilman Barnes' spirit had merged with the land he loved. Po Lin took a final glance at the valley from his Goose, and ordered the pilots to make a maneuver, due northwest, to Fortress Hongcouver. The corporate aircraft ascended.

THE DARK FIGURE FINGERED the algae-covered pilings beneath the dock of the corporate retreat, scanned the moon-drenched peak of Fourth of July Mountain, and waited. When Ming Yaht's corporate aircraft ascended to four thousand feet, *his* explosive device—electronically linked to the altimeter—made its intended connection.

Kaboom!

Ming Yaht's white bird burst into a red ball of fire, and fell forever from the night sky, straight into the unforgiving cliffs above Antilon Lake.

"Karma," whispered the silhouette beneath the dock of the corporate retreat.

But the killer wasn't done yet! Two careless Hong Kong bodyguards continued pacing the pier planks above him, totally unaware of what had just transpired, mesmerized by America's moonlit *Marlboro Country,* and eager to get back to Ming Yaht's courtesy concubine suite in Hongcouver.

Target Number Two tossed a fresh pack of Marlboro cigarettes to *Target Number One,* and climbed the steps toward the pagoda's outdoor deck. "Tell me when you see the Cuban's running lights, Li," he told his comrade in Cantonese.

The killer screwed the silencer tightly to his weapon of choice, and readied for the deed by recalling lines from the Special Forces creed: *"I am a professional soldier. I will fight where my nation requires. I will be called upon to perform tasks in isolation. I will liberate the oppressed."* He waded closer, in a crouched position, placed one gloved hand upon the rocky shoreline, and grimaced in pain. Two cracked ribs, several bruises on his back—it could have been worse. The very same high-tech vest which enabled him to act out his charade in Big Creek Cove, had nearly caused his death by drowning! It was sheer luck that he had come-to in time to shed the heavy thing. He ground his gold crowns together. *"My goal is to succeed in any mission and live to succeed again,"* he pronounced through clenched teeth.

THE HAWK rose quickly from his premature grave, pointed the semi-automatic .22 caliber pistol toward the end of the pier, and pulled the trigger. *Pop-pop!* A head shot.

Marlboro Man Number One—*done.*

The second target sprayed the shore with gunfire.

Nick aimed and fired. *Pop-pop-pop-pop-pop!* A neck shot.

Marlboro Man Number Two—*through.*

Not only did he discover his Rover conveniently packed with all of the Pos' remaining treasures, but a quick search of the grounds revealed no other security people. *Perfect,* thought Nicholas. Gordon retrieved the one item from his personal effects which he could not leave behind—his green beret—and carefully stashed it inside a suitcase filled with crisp currency.

THE TALL DARK FIGURE removed puddles of blood, leaving no evidence of his kills. He kicked two heavily weighted bodies off the end of the dock. A purple pyrotechnic cluster exploded across a faraway sky, briefly illuminating a broad *pay backs-are-a-bitch* smile on the badly burned face of the *former* professional killer. For a moment, he watched the Independence Day celebration's reflection around the one of his own haggard image in the calm, cool waters of Lake Chelan...*and then he walked away.*

HAWK was at peace. Life was strange. In order to live it, both his past and his present had to die. He gingerly reclined behind the wheel of his Rover, took a deep breath, and turned the key.

The cage door swung open.
The Hawk was finally free.
And it was time to fly.

COLOR CLUSTERS rained down around elated passengers aboard *The Lady of the Lake*—some seemed close enough to touch. While the others oo-ed and ahhed, James Shawn Wolf pressed trained eyes tightly to high-powered binoculars. Only he had seen the stray explosion near Fourth of July Mountain, and he had seen nothing but darkness in that direction ever since.

Bill Baker watched his brother drape a jacket around Marla's shoulders.

"Isn't it nice to see Thomas in love again?" Nan whispered.

Bill nodded slowly, then slipped his arm around his wife.

When Wolf's keen eyes tired of scanning Fourth of July Mountain, he turned his attention to swarms of colored running lights fanning out across the bay like wind-blown fireflies, searching for a sign. He could smell Arturos Aquindo's scent on the summer wind, and it consumed him.

The writer handed the pilot two glasses of champagne, and pointed to the chilled chick in the sundress beside him. "Give it a rest, Wolf. It's over. We won."

Wolf lapped champagne and laughed. "Over? I hate like hell to burst your bubble, but we didn't win. All we got was a draw, which was damn good considering the opposition." Wolf sniffed the damp night air suggestively. "And, trust me...they're out there somewhere. The big ones always get away, Writer Man. Put that in your journal."

"Come on, Wolfy," Lyla pleaded with a pouty face. She ran her fingers through the pilot's unruly mane. "Put those damn binoculars down. The best show in the valley is right under your nose!" The braless babe leaned closer, and flashed fleshy cleavage. "Come on," she coaxed.

Wolf curled his upper lip, bit her neck, and nuzzled nooky nonchalantly. The high-powered binoculars hit the deck. "Hands cold, Lyla?" Wolf wetly whispered in her wanton ear.

"Now *that's* the Wolf I know and love," Lyla blurted, as she plunged chilled fingers down the front of the pilot's tan chinos.

Wolf's eyes rolled back in his head. He nearly spilled their champagne. Suddenly, his body grew tense. "Did you say *love?*" the fearless pilot whispered.

Lyla's fingers probed deeper. "Oh, relax. Don't get so paranoid! It's just a little word."

"Get ready, everyone. It's time for the grand finale!" Chef Fish uttered.

Wolf shook his hard head and shuddered. "Some of us are just getting started," he said.

How true.

HANK HODGE had been waiting for the grand finale, too, but by the time the four-minute machine-gun burst of sound and light began, the Walrus was only half a man. He could hardly focus. He was tired. The pills he took were taking too long, and he feared they might fail him.

"C-c-candy is dandy. But liquor is quicker," Hank babbled incoherently. His head spun. "Confusion. Delirium. Damn it— do it!"

Hank Hodge slammed the wood-grained glove box repeatedly until it dropped. He grabbed the .38 revolver and his stash bottle of Johnnie Walker Red from the depths of the compartment, guzzled more liquid courage, and loaded one shell. He spun the cylinder, put the snub nose to his temple...and pulled back the hammer.

Click.

His heavy eyelids blinked rapidly. His weak heart raced loudly. He experienced an inexplicable rush of power, spun the cylinder again...and pulled the trigger.

Click.

Another gulp of scotch ensued...and as he swallowed, a gust of wind cleared smoke from the water, and Hank Hodge saw Ming Yaht's corporate ship materialize before his bloodshot eyes. Suddenly, the Smith & Wesson felt even better in his grip.

This time, he bypassed spinning the cylinder.

Click.

He took another drink, and tried a different approach.

"Shit," he slurred after chipping a tooth on the snub nose. "What f-f-fool s-said suicide is p-p-painless?"

Hank Hodge covered cool chrome with wet lips, and pulled back the hammer once more...

IT HAD BEGUN and, intermittently, night sky grew bright as day sun. Colored fountains illuminated mountains and made the lake a kaleidoscope mirror. Deafening explosions reverberated across the water. Impressed passengers aboard *The Lady of the Lake* whistled and applauded.

BARELY SEVENTY-FIVE FEET AWAY, among dense white smoke clouds, Arturos Aquindo opened the big cooler, and tossed another Budweiser to the twenty-three year old Chinese émigré who had *killed* Nicholas Gordon. Amid color strobes and total darkness, the Latino chipped at a large block of ice with a brass-handled pick, and studied the boy.

Wen Wei Chen's bright, brown, eager eyes drank the elixir of the *meiguo's* skies. His pink lips puffed an American cigarette between satisfying sips of American beer. He leaned contentedly on the stern of the corporation's yacht.

The pockfaced Cuban closed the cooler, grabbed a briefcase, and approached the boy. "The journey has been difficult for you, hasn't it, Wen Wei?" Arturos shouted above the deafening noise engulfing them.

The boy smiled, and bowed to the man who had promised to free him from a sizable debt to the *snakeheads* which had ferried him to the *meiguo's* shores. "Life very hard in Fujian Province, sir. Wen Wei honored to serve Dragon Head—and you."

Arturos moved closer. "And you served us well," the Latino noted, extending the briefcase while keeping one hand behind his back. "After tonight, life will no longer be a struggle for you, Wen Wei Chen. I promise."

The boy's fresh young face glowed with anticipation. Blood pumped through his veins like molten lava rushing to erupt from an active volcano. His young mind raced to comprehend the miraculous realization of the dream—*a new life in America.*

The last vibrant pyrotechnic spider spread its golden legs across the valley's night sky.

Wen Wei Chen watched it, with a child's trusting eye.

Arturos Aquindo's friendly eyes turned cold. The forced smile vacated his face. His sweaty fingers formed a tight grip around the brass handle concealed behind his back.

Wen Wei Chen snuffed his cigarette, and reached for the briefcase.

"Go on, take it. It's your reward. Fifty thousand Canadian dollars," the Cuban said.

The boy sighed as he assumed possession, then bowed.

The sky above them exploded with a final, furious volley of noise and lights.

Arturos Aquindo grabbed his victim's mouth, glared into panic-stricken eyes, and repeatedly plunged the ice pick's cold steel point through the Chinaman's healthy young heart.

"Welcome to the *Beautiful Country, amigo,*" Arturos said, as he dumped the lifeless body overboard.

And then the Cuban began the search for Hank Hodge's cabin cruiser.

THE LADY OF THE LAKE raised her anchor, sounded her horn, and set a course for the fjord-like end of Lake Chelan. A jazz band struck up a tune on the lower deck.

"That was some show. Huh?" Chef Fish said.

"Yeah, some show," echoed Neon, while he watched Wolf and Thomas romancing their ladies along the back rail of the boat.

The curious chef had been dying to ask Neon about something he'd observed earlier in the day. "Why did James Wolf give you that ugly lead doorstop more than a month before your wedding day? Did I, like, miss the joke or what?"

"Wolf might not be around for the wedding. He's thinking about flying the Beaver up to Alaska with some fishing guides."

Neon lowered his head, took Pai's hand, and walked off toward the other couples. "Excuse me, Fish," he said. Michael *Neon* Johnson did not like lying to Baker's chef, but he could not tell him, or anyone, about the gold bars Wolf had appropriated from Ming Yaht's pagoda—especially the one painted battleship gray that was just given to him as a wedding present.

Gary Fisher tucked hands in pockets, and tagged along behind Neon and Pai. "What's up, guys?" he asked the gathering of lovers.

Wolf growled. "The sky's up, Ga-rrry! Why don't you put an egg in your shoe and be—" Lyla pinched the pilot's tender loins. "Owwww! That hurt," Wolf cried.

Lyla smiled.

"We're taking a champagne cruise to Stehekin, just like everyone else on board, Fishman," Wolf said in a more conciliatory tone. "Why don't you get off the AA wagon, have a few drinks, and go troll the lower deck for lonely hearts seeking hot recipes?"

The chef frowned, then confronted Thomas. "Speaking of fish, I've got to ask." He tapped Marla's shoulder. "Are you going to let this catch go back to the Emerald City Sea, or what?" he said loudly. "Inquiring minds wanna know, pal."

Thomas's face turned crimson red. A waiter appeared with several chilled bottles of champagne. Thomas grabbed two, and popped their corks. The Granite Falls gang gathered around with empty glasses, and he filled them.

"Well, Thomas, just what are your two lovebirds' plans? Huh?" Nancy inquired.

Thomas slipped his arm around Marla. "Listen, everyone. I've been keeping this journal, and…"

His brother, Wolf, Neon, Pai, and his English business partner, all moved closer until they encircled the couple. "Come on. Tell us," they demanded as one.

The writer bit his lip. "Ease up, you guys. Listen to me." He gestured to the water, the mountains, and each of them. "This would make a great novel. And all of you would make marvelous characters. I—"

"Don't try and weasel out of the question, Baker," Wolf taunted.

"Tell us! Tell us! Tell us," they chanted.

Marla Decker felt uncomfortable. She bit her nails. Her knees rocked.

The Englishman, Collins, raised his hand and stamped his foot. "All right, then. We've had our fun." He clicked his glass to Marla's. "Give him time, love. I'm quite certain he'll come 'round."

Marla nodded and flashed her natural smile.

Thomas embraced her. They kissed a long while.

The writer cleared his throat. "Miss Decker, would you... *collaborate* with me on my next work?"

Marla took his hand and squeezed it tightly. "Yes, I think I'd like that. I'd like that a lot, Mr. Baker," she sighed.

Wolf howled. "You mean cohabitate, right? There will be no marriage proposal tonight. Right?"

"Not tonight," Baker said solemnly. "But one never knows, do one? *Time* has a way of changing things," he noted with a wink.

THE BIG BOAT rounded the bend at Field's Point, then sailed upon a liquid moon path. The majestic mountainous part of the lake came into sight. Good friends thrust their glasses high into a familiar night sky. One adventure ended...*another began.*

The Granite Falls host offered a toast. "To Chelan!"

Clink-clink-clink.

Once again.

"To Chelan!"